PRAISE FOR

The Brideship Wife

"A wonderful debut . . . This well-researched read marks the arrival of a new talent on the Canadian historical fiction scene."

Toronto Star

"Engrossing."

The Globe and Mail

"A beautifully told, meticulously researched story of the little-known bride ships and the courageous women on board who risked everything for freedom, then fought to get what they deserved. Debut author Leslie Howard brings history to life by masterfully weaving together the social demands of the time, the perilous journey into the unknown, the too often tragic results of colonization, and the hearts and minds of those navigating these troubled waters."

Genevieve Graham, #1 bestselling author of
Bluebird and *The Forgotten Home Child*

"A welcome insight into the neglected history of the marriageable women sent from England to the colonies. The protagonist, Charlotte, is a true heroine. A spellbinding read. Wonderfully suspenseful, right to the satisfying ending."

Roberta Rich, bestselling author of
The Midwife of Venice

ALSO BY LESLIE HOWARD

The Brideship Wife

LESLIE HOWARD

The *Celestial* *Wife*

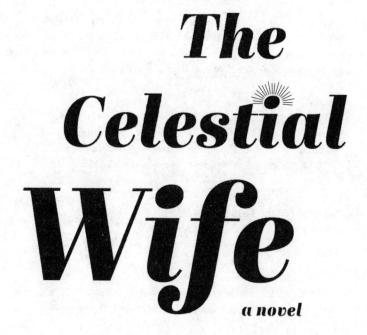

a novel

Published by Simon & Schuster

New York   London   Toronto   Sydney   New Delhi

SIMON &
SCHUSTER
CANADA

A Division of Simon & Schuster, LLC.
166 King Street East, Suite 300
Toronto, Ontario M5A 1J3

This Simon & Schuster Canada edition April 2024

SIMON & SCHUSTER CANADA and colophon are trademarks of
Simon & Schuster, LLC.

Simon & Schuster: Celebrating 100 Years of Publishing in 2024

For information about special discounts for bulk purchases,
please contact Simon & Schuster Special Sales at 1-800-268-3216 or
CustomerService@simonandschuster.ca.

Manufactured in the United States of America

1   3   5   7   9   10   8   6   4   2

Library and Archives Canada Cataloguing in Publication
Title: The celestial wife / Leslie Howard.
Names: Howard, Leslie, 1953- author.
Description: Simon & Schuster Canada edition.
Identifiers: Canadiana (print) 20230485537 | Canadiana (ebook) 2023053922X |
ISBN 9781982182403 (softcover) | ISBN 9781982182410 (EPUB)
Classification: LCC PS8615.O897 C35 2024 | DDC C813/.6—dc23

ISBN 978-1-9821-8240-3
ISBN 978-1-9821-8241-0 (ebook)

If they [polygamists] wish to behave like cattle, it is probably their own affair . . . It would seem wisest to ignore what has no effect on the public at large.

—*The Vancouver Sun*, editorial, May 31, 1947

WEST

Stewart's Landing

Redemption 1964

Hall of worship

Houses for priesthood men

250 acres

EAST

Woods

NO TRESPASSING

Mom's cottage

Radio hut

Small farms and cottages for non-priesthood

SOUTH
to USA

PART ONE

Redemption,
British Columbia, Canada

June 1964

Chapter One

No one else wanted the job, so they gave it to me. Up at five to relay the morning road reports, and back again late in the evening to call in the weather forecast to the off-road truck loggers. It was vital information for the men who hauled raw logs through the treacherous Rocky Mountains to our sawmills in southern BC and across the border in Montana and Idaho. My work was lonely and isolating, but it was my daily pass to the outside world.

I flicked a switch and watched the ancient shortwave radio snort and rumble to life, like an old man's struggle to wake from his nap. I spoke into the mic and heard the eerie echo of my own voice. "Hey, Stan. Daisy here. No snow on the Kicking Horse, but six inches expected on the Crowsnest, if you're heading up that way. Back roads on logging section twelve are clear. Some ice by the river, though."

I stood up to face the large map of western Canada and the northern United States thumbtacked to the wood-paneled wall. Its edges were curled and the print faded, making it hard to see in the early evening light. I ran my forefinger along the route I guessed Stan was taking and thought about the weirdness of snowstorms in June. While it wasn't summer here yet, I could feel its warmth just around the corner. Butter-coloured black-eyed Susans were bursting out in the meadows and ditches.

Static filled the tin-roofed hut and then the words, "Ten-four."

I was supposed to finish up, hurry back to my assigned family, and help the mothers put all the toddlers to bed, but instead I dimmed the lights so no one would know I lingered there, slipped on my headphones, and turned the dial to FM radio. I watched the needle dance until it landed on the station I was looking for: KREM FM out of Spokane, Washington.

"This is Wolfman Jack coming to you *live,* and who's this on the Wolfman telephone?"

"Cindy in Portland."

"Cindy in Portland, tell me who you're lovin'."

Cindy giggled. "Hi, Wolfman, I'm lovin' that new group from England, the Beatles, and I want to hear 'I Want to Hold Your Hand.'"

Wolfman howled his trademark as the song came on. The golden glow of radioland wrapped around me, and I sank deeper into my chair—and another dimension. I took a deep breath, closed my eyes, and let the magic sweep me away.

My mind, dancing with the melody, filled with the image of a boy with dimples and rumpled dark curls reaching for my hand as I looked longingly into his warm, caring eyes. . . .

Lost in a forbidden world, I didn't hear or see the door to the hut open, didn't sense the movement across the old plank floor, didn't feel the warm body beside me until a hand touched my shoulder.

I gasped. And my chair dropped forward with a bone-jangling jolt. I yanked off my headphones and blinked up at the person standing beside me. Relief poured through me at the sight of my friend.

"Brighten! You scared me so much I thought I'd have kittens."

Brighten's eyes were big, round, and a little worried. "Keep your hair on, Dais. I didn't mean to. I just need to talk."

Brighten was my absolute best friend—my only friend, really. Together, we were the daughters of the undeserving: men and women who did not hold the Bishop's favour, either because they didn't give enough money to the church or because they disobeyed the Bishop's teachings. When I was a toddler, my father stopped believing in the Bishop—stopped believing that he was the True Prophet and received messages directly from God—and he quit the church. There is no greater sin, so he was excommunicated. My father lost everything when he left, including my mother and me.

Brighten's situation was different. For some reason we didn't understand, her father had never been asked to join the priesthood. She lived with her mother and father—and three other mothers and their children—in a two-bedroom house down by the creek. It was small and run-down with a chicken coop out back and rusted old cars in the driveway. All the other kids had bunk beds in the basement, but as the oldest, Brighten had to sleep on the second-hand couch in the living room.

We found each other at recess on our first day of grade one, the only two girls standing alone in the playground while the others cut us out of their games. But our similarities ended at our unpopularity. Whereas Brighten was tall and beautiful with auburn hair and amber eyes, I was small, thin, and blonde. Completely unremarkable. The good news, though, was that I had actually grown quite a lot lately and had put on some weight in the right places. Boys noticed me now. Even though it was a sin.

I switched off the radio and gestured for Brighten to sit on the only other chair. "What's wrong?"

"I'm freaking out about the Placement. I'm starting to have doubts."

I shook my head. "Don't. You'll be chosen as the new celestial sister, I know it. Bishop Thorsen practically promised you."

The Bishop's older sister, Charity, had been the first celestial sister years ago. When mothers started having babies at age fifteen and went on to have ten kids or more, our community grew like crazy, and we needed someone to organize it properly. Managing all the businesses the men owned and procuring and distributing food and supplies to all the families was a full-time job. Charity had been unable to have children, so she had what no other woman in Redemption had: spare time and energy.

She did a great job running things. Not long after she started, the Bishop had a revelation: that all scheduling, ordering, payroll, and accounting was now women's work, and would henceforth be the domain of celestial sisters.

When it all became too much for Charity, the Bishop had another revelation: that there would be a total of four celestial sisters at any one time. The sisters would remain chaste before God, but once a sister reached the age of twenty-five, she would train her replacement and then be married and have children. She would heed womankind's highest calling and become a mother of Zion.

Because celestial sisters handled the money and doled out the groceries and pretty much everything else, they were powerful. Girls competed for the jobs, but only the smartest and most capable were chosen. Brighten wanted it bad.

"I was so sure before, but now? I don't know. I don't like the way Brother Earl looks at me. He makes my skin crawl. He watches me when he thinks I'm not looking. Others have noticed too, so it's not just me being vain or proud. Blossom told me that being married to an old fart like him would serve me right for being 'Little Miss Perfect.'"

I smiled as I looked at my lovely friend with her long thick lashes and flawless skin. "Blossom's just jealous. You're prettier *and* smarter than she is. She doesn't mind not being the prettiest, but it kills her that you're smarter. So there's always going to be bad blood. Don't worry, you're a shoo-in for celestial sister."

Blossom, on the other hand, was awful. She was the twentieth daughter of Brother Fred and the first daughter of his seventh wife, Flora, and because her father was a senior man in the priesthood, she had loads of status. She had curly brown hair, a turned-up nose, and her father's build. He was a big burly man who liked to throw his weight around whenever he got the chance, but especially each year at the Placement. People said that Blossom was a chip off the old block. If she became a celestial sister in charge of food distribution, Brighten and I would starve to death.

Brighten pulled a piece of her hair from her long braid and began twisting it into tighter and tighter coils. "It's just that Brother Earl always seems to get what he wants, and I'm scared he wants me. As one of the deserving, he does everything that the Bishop demands and gets rewarded for it."

"Yes. But Bishop Thorsen gets his revelations directly from God, so he'll do *His* bidding. Right? Not just what Brother Earl wants. God sees how good your heart is." I reached over and gave her hand a little pat.

"I've worked so hard for this, Daisy. Fifteen is too young to be a wife and mother. I want a chance to have a job first. If I get placed with an old man, I don't know what I'll do."

Brighten dropped her hair and began to stroke the wrinkles out of her skirt. "I don't like what it's done to my mother—the in-fighting, the bullying. Mom's always so down and worried. I don't want that life."

It was true. Brighten's mom seemed overwhelmingly sad whenever I saw her, which wasn't often. She didn't leave the house much. Brighten admitted that her mom was unable to help care for her large family. She slept a lot, and the other mothers couldn't trust her to look after their children. The Bishop explained that there was something in Brighten's mom that prevented her from feeling the glory of God's blessings. Though she struggled and prayed for guidance, she was not the recipient of God's heaven-sent light. She was undeserving.

I tried to console Brighten. "You've got nothing to be worried about. Celestial sister is all yours."

"Maybe. But what about you? Are you worried the Bishop will marry you to someone you'll find hard to love? Are you hoping to become a celestial wife?"

My heart beat an unsteady rhythm. For girls like Brighten, girls with intelligence and ambition, becoming a celestial sister was the only way to avoid early marriage and motherhood until their twenties. For girls like me, adventurous and romantic—or so I liked to think—becoming first wife to a young man I admired was more important.

But the position of *celestial* wife had not even occurred to me, so focused was I on becoming one young man's *first*. A celestial wife, the Bishop taught, was a man's third, the one who ensured he would get into the highest kingdom of heaven. But I wasn't as interested in the afterlife as I was finding heaven on earth with the boy who'd arrived from Utah last year. "I'm hoping for first wife. I hope the Bishop will place me with one of the new priesthood men. Someone young I can relate to. Someone I can love."

Brighten's eyebrows shot up. "Okay, Daisy. Spill it. Who's the guy you've got a crush on?"

I thought again of the boy with the dark curls and big brown eyes and the way his cheeks dimpled when he smiled. I'd first noticed him in church, but I got to know him—despite the rules against fraternizing—when he was assigned to fix up the derelict "new" cottage where my mom lived.

Correction: the cottage the Bishop banished her to.

I guess I should explain. After my father left, Mom and I lived alone until two years ago when my mother turned down the Bishop's marriage proposal. Apparently, he'd asked her many times before, but she always refused him. After the last time, he forced Mom to move to an isolated cottage on the far edge of Redemption, where "her sin wouldn't infect others," and he put me with my assigned family where I'd learn about God's plan for me.

Plural marriage, hard work, and motherhood are a woman's greatest glory.

Remembering the new guy's shy smiles, his kindness to my mom, our very first conversation, and that time we walked in the woods together—my whole face suddenly felt damp and hot. I looked down to try to cover my lie. I wasn't ready to tell Brighten yet, not until I knew for sure that he felt the same way as I did. "No one. It's a sin to have feelings for a boy. You know that."

She gave me a look that demanded more, but I wanted to

change the subject. I had a deeper, darker secret that I needed to get out in the open before it drove me crazy. I fingered the locket that lay hidden under the bodice of my long dress, dropped my voice to a whisper, and slowly raised my eyes to meet hers.

The idea had popped into my head when I was talking with my assigned father's newest wife. Lavender was only two years older than me, and we had become fast friends. She admitted that she cowered under the covers every time Brother Henry—Father Henry to me—knocked on her door at night. And cried herself to sleep when he left her. She hated him and just wanted to go home to her mother.

That was hard to hear, and her story frightened me.

Over time the idea just kept pushing its way into my consciousness. I wasn't sure where it had come from. It terrified me. I was playing with fire, and I knew I could get badly burnt, but at the same time I was drawn to it. I couldn't turn away from its warmth.

It really took hold last year when they gave me this radio job. I learned it quickly and, once they left me alone, I explored stations up and down the dial to see what was out there in radioland. There was a lot. My favourites were the comedy shows; Jack Benny and Art Linkletter, and especially Red Skelton. But sometimes I caught Walter Cronkite and the evening news. Apparently, there was a war going on in some place called Vietnam, and folks were upset about it. When that got me down, I tuned in to Dear Abby and listened to other people pour out their hearts to her. I wished I had someone like her to tell my troubles to, someone who could tell me what to do. Because Abby was wise. Wiser than anyone I knew, including the Bishop, because his wisdom wasn't his own. Brighten was smart and sweet and deeply sympathetic, but she had about as much experience as me.

And I wanted more.

"Brighten, if things don't work out for us at the Placement, have you ever considered leaving Redemption?"

Brighten looked at me sharply, alarm in her face.

"Of course not! I haven't ever thought of leaving," she exclaimed. "That's nuts. Those people who've left, no one ever speaks to them again. All their friends and relatives—even their own mothers. It's like they died! Not to mention they're excommunicated and banished from the Celestial Kingdom!" Her eyes widened and she slapped a hand over her mouth. "I'm sorry, Dais! I forgot about your dad. I didn't mean it."

I put my finger to my lips and dropped my voice even lower. "Don't worry about it. So, you truly believe everything we've been told, no question? That the Principle is the only way to heaven?"

Brighten looked puzzled, then taken aback, like I'd just said that up was down, and down was up. "I dunno. I guess," she said. "I haven't thought a lot about it. It's all about eternal salvation in return for obedience, right? God wants us, His Chosen, to be fruitful and multiply, and plural marriage was His instruction. The Bishop says—"

"*Never question. It makes us unhappy*," I said, interrupting her. "His sayings are always in our brains. It's hard to ever think for ourselves and to know what makes us truly happy, isn't it?"

Brighten's face dropped, like she had no energy left to keep sweet. "Sometimes I wonder if my mom would be better if she didn't have to compete with her sister-wives and always come up short. She might feel more at home here, like she belonged."

I knew what Brighten was talking about. Everyone wanted to be their husband's favourite wife. They wanted to feel special, to feel loved. So they were always looking for proof of his feelings, and were often disappointed. Their anger and frustration at their husband were redirected to their sister-wives, and there was always one who became the scapegoat for the others.

At my new house, it was Lavender.

I got up and checked the window. I didn't expect to see anyone, but I was always careful. I didn't want to get caught lingering and lose my supper. Last time, Mother Rose punished me with no supper for a whole week.

I settled back in my chair. "What about the outside?" I persisted. "Aren't you dying to see what the world is really like? You could pick your own clothes, go to the movies, listen to music, eat hamburgers and chips."

Brighten's face lit up despite her fear moments ago. "Mmm. You're making me hungry. I haven't had a hamburger since the Bishop banned them. A temptation sent by Satan? I mean, that's ridiculous."

I glanced at the floorboard in the corner of the room, the one that wasn't nailed down.

"Dad sent me a *Seventeen* magazine for an early birthday present this year. The clothes in it are *un-be-lievable*." I saw Brighten's eyes widen. "Tucked inside my magazine was a library card with my name on it. Did you know that there is a library in town where you can borrow all kinds of books to read—for free?" I smiled, lost in a happy daydream. "I'd sure like to visit it, but don't think I could pull it off without getting caught."

Brighten sighed, leaned back in her chair, and crossed her arms over her chest. "Your mom's taking a big risk letting you have the stuff that your dad sends you. If she were caught, it would be bad. For her and you. You'd think she'd have learned by now."

I shrugged my shoulders. "I know. I worry about her. She doesn't seem to care anymore. Does some weird stuff: she says hello to people even though she knows they won't talk to her, *and* she doesn't even try to hide the library books she carries home from town."

"Town" was Stewart's Landing, population two thousand, easy walking distance from Redemption.

"Maybe you should get her some Valium. My mom takes it, like lots of the mothers. There's a doctor in town. He gives Bishop Thorsen prescriptions, no questions asked."

I shrugged. "Knowing Mom, there's no way she'd take it." I got up and switched off the generator. The moon had risen and there was enough light for us to see each other. No one would look at the hut and guess we were there.

I inclined my head towards the radio. "Last night I picked up a signal all the way from Dallas, Texas."

"Where's that?"

"In the States. South, I think. They talk like they have marbles in their mouths. Couldn't understand half of what they said, but the music was boss." I smiled, trying out the language I'd picked up from the station. "There was a prerecorded talent show called *Folksongs*. A singer named Janis Joplin. What a voice! All raspy and shivery. They said she was a real up-and-comer. My point is, she was a girl, just a little older than us when she started, and she was allowed to do things like start a career. Maybe she'll even become famous one day."

It was Brighten's turn to get up and check out the window. Then she turned to look at me, her face stern. "I wish we could go to the States and see her—or go anywhere for that matter. But we will never do that because we can't ever leave. If we tried, we wouldn't survive without money or a place to live. We don't even have any government identification." She paused. "And the punishment would be awful if we were caught. Beatings would be the least of our worries. I don't think I'd survive re-education in isolation."

It was the Bishop's favourite punishment. He locked up the worst sinners in a broken-down trailer where they were forced to study the covenants for weeks with hardly any food. When they emerged, they weren't the same. They claimed that their belief had been restored, but the light in their eyes was gone.

I didn't say anything, just pulled myself to my feet and walked over to the radio, checked that everything was off, and tidied my pen and papers on the desk.

"The Bishop says you can't trust anyone on the outside," Brighten insisted. "They're all evil and live like Satan. We're much better off here."

My face felt prickly hot again and I threw down my pen. "Are we? Even if you're named the new celestial sister, you'll be married eventually. What if we end up as junior wives with a dozen sister-wives? What if we are tied to old men, for time and all eternity, men we can't grow to love? What if I'm always the runt and never get any respect?"

My challenge seemed to make Brighten slough off her early doubts. "That won't happen. You'll be placed with a new member of the priesthood, one who loves you and treats you well. You'll be his first wife, so you'll have status. And I'll be the new celestial sister. We'll both be very happy, you'll see."

As we walked home together—for where else would we go?—I glanced up at the large houses we passed by. Warm yellow lights shone through open front doors as mothers called children to come in for bedtime. While crickets chirped in the deepening shadows, I thought about what Brighten had said. Despite all my insecurities, I knew she was right. I had just needed to air my innermost doubts and fears.

It was true. We *were* better off here in Redemption. I was going to be the first wife of a young man of the priesthood, and not just any young man.

Tobias, the dark-haired, dimpled boy of my dreams.

Chapter Two

The next morning, all I wanted to do was talk to Tobias. I hoped I would be free for a little while after my radio job, but Buttercup, one of my assigned sisters, was sent to find me and bring me right home. I was needed, she said. Mother Hyacinth was in labour, and since she'd been given the day off from her chores, someone needed to pick up the slack.

Me.

My assigned family numbered a total of forty-two people: one father, six mothers, and thirty-five children. I thought of the mothers in groups according to how much I did or didn't like them. Mother Rose and Mother Violet were the worst—both of them sour-tongued and scornful; Mother Hyacinth and Mother Lavender always had a kind word for me, so I liked them the best;

and Mother Fern and Mother Juniper were okay as long as I kept out of their way.

The kitchen was its usual scene of chaos in the morning with the older girls stirring steaming pots of porridge over all four stoves, while the boys carried heavy jugs of farm-fresh milk and homemade apple juice from the industrial-size walk-in freezer. They plunked them down on the wooden picnic table that ran the length of the room.

Oatmeal-raisin cookies were cooling on the counter beside the fifteen loaves of bread baked fresh daily. I knew the cookies were a treat for after church on Sunday and snacking was forbidden at all times, but I managed, with a quick sweep of my hand, to palm a few and drop them into the pocket of my dress without anyone noticing. It was a technique I'd perfected with practise.

The warm smells of brown sugar and cinnamon mixing with the sickly sweet scent of hair spray made me turn around. All the little girls were lined up in front of the big mirror on the wall beside the kitchen while the older girls dragged brushes through their knotted hair, arranged it neatly, and sprayed it in place.

I knocked on Mother Hyacinth's door on my way to the basement. The mothers weren't allowed painkillers during labour, so I wanted to see how she was doing. The Bishop insisted they experience the pure joy of bringing an old soul back to life on earth without the numbing effects of drugs. But it didn't sound like pure joy to me.

Mother Hyacinth looked pale and sweaty when she opened the door, but she gave me a quick smile and a wave before she closed her door again.

I was on laundry detail. In the basement I faced a mountain of

16

dirty sheets, towels, and clothes stacked beside seven old wringer washers. I started sorting. From experience, I knew that the hems of the little girls' dresses had been dragged through the dirt and were impossible to clean. Same as the little boys' knees and pant cuffs, and Brother Henry's church shirts with the yellow stains in the armpits.

Several of the four- and five-year-olds still wet the bed, and the sharp vinegary smell of fresh pee made me want to gag as I dropped their sheets into a tub to presoak them in bleach.

All the bedwetters had to help with the laundry as punishment. The youngest were crying as usual, and I did my best to console them, but it didn't help when Mother Rose came in and slapped six-year-old Tulip across the face and locked her in a closet. She was the oldest bedwetter and she set a bad example for the little ones.

But Tulip was also the daughter of Mother Hyacinth, and I was pretty sure that all the other mothers were resentful of Hyacinth right now, including Mother Rose. Not only was Hyacinth getting time off from her chores, but soon she would be celebrated as a true mother of Zion when she produced a new son or daughter. It was the sort of thing that really set the other sister-wives off.

I knew Mother Rose would leave Tulip in the closet for hours, so as soon as Rose left, I let her out and made her promise not to tell.

The laundry took all morning, so I was kept home from school. "Laundry is more important than school any day," Mother Rose had told me. "Especially for older girls like you. You'll be a wife soon, so you better get used to hard work."

By lunchtime my hands were stinging from the homemade lye

soap and my sinuses were on fire from breathing in bleach fumes. I grabbed a plate of wieners and beans and searched for a quiet place where no one would notice that I was taking a break.

It was hard to find a space to be alone, even in this huge house, but I knew that few people lingered in the hallway behind the kitchen, its one feature being the large *Time with Daddy* chart on the wall. It was here that the six women—my new mothers—came to check their allotted times with Brother Henry.

Since the main goal of our spiritual community was to make babies for God's glory, the monthly cycles of the women were charted. Daddy was assigned to each wife based on their prime nights for conception. When their cycles all synchronized, there was heck to pay.

The lights were low in the hall, so I reached up and flicked on the ceiling fixture. A young woman who had been closely studying the chart spun around, squinting her eyes.

"Oh, it's you, Daisy. You surprised me."

"Sorry, Mother Lavender, I just need a break from the heat and all the awful laundry smells."

"I know what you mean. I hate laundry too." She pointed to the low bench. "Come sit." She said it in a friendly way, not like a command from a mother to a child. Mother Lavender was only two years older than me, after all. "I just came to double-check the chart," she said with a note of apology in her voice. "I need to become a mother of Zion soon, or I don't know what will happen."

I understood. Women who were married but had no children were looked down on, sometimes scorned outright. Lavender had confided in me that she didn't like Brother Henry, and hated their nights together, but that didn't mean she didn't feel the pressure to get pregnant. "Now that you've settled in, I'm sure it won't be long until you are expecting," I said.

"Thank you for your blessed words, dear Daisy. I pray every day for that very thing. I'm sure God will answer my prayers just as He did when I first came here."

I thought back. A year and a half ago, when Lavender first arrived from Cardston, Alberta, as a new wife, she'd cried nonstop for days. "You seem so much happier now than you did then," I said. "Was it hard to get used to married life?"

She must have heard the hint of worry in my voice, because she reached over and grasped my hands, giving them a slight squeeze. "Don't worry, it won't be the same for you. I hadn't wanted to get married till I was older because my mom was sick. She got cancer and I wanted to look after her and help look after all my little brothers and sisters as well."

"I'm so sorry."

"It's okay, I heard she's doing better. She's getting chemo and it's working, so I'm told."

"Chemo? Bishop Thorsen let her go to the hospital?"

"Not exactly. When the Bishop came to Alberta to visit the faithful in my hometown, he found out about Mom's diagnosis. He told the congregation that the cancer proved that Mom was unworthy and unredeemable. He said she had to go—leave the community—and we were never to see her again. I was forbidden to contact her."

I was shocked at the Bishop's cruelty. I understood why sinners were unworthy: they made the wrong choice; but I didn't understand how an illness—something you had no control over—could make you unworthy too. "Lavender, that's awful! I've never heard of the Bishop sending someone away like that. Can't she come back when her treatment is over?"

"No. The Bishop says some sins are unforgivable. That I just have to learn to live without her." Lavender sat up straight and clasped her hands in her lap. "Through prayer, I am."

It all seemed so cruel, so wrong. I felt so bad for Lavender, but I didn't know what to say to make her feel better. I thought of my own mom and how I would feel if I could never talk to her again, feel the warmth of her hug, or hear the soothing sound of her voice. My stomach felt queasy, and I started to hiccup. We sat quietly for a while, my hiccups the only sound breaking the silence, and then Lavender glanced up at the wall clock.

"I should go and get ready for my husband's visit tonight." She got up and smoothed the folds of her skirt. "Some of the women say that if you make yourself as beautiful and desirable as you possibly can, then your husband will give you a baby."

"Good luck," I said, and blew her a kiss. Her return smile quickly faded as the hall door opened. Mother Rose marched straight down the hall without a word and stopped in front of the chart. Her finger followed the date, seeking the name of the mother assigned to Daddy for the night.

We watched her face grow dark as she turned to Lavender. "What a waste of Daddy's time, spending the night with you. And think of the worthy old souls he could be bringing back to life with someone else. You should ask Daddy to be with another mother if you can't do your duty. Or maybe we should encourage him to sleep with more than one wife at a time, like Bishop Thorsen does."

What? More than one wife at a time? I risked a glance at Lavender, who looked like she might burst into tears, but she swallowed hard and said, "I'm sure the Lord will give me his blessing very soon."

Mother Rose scoffed as she pushed past us and headed to her room.

I stared after her. "What's with Mother Rose today?"

"She's jealous, like usual. They all are. I'm the newest, youngest wife. It's the thing I hate the most about this place. The jealousy is overwhelming. They're always doing something to sabotage my time with Daddy—knocking on the bedroom door, claiming that they need to speak to him right away, or that there's some kind of emergency. We never get uninterrupted time alone. I don't like what we do, Daisy, but I understand it's my duty. Why won't they just let us get it over with?"

I didn't want to think about her lying with Brother Henry, so I changed the subject. "I don't get it. Bishop Thorsen tells us all the time that jealousy is a sin. I know that some of the women struggle with it from time to time, but are you saying that the mothers are sinning most of the time?"

"Daisy, open your eyes. Let me put it this way: if your husband came home one day holding hands with a strange woman and then told you that she was his new wife, how would you react?"

"I would try to welcome her, as we are taught to do," I said, ignoring the bad feelings the thought of another woman holding hands with Tobias gave me.

"Would you? Even if you weren't in love with your husband, wouldn't you feel rejected? And what if you did love him? How would you feel as you watched him go to her room at night, heard him call her *sweetheart*, saw him kiss her? What if he took her out on picnics while you had to stay home to do housework and care for all the kids? What then?"

"I . . . I . . ." She had me there. I couldn't imagine living like that. Jealousy would consume me. Perhaps Tobias and I could be like my parents. *I don't need any other woman than my sweet Ruthie,* Mom told me Dad used to say all the time. Maybe Tobias would be like him.

I wished Lavender luck again and went back down to the basement. I just had to talk to Tobias. I had to be sure that he felt the same way about me and that he didn't want anyone else. As soon as I finished the laundry, I left the house.

I ran through the forest trail, my breath hot in my throat, praying I wouldn't meet anyone along the path. I rarely saw anyone out this way, but just in case, I made sure I had a ready-made excuse for being in the woods, with my wild mushroom bag and harvesting knife tied to the belt of my dress.

I picked up my skirts so I could run faster. I was committing another sin for showing my leggings, but today I felt reckless. I was coming to the most important night of my life, the Placement, and my feelings of both longing and worry were building to a fever pitch. My insides felt like they were in a pressure cooker and the shaking metal valve was ready to blow.

If only I knew what Tobias was thinking. Because I was a girl with a bad family history, I couldn't take anything for granted. I hoped that I had moved beyond my parents' sins; after all, that was the whole idea behind my assignment to a new family. By living in a family of true believers for the last two years—one that embraced the Principle of polygamy—I was supposed to be redeemed. I hoped that two years of the Principle was enough to give me the husband that I dreamt of, the husband that only the Bishop could give me.

It had to be Tobias; no one else could make me happy.

Where the path from the radio hut intersected with the path to the main road, my luck ran out. I stopped running and slowed to a respectable pace just as Mother Rose and Mother Violet looked up from their intense conversation during a rare late-morning stroll. Keeping my head down and trying not to breathe too hard, I murmured, "Keep sweet, Mother Rose. Keep sweet, Mother Violet." I sensed rather than saw their frowns.

"Keep sweet, Daisy," they replied in unison, then Mother Rose stopped short.

"Why are you wandering around out here, Daisy? Don't you have laundry and other chores? Didn't Bishop Thorsen decree that God has chosen you for extra duty, that you should never be idle?"

I pointed to the foraging bag hanging from my waist. "Thank you, Mother Rose, for your concern about me staying in God's good graces. I've done the laundry and now I'm gathering mushrooms for supper. After that, I'm going to weed the garden." It was a lie, so I said a quick silent prayer asking for forgiveness.

"Better get at it," Mother Rose answered.

One of them clicked her tongue with disapproval as I continued walking. I was used to it. My parents were tainted by their doubt, and it had infected me too. Bishop Thorsen said doubt was "a cancer in the community" that needed to be cut out, and he often invoked my bad name, making an example of me. For years I'd dreaded Sunday school for that very reason. The Bishop used me to explain the unexplainable. If we were God's special people, then why did bad things happen to us?

Because the Shoemakers were doubters.

No wonder the mothers avoided me at home, except Lavender and Hyacinth, and made their children do the same.

I stepped off the trail into a small glade, pretending to search through the tall grass for mushrooms, waiting for the mothers to leave the area. I thought about what had started all my troubles in the first place, about what had made Dad lose faith and abandon my mom and me.

Mom didn't like to talk about it because it was painful, and even discussing it was a sin. So I'd had to pick up hints and bits of information over the years and kind of piece together the story.

Dad hadn't been brought up in the church; he joined when he was twenty-eight, a few years after he came back from the war. The Second World War. He'd been in a prisoner-of-war camp in Germany and was so sick from starvation and beatings that it took him a long time to get better. In the war camp he'd been forced to construct buildings, so when he got home, he worked in a sawmill. Eventually, he founded a construction company.

His physical wounds healed, but his emotional ones didn't, so when some of his employees told him of a better, calmer, more peaceful way to live, he considered joining our church. While he was still undecided, he met Mom. Mom laughed when she told me this part of the story—the happy part—and said the clincher was when her father, a very senior member of the priesthood in the U.S. church, sent her north to marry. Several men wanted to marry her—including Bishop Thorsen—but she picked Dad for his kind ways and gentle voice. Those were the days when women had a say in who they married.

They had me and everything was great for a few years. Then something happened. Dad and the Bishop had a big fight. I've never been able to figure out what it was about, but it was serious enough to make Dad leave. Leave Redemption, and us.

I miss Dad, but I only have a few vague memories, and the birthday presents he sends every year. I know Mom really misses him, because she refused to be reassigned to another husband. And because she was *legally* married to Dad at the courthouse in town and neither of them wanted a divorce, the Bishop can't make her marry again. Mom will never admit it, but I know she found ways to see my dad from time to time. She used to fix her hair and put on her best clothes, then walk into town. When she came back, she would have a gift from my father for me.

But that stopped suddenly a few years ago.

Since then, the Bishop has pressured Mom to join his family as one of his wives. The last time she said no, he got really mad and told her that God had sent him a revelation. He said that Mom needed quiet solitude to reflect on God's plan for her life.

Mom had to live in isolation. No one was allowed to speak to her, not even acknowledge her presence. I was taken away from her, and she was sent to live in a small cottage on the edge of our community. It was weird being the daughter of the only person in the community who didn't live the Principle according to God's plan. I respected Mom's decision not to marry the Bishop, but at the same time, I just wanted to fit in. I didn't want to be different. I prayed that my mom would start living like all the sister-wives so I could be just like all the other girls.

She wouldn't, so I couldn't, and the rest was history.

Mom and I figured out ways to get around all the new rules and see each other. We knew the risks we were taking, but we felt we had no choice. We were extra careful not to get caught. In fact, we were so good at it, I told Tobias if he ever wanted to meet me in private, to meet me there.

As I approached Mom's secluded cottage, nestled in a grassy hollow with heavy pine woods on one side, I grew happy at the sight. It was a tidy little spot that made me think of fairy tales and storybooks. It had a steeply pitched roof of weathered grey shingles, and green-painted clapboard walls. A fieldstone chimney rose from one side. Mom had planted tulips, irises, and daylilies in front of her kitchen and living room, windows. She had a vegetable garden too. It was where, in partial shade from a gnarled apple tree in the yard, she grew young lettuce and spinach.

I slowed, carefully checking the outbuildings, looking for a sign, any sign. And then I saw it, a slight movement by the heavy-equipment storage shed. I scanned the yard and saw no one, so I turned sharply and ran around the back of the building. A hand shot out and grabbed mine, squeezing tight.

Suddenly, I was breathless and panting.

Chapter Three

"Hello, gorgeous," Tobias said. He stood close to me, too close, and I felt the heat rising from his body as he nuzzled my hair.

He was the boy of my dreams, but even still, his hands on mine startled and shocked me. Holding hands with a member of the opposite sex was a serious sin. The punishment would be re-education in isolation. Tobias's touch thrilled me, but I pulled away in fear.

Then Tobias, with his dark colouring and cleft chin and those oh-so-adorable dimples in his cheeks, smiled at me and my knees turned to butter.

"Have you talked to the Bishop about us?" I asked breathlessly.

Another dazzling smile. "I've done better than that. I wrote to my father in Utah."

"Your father?"

He glanced away, then took a deep breath. "Daisy, I've always tried to be open and honest with you, but there's some stuff I've never told you. Bishop Thorsen knows, but no one else does. I'm supposed to keep a low profile." He paused. "My dad's a member of the Council of Seven. He's powerful. What he says, goes."

Instead of making me feel better, Tobias's news made my worries worsen. I hugged my elbows tightly. I'd had no idea that he was church royalty. When he first came here, he told me that he was from Blessed Town, Arizona, here to learn the construction trade by working for one of Bishop Thorsen's construction companies.

He'd lied to me. Just like I lied to him.

He leaned in close, talking low. I could smell his earthy scent and feel the puff of his breath caress my ear. "I was sent here for two reasons: first, to help mend fences between the U.S. and the Canadian churches. Years ago, there was some kind of power struggle that caused a big rift."

I nodded. "The Bishop told us about that. At worship last Sunday he said that we must begin to reconnect with our families in the U.S. God wants all His Chosen to push back against the evil government's attempts to interfere in our lives. He says there is strength in numbers, so all true believers must unite."

Tobias laughed softly. "I'm just glad that he's finally accepted the fact that our church—I mean the *American* church—doesn't recognize him as their Bishop."

"I don't know about that. He frequently reminds us about the special day God revealed to him that he was the new High Bishop for all the church."

He scoffed. "Yeah, but Prophet Ron in Utah had the same revelation and most people backed him. So . . ." Tobias cocked his ear and held up a finger. He walked to the corner of the building and took another quick glance towards the main road in the distance before coming back. "Bishop Thorsen started this new community so he could be the prophet here without any competition. Okay, fine. But then he refused to send brides south. It's been a real problem."

I let go of my elbows. "What do you mean?"

Tobias's face clouded. "In the church community in Utah, cousins are marrying cousins, and too many kids are ending up in Babyland."

"What's Babyland?"

Tobias loosened his collar. "The special cemetery for kids. Lots of babies are being born with . . . defects. They don't live long."

"Oh!" My head snapped back like I'd been slapped. An image of little white crosses cuddled by teddy bears flashed in my brain and I had to blink back tears. "That's so sad." I was suddenly grateful for the ladies that Bishop Thorsen brought into our community from Cardston, Alberta. *New blood*, he called them. "So are Redemption girls going to be sent to marry men in Utah, now?"

"Yes. I mean, not yet, but soon, I hope. Bishop Thorsen and my father are at least talking."

"Okay, that's good. So you said you had two reasons for coming to Redemption. You're mending fences between the two churches, that's the first one. What's the other?"

"I'm supposed to find a wife." He laughed and took my hand again. "So we've got nothing to worry about. My dad will give his blessing. It's all we need."

"But if your father is so high up in the church, won't he want you to marry one of the Bishop Thorsen's daughters? There's lots to choose from and they're all pretty. He wouldn't want you to marry me, would he?"

Tobias bent low so he could look me squarely in my eyes. "Daisy, you're the one I want to marry. Believe me, there's no one like you. You're so full of fun and energy that every time I see you, I feel alive. My heart is full of joy. I want to feel that way every day. I love you and I want to marry you."

My knees were butter again. I loved the way I could talk so openly with Tobias and that he always listened carefully, never correcting me or telling me what to say or not to say. Tobias's caring ways brought back dim memories of my dad. I hoped we could have the kind of marriage my parents had, full of love and laughter. But thoughts of Dad brought a shadow with them. He'd left us because he no longer believed. Would Tobias one day decide he didn't either? Or would that be me?

I looked at Tobias and saw goodness and earnestness and love in his eyes.

I had to tell him the truth.

"There's something you need to know about me too. My dad, he left the church. He's an apostate." My confession was so painful

I had to hang my head. What was I thinking? Tobias would never want to be tied to me for time and all eternity. I was dreaming in Technicolor. I had a sudden urge to flee.

Tobias's eyes grew soft, and he smiled gently. "I know that already, Daisy. People talk. I'm glad you trusted me enough to tell me, but it changes nothing. I also know that your mom is the daughter of a well-respected senior in the priesthood back home and that you have been redeemed by living with a righteous family. My dad said I could marry anyone from Redemption I chose. He only cares about expanding our family's gene pool, so I choose you."

At that moment I desperately wanted to hug him. And if I were to confess the truth, I wanted to kiss him as well, especially since our future together seemed certain. I consoled myself with the knowledge that I'd be able to do just that in a few short days.

Tobias cupped my hand in both of his, and for a moment I thought he might kiss it, but at the sound of truck tires on gravel he dropped it and shrank back into the shadows.

"We can't be seen together." Tobias's voice was tight.

I pointed to the forest trail. "Go!"

"What about you?"

"I've got a plan. I'll be okay. Run!"

He disappeared into the nearby woods in a flash.

I waited until I saw the truck park at Mom's front door. I caught a glimpse of my mom as she ushered someone inside and closed the door behind him.

My heart was thumping, and I felt a little light-headed. I picked up my skirts and ran for the back of the house before the unknown visitor could look out the front window and see me. I collected the key Mom always left for me by the basement door, and I let myself inside.

Once inside, I was overcome with curiosity. Who was the visitor? Everyone knew Mom was off-limits. The Bishop had called her "a faceless body, not to be acknowledged if you should accidentally run into her." So who was upstairs? I was the only one who ever visited Mom, and even I wasn't supposed to be here.

As silently as I could, I crept up the wooden staircase to open the kitchen door just a crack. At the top of the stairs, I gripped the handle, sucked in my breath, and turned. The old glass knob groaned, but the voices from the living room were loud enough to block the sound.

First, I heard Mom's voice, but then a familiar voice interrupted her. My jaw dropped. Bishop Thorsen!

Chapter Four

Bishop Thorsen hadn't visited Mom since his last proposal. What the heck was going on upstairs?

I tried so hard to hear their words that I barely let myself breathe. Mom's voice, always so soft and gentle, had some power behind it, though I could tell she was nervous.

"I know what you did to my husband. Dan told me and I'm not afraid to speak up," I heard Mom say.

"Water under the bridge, Ruth. And no one listens to you, anyway. You're a ghost, a nonperson," the Bishop retorted.

"Maybe so, but there are doubters out there, and more than

you know. Like you say, people ignore me—so they're not careful around me, and I overhear things. I've heard rumblings from some of the men about Prophet Ron in Utah being the one true prophet, and not you. If they're already starting to doubt you, they'd hear me if I told them what you did to Dan. They'd question your right to be Bishop and they'd question the source of your revelations. They have to know deep down that God would never tell you to do the evil things you do."

"Ha! Prophet Ron is a fake and an idiot. I'm Bishop partly because I'm not afraid to do tough things for the good of the community." He paused; his voice softened a bit. "Look, I'm in the middle of sensitive negotiations with the U.S. church and Prophet Ron, so you trying to stir up discontent right now isn't ideal. Ron has to know that I have complete control over the placement of young brides, no question. If they want a fresh crop of girls from Canada, then they have to go through me first. So if I do this little favour for you, then you're never gonna talk to anyone about this ever again. You hear me?"

"I promise I won't say a word as long as I get what I want."

The Bishop laughed bitterly. "You women are all the same. It's all about what you want, isn't it? Well, if you talk, you'll be very sorry. And so will Daisy."

"I swear I won't."

Bishop Thorsen's cowboy boots thudded across the wood plank floor. I heard the front door open, then bang shut. A moment later, I heard a powerful engine and a spray of gravel as he peeled out of the driveway.

I crept upstairs and found Mom slumped on the edge of the sofa, rubbing her forehead with the heel of one hand.

"Mom?"

She looked up, her face flushed, her eyes flashing with emotion. "Daisy, I didn't know you were here. How long have you been downstairs?"

"Long enough to know that the Bishop paid you a visit, and that you drive a hard bargain. What's going on? Are you okay? I heard my name, and you said something about Dad."

She fanned her face rapidly with one hand and shook her head as if to clear away bad thoughts and feelings. "I'm fine, Daisy. Don't worry about me. You know that the Bishop and I don't always agree on things."

"No kidding."

Mom seemed lost in thought for a moment before she refocused and pulled her face into a smile. "And of course you heard your name. You're going to be one of the new brides in just a few days; this is your special time. I had a few words with the Bishop about your Placement. I want the best for you. And now so does he."

I flopped down on the couch beside Mom and grabbed her hands, squeezing them hard. "Oh, Mom, there's so much to talk about. My dress is almost ready. I can't wait to try it on for you—you were right about the colour, it's perfect. Blossom is so jealous—I can tell by the way she's been glaring at me in the sewing room. She even told me that my nose is too big, that it spoils my looks. That's a sure sign she's jealous."

"I'm happy it's all working out for you, sweetheart," Mom said, laughing, "but let's go down to the den and have tea. We should talk."

"You don't think my nose is too big, do you, Mom?"

"No, dear."

The basement was our special place. We had created a den with two comfortable easy chairs and an old hand-hooked rug. This was our private spot for sitting and chatting, and no one ever knew. We curled up in our cozy chairs, balancing cups of steaming Earl Grey, with its sweet, fruity aroma. While I let my tea cool, I got out the spindle knitter that I had been using to make a long wool coil of gold and blue. Mom had promised to sew it together into a small rug for my trousseau. I tried to imagine it in my new home.

"What sort of living space do you think the Bishop will assign to me and my new husband, if he's a new member of the priesthood, I mean, and doesn't already have a house?" Mom knew I was talking about Tobias, but I didn't want to jinx it by saying his name. I had told her that he was special to me weeks ago, but she'd surprised me by telling me she'd already guessed. She had gotten to know Tobias, just as I had, when he'd renovated her cottage. He talked to her despite the rule against it and showed her a respect and consideration that few in Redemption did.

"I would love it if you and Tobias could live here with me. I told Ray, I mean, the Bishop, that," Mom said. "But we'll see what he decides."

My head shot up from my work. "Seriously? That would be amazing." Mom's cottage was a lot nicer than the arrangements most young families had until they were large enough to have a proper house built for them. Many lived for years in small trailers, or just a bedroom in their parents' big house.

Like most people in Redemption, Mom kept her main floor living space pretty plain: a couch and a table with chairs and a buffet was about it. There wasn't any art on the walls and certainly no books, TV, or radio. But downstairs, it was a whole other world.

Downstairs in her private space, Mom lived like I imagined people on the outside did. Her own watercolours hung on all four walls, nature scenes mostly, along with macramé plant holders spilling over with ferns and spider plants. The couch and two easy chairs were big and soft, with lots of bright throw cushions she'd crocheted herself. She'd even talked about getting a radio but hadn't worked up the nerve yet.

My favourite spot to sit was a big chair in front of a large wooden bookcase beside her loom (she was working on a cool winter scarf for me) and the fieldstone fireplace. Dad had introduced Mom to reading, so the case was full of all sorts of books that Mom had bought for nickels and dimes at the annual library fundraiser in town. Books like *Anne of Green Gables* and *Little Women* were my favourites for years, but now, not so much.

I had no real free time, but when I managed to sneak away from my chores, I read romance novels. There were scenes in them that made me think of boys in a new way. That's when my feelings for Tobias changed. I didn't want to just be friends with him, I wanted him to touch me like Troy touched Isobel in *The Boy Next Door*.

I noticed dark circles under Mom's eyes. "You look tired. Not sleeping again?"

"I've been worried about you. Fifteen is just too young to be getting married and having babies. When you get a chance to talk to your new husband, tell him you want to wait. He has to be patient with you."

I went back to my knitting, using a crochet hook to lift the thread up and over the four tiny nails hammered into one end of the wooden spool. "But almost all the girls want to become mothers. Shouldn't I? Becoming a mother of Zion is the highest calling."

Mom studied me over her mug of tea. "I'm not saying you can't become a mother. Just wait till you're older. Your body is not ready, and neither are your heart or mind. You remember that story I told you about Glory last year?"

I'd tried to block Glory's story from my mind. It didn't help that everyone always said how much we looked alike. She was small and slim like me. Her baby got stuck somehow; I didn't want to remember the details. When the midwife called an ambulance, the Bishop met it at the highway turnoff and sent it away. "*We are the Chosen; we don't need help from outsiders*," he had said.

Glory bled to death and the baby died. When the Bishop explained that God had called the baby's soul back to heaven, we all took comfort in his words. But I'd never understood why God wanted Glory too.

I changed the subject. "What was it like when you got married, Mom?"

Her face took on a dreamy expression. Still cradling her cup, she said, "Oh, that was the most beautiful day. Your father looked so handsome, and I felt so special in my white satin dress. It had a beaded bodice. He drove me to the ceremony in a little horse-drawn buggy."

"You were allowed to wear a white dress with *beads*? Wish I could do that."

"Everything was different then. It was before Bishop Thorsen had all his revelations from God about what we could and couldn't do. Girls had a say in who they married and when. We could even decide when we were ready to ask our husbands for a baby. It was up to us." Mom hesitated for a moment, casting her eyes down.

"You girls went to the Friday night fireside chat with Brother Samuel to prepare for marriage. What did he tell you?"

I pretended to concentrate on my knitting to hide my embarrassment. "He explained that our husbands will be our spiritual heads. They'll lead us and tell us precisely what to do on our wedding night. We just do exactly what they say." Mom let out a long, slow sigh and I hurriedly finished, "Brother Samuel said we were to produce babies as fast and as often as possible so that they can grow up to be soldiers in God's army."

Mom was quiet for a moment. "Things have changed here since Bishop Thorsen became our prophet, and I'm not sure I like it. Now it seems that nothing is more important than having babies. Some of the ladies have told me that they are unhappy about what it's doing to our community."

Sometimes Mom said things I really doubted. Usually I let it go, but this time I called her on it. "How do you know that, Mom? You never talk to any of them."

I was very surprised to hear Mom laugh, and I gave her a puzzled look.

"It's ironic. Bishop Thorsen tried to isolate me because he didn't want me to be a bad influence on the other ladies, but now they see me as someone they can confide in. They sneak over here to talk about what's bothering them, where they're free from the worry that others will judge them or tattle on them. Bishop Thorsen's punishment backfired."

I confess I was more than a little shocked—and curious. "I don't understand. What sort of things do they talk to you about?"

"They are unhappy, Daisy—competing for their husbands'

attention, fighting with their sister-wives over housework and childcare—and they're exhausted all the time. And the Bishop seems to enjoy the in-fighting. He has fun turning women against each other, but it destroys their happiness and peace of mind."

I thought about what she said for a moment. I had seen examples of this within my assigned family. Some of the worst fights were over who got to serve Brother Henry his meals. Last night at dinner, Mother Violet deliberately tripped Mother Fern while she was carrying a plate of food to him. It was a big mess with everyone yelling at one another until Brother Henry slammed his fist on the table.

The Bishop said jealousy was a sin and we all had to work harder to be worthy of God's love. I thought he was right. Didn't the Lord want us to be sweet at all times? If we weren't sweet, wasn't it our own fault if were unhappy? But Bishop Thorsen was mean-spirited too, and proud and vain. I was sure that God didn't like that either.

"You've never really liked Bishop Thorsen, have you, Mom? Why?"

"He claims to be God's one true prophet on earth, but he does things I don't think God would ever want for us."

"Like what, for example?"

Mom thought for a second. "Like his plan to marry twelve-year-old twins in Cardston next month, and other things that I think you are too young to know about."

Mom had a good point. The twins were still little kids. It was kind of gross. I wasn't *exactly* sure what happened between a man and a woman when they tried to make a baby, but I had a pretty good idea.

When we were little, we spent long hours outside playing with just a couple of older kids to watch over us. We got into all kinds of mischief, often egged on by one of the older boys, Jonas. (He was Blossom's older brother. I called him Jonas the Jerk because he kicked boys in the crotch just to laugh at their pain.) He was mean and picked on the girls too, but they knew better than to complain. The grown-ups always sided with the boys over the girls, and tattlers were punished. So the girls learned to suffer in silence.

Jonas made us play a game we called "Father and the Mothers." All the little girls would get on their hands and knees in a row and the older boy would lift their skirts from behind and then straddle them, one after another. He would pound their backsides with rhythmic up-and-down motions, like riding a horse, only really hard till the girl collapsed, crying under the big boy's weight, and he moved on to the next "mother."

Mom set her tea down, walked over to my chair, and put her arm around me. "Daisy, dear, do you have any questions about what to expect on your wedding night?"

After class the other day, Blossom told us that our assigned husbands will make us take off all our clothes and that "it" will hurt like heck. She said we should all just close our eyes tight and pray. But that's not what Troy and Isobel did in my romance novel. Their lovemaking was nothing like our childhood game; it was tender and loving (and very sexy too). That was what Tobias and I would have once we were married: long nights of tender kisses and gentle touching. It would be nothing like what Blossom said it would be. And how would she know, anyway?

"No, I'm good, Mom, I know all about it."

Mom looked a little doubtful but didn't push. Instead, she snuggled beside me in my chair. "I guess what I'm trying to say is that I'm hopeful that you'll marry a loving young man who treats you well—that you have the kind of marriage that I had—but . . ."

I put my arm around her and gave her a squeeze. "I think it's all going to work out, Mom, don't worry."

"But what if it doesn't?"

I shrugged. I didn't want to think about my doubts anymore. And hadn't I just heard her put in the fix with Bishop Thorsen?

"If it doesn't work out, there is another way," Mom said, looking at me carefully. "If you were placed with a man who . . . made you uncomfortable . . . you could leave Redemption. Your dad told me that nonbelievers are not all evil and that life on the outside can be good. It's different, very different, and it would take a lot of getting used to, but you could do it and I would help you get away. There'd be danger. You'd have to be very careful, but you could be happy, Daisy."

It felt like someone had dropped a load of bricks on my shoulders. After I'd talked with Brighten last night, I'd gotten the idea of leaving out of my head, and I didn't want to open that door again. "Mom, if you felt that way, why didn't you take me and leave with Dad? What have we been doing here all this time?"

Mom began to twirl her wedding ring. "Don't think I didn't seriously contemplate it. It was hard to think clearly at the time. It was such a huge step to take. Since my earliest days I was taught that I'd be damned for all time if I became an apostate. I love your father, Daisy. But I was scared to send the two of us to hell for following him. My father forbade me from ever having any contact with him again. He said that if I defied him, he'd call for a blood atonement."

I shuddered. Blood atonement was the harshest punishment of all, reserved for mortal sins that could not be redeemed by the blood of Christ.

How could a father threaten to kill his own daughter?

Chapter Five

As I walked to the schoolhouse on the last day of school, I felt my heart sing. I was going to be rid of the place forever! Last Sunday, when the Bishop explained to us why grade nine would be our final year of school, I was the happiest person in the Hall of Worship.

"No need for any more learning," he told the congregation, who nodded their heads in agreement and murmured their amens. *"Mothers of Zion don't need a fancy education. And the boys only need to know how to follow orders from their supervisors in the sawmills and logging operations.*

"Too much useless knowledge leads to questioning and unhappiness," he reminded us. *"Our teachers don't have high school diplomas, and we all know what terrific jobs they do."*

The whole congregation had erupted in applause.

To be fair, I didn't hate everything about school. I loved Inspection Week, the one time in the school year that the teachers taught from the textbooks that the government sent us.

We spent an entire day preparing the classroom for the inspectors, putting up world maps and posters of the countries we were supposed to be studying. This year we put up posters of ancient Egypt. I was curious about the pyramids and gold-covered mummy cases, but I hid my fascination from the others, who wouldn't understand.

When the inspectors were in the room, Mother Faith told us all about the people who had built incredible stone structures by dragging huge slabs of rock from a distant quarry. Their whole lives were dedicated to their leaders, called *pharaohs*, and to worshipping their sun god, Ra.

The other kids rolled their eyes and smirked at these ancient people who laboured all their lives to please their god, but it made me wonder. What drove the people to work so incredibly hard to prove their faith? And weren't we just like them—devoted labourers—proving our obedience and dedication?

I would have loved to hear more about the Egyptians, but as soon as the inspectors left, we tore down the posters and put up the Bishop's favourite sayings. Things like *Keep Sweet* and *Never question. Questioning only makes you unhappy.*

Inspection Week was my favourite for another reason: it was the only time I felt safe at school. During that one five-day period every year, Mother Faith and the other teachers were completely different. They were good-natured, kind, and patient.

As I paused outside the entrance to the schoolhouse, I searched through my cloth bag for my final piece of homework, a book report on Bishop Thorsen's new Collection of Wise Words and Sayings. The collection was very long—four hundred pages— and I prayed for forgiveness for having skipped quite a few. God would understand. I'd promised Him that I would read it cover-to-cover eventually.

What with all my chores—caring for all the toddlers, doing the dishes after every meal, helping with laundry, weeding the garden, and doing the daily weather and road reports—there was little time in the day, and it was hard to stay up to read at night. My eyes just couldn't do it. They got so heavy they dragged me into sleep.

I felt a looming presence over me and looked up to see my old friend Donald. The boys hardly ever talked to the girls, but we'd been playmates when we were little kids and he never seemed to care much about the rules.

"Hey, Dais, I'm just comin' over to say goodbye. I'm out of here tomorrow."

He'd spoken about this before, but still, I was surprised. I'd never really taken his ideas about leaving Redemption very seriously. His timing surprised me too, but maybe it shouldn't have. The Placement would change the lives of both the girls and the boys turning fifteen this year, but part of me wanted things to just stay the same. It was like, deep down, I didn't want to grow up and leave my childhood behind.

I searched his face, looking for the emotion that he was so good at hiding. "You can't go, Donald. You don't even know what path Bishop Thorsen has chosen for you yet. At least wait for the Placement. What if you're one of the deserving?"

Donald's freckled, fair complexion flushed, and he looked down, kicking pebbles on the gravel driveway. "You and I both know which boys will be invited to join the priesthood. Bishop Thorsen makes it very clear. I see how he talks to them and their parents. He laughs with them, shakes their hands, slaps them on the shoulder. He never does that with me or my dad."

"But anything can change right up to the day of the Placement, the Bishop says that all the time. You can't leave until you know for sure."

"There's no point. Don't you get it? It's all about money. Since my dad hurt his back, he can't work and give money to the church. I'll be expected to work for Thorsen for the rest of my life and give back most of my earnings." Donald coughed and cleared his throat.

"This place is the only home I've ever known. I don't want to leave, but if I stay, I can never get married—can't even have a girlfriend." He blinked and rubbed his eyes hard. "Like I said, I just came to say goodbye. I hope you're happy with your Placement."

"But how will you leave? It's not like you can just walk out of here, right?"

Donald looked at me funny. "What's to stop me? Do you see any walls with barbed wire? It's not physical things that keep us here, Daisy, it's our loved ones and our fear of the unknown. I still love my family, but it's not enough. I have lots of reasons to leave." He turned and pointed west. "I'm just going to walk up to the highway and thumb a lift. The truckers usually stop."

"Good luck. I'll miss you." I had a crazy impulse to hug him or to reach out and squeeze his hand, but thankfully the bell rang and I was saved from doing something stupid. Girls never touched boys. We shared a brief smile before I had to rush for my seat. The thought of being late for school was too painful to even contemplate.

I slid into my wooden seat just as Mother Faith strode into the room and dropped her bookbag loudly on her desk. Everyone looked up uneasily. It was our last day of school ever, but one look at our teacher and I knew it was business as usual. She wouldn't let us go without one last attempt to "make us worthy of the great future we were all embarking upon." I felt the familiar sharp twist in my stomach and swallowed hard.

Time had not cooled Mother Faith's temper in all the years she'd been our teacher. She didn't tolerate impertinent questions or vague answers, and woe to you if your homework was incomplete. Every morning she told us grimly, "I was put on this earth to make you understand God's plan for you, and we can only do this through knowledge of our Fundamentalist covenants." All the courses she taught were centred on that theme.

They bored me silly.

Today, as Mother Faith took attendance, my mind drifted. I was upset about Donald, but there was nothing anyone could do to change his fate. It was up to the Bishop and no one else. Actually, I realised with surprise, it was up to *Donald*. By leaving early, he was changing his fate. And then it really hit me.

Donald didn't believe in Bishop Thorsen either.

I startled when the door to the classroom swung open and Tobias stepped in briefly to have a word with Mother Faith. I shouldn't have been surprised: his visit wasn't unusual. Our school was old and run-down; the Bishop had won funding from the government to build us a new one next year, but in the meantime, Tobias did repairs as needed. He was here a lot.

He wore his construction tool belt and a hard hat, which made him look so cute I thought I would swoon. I felt a sharp pinch on my calf and looked over see Brighten smiling and batting her eyes at me. It was all I could do to keep from bursting out laughing. Brighten covered her mouth and looked away.

Tobias and Mother Faith disappeared into the adjoining cloak-room. I listened to them talking about a leak, followed by the clank-ing of tools as Tobias unpacked. My thoughts clung obsessively to my last image of him, and I was lost in dreamland.

Minutes later I heard my name and jumped to my feet. "Present, Mother Faith," I said loudly and clearly before I sat again, this time on my hands as we were taught to do.

Fidgeting students are disruptive students.

We started covenant studies, but it was hard to concentrate knowing that Tobias was only a few feet away. I did my usual thing of staring wide-eyed at the teacher while thinking of something more interesting—like sewing my wedding dress after school. I could hardly wait. Mom had promised to come to the sewing room to help me with the collar and cuffs. In my daydream I saw myself standing before the entire congregation, everyone whispering about how fabulous I looked and how my dress was the best.

When Mother Faith began writing notes in blue chalk on the blackboard, I unstuck my hands and pretended to copy them, but I sketched my wedding dress instead. First, I drew a round collar, then a wide pointed one. I couldn't decide which I liked the best. *Mom will help*, I told myself.

It was a big deal that Mom had agreed to come to the sewing room after school; she didn't usually like to be seen with me. Ever since I'd been assigned to my new family with six devout mothers as role models, I was supposed to turn my back on my birth mother. It wasn't uncommon for kids to be assigned new mothers if their old ones were found undeserving for whatever reason. Most of the kids did as they were told and shunned their birth mother, but not me. How could I shun my mother when I was full of doubt and questioning too? It seemed that more and more, I was tempted to follow my own ideas of right and wrong, breaking Bishop Thorsen's rules, just like Mom did.

I felt for the locket Mom had given me, the one I kept hidden under my clothes. She'd told me to rub my thumb over it whenever I was lonely for her. I rubbed it now and a quiet calm settled over me.

Suddenly, the room grew dim and the changing light brought

me out of my reverie. I turned to the window, expecting to see clouds blocking the sun, but instead I saw Mother Faith standing over me, her face an ugly crimson. Something was wrong. All the kids were staring at me with fearful faces, including Brighten. She coughed to cover her whisper: "The Principle!"

I jumped to my feet, stepping on my long dress and struggling to pull it free of my sandals. My mind blanked, and I stumbled over my words. "In the Principle of plural marriage, God commands us to be fruitful . . . ah . . . We are the Chosen, so we must go forth and multiply . . . and that is why the priesthood men are superior seed bearers and should have many young wives."

I finished quickly and glanced at Brighten for validation. She looked up at me, her eyes large and moist, but everyone else stared down at their desks, fearful of attracting attention.

I sat back down and had just settled my damp hands under me again when a piece of blue chalk hit me hard in the face. Reaching up, I felt the dry chalk stain on my forehead. I knew better than to cry; it would only make things worse. Mother Faith grabbed a thick ruler and came at me, her eyes flashing.

"That's the best you can do?" she thundered. She was sweating hard, and the earthy smell reminded me of rotting mushrooms. "After nine years of schooling, this is all you have to offer? I always said you were an idiot; the daughter of a degenerate and an apostate. You have no faith. Your heart is full of doubt. You deserve neither this education nor all the sacrifices I've made to teach you." She raised the ruler high and brought it down hard and stinging across my shoulders. "You're a stupid, evil girl."

She raised the ruler again, higher, but it hovered there. Something stopped her. I looked up and I saw Tobias, his face flushed, his eyes red-rimmed and as angry as hers, yanking the ruler from Mother Faith's hand.

"What's going on in here?" he demanded. "Control yourself, Mother Faith! What's possessed you?" Tobias couldn't contain his disgust at her violent outburst. "Stop this right now."

Everyone, including Mother Faith, gasped, their eyes wide at his insinuation. I'd never seen this side of Tobias before; demanding to be heard, taking control, censuring an elder.

The room was silent as Mother Faith shrank back, her face pale, her brow hooded, mumbling that she'd always tried to do her best and treat everyone according to God's direction.

I didn't dare look to Tobias for fear of revealing my feelings for him, but never, ever, had I felt so cherished and protected.

Many of the kids' faces showed a mixture of relief and joy. They slowly got to their feet and walked out of the classroom. It was only ten o'clock in the morning, but Mother Faith had lost control.

Mom met me later that afternoon. As we set up the sewing machines by changing the thread and bobbins to match the colour of my dress, I told her what happened at school. Her reaction surprised me. She clicked her tongue against her front teeth and frowned. Hunching over her sewing, she said, "Tobias shouldn't have done that. The Bishop will see that as a challenge to his authority." She didn't say anything more. Her foot hit the power pedal and her machine whirred to life.

I ran my sewing machine over some unfinished seams. "But he was defending me. He shouldn't have done that?"

"He should have corrected Mother Faith privately, Daisy. Not in front of the class. Tobias needs to know his place. He's not even a member of the priesthood yet. One of the Bishop's wives told me that his father is a very important man in Utah, but that doesn't hold much water here."

I wanted so badly to tell her that I loved Tobias, and that his defence of me had made me love him even more, but I was too frightened to say the words aloud for fear they'd sound silly and childish. Instead, when we both took a break, I told Mom about Donald's decision to leave. "I know you think differently," I said, "but Bishop Thorsen tells us all the time how terrible life is on the outside, how cruel and Godless everyone is. Donald's not like that. How will he make his way?"

"I think Donald will be just fine. People aren't perfect on the outside, but there are lots of kind hearts."

"What are you saying? That Bishop Thorsen isn't telling us the truth?"

"Bishop Thorsen wants us all to live the best lives we can in the service of God. Because of that, he doesn't want anyone to leave, so he bends the truth to suit his needs."

Using a sharp seam-picker to undo my stitching, I admitted, "Sometimes, when you say things like that, Mom, I worry. You don't always think like the other moms. It's not good to be different here."

"Don't worry. I'm already an outcast; what more can they do to me?"

I didn't have the heart to tell her I was talking about me. I still had everything to lose.

Chapter Six

With only three days to go before the Placement I could barely contain my excitement. All the girls turning fifteen that year were part of the ritual, the most important event of our lives so far. We had different dreams for our futures—like yearning to become brides, or mothers of Zion, a goal we had been taught to cherish from our earliest days, or coveting the role of celestial sister—but we all knew better than to gossip about it openly for fear of punishment. A sweet disposition, not a gossipy or ambitious one, is what the men wanted and demanded.

Females are expected to display a pleasant but quiet temperament.

When my radio shift was done, I gulped my breakfast, hurrying through the washing-up for my assigned family. By ten, I rushed over to the Hall of Worship, where all the girls were already gathering for our day-long ritual of preparation and rehearsal. Passing a group of the boys and young men, I gave their faces a quick scan. I felt a surge of warmth when I recognized Tobias, but he kept his head down and didn't try to catch my eye.

I felt blessed knowing that I would soon be married to him, but my heart felt heavy for the girls who would be married to "deserving" middle-aged or older men with many wives and children already. What did they have to look forward to? And what about all the young men? According to the Bishop, most weren't worthy, and they would be sent away.

Inside, the hall was a hive of activity. Eight men struggled to remove the huge baptism tub from the stage while several of the mothers waited with boxes of crepe paper, plastic flowers, and balloons to construct the bridal arch. The women would leave space in the arch for the fresh flowers they'd gather the day of the Placement. They talked softly among themselves because there were men around, but I guessed that they were just as excited and nervous as the young brides-to-be. After the men finally moved the seven-foot-deep fiberglass tub, the women started decorating.

I made a beeline for Brighten, who was sitting in the centre of a group of about twenty girls on the floor below the stage. "Hey, B."

"Hey, Dais." We cupped our fingers and gripped each other's hands in our secret handshake while the other girls reluctantly shuffled their chairs and made room for me.

Blossom stood, stepped up onto the stage, and raised her arms.

Everyone quieted down.

Typical, I thought. Blossom always tried to be the boss. I wanted to say, "Who died and made you queen?" but I kept my mouth shut. There was a pecking order, and I knew it, but that didn't mean Brighten and I had to agree with it.

"You go first, Daisy," Blossom said to me. "Let's see if you can make yourself look less like a little girl so your old-man husband can perform his duty." All the girls except Brighten exploded in giggles and blushes, hiding their mouths with their hands, or burying their faces in the hems of their skirts.

Brighten didn't laugh. Instead, she gave me a sympathetic look.

Now that she was tall, beautiful, and the best in the class, Brighten was accepted by the other girls. Unlike me, she was no longer unpopular, but she stayed loyal to me and our friendship anyway. Maybe if I looked more like the others, I would have been accepted. While their bodies were growing and flowering, mine stayed in childhood, until recently, that is. I'd grown quite a lot in the past months, but they hadn't noticed. Which was why Blossom was trotting out the same old joke.

No one wanted to go first in the dress ritual, but I didn't want to cause problems, so I shrugged it off and walked to the change room. Each of us was to disappear behind a screen and then reappear wearing her wedding dress for everyone to admire.

I squeezed into a tight elastic girdle that flattened my tummy and smoothed my thighs, hooked the sheer nylon stockings to the garters, and stuffed myself into a high, pointy bra with straps that dug into my shoulders.

I thought of Blossom's comment about trying to look alluring.

Ever since I developed the crush on Tobias, I'd been trying to make myself more attractive. Girls weren't allowed makeup, but many did things to make themselves look prettier. They squeezed lemon on their hair and then let it dry in the sun to bring out the highlights, and they mixed baby oil and iodine to use as a suntan lotion. I'd tried them both and they worked well—at least my pale skin looked less like a freshly peeled potato.

I looked at myself in the mirror. The girdle and bra had changed the shape of my body, and a woman stared back at me. I wasn't sure if I was ready for my new look, and I wondered what Tobias would think of it. Would he agree I looked more like a bride and less like someone's little sister?

I pulled the high-necked, ankle-length wedding dress over my head and struggled to button the back. Our choice of fabric colour was limited—light pastels only, because God took pleasure in them— and red was banned outright. I felt like a caterpillar squeezed into a cocoon. The question was would I emerge as a butterfly or just a lumpier caterpillar?

As I stepped out of the change room and onto the stage, I heard everyone suck in their breath.

"Whoa, Daisy! The peach is perfect on you," Brighten squealed. "And the high white collar, wow! Your neck looks so long and graceful!"

"I didn't think crocheted trim was allowed," Rainbow said with a pout. "I would have done that if I'd known."

"There's still time. I can help you if you like." I smiled warmly at Rainbow and swirled my skirt around my ankles. It flared prettily.

"Oh, get over it, Rainbow," Blossom said. "Even if you add the trim, you still wouldn't look as good as Daisy does. She's petite, you're not. The only pot of gold Rainbow has is her gut!" One of the other girls snorted with laughter. Rainbow flushed and turned her head away.

Blossom rolled her eyes. "Don't be so sensitive."

Rainbow didn't respond. Clearly, she was hurt, but I saw through Blossom too. She acted tough so the others would see her as their leader. Underneath it all, she was insecure, always trying to win her dad's approval by being just like him. I guessed it was hard to feel special when you had nineteen sisters.

"Come on, Brighten. It's your turn." Blossom leaned over and gave Brighten a little push.

Brighten held her ground. "Age before beauty."

Blossom's round, fleshy face darkened to a deep crimson while moisture beaded on her upper lip. I noticed the beating pulse in her neck and shrank back, wishing I could slink off to a corner somewhere.

Blossom glared at Brighten. "I don't have to try on my dress because I won't *need* a wedding dress. I'm going to be chosen as the new celestial sister. I'll be favoured by God as one of his helper-maidens on earth, and with His guidance I'll help run this place."

I prayed Brighten would just go try on her dress, but instead she leaned closer to Blossom. "You're not the only candidate for the new celestial sister. I've earned it, you haven't. Everyone knows that your mother did your sewing project for you."

I winced. This was getting tense.

"At least my mother *sews*," Blossom sneered. "Your mother's a nutcase, always trying to get out of work 'cause she says she's just too darned sad." Blossom mimed a sad face. "All she does is sit and stare at walls all day. You come from damaged goods, Brighten. Face it. You'll never be a celestial sister. Better go try on that wedding gown. I hear old Brother Antony's looking for lucky number twenty-five. He hasn't made any new babies for years now, but maybe God will perform a miracle."

As if on cue, the other girls all pinched their noses and let out a chorus of "Brother Antony, eww," before collapsing into stifled giggles.

"Bishop Thorsen is all-knowing and will find the perfect match for poor Brother Antony—perhaps you," Brighten said calmly. "Since you seem to want to wear the pants in the family."

Blossom leaned forward and gave Brighten a sharp push, forcing her chair over backwards and dumping her hard on the floor. Brighten got up slowly and turned to glare at Blossom. My stomach started to hurt. I was sure there was about to be a physical fight.

"Please, everyone, can't we all just get along?" Rainbow said as she hugged her arms across her chest. "This is supposed to be the best time of our lives."

Brighten casually brushed off her ankle-length cotton dress. "We'll just see what happens. It's up to the Bishop now." She looked pointedly at Blossom. "He knows who's deserving and who isn't."

The girls all looked at Brighten with wide eyes. It was true. None of us had any say in our future. Our whole lives were going to be determined by the Bishop. We could fantasize or worry all we wanted, but nothing we said or did would influence the outcome of the Placement.

Unless we walked away. Like Donald.

The mood turned somber, no more jokes or kidding about. As soon as we had all paraded around in our wedding dresses and ooh-ed and ahh-ed for one another, Brighten and I gathered up our things to leave. No one said goodbye.

Brighten looked depressed and I put my arm around her as we left the building. "Don't worry," I said. "Blossom knows that you're the better choice for the new celestial sister and that's why she's so mad at you."

Brighten gave me a weak, nervous smile. "It should be me, but sometimes there're other forces at work behind the scenes, things we don't know about."

We struggled to carry our gowns without wrinkling them or letting them drag on the ground. They had to be perfect for the big night. I thought about the dresses and the ritual around them. Everyone was supposed to say flattering things to each girl on her choice of fabric, colour, and trim, but it hadn't been like that at all. Instead, there was eye rolling and catty remarks. Why?

Because it was what we learned at home.

Chapter Seven

The tension and talk at yesterday's dress rehearsal crowded my brain and I struggled with my emotions. I walked home from my morning radio work very slowly, as I always did. I took the long way, through the forest, across the main road, past the pond, and finally to the centre of our settlement. It was a twenty-minute walk, but I managed to stretch it to thirty. It was my only chance to think, to dream.

How many times had I taken this route? I wondered. Redemption was the only place I'd ever known, aside from the occasional visit to Stewart's Landing. A mere 250 acres of woods and farmland. Lost in thought, I headed towards the centre of the community; some twenty huge homes with large yards surrounding the Hall of Worship. Many smaller cottages, each on five farming acres, stretched off into the distance and the lush valley beyond.

The valley ended in a mountain range that was not actually in Canada but across the border in the United States. This allowed the Bishop to avoid the border control by using a hiking trail through the mountains to a series of safe houses. He moved lots of people to and from his logging and milling operations and one of my jobs was to pack food for them. I stopped and looked off into the distance, wondering if the Bishop would send brides to the U.S. that way, now that the Canadian and U.S. churches were united again, like Tobias said.

The Bishop and the priesthood men had the largest homes in Redemption by far. God rewarded the most faithful, and that was why they made so much money from all the businesses they ran.

They had to fight hard to keep it, though, according to the Bishop, because the government was always trying to steal it.

Twice a year, in April and October, tax inspectors drove the three miles from the town of Stewart's Landing and arrived here unannounced. They didn't even have the common courtesy to stop at the PRIVATE PROPERTY, NO TRESPASSING sign where the road to Redemption left the main highway.

The Bishop instructed us not to talk to any of the tax or school inspectors; he said if we were asked a direct question, we should never tell the truth. That was an easy rule to follow since everyone was terrified of those evil, corrupt men. Anyway, since we were the Chosen, God made us smarter than the outsiders, and it was easy for the celestial sisters to keep the books and hide our money. The Bishop was a real stickler for record-keeping. Once a year every household had to complete a list of everything they owned. Even underwear. Anything that the Bishop decided was more than the family needed had to be donated back to the community. It was a lot of work, but it was for the good of the community.

All I knew of Stewart's Landing was the general store. That's where the celestial sisters occasionally took us to help load a pickup truck full of supplies. We bought flour, sugar, baking powder, vegetable oil, and all the other staples we needed for baking and cooking. We avoided any food that we didn't grow or make ourselves because outsider foods caused cancer. We also bought our sewing supplies and sometimes the sisters let us choose our own fabric to make our dresses. That was always a big thrill.

The one luxury we were allowed was hairspray. We bought it by the crate. It was the only way we could keep our hairstyles in place and avoid punishment for looking slovenly.

I had mixed feelings about those trips into the outside world. On one hand, I was very curious to see the outsiders for myself—I don't know what I was expecting; it's not like they had horns or anything—and I really wanted to see what girls my age were wearing. On the other hand, I was upset when some outsiders treated us like freaks, pointing at us, laughing and calling us *polyg* girls with our *polyg* dresses and hairdos.

I was pulled from my thoughts when I heard laughter and children's voices coming from the edge of the pond. Settling on a large boulder in the sunshine, I positioned myself to feel the warm wind at my back as I watched the kids as they played. The breeze was lovely, and smelled of warm pine woods as it rushed past me towards the water. It was a pity that few people ever came to the pebbly beach. It was a beautiful spot, but no one in Redemption could swim. The Bishop forbade swimming costumes and frolicking in water.

God does not want us to behave as animals do.

Today a small group—two seven-year-olds in charge of a handful of toddlers—had two large pink helium balloons tied together with a ribbon. They'd obviously taken them from the decorations in the Hall of Worship and were tossing them in the air and then hitting them with their hands. The balloons were weighted with a stone small enough to permit them to fly after a good swat, but large enough to keep them from floating away. I laughed out loud at one little dark-haired mop-top who squealed with delight at the game, all his attention focused on chasing the drifting balloons.

I had a soft spot for kids this age, so full of excitement as they explored the world around them. It was a blessing that our community had so many children. Watching them play let me forget about my worries and helped me focus on the here and now.

One of the older boys swatted the balloons towards the little guy on the shore, but the balloons went past him, heading straight out over the water. I sat up and watched as the toddler made a beeline for them, plunging straight in, unfazed. The balloons squeaked and slipped out of his chubby hands, so he stood up and flung himself forward again. This time, he managed to grab the ribbon, but he lost his footing, splashing on one knee in the shallow water. The balloons bobbed down in his tight grip and then rose as he got to his feet, catching the warm wind. They started drifting slowly towards the deeper water in the middle of the pond, taking the little boy with them.

The older boy screamed at the kid to let go, but the little one had already shifted from delight to terror. He held on to the balloons for dear life.

He couldn't swim.

Except for a couple of the young men, *nobody* in Redemption could swim. None of the women swam, except Mom. Dad had taught her, and, of course, she had ignored the rules and taught me.

I called to the older boy, "The little one will drown!"

The older boy just stared back at me, saying nothing. His eyes were wide like he was in shock. I had to do something, so I waded in the water up to my chest but was too weighed down by the heavy layers of fabric I wore to make much progress.

I struggled back to shore in my heavy shoes and long, billowing dress, where I stripped down to my underwear. (God's underwear, as people called it, covered me from neck to ankles.) No one was supposed to *ever* be seen in their underwear, so all the kids shrieked at the sight of me. I might as well have been standing there naked. I felt so ashamed I wanted to cry, but I put that aside. I had to save the little boy.

As I waded back in, I watched in horror as the child lost his grip on the ribbon. The balloons bobbed down gently at first, but then the wind caught them and buffeted them away. Below the bright shrinking orbs growing smaller in the sky, the little boy had slipped silently below the surface of the pond.

Two of the children wailed as they watched the toddler surface and sputter. He slapped the water, instinctively making dog-paddling motions, his eyes wide with disbelief, but he choked on the water forcing its way into his mouth and down his throat.

He sank under the water again. Dreadful, heartbreaking seconds ticked by as I dove underwater for him. Coming up from below, I grabbed the little guy in my arms and gave a mighty kick with my legs. We surfaced in the middle of the pond. Once he caught his breath, he let out a healthy little bellow and tried to wrap his arms around my neck. Floating on my back, I placed him on my chest, and, cradling the toddler's face and head with one arm, I towed him to shore.

I had to blink back my own tears as I tried to comfort the crying children on the beach, telling them that it was all okay, that their little brother had not drowned. Someone ran for towels, and it wasn't long before the little boy was cuddling in my arms, warm and cozy in a dry towel.

I set him down gently and struggled back into my long, damp dress and then dried myself, my clothes, and my messy hair the best I could with a towel. Carrying the toddler, I told the other kids to follow me home. I knew whose children they were without asking. They all had a certain look, like their square-jawed, dark-haired father.

Bishop Thorsen.

I found the toddler's mom, Mother Lily, in the Bishop's

huge, four-storey house built in the shape of an H at the centre of Redemption. Lily shared the massive house with thirty-four sister-wives and one hundred and fifty-six children. The place, with all its inhabitants, reminded me of the community centre I'd seen in Stewart's Landing, but I'd never been inside.

Not all the houses in Redemption were huge and modern—those were just for the priesthood men who had really large families—but I was getting used to big noisy houses full of people. It had taken me a while to get settled among my new family two years ago, especially coming from a house where I had been an only child, but I soon adapted. There weren't any other "onlies" in Redemption. It was another thing that made me different, another reason for people to shun me.

I entered the Bishop's house through the kitchen and felt the tug in my stomach at the smell of chicken soup seasoned with sage and parsley simmering on the stove. It seemed I was always hungry these days. Snacking was not allowed in my house, but I could see things were different here.

The mothers were preparing lunch, and I was shocked to see sliced meats and cheeses on a sideboard. Plates of cookies and platters of fresh fruit were laid out on the table too, and I noticed several of the older children helping themselves while two of the mothers argued about who would serve the Bishop his lunch.

My assigned family ate a lot of beans and rice, and beans and wieners. There was always bread, but we only had fresh vegetables in the summer when we grew them in the garden. Meat and fresh fruit were an occasional treat. Cookies and desserts were for Sundays or special events only. Apparently, the Bishop's family ate like kings and queens every day, or at least on Tuesdays.

Mother Lily, a seventeen-year-old, was slouched on an over-stuffed couch in a corner of the communal living room nursing her newborn. She was surrounded by about forty or so small children. With all the chatter and play, the heat and noise were overwhelming.

The girls, all dressed in long, pastel-coloured dresses, their hair arranged with an upsweep in front and braids in the back, played with a collection of dolls in one corner of the large room while the boys, dressed in black pants and long-sleeved shirts, played with carved wooden construction tools in another corner. What a relief that the Bishop had finally reversed the toy ban. Keeping toddlers happy without any toys to play with had been really hard.

There was no TV, radio, or record player, and instead of artwork on the walls, there were banners with brightly painted slogans. *God Loves Obedient Children*, *Do as You Are Told*, *Never Ask Why*, and *Be Perfectly Obedient or Be Punished Perfectly*.

On one wall, I noticed a large chart drawn on a whiteboard. I'd never seen one quite like it before. It seemed to be for chores. Across the top were headings: bathrooms—one through four-teen, bedrooms—one through thirty, four dormitory spaces, four communal rooms, and the kitchen. Down the side were the moth-ers' names. Large, angry black Xs filled the chart in a haphazard checkerboard.

I tried to catch Mother Lily's attention. "Keep sweet, Mother Lily," I said as the girl glanced up, her face hollow-eyed and pale, mother's milk staining the front of her unbuttoned gown.

"Keep sweet, Daisy."

I set the toddler down while the two seven-year-olds cowered by the door. I told the young mother what had happened.

Lily reached over and gave the toddler a big hug and tousled his hair before her face darkened. "Those two are Hope's and Prim-rose's spoiled brats. Their moms are lazy and useless, just like their kids." Looking over at the two cowering boys, she said, "You two'll get the leather strap once Daddy gets home."

My heart sank as I looked at the two boys fighting back tears. I'd hoped that Mother Lily's gratitude might help shield the boys from harsh punishment, but there was none on display. "It wasn't their fault," I said. "It was an accident. I'm just glad I was there."

Lily didn't want to hear it. She turned away from me to check on her infant. "Thank you for all you did, but they're going to get the licking of their lives. I'll make sure of it." She turned back to me, perhaps remembering who I was, who my parents were. She spoke pointedly. "These boys didn't choose their weak and lazy mothers; that's why we have to be extra vigilant in showing them the right path to God's good graces. They should welcome their punishment."

Our conversation was interrupted by twelve chimes from the large round wall clock. It was lunchtime, and my empty stomach groaned. As if on cue, Bishop Thorsen arrived home for lunch. The door slammed and he stomped in heavy boots across the floor. Mother Lily got up and hurried over to him, talking loudly and gesturing at the boys who were now openly crying, but the Bishop held up his hand, frowned, and pushed past her.

"Enough! Give me peace, woman." He looked over at me.

I knew I was not about to be congratulated for saving the child—I had gone against God's direction by swimming in my underwear, though I would do it again if I had to—but I didn't expect what the Bishop said next.

"Daisy! The Lord has spoken to me about you. We need to talk." He walked to a door that led off the living room and I followed.

It was a small, dark study, sparsely furnished with a plain pine desk and two straight-backed chairs, smelling strongly of Lysol and wood furniture polish. With no carpet on the faded linoleum floor or artwork on the walls, it was cold and uninviting. Bishop Thorsen sat but didn't invite me to. I stood before him, my back to the wall as he looked me up and down me with a hard, expressionless face.

He resembled the other priesthood men: middle-aged and over-weight, with his hair brushed straight back from his face. But there was something different about him, a bearing, a way of holding himself that set him apart. Everything about him gave off a sense of power. I bet he was the sort of man who other men instinctively feared, even if they couldn't say exactly why.

"You're the spitting image of your mother, you know—when she was your age. Can't believe that was twenty-five years ago." A small smile split his face. "I was just a skinny young man back then." He patted his belly. "A lot has changed." Suddenly, his smile was gone. "Your mom—there was something special about her. All the men, young and old, wanted to take her as their bride, but she only had eyes for one man, and that was your father. Seems like you take after her in more ways than one."

I stared at the floor and nodded. My damp, clammy underwear itched and rubbed my skin, but I didn't dare fidget. I heard the Bishop sigh heavily and I looked up. Our eyes met. "I had been thinking that you would make a nice addition to my own little family here. I know the other sister-wives would love you and welcome you with open arms."

My insides churned. *Please, God, no,* a voice in my head screamed. I swallowed hard and glued my eyes to the linoleum. I heard the

Bishop's chair scrape the floor and his heavy footsteps approach me. He stood directly in front of me. I looked up and met his cold dark eyes. He stroked his chin and pursed his lips, looking at me as if I were a prized possession.

"But God sees things differently. You are to be tied for time and all eternity to Tobias. He will be your priest and spiritual leader. Through his grace, you will be pulled up to heaven to sit on a throne alongside him. That is God's will, and I am His one true messenger on earth."

I knew better than to show any emotion in the presence of the Bishop and said nothing. He was standing so close it felt intimate. I could smell his citrus-sweet aftershave and hear his laboured breathing. In that moment I thought about my mom and what the Bishop had said about her. She had told me that he owed her a favour. Was this it? Was this the payback for something the Bishop did to my father?

I suddenly wanted to do cartwheels out of the room. I was to be married to Tobias! I couldn't resist a small smile. But I should have known better.

He stepped closer to me until we were just inches from each other. His voice was low and even. "Don't think your mom got the best of me."

The smile fell from my lips. "No, sir."

He reached around and grabbed my loose hair with his fist and yanked hard. My jaw popped, my scalp burnt, and I was forced to bend backwards to lessen the pain. I struggled to keep my balance.

"What's with your hair, Daisy? You look like a whore. Get yourself fixed up before I change my mind about your Placement."

"Yes, Bishop Thorsen. Yes, sir."

He let go and I turned and stumbled my way out of his office, my thoughts a confused mix of joy and fear.

Chapter Eight

It was my last day working the radio job. Tomorrow was my wedding day, and I was vibrating with excitement. I followed my ritual for one last time. After I signed off, I did the usual. Dimmed the lights, checked out the window to make sure no one was around, and turned the radio dial to the FM station only fifteen miles away, across the U.S. border.

The radio dials blinked hypnotically in the half-light, beckoning me into their forbidden realm. I pulled on my headphones.

"Hi, Wolfman. This is Kim in Atlanta. I want to hear that groovy song about the hot new dance. Can you play 'The Twist' by Chubby Checker?"

"Oh, my, my, this dance gonna make my backbone slip and hurt the Wolfman's sacroiliac, but I dig it. Come on, everybody, let's do the twist!"

The music started, and I couldn't stop myself from moving. I felt like I was full of jumping beans. First it was just in my chair, but soon I was on my feet. Listening to the lyrics that described the steps, I started to twist my body in time to the music, swaying backwards then forwards. The cord on the earphones tied me down, so I ripped them off, turned the sound low, and let myself go. The sense of freedom and pure joy was fabulous. I laughed out loud.

When the song ended, I felt a surge of guilt and quickly turned off the radio just as I heard a knock at the door. My heart fluttered in my chest. No one ever visited me here except Brighten, but she never knocked. Who could be here now? Had they heard my radio? I held my breath. My fingers felt like ice as I slowly pulled open the door.

At first, I couldn't see anyone, then I looked down. My tow-headed five-year-old brother, son of Mother Fern, stood grinning up at me with a gap-toothed smile. "I'm here to get you, Daithy." My name whistled through his teeth.

"Joshua, what a surprise." Relieved, I squatted down to his level so I could read his face. "Do you need me to help you with something?" Joshua was one of the twenty kids in my new family who were under the age of six, and it was one of my jobs to help take care of them. I loved them all, but Josh had a special place in my heart.

"You have to come home now."

"Why is that?"

"It's a secret. I'm not supposed to say." He giggled, his clear blue eyes wide with excitement.

"Oh, you're not, eh?" I smiled and gave him a hug. "How about a hint? Does it involve lots of food?" His eyes flickered sideways in a moment of indecision, then he gave me a solemn nod. "Is there a cake and decorations?" Again, the nod. "Okay, I won't ask you any more questions because it's a secret. Let's go." I grabbed his hand, and we ran down the forest path together.

I was so happy I thought I'd burst. It was tradition for the families to have a shower for the new brides on the night before the Placement, but I had prepared myself for disappointment. I was still the daughter of an apostate, after all. But now, running to what I knew would be my surprise bridal shower, my assigned family made me feel just like everyone else. Of course, I loved my mom, and nothing could ever change that, but at the same time, I loved the feeling of belonging my assigned family gave me.

As we approached the house, I saw the bright lights in the cafeteria-size kitchen go out. Except for little Joshua, who couldn't stop giggling as he stepped aside and made me go inside first, the house was unusually quiet.

When the lights flicked on, most of my forty-five assigned family members jumped out from behind chairs and out of doorways, shouting, "Surprise!" I pretended to be flabbergasted, my hand over my heart as the little children surrounded me, demanding to know if I had been truly surprised. I assured them that I was as they dragged me over to the dining table that ran the length of the huge room.

The remains of supper had been cleared away, replaced by platters of treats. The noise in the room was suddenly deafening as everyone talked and laughed at once. Someone handed me a plate and I began picking at my favourites: pinwheel, sugar, and bird's nest cookies. The succulent, sugary smell of dark chocolate filled my senses, and my eyes went wide at the sight of platters of Nanaimo bars and brownies. At the centre of the table was a massive layer cake with yellow icing. *Congratulations, Daisy!* was written across it in white.

I finally made it, I thought. *I'm truly one of the family and part of the community.* In that moment I felt accepted and loved. It was a wonderful feeling. Belonging was something I had longed for. Once I married Tobias, no one could ever take that from me.

As I stood admiring the cake, I felt the presence of a tall woman next to me. "Keep sweet, Daisy," she said. I looked up and almost dropped my plate.

"Keep sweet, Sister Bluebell," I said calmly, trying to pretend I was relaxed and confident. To have the most senior of the celestial sisters attend your bridal shower was a big deal.

The celestial sisters kept a sharp eye on the daily lives of all the women and older girls. Lists of sins were kept, and when necessary, the sisters spoke to the Bishop and recommended a punishment that would correct bad behaviour. No matter how hard I tried to stay out of the Sinners Logbook, I wasn't successful. Either the sisters had grown eyes out the back of their heads, or snitches were rewarded for tattling.

"Congratulations on your marriage tomorrow," Sister Bluebell said. She spoke through tight teeth that I took for a smile. "I don't think I'm betraying any confidences by telling you that I've heard that you are going to be especially blessed."

Sister Bluebell was overseeing the ceremony tomorrow, so Bishop Thorsen would have shared all the details with her. She had to know that I was to marry Tobias, the son of a member of the Council of Seven. I wanted to appear happy, but not over the moon. I was superstitious: if I celebrated too soon, it wouldn't happen. "I believe Bishop Thorsen has found the best possible husband for me, and I will do as I am directed."

"Good girl," Sister Bluebell said, patting my arm. "I wish some of the other girls were as mature and sensible as you." I nodded piously just as Sister Bluebell caught the eye of someone else and headed off to speak to them.

I wandered back to the table where a group of my cocky older brothers and their friends had gathered, grazing, pushing the girls out of the way. I was just reaching around them for another Nanaimo bar when one of the boys gave me a hard slap on the back. Jonas the Jerk, Blossom's brother.

"Congratulations, Daisy," he said with a smirk. "Wish I could be there to see you get what's coming to you. Your new husband's gonna ride you till you're raw." He laughed loudly.

I looked at him calmly. "Why? So you can see what a real man looks like?" I backed away into the hall off the kitchen, leaving Jonas to close his gaping mouth.

What was he doing here anyway? Wasn't he missing Blossom's bridal shower at his own house? I looked around for Lavender, even checked her room, but I couldn't find her, so I sat by myself for a while, trying to push a hornet's nest of new fears and worries from my mind. I took a deep breath. I had nothing to be afraid of. I would have a good marriage with a loving husband who would adore me and hear my concerns.

Tobias and I had something special, something that few husbands and wives had—a relationship built on mutual love and respect that came from shared values outside our religion. We believed in basic fairness, and that men and women should have equal status in a marriage. We thought life should not be all hard work, but that there should be time for fun and laughter every day. We saw things the same way and we connected on a deeper level.

God wanted us to be together. Tobias and I were promised in the pre-life, and God would make His wishes known through His vessel, Bishop Thorsen.

Tomorrow was my big day, the day I would become a some-body in the eyes of the rest of the community. I would be the first wife of a new member of the priesthood and happily married to the kind, gentle Tobias. I crossed my fingers and prayed.

Daisy and Tobias together, for all time.

Chapter Nine

It was a cool day for the end of June, but when Brighten and I walked into the Hall of Worship, we felt like we had stepped into a steam bath. The air was stifling. Right away, my stomach didn't feel quite right, and I rubbed my clammy palms on the long skirts of my bridal dress. My tight nylon stockings made my legs feel like they had been stuffed into sausage casings. The garters that held them in place dug into my upper thighs.

As hot and uncomfortable as I was, I loved showing off my beautiful dress. I caught the admiring glances from some of the mothers and I knew it was a standout. Mom had helped me get dressed and do my hair over at her cottage, but, as a nonperson, she wasn't allowed to come to the hall and see me marry Tobias. I promised to bring him back to her place after we were husband and wife, and Mom said she would have tea and cake ready for a little celebration. I still hadn't heard if we were going to be allowed to live with her, but I figured the Bishop would tell us tonight. I crossed my fingers again.

"Ugh. Why can't someone open a window?" Brighten said. "So many sweaty, nervous people."

The mood in the vast space was electric. Hundreds of the Chosen filled the wooden chairs in front of the stage where the Arch of Flowers stood resplendent. The room buzzed with anticipation and speculation. The brothers, all wearing the starched white shirts and black pants of bridegrooms, sat apart at the front.

"There they are." Brighten pointed at the men. "Those are the ones getting a new wife." We both stood on our toes to get a good look.

I rarely saw the priesthood men all together and I took a moment to observe them. Two were caught up in animated conversation, their faces flushed, one with excited bulging eyes, the other with beaded sweat dripping from his upper lip. Were they hoping for a lovely new wife who would be submissive and obedient, or were they worried about household discord and anticipating battles at home?

Men and women rarely mingled socially, so tonight, the Bishop would forever bind each brother to a fifteen-year-old girl they'd only ever met in passing. They would then lead their new brides into one of the celestial chambers upstairs and complete the celestial union. Were they as nervous as we were, or was it something else that I saw in their faces?

Brighten inclined her head. "That's him," she said with a shudder. "Brother Earl, the one who always watches me."

Brother Earl was seated closest to Bishop Thorsen, an indicator of his power and influence. Despite the heat, I shivered. There was something about the man that I didn't like. Physically he looked very much like the others. All old men, ranging in age from forty to seventy, bellies sagging over groaning waistbands, hair generally short and thinning. They all seemed very pleased with themselves. God and the Bishop had found them to be deserving, and they waited patiently for their just rewards.

But Brother Earl managed to stand out. It was his eyes, I decided. Always watching, always alert, like a dog on the lookout for any chance to display dominance over the pack. He turned and looked directly at us. I felt my nausea grow, made worse by the prickly heat.

Brighten gave me a knowing look and pointed discreetly. "There are the new priesthood men." Directly behind the brothers of the priesthood sat the younger men, hoping to be found deserving and rewarded with their first wife. They also wore the standard outfit of dark pants and a white shirt. Their faces were flushed in the heat, their hair trim and neat and shining. Turning in their chairs, they craned their necks to cast hopeful, hungry glances at the girls. I felt a surge of emotion when Tobias caught my eye and smiled.

"That's the guy you've been pretending not to have a crush on. Right?" whispered Brighten. "I've got to hand it to you. He's got to be the cutest guy around. A real honey."

My heart felt like a butterfly in my chest.

We took our seats with the rest of the new brides at the back of the room. The mothers sat off to one side, their faces glowing with pride as they watched their daughters line up like prize calves at the fair.

I had come to the Placement ceremony every year for as long as I could remember. To me it had always been like a big, fun party where everyone guessed which deserving brother would be assigned which bride. We all had our favourites. But I had had no idea of the incredible emotions that the participants were feeling. Now I knew. It hadn't been a game to them, and it wasn't a game to us. This night would determine how happy and fulfilled we would be for the rest of our lives.

Bishop Thorsen, in place onstage beside the Arch of Flowers, rang a tiny bell and the room instantly fell silent. "Believers of the First Order," he began. "Welcome to the Placement. 1964 looks like a bumper crop. Twenty-two sweet, beautiful girls. God has truly blessed His Chosen people."

A round of cheering and applauding followed.

The Bishop beamed back at us. "Before we get started, we'll enjoy a little entertainment from Mother Sunshine. I hear she wrote this song herself. Come on up here, Sunshine."

Brighten moaned. "Oh, *please* not her!" Mother Sunshine, an older, heavy-set woman who was already perspiring, struggled up the steps to the stage carrying a large black-and-silver accordion.

Frozen smiles appeared as she sang her lyrics in an off-tune soprano.

I blocked out Sunshine's song, letting my mind drift. I thought about the music I listened to on the radio, the exciting rhythms, catchy beats, and expressive lyrics. It always made me feel like moving my body or succumbing to my emotions—urges I had trouble resisting. Dancing was forbidden in Redemption, and the whole thing left me feeling ashamed after I did it. As much as I loved it, once I was married, it would be time for me to quit.

Unless Tobias thought differently.

I sighed softly and tried to focus on the performance onstage.

Leaning in close, Brighten whispered under the cover of light applause, "Once I'm appointed a celestial sister, I'm going to ban Mother Sunshine from singing in public." We covered our mouths with our hands to hide our giggles.

The marriages were announced and conducted in order of the seniority of the men, with the highest-ranking first, but Bishop Thorsen occasionally mixed things up to add a little drama. I knew that the prettiest girls were always chosen first, assigned to the most deserving brothers. Brighten and I were considered to be in that group too, so when our names weren't called right away, I felt a surge of confidence. Neither of us was to be paired off with a senior priest. I was being saved for Tobias, who had no seniority, and Brighten would be named the celestial sister. Things were going according to plan.

Each bride stepped forward to the applause of the crowd as Mother Sunshine strummed the "Wedding March" on a zither. Under the Arch of Flowers, the brides joined hands with their assigned husbands in the special sacred handshake and obediently repeated the vows that the Bishop recited. Though all the girls hoped to please their parents and the entire community by fulfilling the destiny that had been theirs since birth, only some seemed happy about it. Most were fighting tears. A few turned lost, bewildered eyes towards their mothers one last time before being led away by their new husbands.

More girls were called up, including Sparrow, seated next to me, who stifled a sob. I watched her walk woodenly up to the stage with her head down. She shuddered as Brother Richard, an overweight, balding man of fifty-five, reached out and grabbed her hand before leading her to the altar.

More girls were called up, until only eight were left. The young men who were receiving their first wife stepped forward. There were five of them, including Tobias. I sat as tall as I could, straining to see.

"Tobias, come on up to the Arch of Flowers," the Bishop's voice boomed.

My throat felt so tight I could hardly swallow. I felt for the locket under my clothes, the one Mom had given me, but remembered I'd left it at her house. It was forbidden. Brighten reached over and held my hand.

"Your new wife is . . ." The Bishop paused for effect, and I began to slowly rise from my seat. "Rainbow."

I hung in the air, half-risen, until a sharp tug from Brighten brought me down to earth.

Rainbow squealed, jumped to her feet, and made her way to the front as Mother Sunshine strummed the zither. I sat rooted to my chair, disbelieving, feeling an oppressive chill in the room that was sweltering just seconds before.

Tobias looked at me and our eyes locked. His face was flushed and his eyes dark. Did I see a slight shake of his head? If I did, it didn't last long. He turned his back on the crowd to say his vows to Rainbow.

Rainbow.

My stomach turned sour, and I was filled with terrible, horrible thoughts. Unkind, jealous, sinful thoughts.

Brother Earl tried to catch my eye and then smiled encouragingly at Brighten. Was that triumph on his face? I looked away. If Brighten was the new celestial sister, was I going to be *his* bride? *Please, Lord, do not tie me to that man for all eternity*, I prayed. *I don't think I will survive.* A headache took root around my temples.

Soon, there were only three girls left: Brighten, Blossom, and me. "Good luck," I said to Brighten. My voice sounded unfamiliar, dry and hollow, like it came from some deep cavern inside me. "When you are the new celestial sister, do what you can to help me."

"I promise." Brighten squeezed my hand again. We held our breath.

Blossom leaned over, and in a low voice said to Brighten, "Have a great night with Brother Earl."

My headache throbbed. I leaned forward and massaged my temples. "Don't worry, you'll be rewarded for your years of hard work," I told Brighten.

Blossom smirked. "Oh, she'll be rewarded all right."

Everyone leaned forward in their chairs to get a better look as Bishop Thorsen made his announcement. "There are only three sweet young brides left to be placed. Which one will be the new celestial sister? Wish I was a betting man."

The crowd laughed.

"In all seriousness, everyone knows that I get my revelations directly from God and that the choice of the new celestial sister is a very important one. We know how much I depend on those saintly women who postpone matrimony and motherhood for a few years so that they can remain chaste maidens and work for us all. They are the ladies who take care of the million little details that keep things running around here. They leave me free to serve God. Only the best are chosen.

"You girls, come on up. And you, Brother Earl, you come up too." Bishop Thorsen beckoned us all onstage.

People clapped in rhythm as we made our way to the front. The Bishop had us stand onstage holding hands as he reviewed his notes, drawing out the tension as long as he could. I felt Brother Earl's grip tighten painfully and I winced, looking over at his curdled-cream smile.

Brighten and I exchanged frightened looks, then I dropped my head and shut my eyes tight.

Help me, Lord.

"The new celestial sister is . . . Blossom!"

Blossom squealed and clapped her hands. Pride glowed pink in her cheeks as she gazed triumphantly at Brighten.

Beside me, Brighten stood still as a statue, her hand still grasping mine.

Smiling ear to ear, Bishop Thorsen continued with his announcements. "Brother Earl, your new wife is . . . Brighten!"

My head snapped up as if an electric shock had run through me. Our eyes wide, Brighten and I stared at each other in disbelief. I watched Brighten's mouth form the word *no*.

Shouts of *amen* rose from the crowd until the Bishop held up his hands for silence.

"We still have one more sweet young bride. Daisy here is unassigned."

All eyes turned on me. I wanted to run and hide.

Bishop Thorsen adopted a very serious and pious manner, looking out into the crowd and not at me. "Some of you may not know it, but our little Daisy here needs special care and attention. She suffered evil outside influences as a child and is not yet fully redeemed."

He turned and looked deep into my eyes, smiling. "God has spoken to me. I am to be Daisy's guide, as we were promised to each other in the pre-life. Our souls crave each other. I will take her on as another wife for myself, where I can give the close spiritual oversight she needs."

The crowd jumped to their feet and cheered, while Brighten and I, our faces wet with tears, stumbled forward to the Arch of Flowers.

The Bishop announced that he and Brother Earl would take turns performing the ceremony. Brighton was married first, and when it was my turn, Brother Earl told me how to perform the Patriarchal Grip with the Bishop.

My stomach roiling, I took Bishop Thorsen's right hand and entwined my baby finger with his. Next, the Bishop and I placed our index fingers on each other's wrists. His hand was surprisingly soft and damp, and I had to fight the urge to pull away in revulsion. If the Bishop noticed that my hand was trembling, he made no attempt to calm me.

I felt as if I was in a trance, as if none of it was really happening. Someone would come and wake me soon and the nightmare would be over. At one point I dropped the Bishop's hand and searched the crowd for Tobias. I was sure he would come and rescue me, like the princes in the fairy stories my mom read to me when I was little, like he had in the classroom.

But he didn't come. Tobias had left with Rainbow. They had gone up to the bedrooms to complete their union. Tobias and I were over. He was another girl's husband now.

The clamour of the crowd mixed with the blood roaring in my ears. The floor of the stage shifted under my feet. Just as I thought I was going to faint, Brother Earl grabbed my hand roughly and gave it back to Bishop Thorsen in the Patriarchal Grip.

Brother Earl read from an elaborate scroll. "Bishop Thorsen, do you take Sister Daisy by the right hand and receive her unto yourself to be your lawful and wedded wife for time and all eternity, with a covenant and promise that you will observe and keep all the laws, rites, and ordinances pertaining to this Holy Order of Matrimony in the New and Everlasting Covenant? And this you do in the presence of God, angels, and these witnesses of your own free will and choice?"

"I do," Bishop Thorsen said.

Then it was my turn. Brother Earl repeated the vow, but I said nothing. I refused to answer. Brother Earl pinched my arm until my eyes watered and I heard myself echoing the Bishop's vow.

"By the authority vested in me," Brother Earl said, "I pronounce you husband and wife for time and all eternity, and I seal upon you the blessings of the holy resurrection with power to come forth in the morning of the first resurrection clothed in glory, immortality, and eternal lives, and I seal upon you the blessings of kingdoms, thrones, principalities, powers, dominions, and exaltations, with all the blessings of Abraham, Isaac, and Jacob, and say unto you: Be fruitful and multiply and replenish the earth that you may have joy and rejoicing in the day of our Lord Jesus Christ."

Over the cheers and applause, Brother Earl turned to the Bishop and said, "You may kiss the bride."

Bishop Thorsen pulled me to him and kissed me so hard I could feel his teeth through our lips. I recoiled and he pressed his tongue in my mouth. The taste of his saliva did it to me. My stomach heaved and I managed to pull away in time to avoid vomiting in his mouth. Instead, I spattered the Bishop's shiny black cowboy boots with a mass of reeking yellow vomit.

Gasps rippled through the crowd and an involuntary, "Ohhhhhh," rose up to the rafters. Then a hush settled over the entire congregation.

I wavered on my feet, stunned at my lack of control. My body's reaction had put the lie to the Bishop's claim that God ordained we be together for all eternity. All eyes stared questioningly at the Bishop, and we watched, transfixed, as his looks and manner changed before our eyes.

It was as if a benign mask had been pulled from his face. His eyes bulged from a mottled, sweat-streaked visage and he wore a look of fierce hatred directed solely at me. My inability to control myself had humiliated him in front of his flock and left them with questions he couldn't easily answer. He was livid.

"The Placement is finished. Go home." Ignoring the splatter on his boots, he stomped off the stage.

Chapter Ten

Backstage, Brighten and I were met by Celestial Sister Bluebell with a clipboard. "You two the last?" She didn't wait for an answer. "We're pretty backed up right now. People are taking too long in the bedrooms. It's not a hotel, for crying out loud. You girls go wait in the office and I'll call you when we're ready." She opened a door to a small room with two desks and a few wooden chairs, switched on a harsh overhead florescent light, pushed us inside, and slammed the door behind her on the way out.

I fought tears and stumbled into Brighten's arms. "I can't believe this. It's a nightmare. The Bishop is never going to let me forget what I did out there. My entire life is ruined."

We sat in silence for a few moments, our eyes wide, staring at the wall in disbelief. Suddenly, Brighten was very, very angry; angrier than I had ever seen her. "This is not what was supposed to happen." She brought her fist down hard on the surface of a desk. "This is not how my life unfolds. I did everything I could to earn the role of celestial sister, but it wasn't enough. I've seen what it's like for my mom, and now it's my turn. I don't think I can stand it, Daisy."

"We have no say in our lives here, no power, no control. It doesn't matter how hard we try," I said, "nothing will ever change."

Brighten let go of her anger and seemed to fall into some kind of helpless state of shock. She sat motionless, then turned a deer-in-the-headlights stare on me. "But what can we do?"

I wasn't like Brighten. I had no great ambition. I just wanted to marry for love. I thought about what Mom had said, that the Bishop owed her a favour. What went wrong?

There's another way, I heard my mom say in my head.

"Brighten, look at me. We can run. Right now, before they come to get us. No one will think we ran away on our wedding night. That's never happened before. They'll be disorganized. It'll give us a few minutes' head start. If we're fast, we can catch a ride on the main highway with some trucker and be gone before they've figured it out." My breath came in short bursts. My body was itching to move, to run.

"But how would we survive? And our moms, what about them? We can't just leave them. They depend on us."

"They do, but more than anything, they love us. They'll want what's right for us. We'll find a way somehow, we won't starve. Come on, Brighten, we don't know how much time we've got. They could come for us any minute."

Brighten thought for a minute, her mouth a grim line, then, slowly, she nodded.

As if on cue, the door swung open. "You, come with me," said Bluebell as she reached for my arm.

My new plan galvanized me, helping me to hold fear and dread at bay. I looked at Brighten with fresh conviction. "It's not too late. Hold tight," I whispered, before I was marched down the hall to a bedroom.

As I entered, two mothers left the room with armloads of linen for washing. Musky, sweaty human smells hung in the air. I gagged and coughed. One pulled an aerosol from the pocket of her long dress and filled the room with a sickeningly sweet floral smell. I felt my stomach muscles tighten and bile percolate into my throat again.

As if realizing it was me for the first time, Bluebell acknowledged me by name. "Keep sweet, Daisy."

"Keep sweet, Sister Bluebell."

"Didn't I promise you that you were going to be specially blessed tonight? What an honour to be chosen by the Bishop himself. At least your children won't carry the stigma you have." She gave me one of her thin-lipped smiles. She didn't seem to know of my humiliation onstage. While I struggled not to show my anger, she inspected her clipboard. "Someone's talked to you about what to do tonight, right?"

"No, no one's talked to me."

Bluebell rubbed the sides of her eye sockets with her thumb and forefinger. "Honestly, do I have to do everything around here? One of the mothers was *supposed* to talk to you about tonight. What to do when your husband arrives?"

I looked at the floor and shrugged.

"Okay, listen up. The last thing I need is another meltdown from one of you girls. I don't make the rules around here. I'm just doing my job. If you don't do as you're told, I get the blame. Got that?"

"Yes, Sister Bluebell."

"After I leave you, take off your dress and hang it on the hook behind the door. Then sit on the bed and wait for Bishop Thorsen. Listen to his instructions and do exactly what he tells you. And be quick about it. The sooner he's done, the better. He has to be at the wedding banquet in one hour, so just do your duty and get it done. No fuss. No muss. Got that?"

I felt my stomach begin to ache again. It gave me an idea. "Yes, Sister." I struggled to keep calm.

"Good girl." Sister Bluebell turned to leave but stopped at the door, her hand on the knob. "One more thing. The Bishop is sensitive about the extra weight he's gained. Whatever you do, don't look at his belly. In fact, when he takes his clothes off, tell him how handsome he looks. A real man."

"I don't feel so good. I think I'm going to throw up. I've got to find a toilet."

Bluebell scowled. "Oh, for heaven's sake. What a mess this Placement night has turned into. The mothers are going to hear about this, that's for sure." Opening the door, she said, "The bathrooms are 'round the corner and down the hall. Don't be long."

I stepped into the hall, closing the door behind me. I turned the corner and walked straight into the soft, doughy belly of the Bishop. He reached out and grabbed my arm, twisting it hard. I yelped in pain and fear.

"You little bitch!" he hissed into my ear. "You thought that was fun, did you? You wanted to make a fool out of me, to get back at me for not giving you to Tobias? I'm going to make you pay for this. You will be very, very sorry." He twisted my arm harder, and something popped in my shoulder.

Sister Bluebell came around the corner, her face buried in her clipboard. The Bishop dropped my arm as she looked up. "Oh, Bishop Thorsen. Daisy will be right with you. She just needs the washroom, then she'll be right back."

He released me with a shove, and I lurched down the hall, swallowing hard and swiping at the sweat on my forehead. I burst into the washroom and collapsed in a stall, purging the little that was left in my stomach. Struggling to open a large wood-framed window, I took a few gulps of fresh pine-scented air until I felt more myself.

How had it all gone so wrong? It was like a story my mom read to me when I was little. I was Alice in Wonderland. I'd fallen down a rabbit hole into a nightmare world that I couldn't find my way out of. My worst fears had come true, and I needed a plan.

A gust of wind caught the open window and blew it wide. As I moved to shut it, I looked outside. It was only four feet to the ground. Wiping my wet cheeks with the backs of both hands, I turned and ran down the hall to the office where I had left my best friend. I burst through the door and Brighten looked up, startled.

"There's a big window in the bathroom close to the treeline. It's a short drop to the ground," I panted.

Brighten jumped up and grabbed my hand. "I can't be with Brother Earl. Let's do it. Go!"

There was no one in the hallway, but we heard voices coming from the backstage wings. "—leave until the last girls go in, so stop complaining. Just keep cleaning up the—"

We silently opened the bathroom door and searched for a skeleton key to lock it from the inside, but there was none. Brighten pushed the window open as wide as she could and motioned for me to step into her cupped hand for a lift.

"On three," she said. Brighten gave me a small boost on "one," a larger boost on "two," and then we heard a toilet flush and the bolt on a stall door snap back.

Brighten dropped my foot but there was no time to close the window.

Rainbow emerged from the stall, dressed in a floral chiffon

robe. "Hello, girls! Isn't this wonderful? I just keep pinching myself. Have you been as lucky as I have? I can't believe I was assigned to the best-looking, youngest brother—Tobias—and as his first wife too! He's so kind and gentle." Rainbow was large-eyed and loose-limbed. Her skin was glowing.

I couldn't bring myself to say anything. I knew that if I stayed in Redemption, I'd spend the rest of my days listening to Rainbow talk about her fabulous marriage to Tobias and how much she loved the status of first wife. And once a year I'd be expected to congratulate her on the birth of another adorable baby with dimples and dark curls, just like his father.

I couldn't do it. And with all my heart I knew God didn't want this for me either.

Brighten grasped her in a hug. "Congratulations, Rainbow. You deserve to be blessed! But you better hurry back to him. You're a .wife now. You have to see to your husband's every comfort."

Rainbow looked stricken for a minute. "Of course. Thanks, Brighten." She quickly washed and dried her hands. When she opened the door to leave, she said, "Someone should close that window in case it rains."

"We'll take care of it," I said.

As soon as she was gone, we stepped up to the window once more, but as Brighten got ready I suffered a stab of fear and doubt. What would God think of our actions? Would Brighten and I be doomed in the afterlife?

Brighten shouted, "Just go!" and crouched to give me a boost.

I didn't think twice. I stepped into her hand, and she hoisted me onto the window ledge. I slid out the window and down the side of the building. My dress snagged on a nail as I fell, and I heard a tearing sound as I landed on the soft earth below. Juniper bushes ripped at my stockings, shredding them as I tried to pull away.

Brighten tumbled out the window, landing hard beside me. She insisted she was fine, but she limped after me as we stumbled through the forest. Low brush snagged and tore our billowing dresses as we ran but we didn't care. We didn't plan on ever wearing them again.

The sun was gone but a full moon rising lit our way. When we reached a cluster of houses, Brighten grabbed my arm and whispered in my ear, "We can't run away with nothing but ruined wedding dresses. Grab some clothes and I'll meet you at the bridge. As fast as you can, Daisy. Promise."

"I promise."

I turned onto the narrow path through the woods and ran to Mom's house as fast as I dared through the deepening shadows. What had I done? Was this crazy? If we were caught, the punishment would be awful—a terrible beating, then the Bishop would force me to go to bed with him every night until I was pregnant.

It was simple.

We couldn't get caught.

Chapter Eleven

When I got close to Mom's, I took the fork in the path that went around back, right to the basement stairs. The house was all lit up. Then I remembered: Mom was expecting me, along with Tobias, for a wedding celebration.

A wave of sadness washed over me.

I found the key hidden under the rock by the back door and quietly stepped inside. I desperately wanted to talk to Mom, could even feel the hug I knew would be coming, but something made me pause before calling out to her.

I was just starting up the basement stairs when I heard a conversation from the living room through the open door. Mom wasn't alone.

"You saw for yourself that she's not here," Mom said. "You let down your side of the bargain, Ray. I thought we'd agreed on Tobias. What happened?"

The Bishop!

I started digging frantically through Mom's laundry basket for the outsider clothes she wore when she went into town, keeping an ear out for the conversation upstairs.

"Tobias turned out to be a little shit disturber. He asked his father to bless his choice, taking me out of the picture. He's trying to undermine my absolute authority and establish a power base for himself and for the leaders of the Utah church. That can't happen. I gotta stop them from worming their way in here."

"Ray, you're acting paranoid. That boy is interested in my daughter and nothing else."

"Oh yeah? What about undermining Mother Faith in the classroom? You gonna tell me that boy ain't got ambitions here in Redemption? No, sir. I had to put that boy in his place."

So that was it—Tobias's letter to his father. The Bishop had had no revelation from God about me. He was punishing Tobias for trying to subvert his authority. The Bishop was a fake and a fraud.

I checked the clock on the wall. I had to go, but again I wavered. Glancing around the room, I felt a wave of nostalgia. The old teapot, my favourite chair by the bookcase, my spool knitting project—the den was full of reminders of my special times with Mom. The outside world was a big place filled with the worst kind of sinners, and not one of them knew me or cared for me. I felt a pang of longing for my mom so strong it took my breath away.

I heard her say upstairs, "You owed me a favour."

"Yeah? Well now you owe me one. Daisy tried to make a fool out of me tonight and I'm going to make her pay for that unless you tell me where she is right now." The Bishop's temper was rising, if his voice was any indication.

Mom coughed nervously, then she took on the soft, sweet tones she used only when she talked to men like the Bishop. "I'm sorry, but I honestly don't know."

I forced myself forward, overcoming my fear. I was running away with Brighten, the most capable, intelligent person I knew. Together we'd make it work. I ripped off what was left of my mud-spattered wedding dress, not even bothering to undo the covered buttons I had so painstakingly sewed on the back. Next came the stockings, full of ladders, and then the tight girdle and painful, pointy bra. I kicked them all into a heap on the floor, a pile of old rags no one would ever want again.

I was still hunting through the laundry when I saw a neat, folded pile of clothes on the couch. There were jeans and a baggy sweatshirt, a blue pea jacket and a pair of Mom's old penny loafers with socks stuffed inside. On the top of the pile of clothes lay my locket.

How did Mom know? Someone had told her, and she'd guessed I'd come here? Did she know what I was about to do?

I was getting dressed when I heard the Bishop again. "We'll find her. She's with her friend Brighten. They won't get far. And when we grab them, I promise I will make an example of them. No one will ever try this stunt again."

"What if you're too late? What if they've already run away— made it to the outside world?"

"You'd like that, wouldn't you? You want your daughter to live your dream—living with that apostate husband of yours."

"Yes!" Mom's voice had changed. It came through loud and strong. "It was my dream, and nothing would make me happier if Daisy managed to do it."

I heard the unmistakable sound of an open hand striking flesh, hard. Then Mom sobbed.

"I'm gonna hunt those little bitches down. And when I find them, I'm gonna drag them back here by their hair, throw them in a hole, and make sure they never see the sun shine again."

Blind with fury, I pulled on Mom's clothes, stopping briefly to grab the snow shovel in the cubby behind the stairs. When I snuck into the living room from the kitchen entrance, the Bishop had his back to me, his hand raised as if to strike Mom again.

Though I tried not to make a sound, he heard me approach from behind. As he started to turn towards me, I rushed forward and hit him hard on the head with the flat bottom of the shovel. He groaned, collapsing onto all fours, then slumped forward on the floor, unmoving.

Mom and I looked at each other for a few moments in disbelief. The Bishop had just left a handprint on her cheek. Now he was out cold on the floor.

"Run, Daisy. Just go. Now!"

"But what about you?"

"I'll be all right. When you get somewhere safe send a note to

Sybil, the librarian in town. Tell her you've made it, but don't tell her where you are. She'll find a way to let me know."

The Bishop began to stir. He groaned, pulling himself back onto all fours. His hand shot out and gripped the shaft of the shovel, wrenching it from my hand. I staggered back, almost falling, but steadied myself.

He got to his feet, stepped towards me and raised the shovel over his head as if to hit me, but his movements were jerky and uncoordinated, and his left arm trembled.

I saw my chance.

Without long skirts to constrain me for once, I took a step forward and planted my knee as hard as I could in his crotch. He cried out, doubled over, and dropped the shovel, collapsing to the floor again. Grabbing the shovel, I hit him on the head a second time. Blood spurted from the wound I opened on his temple. I turned and ran.

Despite the full moon, I tripped over logs and slipped on wet, grassy ground. Finally, I found the creek bed and followed it to the crossroads. Under a lone streetlight, I could see a figure standing on the bridge above me, the bridge where the road to Redemption met the main highway. It was Brighten. Putting two fingers in my mouth, I got ready to let out a short, sharp whistle.

But something stopped me.

Chapter Twelve

The roar of an engine and screeching tires shattered the silence. From below the bridge, I couldn't see much, but through the gaps in the planks, I saw a moving light and four figures. There was a muffled cry, and five shadows ran west. I heard a scuffle, grunting and swearing, and then:

"Fuck! She bit me!"

"Just get her in the car and hold her hands, for crying out loud."

I hung back in the shadows, cringing with fear. What should I do? How could I save Brighten? My brain was sluggish. It was hard to think.

I heard more grunting and heavy breathing.

"No, no," Brighten shouted. "You can't stop me. I have a right to leave if I want to."

"You belong to Brother Earl now. If you don't like it, you can complain to the Bishop and see where that gets you. Where's Daisy?" The voice was male, gruff. I didn't recognize it.

"Take me to see the Bishop. I want to talk to him. Now!"

What? Why? Then it dawned on me. Brighten was trying to divert them. She must have guessed that I was nearby; she was trying to get the men to leave so I could get away. I felt sick that Brighten was sacrificing herself for me, but it made me more determined than ever to get away.

"One of us should stay here in case she shows up."

"I'll do it." I heard a car door open and close and saw the shadow of a lone figure walk slowly across the bridge.

The car with Brighten drove away with a squeal of tires. I moved out from under the bridge and began a slow, careful climb, using a large metal culvert for footing. I made it up the slick grassy slopes of the riverbank without a slip or a sound. I spotted the man who'd stayed behind to catch me.

Keeping to the shadows, I looked for the easiest way to get past him. He was leaning with his back against the bridge railing, looking as though he didn't have a care in the world. As if he weren't trying to trap me, kidnap me, and take me back to the Bishop who would—

The man shifted, and the light from the solitary streetlamp caught a familiar silhouette. I froze as he turned his face in my direction. I could see him clearly. My heart broke into a thousand pieces, and my old life fell away.

Tobias.

PART TWO

Nkwala, British Columbia

July 1964

Chapter Thirteen

Picking cherries was hard work.

We were paid half a dollar for a twenty-pound basket of cherries, and on good days I pocketed ten dollars, cash. For the first time in my life, I had money that I'd earned myself. It was such a good feeling. I could decide what was important to me and how I wanted to spend it. Today, I was determined to treat Saffron after all the help she'd given me. She'd saved my life, after all, not once but twice. She was the first person I saw that morning when I woke up frightened and alone in the woods, after running away from the only home I'd ever known. From the love that would never be mine.

From Tobias.

Later, Saffron helped me get away from the "God Squad" too—the relentless, angry men sent by the Bishop to find me.

On a rare day off, Saffron and I headed to the Apple Dumpling Café for breakfast, just the two of us. The place filled up quickly, but we managed to get a quiet table for two in the corner by the kitchen.

"Are Jean and Marilyn coming?" I asked.

Saffron rolled her eyes. "They had another one of their fights last night. Marilyn demanded a ride to Kelowna this morning. She's out of here. I think she means it this time." Jean and Marilyn were the couple that Saffron and Lance had been travelling with when they found me, a few kilometers outside Redemption. I wasn't surprised they were breaking up; there had been tensions, jealousy. I recognized the signs.

"That's sad."

"No it's not. Trust me. They weren't made for each other."

"What about Lance?" Lance was Saffron's boyfriend. I hadn't seen him for a few days either.

"Nope."

As Saffron and I checked out the menu, the warm, spiced atmosphere of the café wrapped around me like a soft blanket. The sweet smells of cinnamon and caramelized maple sugar were so strong that I could taste them just by breathing in. I felt spoiled. I didn't have to make the food, serve it, or do the dishes after. This must be what the Queen's life was like, I thought.

The place had a nice feeling. I liked the small tables with bright yellow arborite tabletops and matching vinyl chairs. An ice cream bar with a stainless steel soda fountain ran along the back wall next to a double-hinged door leading into the kitchen.

A plump older woman with a limp came over as soon as we sat down. She took our order and poured two coffees without asking. Obviously, no one ever said no to coffee in this place. I looked at my cup uncertainly. Following Saffron's lead, I stirred in two heaping teaspoons of sugar and lots of cream. I took a small, unsure sip.

"Oh! It's good! I like it."

Saffron looked at me, her eyes wide. "You've never had coffee before? What kind of bizzarro place did you grow up in?"

I swallowed and looked out the window. Was it time I told Saffron what I was really running from? The idea of unburdening myself was so appealing. It was hard to be physically apart from those I loved, but it was even harder to be alone with my thoughts and feelings.

I couldn't stop thinking about Brighten. Bishop Thorsen said he was going to make an example of her. What did that mean? What was her punishment? I felt guilt-ridden whenever I let myself dwell on it, because hadn't it been my idea to run away?

Wasn't it all my fault?

For three weeks I'd lived in a constant state of fear, expecting to hear the hollow clomp of the Bishop's cowboy boots behind me every time I set foot in Nkwala, a tiny town in the Okanagan Valley. I worried that he'd never stop looking for me to get his revenge, and I wondered if the squad had figured out how I'd made my escape and where I was headed. Dark-coloured pickup trucks made me sick with anxiety, and I jumped whenever one passed by.

But I was also dying for news from home. I'd sent the librarian in Stewart's Landing a note asking her to tell Mom I was okay, but I didn't dare put a return address on it. Was Bishop Thorsen punishing Mom like he was punishing Brighten?

On the positive side, I was grateful to be alive, grateful to be safe. Grateful to be away from Redemption, marriage to the Bishop, and all the rest of it. The outside world offered many of the things that Brighten and I had dreamt of, and I was beginning to enjoy them. Things like jeans and beaches and restaurants and radios. After all I did to get away, I refused to let fear and guilt ruin my chances of a happy life. I would do everything I could to help Brighten and my mom, but I was determined to live life to the fullest despite everything.

I didn't want my old life to infect my new one.

So I held back. I didn't tell Saffron about the "bizarro" place I came from. I didn't want her to be my friend because she felt sorry for me, but deep down, I think I was afraid Saffron would think I was some kind of freak like the people in Stewart's Landing did. The ones who used to laugh and call us *polyg girls*, like we were lesser beings. I didn't want to think Saffron was like them, but how could I be sure? I wanted to be accepted as an equal. How ironic was it that after running away from everything and everyone I ever knew in Redemption, I still wanted to fit in here?

All Saffron knew was that I was from a small, religious community. I didn't tell her about plural marriage or the custom of marrying off young girls to old men. I hid the things I knew would be strange to her. The things that were becoming increasingly strange to me too, now that I was living on the outside.

With perfect timing, the older woman appeared, interrupting our conversation to set down giant plates loaded with pancakes, scrambled eggs, maple sausages, and hot buttered toast.

Saffron laughed. "Whoa, now we've got a problem. Like, how we're going to be able to get up and walk out of this place."

After three pancakes with maple syrup and two pieces of toast, I set my fork down to take a breather. "Do you remember when we first met? When I told you I was running away from home? You said that you were all running from something. Well, I've been wondering what Lance is running from. I mean, I haven't seen him in days. But even before that, he seemed distant."

I checked her face for a reaction, worried that I'd opened a fresh wound, but she seemed fine with it. Had she and Lance broken up? Until now, they'd seemed inseparable.

"That's what I was going to tell you. He left. He got tired of running from himself, and who he really is."

"I don't understand."

"You've had a sheltered upbringing. Maybe you won't get it, but Lance prefers men to women. He couldn't deal with it and was trying to hide it by being with me. I told him to go with it, be proud of who he is. So, he's going to Vancouver to be part of that scene—live and let live."

I wasn't really sure what Saffron meant, but I remembered the Bishop preaching something about the sin of men loving men. An *abomination*, he'd called it. I remembered his Sunday school talk to all the older children quite clearly.

Homosexuality is a terrible plague, a devil-sent lust that destroys souls.

I took a sip of coffee and shook off the voices in my head that weren't my own. "So, that's good, then? You're okay that he broke up with you?"

Saffron snorted. "He didn't break up with me. He stopped living a lie. And yes, I'm okay."

We finished up, and against Saffron's protests, I paid the bill. I felt a little smug that I knew enough to leave a tip and dropped a dime on the table. We split up, agreeing to meet later at Willow Park for the regular Saturday night bonfire and cookout with all the other pickers. Saffron headed over to the thrift shop while I wandered off to the General Store. The day's excitement wasn't over yet. I had something very special in mind.

The ferry was coming in and I stopped to watch it nose gently into the dock. It was a barge—a brightly painted gleaming-white superstructure. It squeezed about twenty cars and thirty foot-passengers on board for the forty-minute trip from a town called

Kelowna. It sailed south on Okanagan Lake, passing Rattlesnake Island on the left, before finally pulling into a horseshoe-shaped cove called Commando Bay. The hand-carved wooden sign on the dock read:

WELCOME TO THE UNINCORPORATED VILLAGE OF NKWALA, POPU-LATION 800. A NUCLEAR-FREE ZONE.

As I turned and walked along, I could taste chalky clay dust on my lips and smell the sweet pine scent of a giant ponderosa growing by the high-steepled Anglican church. Across the street was the Nkwala and District Museum. A banner proclaimed that it was maintained by volunteers from the Imperial Order of the Daughters of the Empire.

I arrived at my destination, and I felt my heartbeat quicken. Ever since I'd noticed that tourist on the beach, I knew I had to have one just like hers. I'd stationed my towel near the girl and watched with fascination while she casually set the pocket-size device on her towel and used a small dial to turn it on. I looked carefully. There were no electrical cords attached to it, but once the telescope antenna was raised, music blasted from some hidden speaker. And it wasn't just any music. It was rock and roll from a station called CFUN in Vancouver.

I was "knocked out," a phrase I'd learned from Saffron. Working up my nerve, I had asked the girl what the thing was.

"It's called a transistor radio and it runs on a battery. I love it 'specially 'cause it has an earpiece so my parents don't even know I listen to it late at night," she'd said proudly. She'd told me they cost ten dollars at the store in the village.

The only radios I'd ever seen—in the Simpson Sears store window in Stewart's Landing—were built into big pieces of wooden furniture, but this was light and mobile. It was magic, like having a rock-and-roll band in your pocket.

I had to have one.

The sign on the door read NKWALA GENERAL STORE AND LIQUOR SALES. Underneath was a smaller sign that said, OKANAGAN AND SIMILKAMEEN DISTRICT LIBRARY, NKWALA BRANCH. Below that, an even smaller sign read C. B. TUTORING SERVICES. I paused, wondering how such a small building could house so much.

The bell on the door jingled as I pushed it open and went in, pausing to let my eyes adjust to the dim light. I saw the object of my dreams on a high shelf behind the cashier. As I pulled a wad of soiled, folded notes from my pocket, I got in the line behind a middle-aged man with slicked-back hair who'd stuffed himself into a grey suit that might have fit ten years ago. On his feet were polished lace-up oxfords.

Something didn't feel quite right, and I didn't need the hot prickles in my stomach to tell me that. The men in this village were either farmers or tourists and they dressed for it. No one had polished shoes with all the dust around. The people who wore suits— the lawyers and businessmen—they lived in places like Kelowna or even Peachland across the lake, not Nkwala. Who was this guy? Where did he come from, and what was he doing here? The prickles in my stomach got hotter.

Was this someone Bishop Thorsen sent to find me, or was I letting my imagination run wild? He didn't look anything like the members of the God Squad, big goons in black pants and shirts. Maybe he was just a travelling salesman. Saffron said that they came here sometimes, selling layaway plans on Maytag washing machines and the Encyclopedia Britannica.

I shifted uncomfortably from one foot to another, not knowing if I should run and hide or try to get a better view of the man. As if he read my mind, he turned and looked me square in the face, smiling.

"Didn't expect it to be so busy in this little village," he said. "Are you a local?"

I felt a wave of heat under my skin and immediately dropped my eyes.

A woman must lower her eyes when speaking to a man.

"Not really," I mumbled. I didn't want the man to think that I lived here, that it would be easy to track me down.

"Just visiting from Vancouver, myself. You? Where are you from?"

I froze, not knowing what to say. Was he just being friendly or—

"Next," the cashier called out.

He paused as if he was about to say something, then stepped forward to unload his basket.

I took the opportunity to bury myself in the aisles, pretending I'd forgotten something. Hiding behind the cigarettes, I watched the man through stacks of Rothmans and MacDonalds as he paid for his items. He looked around for me, scanning the aisles, moving out of sight until finally the small bell over the front door told me he'd given up and left.

Relieved, I went to the cashier, paid for my purchase, and, holding my new transistor radio close to my heart, glanced through the store window into the parking lot. The man was sitting, *waiting*, in a brown car with winged taillights, watching the store. On one hand, I was relieved that his car was not a truck, but on the other, I knew he was waiting for me.

I couldn't very well go out the front door of the store with the strange man waiting outside, so I turned around and walked back through the grocery aisles. They were stocked full of cans of Campbell's Soup, boxes of Kraft Dinner, and tins of Spam. At the back was a glass door. Looking for a way out, I pushed the door open and immediately felt the tickle of dust on the end of my nose. I smelled old books: the unmistakable odour of dry paper and old glue.

A woman was seated at a desk a few feet from the door. A sign on her desk read MISS CAROL BRAID, HEAD LIBRARIAN. I glanced around the small room, looking for the other librarians, but couldn't see anyone else.

Miss Braid's head snapped up the moment she saw me. Quickly refolding her cheese sandwich into wax paper, she ran her tongue over her front teeth and gave me a dignified nod, then a warm smile.

A black-haired woman in her late thirties with cat's-eye glasses, she was wearing a light-blue cashmere skirt and matching sweater set. A jewelled clip and chain held her cardigan draped over her shoulders, boldly showing her bare arms. She was lovely.

"Welcome to the library. Is there anything I can help you with?" She gently but firmly pushed a library card application across the desk towards me.

I picked up the form, pretending to study it. A flash of memory hit me hard—my mother, coming back from one of her forbidden trips to the library in Stewart's Landing, exclaiming what fabulous places libraries were and how she loved them. I felt tears in my eyes and blinked hard.

"This is just what I was looking for," I said. "I'll fill it out and bring it back soon. Okay?"

Miss Braid's eyes, made large by her thick lenses, looked strangely feline and eager. "Absolutely. We are especially pleased to attract younger members. We've been getting in some of the new—what do you kids call it . . . *hip* books for the teenage crowd. We just got in Joseph Heller's *Catch-22*." She flushed with pleasure, lowering her voice. "I've read it myself and it's wonderful. Have you heard of it?"

I folded up the paper application and stuffed it into the large bib pocket of my overalls. "No, but this is great, thanks." I was just turning to go when I noticed a brochure on a small table beside her desk: C. B. Tutoring Services. I paused. At the thought of Mother Faith's stinging hand-slap, I hesitated to pick it up.

"Help yourself to that too," Miss Braid said, pointing. "This is how I spend my evenings. Lots of orchardists here are new immigrants and need help learning to read English, and there are quite a few locals who didn't finish high school. I help them get their equivalency."

"Equivalency?"

"It's a high school diploma for older students, based on a combination of work experience and curriculum study." She reached out and picked up a copy of the brochure, handing it to me. "Go ahead, keep it," she said firmly.

I thanked her and asked if there was another exit. She showed me to the back door. I thanked her again and promised to come back. Looking around cautiously, I noticed a high fence blocked the view to the parking lot. I hurried over to Willow Beach and my favourite spot—a park bench mostly hidden by the cascade of drooping branches and leaves from the huge old tree that gave it its name—to withdraw from the outside world I'd risked everything to escape to.

In the cool dark shade, I could look out of my willow tree

bower, but on the beach in bright white sunlight, no one could see in.

I turned the round dial and the radio suddenly blared to life. "Welcome all you rock and rollers, to 1410 AM, CFUN radio." Then I heard what sounded like the Beach Boys singing "...*fun* ...*fun* ...*fun*." The announcer broke in again. "And number one this week, here's the Beach Boys with, 'I Get Around.'"

I quickly turned the volume down, afraid of getting into trouble like I would have back home. I found the earpiece and attached it to the radio on one end and my ear on the other. I stretched out on the wooden bench, looking up the beautiful tree canopy. A cathedral of green leaves and golden light shimmered with the vibrations of the music as if it were plugged directly into my brain.

I tried to relax but I still felt jangly after my encounter with the strange man.

What if he came after me and tried to kidnap me? Stuff me in the back of his brown car? Who could help me? Lance was gone, Jean was out of town on his ranch, and Saffron wasn't much bigger or stronger than me. The police were out of the question, I was terrified of them.

So, I prayed.

I was struggling with my faith and my need for forgiveness for hurting the Bishop, but even more for abandoning Brighten and my mother. The one thing I was sure of was that I no longer wanted the Bishop or anyone else to be my spiritual leader.

I took deep breaths and I tried to think calming thoughts. Finally, the heat of the afternoon, my big breakfast, and the music in my ear lulled me into a good long sleep.

But my dreams betrayed my inner turmoil. The past came rushing back.

———

Redemption. The night of the Placement.

In the light of a solitary streetlamp, I saw Tobias on the bridge.

I'll never forget what he said to me.

And so I ran.

Then I was crawling, army-style, through a long pipe, terrified that I wouldn't fit, that I'd get stuck and no one would ever find me. But I broke free, running, running till my sides ached and my breath felt like it was scorching my insides.

I found a hole in the fence, and I crawled through it, stopping at the side of the highway. Bending over, I massaged the sharp, stabbing pain in my right side. At the sound of an approaching car, I stuck out my thumb.

But it wasn't a car. It was a truck. A Dodge like the men of Redemption drove. I hid in the bushes until it passed.

An hour later, I found myself at the side of the road, walking into the deepening darkness. I guessed it was around ten o'clock in the evening. There weren't many cars travelling this way at night, so when I heard the sound of another vehicle, I looked for cover. This wasn't a powerful V8 engine, but something much smaller. It sounded like a sewing machine on wheels. I turned to face the oncoming headlights and stuck out my thumb one more time. The car couldn't have been doing more than about forty miles an hour, so the driver had plenty of time to react.

The vehicle stopped. The driver leaned over and opened the passenger door from the inside. I didn't hesitate. It wasn't until I closed the door behind me that I saw the sticker on the dash: *property of the Government of Canada.* I thought my heart would stop.

"Where ya going?"

A kindly-looking middle-aged man sat across from me. He was short, his foot barely reaching the gas pedal. His smile rested comfortably on several chins, in a round face framed by thinning red hair. A loosened tie hung over his long-sleeved blue shirt that was tucked into white polyester pants. He wore a wide white belt and matching loafers.

I gripped the door handle and tried to smile through my fear.

Government is an evil beast. With God's guidance, we will bleed the beast.

"Just up the road a bit. It's a really small town; you've probably never heard of it."

"Try me. I know most of the towns around here. I travel all over doing tax audits."

I'd never been this far from Redemption and didn't know the names of any of the nearby towns. I searched the interior of the car for some inspiration.

Never tell the tax man the truth.

"Fordston. It's really little, just a few families, named after, ah, Willy Ford, the founder."

"Well, you got me there. Never heard of Fordston, nor Willy. Relatives of yours?"

"Sure, I mean, yes, just on my way to visit my grandmother, she's a Ford."

"I'm Matt, by the way." He took a small pudgy hand off the steering wheel and offered it to me.

I tried not to wince as I shook it. "Daisy." As soon as I'd spoken, I regretted it. I'd told the government man my real name. "Daisy Ford," I said.

Matt put the car in gear and revved the engine. We were off with a lurch. After a few quiet miles he cracked a window. "Interesting perfume you're wearing."

"Oh, sorry. Skunk."

"Figured." He gave me a long sideways look. "You know, I would have pegged you for one of those polyg girls, from Bountiful or Redemption."

I swallowed. "Why's that?"

"It's the hair. All those girls wear it the same way with the big upsweep in front. Don't know how they manage to get it to stick."

I didn't like the direction the conversation was going, so I forced a laugh and tried to appear calm. I kept my focus on the air freshener shaped like a fir tree that hung from the rearview mirror. It made the car smell sickly sweet, but it was better than skunk. "Well, I'm not one of them. . . . My hair, it's just the latest style, that's all."

"It is? I thought all you girls were wearing it long and straight these days, like that singer, what's her name? Marianne Faithfull. Ever heard of her?"

I relaxed a little. "I have. She's boss. I really like her songs."

"Haha. Boss. You kids come up with the darndest expressions. I'm not as interested in her music as I am in how she looks in a miniskirt. She's one hot mama. That's what the kids say today, right? A 'hot mama'?" Matt took his right hand off the steering wheel and rested it on the stick shift. I moved my knees as far from the stick shift as I could.

"I guess."

Matt seemed to get the message and put both hands back on the steering wheel. I didn't want to talk about myself, so I turned my head and stared out the window. There was enough light to see the silhouettes of spindly fir trees fly by. Silence hung heavy in the car for another few miles.

"I bet you'd look great in a miniskirt, a pretty bit of a thing like you."

I glanced at the photo stuck to the driver's-side dashboard and pointed. "Yours?"

Matt sat up straight and puffed out his chest. "You bet. That's twelve-year-old Brenda, ten-year-old Benjamin, and that cute little button is eight-year-old Sally. They're all smart as whips and good in sports."

"You must be so proud."

"Sure am."

"I guess it's hard when you have to travel for your job. You must miss them a lot?"

Matt looked at me square on. He had a wolfish grin on his flushed face. "Travelling has its perks. At home I'm a perfect husband and father, but when I'm away, I'm a bad boy."

His laugh was high-pitched, and it made my skin crawl.

"Are you one of those modern girls? You know, the kind that burn their bras. Are you a bra burner, Daisy?"

His questions made me shudder. I moved as far from him as I could. Turning my gaze back to my side window, I said nothing. I'd been away from Redemption for only a few hours and already I had met one of the terrible sinners that Bishop Thorsen warned us about. What was next? Was my life on the outside going to be one of endlessly beating back the forces of darkness?

The car's high beams picked up a small road going off to the right just up ahead. "There's the turnoff to Fordston. You can let me off here."

"Already? We were just getting acquainted." Matt reached for my knee but failed to connect.

"Yeah, it's a real bummer. I better get going. Grandma Ford'll be waiting for me, along with Uncle Ed. He's the one who likes to hunt. Has a big gun collection. I'd invite you in for coffee, but Uncle Ed has a really quick temper, and he doesn't trust strangers."

The car came to a skidding stop. I jumped out, and with relief, gave Matt a curt wave.

As I turned to walk away from the car, I heard Matt grind the gears and hit the gas, peeling off. After distance swallowed the sound of his engine, the song of crickets filled the still night air. The world was midnight blue. A wave of profound loneliness swept over me with a weight that I could physically feel.

Just a few hours ago, I had been thrilled at the expectation of being placed with Tobias as his first wife. Brighten had been looking forward to being appointed the new celestial sister. Now, she was a prisoner, enduring a punishment I couldn't bear to think about, and I was lost and alone in the middle of nowhere.

Chapter Fourteen

I woke from my dream under the willow tree at Willow Beach to the sounds of the other pickers setting up the food and a bonfire for the evening's fun. A wave of relief swept over me. I was with my new friends on the beach, on a rare day off from cherry-picking. I was a long way from Redemption, and I was safe for now.

Had been safe, I corrected, remembering the strange man in the general store.

The pickers mostly spoke French, because so many were from Quebec. Jean called them Quebecois, and I heard his voice above the others, laughing and calling to his friends, obviously happy to have other French speakers to talk to.

I peeked out from my willow curtain and caught Jean's eye. He gave me a surprised but friendly wave. He didn't look like a man who'd just lost the love of his life, but I knew from experience that he was hard to read. He kept his emotions to himself. If he was nursing a broken heart, he'd never let on.

Saffron told me that the Quebecois pickers came every year. It was a rite of passage for them; pick fruit, live free, and have a good time, before heading home to their colleges and universities, slogging it out through another cold Quebec winter. They were full of fun and very resourceful.

I hoped there would be fire dancing. Last Saturday, after the bonfire grew big, a couple brought out special staffs that they lit on fire at both ends. They danced and whirled the staffs high in the air, the trailing flames drawing yellow and red circles and fanciful images in the dark sky. I'd kept thinking about how much my mom would have loved their show, and how much the Bishop would have condemned it as demonic.

I looked over to see Saffron, dressed in a miniskirt and bikini top under a white knitted vest, waving a spatula over an outdoor grill. Last time, one of the guys had roasted quail that he'd shot. These scurrying, comical birds were everywhere, but I couldn't bring myself to eat anything so charming and adorable. I stuck to the hot dogs.

"Hey, Saffron," I called as I emerged from my little natural den, "wait till you see what I bought." I hung my new transistor radio from its strap on a nearby branch and cranked up the volume. A look of pure joy lit up Saffron's face. Bringing music to the party was obviously a cool thing to do. Saffron flung her arms around me and gave me a huge hug while Jean and the other pickers smiled and nodded.

A dance party broke out. I didn't join in. I'd never danced with anyone but Brighten, and no way would I ever consider dancing with a group of men. I stood off to the side for a while, watching. Finally, I couldn't resist the urge, so I backed off behind the willow curtain where I was free to try out the new dances. The Pony was an easy two-step hopping from side to side, the Hitchhiker was pretty much what you'd expect, the Jerk hurt my back, and the Watusi, I couldn't figure out at all.

I had paused to catch my breath when I noticed a man walking barefoot across the sand towards us, carrying his brown leather shoes, his grey suit pants rolled up. It took a few moments to register who he was, and then I stepped well back under the cover of the willow tree.

He reached up into the maple that held my new radio and switched it off. To stop the protests from the dancers he waved a handful of money in their faces. "I'm looking for a girl named Daisy Shoemaker. Fifteen; slim; long, straight, ash-blond hair. I have reason to believe she's in town. She may be just passing through or staying for a while. I've got two hundred bucks for anyone who leads me to her."

There were blank faces. I sucked in my breath. No one said a word.

"She's not in trouble or anything, I just need to talk to her."

Saffron spoke up. "We don't know anyone by that name, and you're crashing our party, man."

He ignored her and turned to some of the male pickers, letting them get a good look at the money. "Are you sure? Two hundred bucks could mean the rest of the summer off for one of you."

Saffron walked over to the man and poked him hard in the

chest with her index finger. "Look, man, I already told you that we don't know anyone by that name. You need to blow this pop stand. If you're not gone in two minutes, I'm calling the police. I'll tell them that there's a man here offering money for a young girl."

I couldn't see the man's face well enough to know the effect of Saffron's words, but he turned on his heel and walked off the beach. He was gone, for now at least. But would he be back?

I sighed with relief. Saffron was something of a guardian angel for me. Since that first morning after my escape from Redemption, she'd been guiding me to safety.

———

That first morning after my escape, I woke when something droned lazily near my ear. I gave it a half-hearted swat and the sharp scent of dry grass and warm earth filled my nostrils. Blinking at the sun, I opened my eyes. I had absolutely no idea where I was, but knew I wasn't alone. There was movement nearby; soft footpads stirred the grass as a pair of bare feet came into view. They were distinctly female, and each toenail was painted a different colour.

I held myself still as I could, hoping I wouldn't be noticed, but a head followed the feet into my little sleeping nest. "Oh, hello," said a woman with a mass of curly blond hair. "Sorry to wake you. We're just shroom hunting." She laughed. "I promise we'll leave some for you and whoever else is with you. Go back to sleep. We'll be moving along soon."

I blinked at her, wide-eyed, and pushed myself up onto one elbow. "What are shrooms and who is we?"

The woman laughed again, a deep belly laugh. "That sounds poetic, don't you think? Like a song lyric? What are shrooms and who are we?"

Confused, I said nothing.

"Shrooms are mushrooms. We hunt all kinds. They grow best in the fall here, but if you know where to look, you can find them earlier. There's some that are great to eat, so we fry them in a little butter—so far-out—and some we use to make a special tea." She gave me a wink. "I'll brew you some, if you like."

I sat up and the woman squatted down, so we were at the same level. "I'm Saffron," she said with a wide, goofy smile. "What do you call yourself?"

"Daisy," I said. "Daisy Ford."

"Well, Daisy Ford, come meet my merry little band." The woman offered her hand to pull me up, but I held back. She saw my hesitation. "Running from someone? Don't worry, we all are. Listen, Daisy, no matter what kinda bad shit you've got going on, you're safe with us." She stood, spread her arms wide, and twirled, her hair shining in the sun like some sort of unkempt halo. "We're all about peace and love."

I knew from experience that the best lies had some truth to them. "I ran away from home," I said. "I hitchhiked but a creepy guy picked me up, so I made him stop and let me out. I ended up here."

She stopped spinning and slipped her arm in mine, speaking gently. "Don't be scared. I'll tell the others that you're all on your own. They'll help. Believe me, I know what it feels like to be at the mercy of a man."

I saw kindness in Saffron's eyes and felt a connection with her. I couldn't quite put my finger on why; it was just instinctive, I guess. It was like those feelings you get when you meet someone for the first time, and you just seem to click. Like when Brighten and I found each other that first time on the school playground in grade one.

We walked farther back into the bush, away from the highway, and I felt my body relax.

We were in an area of rolling grasslands dotted by the occasional birch or alder tree and sumac bushes with their odd, cone-like red fruit. The day was *already heating up, so I took off my peacoat and held it in front of me, like a shield. Saffron led me to a pullout where I saw a weird vehicle parked. Upon closer inspection, it was a Volkswagen van painted in a brilliant cascade of pink, yellow, and blue flowers.*

"Lance," Saffron called. We approached a slight, thin man dressed in a worn slouch hat, sandals, white cotton pants, and a white homespun shirt. "Come meet Daisy, she's lost and needs our help."

Lance turned towards us, did a little pirouette with one hand in an arch over his head, then whipped his hat off and bowed low to me. "Sir Lancelot at your service, my lady."

I didn't know what to think of him. He looked and acted nothing like the men in Redemption. I nodded and forced myself to look him full in the face.

Women must be meek in the presence of men and cast their eyes downward.

A young woman and a tall, lightly bearded man walked over to us from a clearing nearby. When the woman saw me, she looped her arm in the man's and leaned in close to him.

Saffron gestured towards me dramatically. "This is my new friend Daisy. I just found her in the woods, like the wildflower she is." She giggled.

The woman nodded, while the man seemed only vaguely interested.

"Marilyn," the woman said, by way of introduction. I figured Marilyn to be the same age as the others, twentyish or maybe a little older. She was really pretty, with long, straight dark hair, strong cheekbones, and a high forehead. I was in awe of her, perhaps because she was so beautiful, but she looked at me with distrust, narrowing her green eyes and frowning. "So, what log did you crawl out from under? Why are you here?"

All eyes turned on me.

Outsiders had such a blunt way of talking. The women in Redemption usually softened their message with sweet words. I didn't know how to respond, and thankfully, Saffron spoke up for me.

"She's a runaway, like I was. She's ditching her square parents and that whole weird conformist crap that goes with their generation."

I watched the group's interaction carefully. I could see that the bearded man was their leader by the way everyone kept looking up at him, waiting for him to speak.

"I'm Jean," he said, putting his hand out to shake mine, but I couldn't bring myself to touch him. I just stared at his hand as if it were the devil's paw. He dropped his hand and looked at me hard, with puffy, shadowed eyes, the kind you get when something's bugging you and you're not sleeping well. He made me afraid.

I was glad the jacket I was holding covered my trembling hands. My mouth was dry. I managed to peel my tongue off the roof of my mouth and say, "Hi, John."

"Not John—Jean," he said, his voice rough and tight. "I'm French."

"Jean is a French name? I'm sorry, I don't know any French."

Jean sighed. "No wonder the Quebecois get so fed up with you English Canadians. How can you live in this country and not know a single word of French?"

A burning blush crept up my neck to my cheeks. I lowered my eyes. "They didn't teach it at my school," I mumbled. The silence that followed was broken by the sound of my stomach loudly rumbling, making me blush even harder.

Saffron put her arm around me, and I felt the warm comfort of her body. "Come with us, sweet Daisy-flower. We've got some cherries to munch on in the van while we head to our camp to make a big meal and crash. You can share what we have. What's ours is yours." She turned to the others and looked straight at Jean. "Right, guys?"

Jean scowled as he lowered his large frame onto a log and set his mushroom bag down.

"The van is pretty full already and it's a long drive." He paused, squinting at me. "How old are you, anyway?"

Always tell outsiders that you are older than you are.

"Eighteen."

"You sure don't look it."

"That's because I'm small."

He lowered his head, poking at the ground with his knife. "And what happens if I leave you here?"

I didn't even want to think about that. We were still close enough to Redemption that the Bishop's men would be out scouring every campsite and pullout in the area. "I guess I'd hitchhike. I can't trust the men who pick me up, though. Some of them are—" I paused uncomfortably.

Jean sighed heavily again. "Merde. I guess I can't just leave a young woman by herself out in the middle of nowhere." He looked annoyed that I'd presented him with a moral choice, and I watched with curiosity as he fingered the cross that hung around his neck on a gold chain. "You can ride along until we hit civilization, if you promise to be quiet and just sit in the back."

"I promise." I turned to Saffron. "Where're we heading?"

"Fruit-picking in the Okanagan Valley," she said. "It's the perfect place to get lost if that's what turns you on. We've been doing it every summer for three years now. Lots of jobs and you can just pitch a tent in the orchard and live for free—all the fruit you can eat—and then hang out on one of the beaches after work." Saffron held her arms like airplane wings and ran a circle around me. "It's phantasmagoric!"

Jean's brooding face broke into a wide smile. "For once Saffron's not exaggerating. What she says is true."

"I've never heard of it. The Okanagan Valley, I mean."

"Mon Dieu. You're like these little mushrooms I've been picking. They like to hide in the shade, under rocks and leaves, never see the light of day. In French they are called champignon. Maybe I should call you that, le petit champignon."

"I love it. 'The little mushroom,' that's our Daisy," Saffron said. "Come on, everyone, let's blow!"

Marilyn gave me a hard look before climbing into the van's passenger seat and slamming the door behind her.

As I munched cherries, I watched Jean and Marilyn from my seat at the back. The van's engine was loud enough to drown out most of the conversation, but I got the gist of it. While Jean drove, Marilyn talked, sending dark looks my way and occasionally gesturing to car pullouts at the side of the road.

When men talk, women listen.

We drove towards the dazzling ball of the western sun. The van was stifling. It was an old winding highway and the rocking motion set my stomach on edge. It was a relief when we finally pulled into a clearing to camp for the night. I didn't want to cause any more trouble, so I tried to keep out of the way. Saffron noticed that I was quiet.

"Don't let Marilyn bug you. She's slow to trust. Had a tough childhood— only child of a single mom. She grew up dirt poor, so she stresses about money, insists everyone earn their keep."

I took the hint and asked Saffron what I could do to help. Behind a small door in the back of the van, she showed me a storage area with a box of tinned food and a few fresh things. I hunted through it. Putting together a meal made out of odds and ends was what I was good at.

There were canned beans, tomato soup, corn, onions, garlic, and other spices. I found a sad-looking green pepper and a few overripe tomatoes, as *well. There was no meat, but I figured some lentils could substitute—and of course, I knew which mushrooms to pick and throw into the mix.*

A portable stove was lit, and I made a big pot of chili. I'd done it so many times for my huge "family" in Redemption, I could do it in my sleep. After dinner, Lance went into the van and rooted around before coming out with a small bag. "Dessert," he called, and held up the bag for the rest of us to see. I was still hungry and hoped it was cookies or squares. Anything sweet.

I was sorely disappointed.

While the others drank the magic mushroom tea that Saffron brewed, I turned and surveyed the darkening woods, wondering if I should make a run for it.

"Just ignore them, Daisy. I don't like taking the tea, and you can choose not to too," said Jean. He began to build a fire as if he'd done it a thousand times before. After he got it going, he got up and went to the trailer, coming back with a mug of something. I could smell a fruity, musty smell and guessed that there was wine in the cup. Some of the priesthood men back home had it at festival dinners. They argued that it made them uninhibited, and more likely to sleep with their wives, so it was a good thing.

Protect me, Lord.

I took a deep breath and tried to stay calm. This was my chance to get some information. I had a basic plan roughed out in my mind, but I needed to fill in the gaps.

I broke the silence but carefully avoided making eye contact. "I plan to get a job and find a place to live as soon as possible once we get where we're going. Where exactly are we going? I don't want to bump into anyone I know."

Jean tossed another log onto the fire with an air of resignation. After taking a long drink, he said, "It's about four hours' drive from here, then we'll catch a ferry. I wouldn't worry about meeting anyone you know. We're going to a small village called Nkwala. No paved road in, just boat access or a four-wheel-drive dirt road through the provincial park. Pretty remote if you're into that." We talked a while longer, about why he'd chosen Nkwala. Jean sighed heavily and stood up. He looked annoyed, like maybe he'd said more than he'd intended. "I'm going to go sleep in the van. When you're done here, put water on the fire. Bonne nuit, good night."

He was gone before I had a chance to reply, leaving me with the others, sleeping off the effects of the tea.

I walked over to the pile of blankets and pillows that Lance had brought out and picked up one of each. The three of them lay still with their eyes shut, not moving except for their breath, which came in shallow puffs.

Saffron sat up abruptly. "Daisy, is that you?" She looked at me with hollow, unseeing eyes. "Be careful," she called after me. "Your face is glass, and we can all look through it."

Chapter Fifteen

With Jean helping Saffron and me, fruit-picking got a little easier. We had trouble moving the heavy ladders, but Jean always stopped what he was doing to move them for us. His presence also eased my mind after seeing the strange man in town. Knowing that Jean had pitched his tent a short distance from us made me feel safer. It was like he had assumed the responsibility of watching out for me, just like Saffron had.

We were up with the sun, starting work at five, picking till one or two in the afternoon before it became too hot. With wicker

backets tied around our waists, we hung from the high ladders filling the baskets as fast as we could.

I learned to open my hands wide, letting the cherries fall
between my fingers, then tug hard. If I did it right, I would harvest a handful of large, deep-purple Bing cherries, their stems still
attached. Once the baskets were full, we pulled drawstrings in
the basket's cloth bottom and let the gorgeous, plump fruit drop
unbruised into the large bins below.

There was something peaceful and soothing about the whole
thing. The clean air, the dry heat, the gentle birdsong, the repetitive,
hypnotic physical movement. It turned out to be a balm to my soul,
a way to turn off my worries and homesickness, to live only in the
moment, calm and relaxed.

In the evenings, Saffron, Jean, and I lit a charcoal hibachi and
cooked hamburgers or fish for supper, then we got comfy on three
old lawn chairs perched on a cliff overlooking the lake. We sat in
awe of Mother Nature, watching the sun go down and turn the
sky at the horizon shades of peach, pink, and violet. Then the vast,
twinkling Milky Way would come out to play in the velvety sky
with its shooting stars and the Big and Little Dippers almost right
overhead.

We all loved it, so it was noticeable when Jean seemed a little
dejected one evening.

"I want to plan my new vineyard. I need to buy some good
rootstock, but I can't find any. No one around here sells it. Everyone thinks I'm nuts when I ask about it. Maybe I could bring it
in from California, but I'm not sure how. The last thing I want to
do is to ask my brothers for help. They would laugh as hard as my
dad did."

———

That first night with Saffron and the gang, after everyone else had sipped their mushroom tea and gone to bed, I had asked Jean why he chose Nkwala. Jean had poked the fire with a stick and we both watched sparks drift skyward like dozens of blinking fireflies in the dark. "It's near my ranch."

I was startled. "You have a ranch? How? I mean . . ."

"How can someone like me own a ranch?"

"I just meant that you're young and I guess ranches must cost a lot of money."

"I bought it last year with the money my mother left me in her will."

I looked up sharply. "Oh—sorry your mom died."

He flung the stick into the fire, the flames flaring up, giving his face a golden hue. "Me too." He took a long drink of his wine, then he got up, rescued the stick, and aggressively poked the fire with it. "Thanks to the ranch, my dad is now convinced that I'm an idiot."

"Why?"

"It's a long story. I want to clear the land and grow grapes, make wine." He shrugged. "My dad is French. He thinks that the only good wines come from France. Only a fool would try to be a winemaker in Canada. Maybe he's right."

❦

Recalling that previous conversation, I tread softly. "Why would your brothers laugh?" I asked. I tucked my arms into the cardigan I'd brought with me.

Jean sighed and slumped forward. "I am, what you call, the black sheep of the family. My two brothers were good at school and sports." He shrugged. "Good at everything. They run the family vineyard and winery in Provence. I was the one who couldn't sit still in class long enough to learn anything. I prefer to get my hands in the dirt and do things myself, but my brothers wear suits and never leave their desks. They call me a 'paysan.'"

I wrinkled my brow. I had no idea what a paysan was, but I said nothing. I didn't want the others to know what little education I'd had.

"Your brothers sound like a couple of real little shits," Saffron said. "Who needs brothers like that?"

"I do." Jean rubbed his forehead. "I'd hoped I could do it all on my own," he said, "but I think I'm going to have to ask them to give me some rootstock. They'll tell my dad and he'll remind me what a disappointment I am and how humiliated he was that I dropped out of law school in Vancouver." Jean kicked a rock over the edge of the cliff. We heard the faint splash far below.

"I'm sorry, Jean," I said. "If it helps, I know what it's like to be the outsider. The person that everyone else treats like a loser. I was the scapegoat for my whole community. It's one of the reasons I ran away. It's hard, but going your own way will work out for you in the end." I summoned a small smile and gestured at the beauty around us. "It has for me."

Jean smiled warmly. "Maybe I can learn from you."

Saffron giggled and stood up, thrusting her fist in the air. "Look out, world, here comes Daisy," she shouted. I flushed with pleasure. No one had ever suggested that I had something to offer the world or that they could learn from me. Maybe it was true. I had paid my dues and I was tired of running.

⸎

Tucked into my tent near the cherry orchard, I was vaguely aware of a big rainstorm overnight but didn't wake until early the next morning when I was jolted from my sleeping bag by the deafening *whump-whump* of a helicopter directly overhead. Pulling on my overalls and covering my ears, I ran outside. Looking up I saw a bright yellow helicopter hovering just over the cherry orchards, its great blades sending small water droplets spraying off in all directions—a painful, penetrating shower of tiny water bullets.

Saffron came running from her tent, laughing. She grabbed both my hands in hers. "Far-out, eh?" she yelled in my ear over the throbbing sound. Pulling me in the direction of the orchard owner's house, she shouted, "Hardeep said we can wait inside. We have the morning off while the choppers dry the cherries."

She must have taken the look on my face as a request for more information. "They have to get the rain off the cherries before the sun comes out and heats them up," she said, "otherwise the skins split and Hardeep can't sell them to the co-op."

I didn't argue. The idea of a morning off, curled up on the couch in Hardeep's cozy house, was heavenly to me. I'd often admired the old house with its wide, covered veranda, cross-paned windows, and river rock chimney. I was dying to see inside.

The day was cool after the storm, and when we settled in the front room, we were thankful to find a crackling fire and a big pot of fresh coffee on the pine coffee table. Saffron and I crashed on the plush couch, sipping our hot drinks. I'd never stayed at a big fancy hotel before, but I guessed it would be a bit like this: a warm room, a soft place to sit, and all the coffee you could drink.

We sipped in silence for a while as we woke up. "Where's Jean?" I asked.

"Helping Hardeep move the ladders out of the way." Saffron got up and wandered over to the window, looking out at the dreary cloudy day, rain streaks blurring the view. "I've been thinking about things."

"What things?"

"The future. Before Lance decided to leave, he was looking into a job he saw posted here. Every winter until now, Lance and I hitchhiked all over, wherever our hearts took us, wherever the action was. Without him it wouldn't be so easy—like you discovered. So I've decided that at the ripe old age of nineteen, it's time to settle down here for good. You should think about it too."

Saffron's comments about settling down and moving beyond her vagabond lifestyle made me think of the time we travelled together in Jean's van on our way to Nkwala and she filled me in on her past.

———

Saffron had dramatically opened her hands wide. "Meet Miss Linda-Ann Cranston. Only child of middle-class parents from Calgary. Mom's a housewife and Dad sells life insurance. We lived in the burbs, went to church every Sunday. We did not listen to music, dance, drink, smoke, or eat any food with a spice in it. Favourite TV show? The Andy Griffith Show *with Opie and Aunt Bee. If I hadn't left and become Saffron, I'd have died of boredom."*

I'd laughed. "I like Saffron way better."
"So do I."

∽

I looked at Saffron curled up on Hardeep's couch. "I don't know what kind of job I could get," I said.

"It's not hard here. There's plenty of places that need help but not many people looking for full-time work. No one wants to commute from Kelowna. The ferry is expensive and too much of a hassle."

I shrugged.

"Cheryl, that dark-haired girl with the groovy clothes who works at the Apple Dumpling? She told me she's going back to school in the fall. There'll be a job there."

"I don't know." A whole new world of fears opened up inside my head. I didn't think I was ready for a full-time job in the outside just yet, but at the same time, I felt the lure of the money, not for the things I could buy, but for the freedom and independence it offered. Besides, I couldn't camp outside in the winter. I'd have to pay rent somewhere. I changed the subject. "What kind of job are you trying to get?"

"Not trying to get—will get. Working for BC Ferries, using the radio to manage ferry traffic in the bay. I think I'm going to put on my old Linda-Ann clothes from my past life and apply. Linda-Ann will knock their socks off. I have all the requirements: I'm an adult, a Canadian citizen, and I speak perfect English. There's just one minor glitch."

"What's that?"

"I don't know anything about radio systems. Like ship-to-shore, shortwave, CB, all that."

"I know."

Saffron whirled from the window, her big blue eyes bulging. "You do?"

"It was my job back in Redemption. I can show you if you like."

"Linda-Ann would definitely like that, and Saffron would owe you one."

"No problem," I said. I'd been waiting for a moment like this. I'd wanted to tell Saffron the final details of my past—about plural marriage and sister-wives and marrying at fifteen—but I'd always held back. I was insecure and I felt shame. Before I told her, I'd wanted to be sure I could trust her not to tell anyone, and to understand with no judgment. It was time. And who better to understand what I was running from than Saffron, who saved me from abduction by the Bishop's men?

———

On my second night of freedom, after I'd cleaned up my chili, I'd settled down near Jean's small fire. Saffron and the others were sleeping off their mushroom tea again, but I couldn't sleep. Lucky, I guess. Because soon I was startled by the roar of an engine.

I sat up to see the headlights of a truck as it turned off the highway and parked nearby. The driver killed the engine and two men got out. I knew them right away by their look. They were dressed the same: black pants held up by white suspenders, black T-shirts, and matching ball caps with a bright red R on the front. They were the Bishop's private security team. Everyone in Redemption called them the God Squad because of their reputation for being ruthless in the name of the Lord. I scrambled to my feet and ran.

I wasn't thinking. I just ran wildly into the woods, with no idea where I was going. All I knew was that I was never going back. Not after what Tobias had said to me that night on the bridge. I knew that going back to Redemption would kill me one way or another.

Tree branches swiped at my face and body as I stumbled along in the semi-darkness, keeping low in case my ash-blond hair caught the moonlight and gave me away. My foot snagged on a large tree root, and I went forehead-first into the thick spongy bark of a large ponderosa pine. The world spun for a moment as I lay stunned, feeling warm blood trickle down my cheek like a tear.

When my head cleared, I heard voices. Jean was saying something; he was talking to the men with the truck. They would tell him lies: that I was a spoiled, willful teenager running away from a loving home; that my parents were desperate to have me back; that my poor mother had been crying for days, so my father hired private detectives to find me. I couldn't hear what Jean was saying, but I prayed that he wasn't falling for it.

The beam of a flashlight swept past me, just over my head. I lay perfectly still until it arced away from me, and then I took off again, running in short spurts from tree to tree.

The land suddenly sloped downhill, so I tried sliding on my bum on the loose scree, but I soon gathered too much speed and lost control of the descent. Gravity took over and I tumbled like a limp rag doll until I landed at the bottom of a long slope, scraped and bruised. I knew that the crunching sounds of the sliding rocks might have attracted the men, so I stayed as still as I could and listened.

My heart was like a drum in my ears, and I had to wait for it to calm down before I could hear anything. The noises around me didn't seem man-

made, but that brought me no comfort. Scurrying, scratching noises came from the scree slope and from the bushes nearby, and something smelled gut-churningly rank.

I felt dampness beneath me, and I could hear water trickle nearby, so I wondered if I was smelling the carcass of a steelhead trout on the riverbank. I didn't want to think about bears, but I knew there would be plenty around here.

I crawled away to dry land and must have slept. I awoke with the first rays of dawn. Looking around, I found myself near the edge of a little stream. I washed as much dirt, grime, and blood off my face as I could. I took off my pea jacket and splashed ice-cold water on my raw and stinging scrapes. I cupped my hands and took great greedy gulps of the clear, cold water.

With the full light of day, I saw that I was on the side of a small mountain that sloped down into a green, irrigated valley. I hiked down to the nearest bluff and looked out over the patchwork of farmers' fields below. I could pick out a narrow deer trail that led down towards the farms and what looked like a small cluster of buildings. I made my way over to the trail and began walking.

Late afternoon the next day they got me. I'd let my guard down and didn't see it coming. I was walking along a road headed west when a black pickup truck pulled up beside me. A man inside opened the passenger door and jumped out. He grabbed me in a headlock, clamped a hand over my mouth, and shoved me into the middle of the cab. He jumped in beside me, slammed the door, and the driver hit the gas.

It took me a minute to grasp what was happening, but when I did, I fought for my life. I jammed my elbows as hard as I could into the ribs of both men and felt the truck swerve before the driver recovered. Diving for the door handle, I managed to pull the lever. The door swung wide.

The driver swerved off the road and yelled at the other man to get me out of the truck.

The guy who'd grabbed me off the street hauled me out of the truck after him and we stumbled together onto a recently plowed field. The black soil gave off the overwhelming reek of decaying mushroom fertilizer. I gagged but managed to hold on to last night's dinner.

The driver joined us and together they held me by the arms. When I struggled, the driver shot his hand out from his side and slapped me hard across the face, sending me reeling into the rotting pulp below. I sat in the mulch, my face stinging ferociously, too stunned to move.

"You will come with us and do as you are told," the driver boomed. "You, woman, are infested with Satan's spores. You should be grateful that the Bishop cares enough to save you. Especially after what you did to him."

My brain began to work. What had I done to the Bishop? I'd hit him twice with the shovel, but he was moving when I'd left him. Had I injured him permanently? Would God forgive me?

"I didn't do anything bad to the Bishop. He hit my mom. I was just trying to protect her."

The driver's face turned purple in the low twilight. "Nothing bad? You call that nothing? You cracked his skull!" He could barely contain his fury.

The other man broke in. "Some say he don't get revelations from God no more. That crack in the skull did it."

I started to shiver uncontrollably. This was so much worse than I could have imagined.

"If it were up to me," the driver said, leaning in close, "I would deliver the Lord's ultimate punishment on you, right here, right now, in this putrid farmer's field. You don't deserve the Bishop's love and forgiveness."

As the guilt poured into me, the fight went out of me. When the men told me to get back into the truck, I followed their instructions like a lamb. We bumped along the highway, driving long into the night.

I dozed off, only to waken to the men discussing our route. The Bishop had instructed them to make a show of my arrival and that meant not arriving back at Redemption in the middle of the night. They decided to take a long route back, going west for a while, then circling back around to arrive mid-morning.

At dawn we stopped at a public campground and pulled up to the free toilets and showers.

"Get out," the driver said to me. "You stink. Get yourself cleaned up." He reached into the glove compartment and pulled out a long, pastel-peach dress. I knew it at once. It was my wedding dress, carefully cleaned and mended. I felt the bile rise in my throat.

"Put it on. The Bishop will consummate your marriage first, clearing your path to redemption with your rebaptism. Then the real punishment begins."

With the weight of the world on my shoulders, I grabbed the dress and hauled myself into the lady's washroom. There was only one entrance, and the truck was parked right in front of it, so there was no way to run. I tossed the dress on the counter, went into a bathroom stall, and sat dejectedly on the toilet.

How had it come to this so quickly and easily? After all I'd been through, to have them just drive up and grab me off the street? I should have been more careful. I'd never felt so low in my life.

As I sat staring at the scarred cement floor, fighting tears, someone entered the washroom and sat in the cubicle beside me. Looking over, I recognized sandaled feet and ten toenails painted different colours. I gasped.

"Saffron?"

Chapter Sixteen

I'd just finished "explaining" to Saffron about the men waiting for me outside, the ones "sent by my strict parents to find me," when the door to the washrooms was yanked back on its hinges and at least a dozen girls trooped in. Talking and laughing excitedly, they were dressed in an odd assortment of outfits. I was struck with how carefree and genuinely happy they all seemed compared to the girls in Redemption.

I tried not to stare as they lined up at the mirror, applying makeup and doing their hair. A familiar cloud of sticky-sweet hairspray filled the air and I stared transfixed for a moment until Saffron gave me a push towards the showers. "Hurry up, this gives me an idea. We're going to try something."

When I'd dried off and dressed in my underwear, Saffron dug into her huge purse and pulled out a long paisley shawl with a fringe. She tied it at one of my shoulders, letting it hang to my knees like a dress. Next, she fastened a silver chain-link belt around my waist to hold the shawl in place.

She pulled the big floppy sun hat off her head and helped me tuck all my hair up under it. Finally, she fished around again in her bag until she found a pair of oversized sunglasses and handed them to me. I was transformed. I could pass for any one of the girls in the room.

I could see what she had in mind, but I wasn't sure I wanted to try it. I didn't want Saffron hurt. "You don't have any idea how bad these men are," I said. "They think they're doing God's work and they'll stop at nothing."

Saffron looked at the red welt forming on my cheek. "They're a couple *of real shits if they have no problem hitting a girl, but they have to be careful. We've got a lot of witnesses here."*

Before I could say anything more, she asked one of the girls if she could borrow a little pancake makeup and used her fingers to spread it over my red, aching cheek. Her finishing touch was lavender-coloured lipstick that made me look like a model in Seventeen *magazine.*

We tossed my torn clothes and shoes in the garbage, and I headed for the door in bare feet. At the last moment I grabbed my old wedding dress and hung it on a nail by the washroom door. If the men glanced in through the opening, they'd see the dress hanging there and assume I was still in the showers.

"Whatever you do, don't look at the men. Stare into my face like you're fascinated by what I have to say. Let me do all the talking. We'll pretend we're deep in conversation and couldn't care less about Tweedledum and Tweedledee. Got it?"

I nodded with a confidence I didn't feel and felt my knees weaken. Saffron linked arms with me, pulled me close, and threw open the door to the outside.

We stepped into the bright sunlight, directly in the path of the man who'd grabbed me off the street. Saffron suddenly erupted in laughter and pulled me even closer to her. "Isn't that just the craziest shit you've ever heard, Judy? So, I said to him, Who you tryin' to kid, man? I'm not falling for that old trick." She laughed loudly again.

I don't know what else Saffron said. My ears began to roar with the sound of my blood rushing. We passed the Bishop's man, and I fought the urge to look back to see if he was following us. When I saw Jean's van parked nearby, I focused all my energy on walking calmly to it.

Saffron raised her voice, but she kept the tone calm. "Jean, start the van."

Jean was dozing in the driver's seat. He woke and looked around, confused.

"Jean, start the van." Saffron's voice had more urgency this time.

I saw Jean focus on us and then look past us, towards the washrooms. His eyes widened, clearly recognizing the truck and the men from our campsite. I had no idea if they were closing in on us or not—I didn't dare turn around—but Jean jumped into action. He started the van and stepped out of the cab to slide the side door wide for Saffron and me.

This time I didn't hesitate in accepting his help. Saffron and I leapt into the van and flattened ourselves on the floor while Jean slammed the door shut behind us. In a second we were off. As the van roared out of the campground, I couldn't resist lifting my head to peek out the window.

The Bishop's man stood with his hands on his hips, eyes squinting as he watched Jean's van disappear down the road.

⤜⤛

Tucked safe in Hardeep's house, waiting for the helicopter to dry the cherries, I told Saffron what I'd been too scared to confess when she'd rescued me from the ladies' washroom. I told her about growing up in Redemption, about the child brides and the obsession with having huge numbers of children, about the sham school and the endless work and punishments. Then I told her about my mom and Brighten, and how I missed them and needed to get them out of there. Finally, I told her about my fear of being found again and dragged back.

I didn't tell her about Tobias. About our reckoning on the bridge, when the truth came out. That pain was still too raw.

"We'll never let them take you back! That'll never happen!" Saffron said, slamming her fist on the table, making our coffee cups jump. "I'll give 'em the ole kung fu."

I jumped too.

She laughed and said, "Jean and I will protect you. The Bishop and those other assholes can just go pound sand."

Before long I joined in the laughter, more with the relief of having it all off my chest and imagining Saffron engaging in combat than anything.

Jean came in, his curly hair wet and his clothes soaked through. "What's the joke?"

"Nothing. You wouldn't get it. Girl stuff." Saffron winked at me and waved him away. He helped himself to coffee, and stood with his back against the fire, looking a bit like a half-drowned cat. Staring into his coffee, he seemed miles away. I sensed his unhappiness and felt sorry for him. It must feel awful to lose a parent's love and respect. I had always had the blessing of a loving, caring mother, at least. Without it I would have been lost.

But what about my dad? I had a father who cared enough to send me early birthday gifts every year. Even if he did leave Mom and me, even if I hadn't seen him in years, I had a father who thought of me. A father who, like me, didn't believe in the Bishop anymore.

I shifted on the couch and heard the crinkle of paper in my pocket. Reaching in, I pulled out the library card application form and brochure that I'd picked up at the library the other day. I smoothed out the worst wrinkles and selected an HB pencil from a mason jar on the corner of the table. I'd made a plan, and joining the library was my first step towards a proper education.

I started filling out the application, but before long, I let out a long, slow groan.

"What?" Jean said.

"I need an address, a permanent mailing address, in order to get a library card. I can't just write 'Pup Tent Number Two, Hardeep's Cherry Orchard.'"

"Not a problem, use my address at the ranch."

"Can I?"

"Bien sûr, of course," Jean said.

"You'll be official," Saffron said, nodding excitedly. "You'll have ID. You'll be able to prove you belong here. You'll be a . . . Nkwalian."

"Is that really a thing?" I asked.

"Of course not, I made it up."

⤫

The next day, right after work, I went to the library, my application heavy in my pocket and a lump in my throat. I didn't know what I was so nervous about, especially since the librarian had been nice to me. I just had this uneasy feeling that I didn't really belong in a house of learning, that I was an imposter who would be discovered and told to leave. I was fearful of getting into trouble. It was so easy to do, back in Redemption.

My worries proved silly. Miss Braid was just as enthusiastic and warm as the first time we met. I told her what I was looking for and she was more than happy to give me all her time and attention.

She adjusted her cat's-eyes glasses on her freshly powdered nose and loaded a spool of thin black film, from one round reel to another, into some sort of odd machine with a flat front screen. It reminded me of the first television set I'd ever seen in the window of the furniture store in Stewart's Landing. There'd been an animated cartoon flickering on the screen, a large bunny with big teeth and bigger ears. He'd looked so funny. "*The Bugs Bunny Show*," I'd heard a passerby say. Oh, how I'd wished I could go inside the store and watch.

Miss Braid interrupted my daydream. "Thanks to a recent project by the Canadian Library Association, we have every newspaper in the country on microfilm, including the *Stewart's Landing Chronicle* that you asked for. We may be small, but we are up-to-date with all the latest research tools." Miss Braid beamed and patted my arm as if to reassure me.

"You can start first with the card catalogue, and when you find what you're looking for, you can access it on this microfilm reader just the way I showed you. I had this baby flown in all the way from Vancouver." She dropped her voice even though no one was in the library. "They don't even have one of these at the big library in Kelowna yet. Not that I'm competitive, mind you. Let's just say, if you snooze, you lose."

I thanked her and settled down at the card catalogue. I'd expected my search might take several hours or even days, but I immediately found a newspaper article under: Shoemaker, Dan. The microfilm reader was not hard to figure out, and I quickly brought up the article.

May 1, 1964
War Hero Returns to Site of Escape

Local war hero Captain Dan Shoemaker recently returned from a visit to the German stalag where he had been imprisoned for three years during World War Two. He told this reporter that he hoped that the excursion would help to rid him of the ghosts that had haunted him for years. He'd also visited the old construction site where, in 1944, he'd led a prisoner revolt that resulted in freedom for ten of his fellow slave labourers. As the last to escape, Captain Shoemaker was recaptured, then starved and beaten for his role in the uprising.

He never completely recovered, and deteriorating health forced him to take an early retirement from his job of the last ten years as the manager of the Stewart's Landing Sawmill. Prior to working at the mill, Dan owned his own company, Shoemaker Forest Products, but sold that when he left Redemption in 1954.

At the recent homecoming party attended by many local friends and colleagues, speakers said that they had missed his warm, generous spirit and wish him well in this next phase of his retirement. He plans to spend it fishing, plying the local lakes in *Ruthie*— the houseboat he painstakingly built in his spare time.

George Snelgrove, staff reporter
Stewart's Landing Chronicle

I read and reread the article at least ten times. Never had I learned so much about my father than I did from that one short newspaper article. Mom had made vague references to Dad's wartime experiences, but when I asked pointed questions, she always clammed up, telling me that the subject of Dad was off-limits and the less I knew, the better. Since Mom's father had threatened a blood atonement on her if she ever had contact with Dad again, she was afraid that I might let something slip.

Had I known all this while I was growing up, it would have helped me deal with the endless taunts about my father. While the people in Redemption thought he was the lowest of the low, outsiders called him a war hero. Oh, how I wished my mother had told me.

The war was something I had very limited knowledge of, but what I did know now was that my father, my own flesh and blood, had been a leader, freeing his fellow prisoners. I was so proud that I decided to find him right away. I wanted to make up for lost time. But how was I to go about tracking him on a houseboat?

Maybe I'd work up the courage to ask Miss Braid. In the meantime, I searched in the card catalogue for stories about Redemption. I found a recent one and pulled up the microfilm.

July 15, 1964
Tragic Drowning in Redemption

A young woman has drowned in the religious community of Redemption just after church service on Sunday. No additional information was released, but Bishop Thorsen wishes to thank the greater community for their prayers at this difficult time. The deceased has been identified as seventeen-year-old Lavender Sanderson. The police have issued a statement labeling the mishap as an accident. No foul play is suspected.

My mind raced back to the last time I had visited with the youngest wife in my assigned family, and I struggled to remain calm. Lavender had been distraught over her inability to get pregnant—and Mother Rose had scorned and mocked her.

How could she have drowned? None of the women ever went anywhere near the pond for the very good reason that they couldn't swim. Had one of the children gone back to the pond, and this time Lavender intervened? It seemed unlikely, but it was possible. Or was she so distraught that she'd hurt herself?

I immediately thought of Brighten and her marriage to Brother Earl. What might Brighten do to escape her situation? Fear for her exploded in my brain like the brilliant flash of fireworks I'd seen at Willow Park on Dominion Day.

Chapter Seventeen

I was still thinking about all that I'd learned in the library as we sat on our lawn chairs staring off into the distance. Ghost-like pale-blue hills were silhouetted against a cobalt sky. The long lake, the colour of slate, sparkled and shimmered, cutting a jagged swath through the desert-dry landscape.

Saffron and Jean were full of fun that evening, but I felt lost and low. What happened to Lavender? How could I help Brighten and my mom? Would I be able to find my dad? My head swam with overlapping waves of worry.

Saffron got up to light two sweet-smelling sandalwood incense sticks in a large glass ashtray. As she sat back down, she leaned over and poked me in the ribs with her elbow. "What's up?"

"Just thinking about weird family stuff," I said. "I want to try to find my dad. I think he can help me figure some things out."

Saffron nodded sagely. "We should talk about that sometime. Maybe tomorrow. But tonight?" She flapped a dismissive hand in the air, her slew of brightly coloured bangles jangling on her wrist. "Tonight, forget it, Daisy. We don't get to pick our families. If we did, I'd have been born to hippie parents living in Marrakesh who loved to dance, eat exotic foods, and explore the universe. Tonight, let's celebrate good friends."

I couldn't resist a small smile. Saffron always knew how to cheer me up.

Jean picked up Saffron's point. "None of us are very happy about the people we came from, but I've got one relative who's actually a pretty good guy, my mom's brother, Uncle Pierre," he said. "When my mom got sick, he wrote to her and suggested I come and live with him in Vancouver for a while. He knew my dad and I didn't get along. He was cool about me quitting law school. *'Being a lawyer is not for everyone,'* he told me, and he should know, he *is* one."

Jean stood up. I was surprised to see a big, eager smile on his face. "Long story short, it's my nineteenth birthday on August ninth. In my family, nineteen is a big deal, a fun celebration, but of course they won't be having one for me—so . . ."

He reached into his back pocket and brought out his wallet. He held out some small pieces of paper. "Uncle Pierre sent me these— three tickets to the Beatles *live* in Vancouver!"

Saffron and I stared at each other in disbelief, and for a moment

I couldn't breathe. Then we shrieked and started jumping up and down and hugging each other. Saffron hugged Jean while I hung back awkwardly, then we leaned in close and examined the tickets.

The Beatles, August 22, 1964,
Empire Stadium, VIP seating, $5.25.

It was a dream come true.

But how could I go to a concert when Lavender was dead and my father was out there somewhere? When Brighten was married to Brother Earl and my mother was all alone?

But I needn't have worried. The Beatles concert would bring me face-to-face with my past.

∽

I pinched myself a dozen times as the three of us piled into Jean's van, took the ferry across the lake to Peachland and headed south, then west to Vancouver, a five-hour drive.

I didn't tell the others that it was my birthday too. I would turn sixteen the day of the concert. It was Jean's special treat, and I didn't want to steal the spotlight, but I savoured the secret knowledge that it was my day as well.

Saffron had suggested we get some new cool clothes, or "threads" as she called them. I was excited to buy something high-style, but in the end, I settled for a new pair of Lee jeans, a white tee, and a matching jean jacket. There was absolutely no way that I was ready to show skin.

A woman must cover herself for all but her husband.

When I saw Saffron's new dress, a maroon velvet granny gown with a low scoop neck, puff sleeves, and an empire waist, I thought it looked beautiful on her. It was the very latest style, but I wasn't envious. I would never wear another ankle-length dress as long as I lived.

We drove through rugged mountains on a very curvy road full of switchbacks, so that when we hit the wide, flat Fraser Valley, my stomach was happy for the first time since we'd started. After pitching our tents in a provincial campground just out of town, we headed into the big city for dinner.

I cringed and ducked when we drove under the broad river into a tunnel that seemed to go on forever, before emerging into a wide road with more cars than I'd ever seen. Jean managed just fine, but I had to bite my tongue a few times to stop myself from shouting, "Look out." One time, I embarrassed myself by pointing out the window and exclaiming, "Look, a bus!" They laughed.

Darkness had fallen by the time we reached downtown, but the many neon signs lit up the night and created a whole new and fascinating world. With vivid neon colours in reds, blues, and greens, the signs were like a parade of exotic, flashing images reflected in the rain-slick streets.

A huge red *W* glowed on an Eiffel Tower–like structure above the Woodward's store; it and the pulsing Stanley Theatre sign with its green maple leaf made me want to stop and see the show. But the most incredible sight by a long shot was the Vancouver Sun building with its domed roof and six brilliant yellow lightning bolts seemingly suspended in midair above it.

Saffron wanted to buy new shoes to match her dress, so we stopped at the Hudson's Bay store on Georgia Street. Despite the light rain, I hung out the van window, looking up. "How many storeys does it have? It's huge."

"I don't know, maybe five or six," Saffron said.

"That's a *lot* of stairs," I said.

Jean and Saffron looked at each other and smiled. "They have an elevator and an escalator," Saffron said.

"I knew that."

"No you didn't."

The escalator turned out to be a moving staircase. Jean and Saffron hopped on, and I followed behind, but before I knew it, it was time to get off and I had no idea how to do that. I managed to stumble and crash into Jean from behind. He took it well, but I'm sure I turned the colour of the borscht Mom used to make.

The exotic smells of perfume blends and skin-care lotions filled the air, and I shivered with excitement. The store had more clothes than I'd ever seen in one place, and as we made our way to the shoe department, my head swivelled, taking in the glittering jewelry, leather handbags, and embarrassing displays of lady's fancy underwear.

The best part, though, was the elevator ride back down. I'd never actually been in one before and I was dying to try it. Our large car had its very own operator who called out a list of items for sale on each floor as we descended. It was like a private tour of the department store. I hung on tight, but my knees felt wobbly at each floor.

Afterwards, Jean said he was taking us to Chinatown for dinner. I was expecting something like Mrs. Lee's little café in Nkwala, but boy, was I wrong. During Inspection Week at school two years ago, we actually got to study China. I loved it and fantasized about seeing it one day. When we got to Chinatown, it was just as I'd imagined the real China would be.

Entire streets were lined with elaborate Chinese-style architecture, including a pagoda with curved, yellow-glazed tile roofs trimmed in red. Crowds shopped in open-air fruit and vegetable stalls, stacked with produce I didn't even recognize, but I didn't have time to ask questions because Jean was starving and wanted to take us to his favourite place, the Ho Inn. And what a place it was!

I was happy to let Jean and Saffron do the ordering as I sat mesmerized by the waiters rushing back and forth with giant platters loaded with chicken, beef, seafood, and every kind of vegetable I could imagine. When the steaming platters were brought to our table, I managed the chopsticks well enough to keep up with the others. We ate until our stomachs were full to bursting. When the bill came, I could hardly believe we'd had a feast for a dollar each.

We slept in the tents that night, and the next day was the concert. Jean had to park a long way from Empire Stadium because twenty thousand people were also headed there. I couldn't even imagine that many people in one place.

We joined the crowds outside pushing to get in, and I had a moment of panic when I saw how many police officers and security guards there were. I hung back until Saffron noticed and circled my arm in hers. "Just ignore them; they aren't looking for you, you're just one more teenage girl here to see the Beatles."

With a rush of adrenaline, my mouth went dry, and my knees wobbled.

Police are the soldiers of Satan.

We were thrilled with our seats, on the grass to the right of the stage, close enough to see the faces of the Fab Four. The Righteous Brothers came on while we waited for the main event. I loved them and their great harmonies, but people weren't listening. I could feel the impatience of the crowd. It had its own kind of electricity, like a room full of six-year-olds waiting for the bell on the last day of school.

The girl next to me leaned over during the mild applause. "I don't give a fig about these boys. I came to see Paul. I'm in love with him. I'm going to make sure he notices me." I looked over at her. Her eyes were wide, the pupils dilated, and her face dewy and flushed. She'd obviously done her best to look special. She wore a bright pink dress with a Peter Pan collar, her hair in an elaborate French braid that must have taken a long time to do. I knew how much work they were—I'd done plenty of those braids for my little sisters.

I looked around at the others near me, mostly girls, but some boys. Many looked like they were in their Sunday best, prim blouses and suits, smart dresses. A few girls even wore white gloves and carried purses. It seemed like the new mod British styles I'd seen on TV hadn't made it to Vancouver yet.

A wiry, ginger-haired man walked onstage and introduced himself as Red Robinson. "It gives me a great deal of fun to present . . . *The Beatles*."

The whole place erupted in a cacophony of screams. The noise level was astonishing, like someone had let loose a dozen roaring, fire-breathing dragons.

Four young men with long hair, matching dark suits, and black boots walked swiftly onstage and grabbed their instruments. My pulse throbbed when they opened with "Twist and Shout," and I screamed long and hard along with the rest.

Saffron cupped her hands and shouted, "My mind is totally blown," as the four mop tops shook their long hair in unison and a large crowd of girls made a rush for the stage. Saffron pulled me to my feet, and we danced where we stood, laughing with sheer joy and the zaniness of it all.

I looked over at the girl beside me. She was overcome, ripping her elaborate hairdo apart, sending bobby pins flying. Weeping, she cried, "I love you, Paul," over and over, then she was gone, joining the surging crowd of girls trying to break through the barricades and rush the stage.

Soon Red Robinson was back with a handheld microphone, one hand stretched out like a stop sign to the audience. "Ladies and gentlemen—"

"Get the fuck off our stage! Nobody interrupts the Beatles," said John Lennon in his thick Liverpool accent.

Beside me, Saffron hooted with delight, but I was shocked by his language.

"John . . . John, I'm sorry. Your manager sent me. It's getting too dangerous." Red looked tense and apologetic, but also determined.

John nodded. "Okay, carry on, mate."

Red turned back to the audience and asked everyone to please sit down and move away from the barricades.

"One—two—three—four," John called out, and Empire Stadium rocked with "She Loves You." The crowd was jubilant, but it was when the band played "Roll Over Beethoven" that I felt like one of the shooting stars that we loved to watch in the night sky, exploding in a fiery ball, spinning out of control.

Suddenly, the music stopped. All I could figure was that the crowd had turned into a frenzied mob and the police had halted the show. The lights came up and loudspeakers asked everyone to exit the building calmly and quickly. We were seated near the front, so were among the last to leave.

When it was finally our turn to exit the nearly deserted stadium, my bladder complained. "One sec," I said. "I've got to visit the ladies' room."

Saffron pointed to the closed ticket booth. "We'll wait there for you."

I entered the empty bathroom and hurried into the first stall. As I relieved myself, I heard the heavy door open and slam shut, but I didn't think much of it. Washing my hands, I noticed a flicker of movement by the door and turned my head to look.

A young woman in a long, old-fashioned dress stared back at me. Rainbow.

Chapter Eighteen

She stood there in the shadows, her body blocking the door, making no move to either come in or to leave.

"Rainbow! What are you doing here? Is everyone okay? Mom? Brighten?"

She stepped forward. "They're fine, Daisy, both doing well. Tobias drove me here. We wanted to talk to you. We both miss you so much."

My wet hands hung limp at my sides as I stared at her in disbelief. "How did you find me?"

"The Bishop's men said you made off in a Volkswagen van painted in bright flowers. Tobias asked friends to keep an eye out for it. It was spotted yesterday, downtown, by the Bay. We drove all night to get here. The van was seen again parked near here. It wasn't hard to figure out where you were. I was watching the exit when I saw you. Nothing like the ladies' room for two women to have a private talk, right?"

She tried to smile, but I could see fatigue in her greying complexion and puffy eyes.

"Tobias is here?" My mind flashed back to the last time I'd seen him, illuminated in the light of a streetlamp on the bridge.

Rainbow took a step closer to me, her eyes glistening with intensity. "Tobias is determined to save you, Daisy. He wants to marry you."

I felt a prickle of heat. "He already has a wife. And I don't need saving or marrying."

She teared up as she made a sweeping gesture with her hands. "How can you say that? Look what's happened here! Hundreds of teenage girls were out of their mind. They threw themselves at the long-haired members of a rock-and-roll group. They idolize these men, treat them like gods, but the men use them and then toss them away. Is that the kind of life you want, Daisy?"

"I wasn't one of those women."

"Why would you even want to be part of this?" she cried. "Come back to Redemption and feel the warmth of a big loving family. You could have a husband who loves you, takes care of you and treats you well. You won't find what you are seeking here. People on the outside are depraved."

"You know what's depraved? Fifteen-year-old girls being married to old men! And why do you care so much? You want to share Tobias with me? Or is the Bishop behind this?"

She shook her head. "The Bishop doesn't even know we're here. But we know he would welcome you back with open arms and reassign you to Tobias to prove that there are no hard feelings. We came because we care about you."

I sighed. "Do you love Tobias?"

"Yes," she exclaimed. "With all my heart."

"Then how can you stand there and ask another woman to share him with you—to live with the two of you day in and day out? How could you not be crushed by the hurt?"

"You have always been so good to me, Daisy. You stood up for me lots of times, and always had a kind word, not like the others. Not like Blossom. You're a fine person, and you deserve eternal life in the Celestial Kingdom." Large tears began to roll down Rainbow's cheeks, and she swiped at them like a child.

"Tobias is an important member of the priesthood now. He recently married my little sister and will be assigned his third wife soon, his celestial wife, the one who ensures he gets to heaven. Daisy, Tobias has given me a say on who it is. Sharing Tobias with other women would test my devotion daily, but not you."

A man's third wife is his celestial wife and ensures he will get into the highest kingdom of heaven.

My jaw dropped. Celestial wife? Bishop Thorsen said there was no higher calling for a woman than that. For a fleeting moment, I imagined what life would be like waking up next to Tobias each morning as his most highly favored wife—redeemed and rewarded—but then I envisioned the chart on the wall labelled "Daddy Time" and knew that I could never share my husband. Could never live the Principle and be forced to compete for affection and attention.

One look at Rainbow's hopeful, pleading face made me feel sick to my stomach. Had Tobias put her up to this? I didn't need to know. I didn't want to know. I changed the subject. "Tell me about Brighten and my mom."

Rainbow smiled through her tears. "Brighten is fine—good even. Bishop Thorsen has devoted his valuable time to her re-education. She's adjusted her thinking and is going to be rebaptised in a couple of weeks. Everyone is supporting her and cheering her on."

"Re-education through isolation? How do you even know how she's doing? Have you seen her?"

"I visited her, in her room—such a lovely big room, bright flowered drapes with a matching comforter—all to herself."

I wanted so much to believe Rainbow. I knew she wouldn't lie to me, but how much of what she told me were the Bishop's lies?

"You had a long talk with her, in private?"

"I did, and with your mom. They are both doing well, and they really miss you. Here, Daisy." She reached into her pocket to retrieve something. She took my hand and dropped the object into it—the locket that Mom had given me years ago. "Tobias is waiting. You can be back with your mom and Brighten by tomorrow evening. I know how much you've missed them. It must just break your heart."

It was my turn for tears. Rainbow knew my weak spot. I had a moment of crisis when doubt and uncertainty crept in, but then—

"What happened to Lavender?" I said quietly.

"Lavender?" Rainbow looked momentarily flustered. "She . . . she drowned."

"I know that. But where did it happen? She couldn't swim. She wouldn't have gone swimming in the pond, so how did it happen?"

"It was an accident. No one meant for it to happen. Her dress—it got tangled around her head. No one noticed till it was too late."

But where? It made no sense. And I couldn't bear to hear the lies.

"Rainbow, I know you don't want to hear this, but I don't believe in the Bishop anymore. I don't think God talks to him or gives him revelations. The Bishop does what he wants and then he says God told him to, but he lies. He lies to all of you. The Bishop directs people to live unhappy lives in blind obedience and encourages old men to have sex with young girls against their will. I don't need the Bishop to tell me what God wants for me. I know what He wants."

Rainbow gasped, dropping my hand as if burnt.

"God wants people to be free, to make their own choices, to find their own kind of happiness. God wants us to be loving and kind and to use our common sense. God loves everyone equally," I said. "Except maybe Bishop Thorsen, who has it in for your husband."

I walked around Rainbow and opened the washroom door.

"Daisy, please, don't . . ."

"Goodbye, Rainbow. Go home with Tobias and give my love to Mom and Brighten. Tell them that I'm doing well."

I turned and ran straight to the ticket booth where Saffron and Jean were waiting. I didn't look back.

Saffron put her arm around me. "Everything okay, Daisy-flower? You look like you saw a ghost."

I put my arm around her waist. "I did. But everything's okay now."

That night, I went to sleep with the Beatles still ringing in my ears.

And I dreamt of the last time I saw Tobias.

———

The man shifted, and the light from the solitary streetlamp caught a familiar silhouette. I froze as he turned his face in my direction. I could see him clearly. My heart broke into a thousand pieces, and my old life fell away.

Tobias. He wasn't here to save me—he was here to capture me and take me back.

I held my breath as I waited for him to turn away. When he did, I inched my way back down the slope to the water. Creeping along the edge of the creek, I soon disappeared into the undergrowth. Making a wide loop, I circled back towards the road as fast as I could. Moving west, I had the highway on my left and a big drainage ditch and a deer fence on my right.

A gut-churningly sour smell made my eyes water and my throat constrict. A skunk had sprayed, and somewhere close by. I ran out of the bush as quickly and quietly as I could to escape it.

The sour, biting odour was so strong it suffocated me. Seized by great hacking coughs, I doubled over wheezing, gasping for breath. I kept jogging west, away from the bridge, but stumbled as I went, fighting the urge to retch.

Consumed by my own misery, I didn't hear the pounding feet rushing towards me. A hand came out of the darkness and gripped my upper arm, spinning me around.

Tobias shook me. "Daisy, stop! What are you doing?"

"Let me go!" I tried to yank my arm away, but he held on tight. I felt a stab of pain shoot through my shoulder where the Bishop had twisted it. I cried out.

Tobias dragged me back to the bridge towards the streetlight. He glared *at me, hands on hips. His posture seemed to demand an explanation. The light played on his handsome features, his dark brow creased and brooding, his eyelashes casting shadows on his cheekbones. He ran a hand through his hair, and something in his face shifted. His glare was masking genuine concern, and I felt myself dissolve.*

"Daisy, this is crazy! What are you doing? I'm just as disappointed as you that we didn't get married. But running away isn't the answer."

"That's easy for you to say!" I cried. "I can't live the Principle with the Bishop! His family, the wives, they all hate one another. They fight all the time, and they do mean things to one another's children. It's awful." Tears coursed down my cheeks. "I can't sleep with him, Tobias. Don't ask me to." Even saying the words filled me with shame and I couldn't look Tobias in the eye.

"Don't cry," he pleaded. "We'll find a way. I love you too much to let you go." I felt the gentle touch of his fingers on my cheek, and then the press of his lips on mine. The kiss was warm and soft and lingering, and I didn't dare breathe. I was shocked and thrilled to my core. For a man to kiss a woman who was not his wife was one of the greatest sins of all—and I wished he would never stop.

I waited for God to strike me dead.

Instead, I felt Tobias's hands on my shoulders as he ended the kiss.

"I'll work extra hard, Daisy. I'll volunteer, give even more tithe money than the usual thirty percent. The Bishop rewards that, and he knows I want you to be one of my wives. He'll reassign you to me eventually."

Eventually? Was he crazy? "But that could take months or even years. And what if he doesn't ever transfer me? And I have to live with him forever? Because he's really mad at you, Tobias, for the letter you wrote your father. He thinks you don't respect his authority, and as long as he feels that way, he'll never give you what you want."

Tobias shook his head. *"Where are you getting this stuff? Bishop Thorsen came to see me to tell me the Lord had spoken to him and said I should be rewarded. He said that I had a bright future in the church, in Redemption, but that you were unworthy of me."*

I took a step away from Tobias. *"Do* you *think I'm unworthy of you?"*

He avoided my eyes. *"He said that you haven't done enough to be redeemed in the eyes of the Lord. You are still tainted by your apostate father. That makes you unworthy, Daisy. You can't be a first wife, so you couldn't be mine. Especially given my higher status. But you could be made worthy by living the Principle with the Bishop for a while."*

The muscles in my stomach tightened painfully as though I'd been punched. I held a cry in my throat as I struggled to contain my emotions. Tobias had accepted Bishop Thorsen's lies without question because he had flattered him and rewarded him. Tobias had told me he loved me—would do anything for me, but he wasn't willing to go against the Bishop and save me from a living hell.

I was scared to ask the question, but I had to know the answer. *"Is that what you want?"*

"Daisy, I want you, and I'm willing to wait however long it takes for the Bishop to redeem you."

The sound of a car approaching from Redemption made us both turn our heads.

Tobias looked up, recognized the vehicle, and stepped away a few yards to wave them forward. The driver seemed hesitant. Once he crossed the bridge, he wasn't in Redemption anymore—he was on the outside, where there were different rules and different rulers. Tobias continued to focus on the car, waving it on with both hands.

That's when I ran.

I was a good twenty yards down the road before I felt Tobias bearing

*down on me again, his feet pounding the asphalt, his breath in hot puffs
against the back of my neck. This time he grabbed my arm angrily and
yanked me hard.*

*"Stop it, just stop it! You're acting crazy. You're coming back with me
right now. We'll find a way to work all this out."*

*"No!" I tried to push him away while scanning the side of the road for
some sort of escape. A large ditch and high deer fencing blocked any chance
of running and hiding in the fields beyond. Then I saw it.*

*A narrow drainage pipe ran from the ditch under the fence and into
the field.*

*I stamped on Tobias's foot and dropped hard to the ground, twisting my
body sharply as I fell. Tobias cried out and wasn't able to hold on to my arm.
I dove into the pipe. Crawling army-style in the darkness, I moved as fast
as I could. A firm hand gripped my foot, but I kicked hard, and it was gone.*

*Tobias was too big to follow me into the pipe. When I came out on the
other side of the deer fence I didn't even look back. I ran.*

Chapter Nineteen

We drove back to Nkwala the next day. Through my tears,
I watched the scenery out the window, and noticed some
changes in the world around me. The angle of the light was slant-
ing as the sun was beginning its journey to its winter home in the
south. Grass was brown and dry and some of the trees we passed
had stopped trying to keep their leaves bright and green. It was
inevitable—there was no such thing as an endless summer. Autumn
was coming, and with it, the end of the picking and tenting season.

As if reading my mind, Jean told Saffron and me of his plans to go back to France in September. He'd be gone for some time, maybe even a couple of years. He was going to buy his rootstock and nurse his vines past infancy so they would travel well when he finally brought them to his ranch.

Saffron would be starting her new job soon too. It was time for me to figure out what I was going to do with the rest of my life. Nkwala was beginning to feel like a place where I could fit in and be accepted—like home. Was that true? I wondered. And I realised that my definition of home was changing. Home isn't where you were born, it was wherever you felt safe.

Home was wherever you stopped running.

I thought of the girl at the concert hysterically pulling her hair braid out. She desperately wanted Paul McCartney to notice her, to love her, and save her from a mundane life she didn't want. I was just like her a few months ago, wanting Tobias to save me. But Tobias couldn't save me then, and I didn't want him to save me now.

I had to take my destiny into my own hands.

When the girl at the concert got caught up in the mob trying to storm the stage, she was like the people in Redemption caught up in Bishop Thorsen's fervor. I never wanted to return to that blind obedience. I still had my faith, but it'd changed. I no longer placed my faith in an earthly prophet subject to human foibles. I felt a new kind of spirituality rising within me, one that didn't rely on rigid rules. It was about freedom and self-expression, love and acceptance.

I'd already figured out that education was my way forward. I had a craving to read and learn about the world. If I was ever going to be able to help Mom, Brighten, and others leave Redemption when they were ready, I needed to understand the law.

In Redemption I had no choice; I was to be a wife and mother, full stop. But now, like a brilliant summer sunrise, the horizon was opening up to me. There was no longer just one path, there were many. I just had to decide for myself which path to choose.

When we got back to Nkwala, I planned to stop in at the Apple Dumpling and enquire about a job, then I'd talk to Miss Carol Braid about her night school and the high school equivalency she'd mentioned. Maybe she could help me find my dad. If anyone knew what I was going through, it would be him.

I thought about my mom and Brighten, wondering where they were at that very moment. Were they truly happy as Rainbow claimed? Maybe what Rainbow said was true, but I struggled with doubts. I had to find a way to connect with them in a way that wasn't dangerous for any of us, and I needed to do it soon.

Chapter Twenty

Saffron's first day of work sounded like fun to me, but she was a nervous wreck. She begged me to take the day off from picking—it was apples now—and stay with her. I was more than happy to do it.

The new job required more skill than she'd thought. As well as ferry traffic in the harbour, she was responsible for monitoring the emergency channels for all marine traffic, sea planes, and water bombers during fire season, as well as the long-haul truckers using the mountain road through the provincial park into town.

We climbed the long switchback stairs that led us to the attic room above the Anglican church, chosen for its uninterrupted view of Commando Bay and the ferry dock. The day was pristine and the lake languid. A few small Hobie Cats drifted lazily in the light breeze, their sails limp, while a row of pleasure boats bumped hypnotically against the dock. A day with little action was just what Saffron needed.

It felt great to be the one giving the advice and encouragement instead of the one always needing it. I made sure Saffron knew how to find the open emergency or calling channels for all the radios: VHF, ship-to-shore, shortwave, and CB. Once those were dialed in, it was just a matter of listening for any general traffic or emergency calls, responding, and then forwarding them to the authorities if needed.

"A piece of cake," she said to me once we were all set up, but I noticed she'd lit her third cigarette in a row. The marine channel squawked, and Saffron jumped, but it was just the ferry captain calling in his position off Rattlesnake Island. It would be a while before it docked in our little bay.

I gave Saffron a guilty look and reached over and switched on the AM radio. "Might as well relax and enjoy ourselves while we wait for the ferry," I said. I fiddled with the dial, trying to find the right station. With the tall antenna on top of the church steeple above us, I expected the reception would be good, and it was.

The hot new song by Roy Orbison, "Pretty Woman," came in loud and clear.

"I love this one," I said. We both pulled our chairs close to the speaker. "He's got a gorgeous voice." Saffron nodded. I couldn't bring myself to say "sexy," but I thought it.

I held up one finger. "Wait for it . . ."

Roy finished a verse, then growled into his mic like an alley cat on the prowl. We both exploded into belly laughs.

The song finished and I turned the volume down during the commercial break. We sat back in our chairs enjoying the afterglow of a great laugh when I heard a voice, a voice from my past coming through the radio. I sat up sharply.

"Brighten?"

I ran to the CB radio and turned up the volume.

"I repeat. Chuck, Brighten here. You need to pull all your guys out of logging sector five. There's an out-of-control forest fire coming up the backside of Mural Mountain. The water bombers are coming in off Kootenay Lake. Do you copy?"

"Chuck here. Ten-four."

PART THREE

Nkwala, British Columbia

August 1969

Chapter Twenty-One

At the end of my shift, I turned up the radio dial and sang along with John, Paul, George, and Ringo as they told the world that "all you need is love." Then I hung up my apron, turned off the radio, and closed and locked the door to the Apple Dumpling. It had been five long years since I'd seen the Beatles live in Vancouver. Five years of looking for my father and worrying about Brighten and my mom under Bishop Thorsen's thumb, with little progress made towards solving either problem.

How do you track down someone who lives on a houseboat? Not even Miss Braid could help with that one.

I was discouraged. Something had to give, and soon.

As I trudged towards Okanagan Lake, the dry heat clawed at my skin, sucking up every last bit of moisture and leaving a salty residue. Even the inside of my nose felt scorched. Each blink of my eyes made me think of wiper blades dragged across dry glass.

I was soon dripping with sweat as I mounted the last flight up to the small room at the top of the church bell tower. "Hey, Saffron, I brought Cokes." I pushed open the old wooden door with my foot and stepped into the small dark radio room with its clear view of the ferry dock and the glistening bay beyond.

"Groovy, Dais. I'm parched." Saffron observed a small sailboat catch the wind and scoot out of the way of the approaching ferry.

She flipped a switch and the vast radio system squawked. "All clear, Captain Richards. Local traffic is out of the way."

I felt the familiar thrill as I watched the large vessel glide gracefully into view, then heard the grind of gears. We could feel the vibration as the huge engine shuddered into reverse and churned up the lake water before gently nosing the dock and coming to a full stop.

I set the glass bottles down on the desk with a thump. Grabbing the opener that hung on the wall, I flipped the caps off. The contents bubbled up and overflowed. Laughing, we dove for the bottles, covering the openings with our mouths.

"Oh man, this is soooo good," Saffron groaned. "How hot is it today, anyway? Feels like a hundred."

"Over," I said with a weary sigh. "A hundred and three in the shade, according to the thermometer at the Apple Dumpling. You want to go swimming later?"

"For sure. Meet you at the nude beach at six," Saffron said, a twinkle in her eye.

"I'll meet you at *Willow* Beach."

Saffron shrugged. "Have it your way, but some of those regular guys at the nude beach are real babes." She got up to leave, Coke in hand. "I've gotta get some work done on my articles for the *Georgia Straight*. I'll catch you after your shift."

She struggled to close her bulging tie-dyed cloth bag and blew me a kiss. As she clomped downstairs in her Birkenstocks, I flipped on the radio, comforted as always by the blinking lights and bobbing dials. There wouldn't be any radio action that I needed to pay attention to for a while; the big ferry was on its lunchtime layover.

"This is Flower calling Daylight." I repeated the call and was rewarded when a crackle came over the radio.

"Daylight here."

We flipped to another frequency for privacy.

"Hey, Brighten."

"Hi, Daisy." Brighten's voice was flat, subdued.

When we reconnected after the Beatles concert five years ago, I noticed the change in her immediately. Since then, she'd grown even more withdrawn and dejected. I knew it had something to do with what happened to her after the Bishop's men hauled her back to Redemption, but she always sidestepped my questions about her punishment. She said that she'd been through a period of re-education, but that was behind her now. I'd stopped pressing her for answers that she wouldn't give. She had no problem reassuring me about the Bishop's injuries, though. He was back to himself again, so I could ease my conscience on that count.

"You don't sound so great."

"I hate this place. I can't take it much longer."

Brighten and I had talked just about every week for five years and we were closer than ever. Taking over my old job was supposed to have been a punishment for Brighten, but it had actually been a godsend. I couldn't imagine how I would have survived my struggles to adjust to my new world without our radio visits.

I don't know how she would have survived either.

I leaned closer to the mic. "I hear you, Brighten. Listen, I've been doing some research for a while now, reading books at the little library here. I thought maybe I could find something that would help you leave Redemption. If there were a law against how Bishop Thorsen runs things, then the police would have to do something, right? Well, I did find a law. I just can't figure out why the police don't charge anyone."

Brighten didn't seem to hear me. "I was doing the grocery shopping in Stewart's Landing yesterday. Blossom was with me. She was supposed to watch me, but she doesn't seem so interested in doing that anymore. She's changed.

"She had to make a deposit at the bank for the Bishop, so she left me alone to shop. I talked to someone, an outsider, the woman who runs the grocery store."

I felt my heart quicken. Brighten had always been the smartest girl, maybe she'd find her own way out. "Good for you! That took nerve."

"I knew I was taking a risk, but I had to try. I told the shop-keeper that I was very unhappy in Redemption, but that they wouldn't let me leave. I was trapped and needed help."

I felt a rush of adrenaline. "And?"

Brighten's voice sagged. "She said she didn't want any trouble. Ray Thorsen was the biggest businessman around. Without him, Stewart's Landing wouldn't survive. She said that no one wanted to get on the wrong side of him. It's true, Daisy. Everyone in town seems to like him. Even the police. The cops play pick-up hockey with him and a team of young priesthood men every Tuesday at the arena. He even sponsors their charity golf tournament."

"That sounds about right. The Bishop tells everyone to fear the police, but he makes friends with them because they have power he can use to his advantage. So the shopkeeper wouldn't do anything to help you?"

"No, and she told me never to come into her store again."

No! How long would it take Brighten to work up the courage to ask for help again? It was all so frustrating. "Oh, Brighten, I'm so sorry."

"Yeah, well, life is pretty rotten for me right now. Anyway, your mom sends her love. She's fine but she worries about you. Wants you to be very careful about who you talk to. The Bishop can't find out where you are."

"Tell her I'm being careful, and I send my love right back to her."

"Sure."

"Something else is bugging you," I said. "I can tell."

I heard a small choking sob. "I'm expecting again, Daisy. I have been for a while now. I didn't take it seriously at first because of all the other times, but this is different. I don't think I'm going to lose this baby like the others. It's too far along." Brighten's voice became high and tight. "Don't get me wrong, I'm happy I'm going to be a mother. It's just that the timing is all wrong. This changes everything. If I can't get out of here before the baby comes, I'll never leave."

Tears stung my eyes. Brighten had had three miscarriages since her marriage to Brother Earl. My worst fear was that her next pregnancy would eventually go full-term. "Why? What do you mean?"

She blew her nose. "If I run away after the birth, Brother Earl won't let me keep my baby. He'll hunt me down and he'll get custody. What if I have a girl? Bishop Thorsen controls everything and everyone in town. I won't be able to fight it. You have to help me, Daisy. You've got to get me out of here before my baby comes. There's no one else who can."

Brighten's news left me completely bummed. How could I help her? I owed her so much. I was the reason she'd been trapped in Redemption for the last five years, and she was the reason I was free. In the early days of our reconnection, our soul-baring talks helped me get through my homesickness. As much as I wanted to build a new life on the outside, I missed the familiar things from my childhood: the community lunches after church every Sunday, the big gatherings to welcome guests from Utah, the Friday night sing-along after supper. And then there was my mom. Oh, how I missed her and our secret chats in the basement! At least we could still connect through Brighten. She comforted me, made me feel less alone.

But what had I done for Brighten in the last five years?

When I finished my shift, I visited the library before meeting Saffron for a swim. I wanted to review my research notes. Perhaps there was something I'd missed in the months I'd spent poring over books and articles after my regular schoolwork was done.

I'd worked hard these last years to get my high school equivalency and I didn't think I could have done it without Miss Braid's help. Thanks to my education in Redemption, there were holes in my knowledge big enough to drive a logging truck through, and the librarian helped me fill the biggest ones.

I hadn't known, for instance, that there had been a great war, *the war to end all wars*, before the one that my father fought in. That the Allies dropped nuclear bombs on Japan, big enough to destroy whole cities. That the American president John Kennedy had been assassinated, or even that vaccines had been developed to prevent many major illnesses. All of this and much more was news to me. Carol Braid never judged. Instead, she patiently helped me to fill in my gaps and carry on.

Ever since I'd received my high school diploma, I'd been commuting to the new community college in Peachland across the lake three or four days a week. Next semester I'd be taking two prelaw classes. I hoped they would help me find a way to help Brighten.

In the course of my research, I'd asked Miss Braid to order in materials from UBC. Behind her cat's-eyes glasses, her pupils had grown big when I'd told her my little white lie. I was doing a big research paper on polygamy, I said, for a class I was taking.

She'd seemed thrilled. "Most people just want my advice on a good thriller or a beach read," she'd told me as she'd grabbed a sharp HB pencil and began to scribble notes furiously.

She did a great job finding stuff. I read about polygamy throughout history and the different peoples who practised it, including some followers of Islam and certain native tribes in North America. It wasn't always practised for religious reasons—some men had more than one wife for practical reasons—but the first Christian missionaries in Canada strongly condemned it.

I read about Joseph Smith, the founder of the Mormon religion, and I devoured volumes on the history of the church. I was really surprised by the old stories of violence—awful, pitched battles between believers and nonbelievers—as well as terrible bloody fights between the followers of different prophets. The blood atonements, murders of sinners in the name of the Lord, were the worst. Some Mormons believed that the atonement of Jesus didn't redeem an eternal sin, and that the sinner's blood had to be shed on the earth as a sacrificial offering. Even reading about them made me cringe with discomfort. How could God sanction all this killing?

It was simple. He didn't.

God hadn't called for the death of sinners. But my grandfather had. He'd threatened a blood atonement on my mother if she followed my father.

When the Mormons moved north from Utah looking for freedom, they brought "the Principle," plural marriage, with them. But in 1890, polygamy was outlawed in both the United States and Canada. I'd found the law that I was looking for, but I had no idea what to do next. Bishop Thorsen was breaking the law, but the police did nothing. Why? How could I get someone in power to listen to me?

I wondered a lot about truth and my understanding of it. As a child, I had been terrified of the prophecy of the End of Days, the Great Destruction, when all but the righteous would perish in a burning apocalypse. It was a fear that had haunted me and filled my sleep with nightmares when I was little.

I hadn't had the nightmare for years, but after running into Rainbow at the Beatles concert, it started again. I'd dreamt I was in a life raft on the edge of a vast whirlpool. While massive firebombs went off overhead, I paddled like mad to keep from being sucked down into the swirling vortex. But the force of the water was too great. As soon as I was pulled under, I woke with a cry. Exhaustion left me trembling.

Now, my education provided me with a frame of reference, a way to challenge what I was told was God's truth and rid myself of these lifelong fears.

I dropped my bag and set up my notes on one of the three tables for library patrons. I tried to focus, but Brighten's news kept me from concentrating. "Miss Braid?" She looked up. "Can I run something by you?"

"Of course." She came over and sat next to me. "You look confused."

I sighed and put an elbow on the table, cradling my chin with one hand. "I am."

"Okay, maybe I can help you sort it out. Try me."

"Here's the thing. Canada made polygamy unlawful in 1890. I found the actual law."

"Okay."

"So why has no one ever been charged with the crime? Thousands of polygamists live in Canada, mostly right here in our province. They do really bad things to women and girls in the name of their religion. Why is there a law if the police ignore it?"

Outsiders have made laws that benefit the warriors of Satan.

Miss Braid rarely looked perplexed, but she did now. She wrinkled her nose, then removed her glasses and gave them a quick polish on her cashmere skirt. "That's a good question. I don't know the answer. You've done a great job with your research, but I think you are at the point where you'll need some legal help to draw final conclusions for your paper."

"You mean a lawyer?"

Miss Braid nodded.

For the past five years, I'd been afraid to talk to a lawyer, or anyone in a position of authority, because I was a teenage runaway and I feared I'd be sent back to Redemption. Now that I was of legal age, it was clear that I had to do something.

I couldn't keep hiding.

Chapter Twenty-Two

I sat on a towel in the lovely cool shade of the big willow tree, waiting for Saffron. She approached the beach wearing a tiny white string bikini that showed off her tanned, fit body, causing many heads to turn in her direction. Her giant floppy sun hat was pulled so low she could barely see where she was going. Lifting the brim, she saw me and waved as she always did. Like she hadn't seen me in years.

"Hello there, little Daisy-flower." She dropped her large beach bag next to me, kicked off her yellow plastic thongs, and flopped down into the warm sand. Immediately rooting through her bag, she stopped short and looked up at me. "Let me ask you a question."

"Hm?"

"You must be wondering why no celebrations."

"What do you mean?"

"Did you honestly think that Jean and I would forget about your twenty-first birthday and do nothing about it?"

"Well . . . I was expecting a card or something." In truth, Brighten's pregnancy news was all I could think about.

"A card! I think we can do a little better than that for our sweet Daisy-flower."

"That's nice."

"No, it's not nice—it's phantasmagoric! Buckle up and hang on to your magic carpet, little girl, because Jean and I are going to take you all the way to New York to attend a massive music festival they're having there on a farm. We are going to tune in, turn on, and drop out." She held both hands up in the classic V for peace sign.

"Three days of grooving to great live music—some big names— the Who, Jimi Hendrix, Janis Joplin. It'll be a happening, a love-in like Monterey, but bigger." She leaned in close to me as if sharing a big secret. "They're expecting fifty thousand people."

"But how?"

"It's all arranged. It's my annual vacation and I found some of our friends at BC Ferries to take your shifts, so you've got two full weeks off before school starts. We'll drive Jean's van out to New York, and he'll meet us there."

"He's done with vintner's school?"

"Yup, so he'll drive back here with us. The kicker is my news-paper will pay for the gas if I write some columns on the whole groovy scene."

She pulled her hand out of her bag and handed me a piece of paper. Unrolling it, I saw it was a poster. There was a drawing of a white dove perched on the neck of a guitar.

Woodstock Music and Art Fair, An Aquarian Exposition.
3 Days of Peace and Music.

"This is going to make the Beatles concert look like a day trip to a nursery school," she said.

"I'd love to go but . . ."

"You're worried about your friend Brighten. I know. Look, Daisy, you've been struggling to find a way to break Brighten out of her jail and you haven't come up with a solid plan. Right?"

"Right."

"Maybe what you need is a complete change of scene. Your brain is stuck in a rut. Free your thoughts. Let your mind roam and your creative juices flow."

"I suppose that could be good."

"Not good—perfect. Tell Brighten you'll have to miss next week's call, but you'll be back the following week with a new, solid plan. It's a deadline. You'll force yourself into action."

I jumped to my feet. "I think you're right. This is exactly what I need. Come on!"

"Where are you going?"

"Home to pack. Let's go."

I was so proud of my new driver's licence that I couldn't wait to show it at the border. I had it out and ready, but the U.S. border guard at the tiny crossing at Orville, Washington, just glanced at Saffron's licence and waved us through.

I checked out my picture as I was tucking it back in my wallet. Man, I'd changed from the small, thin runaway I'd been five years ago. My hair, while still ash blond, was much fuller and trimmed to shoulder length. Instead of the upsweep in the front, I had bangs that brushed my pale brows. My face had grown sharper, with high, flat cheekbones and a strong jawline. I loved that people said I reminded them of Joni Mitchell.

Saffron and I didn't want to miss a minute of the festival, so we planned to drive nonstop for four days and nights with a few pit stops. Washington, Montana, South Dakota, Minnesota, Illinois, Ohio, and Pennsylvania all flashed by me in an exhausted blur.

We drove and slept in four-hour shifts. When it was my turn to rest, I curled up on the bench seat in the back and marvelled that I'd once fit there so easily. Now my feet hung over the edge when I stretched out, and I could only lie on my side—it was too narrow to lie on my back as I had.

I didn't really focus on our surroundings until we pulled into the town of Woodstock, New York. From that moment on, I was overwhelmed by the most incredible array of new sights and sounds that I had ever experienced in my life. I really *was* Alice down the rabbit hole. The difference was, this rabbit hole wasn't scary, it was full of peace and love.

For several miles before we hit town, we'd had to maneuver Jean's van around abandoned cars that were broken down or out of gas, cars parked half blocking the road, and others creeping along looking for parking.

"Let's keep going as far as we can," Saffron said, "so we don't have to walk too far to the main stage."

"It'd be good if we knew where that was," I replied.

"Good point, I'll ask a local." She rolled down her window and hot, sticky air wafted in. It smelled of clover and fresh-cut grass and had an unmistakable earthy, black loam essence to it. It made me think of grazing cows and hay barns.

Saffron pulled up beside a man who looked to be in his mid-fifties, with slicked-back, neatly trimmed hair and large black glasses. I could smell the sharp bite of his sweat and felt a sudden wave of unease. He was a dead ringer for Brother Earl, Brighten's husband. Whenever I was reminded of Brighten, a rush of intense frustration ripped through me. I breathed deeply and told myself to let it go.

He leaned in the driver's window to give Saffron directions. "You girls gotta get this rig turned around," he said. "The festival's moved to Bethel—couldn't get a permit here. Out at a farm belonging to Max Yasgur. Just follow the crowds—and call your mothers when you get there."

I smiled wistfully. He tapped the roof of the van as a goodbye, and Saffron put on her signal light, waiting for her chance to merge back into the snaking traffic.

Another tap on our roof, but gentler, almost apologetic, this time. Saffron stopped short. All I could see was a shaggy head of dark curls inching through the driver's window. There was a murmur of voices, and then Saffron said, "Sure, hop in."

The middle door of the van slid open, and two grinning guys threw their backpacks in before climbing inside. The smaller one slid the door shut as we moved out into traffic.

The other one, with dark curls and brilliant blue eyes, had a wide, easy grin. "This is totally far-out. Thanks for the ride. You chicks are something else. I'm Sam and this is my little brother Nick."

They were both long and slim, and they spoke with a slow drawl that I'd heard on phone-in radio shows. It marked them as American southerners, and it was charming.

We introduced ourselves, and Saffron shot me a wink. I knew what she was thinking. I was thinking the same thing.

From there, things got crazy. Not only were cars *everywhere*, but people too. Whole families and communes had set up camps all along the side of the road with places for cooking, laundry, and bathing. Most were young hippies with lots of hair, wearing flowing robes or tight bell-bottom pants in bright colours, but also ponchos, chunky jewelry, huge woven belts, large hats with feathers, leather boots or bare feet—or they were dressed in nothing at all. People danced nude and swam nude. I saw a juggling group who wore *next* to nothing, along with poets, healers, and yoga instructors—all bare. There were so many naked people around, I finally lost my inhibitions and stopped noticing.

Who am I kidding? I noticed.

I noticed *everything*.

We saw a sign that read BUS PARKING and decided that Jean's little Volkswagen van qualified. We battled our way through a long line of cars and turned off-road onto a big grassy field. Low-slung vehicles would never have made it without getting high-centred, but we managed, parking next to brightly painted school buses and delivery trucks.

The moment I stepped out of the van, I was overwhelmed by the distinct, sickly-sweet scents of marijuana and hashish. As Saffron's good friend, I knew the smell well. Weaving our way through the crowds, we dodged lit spliffs, clouds of smoke, and stumbling but friendly concertgoers.

We came up the backside of a small hill, moving towards the restless hum in the distance. When we crested the hill and looked down, the sea of humanity below us took our breath away. As far as the eye could see were people, swaying, dancing, laughing.

We stood in awe, gaping at the scene before us. The collected humanity reminded me of vast fields of prairie grasses, bowing down and rising before the wind.

"This can't be just fifty thousand people," I said in awe.

"No way," said Saffron. "Lots more—this is one far-out trip."

Nick turned to me, his sweet blue eyes wide. "How many do you think?"

"No idea. Gotta be a hundred thousand, easy." We stood in silence, trying to wrap our heads around it. Everyone was happy and mellow, calmly standing or lying back on blankets on the ground.

We were close enough to see the huge stage in the distance, where stagehands scurried about, setting up for the first musicians. The audience wasn't impatient, though. When an announcer stepped to the mic and apologised for the delay, he was greeted with a ripple of light applause.

A shirtless man in tight buckskin pants and moccasins appeared beside us. He held open a dark leather pouch to reveal several small plastic baggies tied with multicoloured ribbons. "Any of you cats into a dime-bag? I've got Gorilla Glue and Blue Dream from Maine. Only the best."

Sam pulled out some cash from his back pocket. "My treat, a thanks for the ride."

He soon rolled a joint and began passing it around. I watched Saffron expertly take a long, deep toke, her voice box squeaking a little as the smoke slid through her vocal cords.

Then it was my turn. I had never taken any kind of drug in my life, mindful of the Bishop's admonishment that drugs were a direct path to the worst kind of behaviour: hysterical laughing, binge eating, lascivious dancing, and sex outside marriage.

I took the joint from Saffron, pinching the white wrapper between my thumb and forefinger to contemplate it for a minute. Heavy, sweet wisps of smoke swirled around me like phantoms. "What the heck," I said, and took a light sip, holding the smoke in my mouth before drawing it into my lungs.

We passed the joint around for a while and I took a few more puffs. I was surprised how unaffected I seemed by it. I wondered what the big deal was. I looked around. Why was everyone so into it?

Inwardly, I smiled. Of course, God hadn't struck me dead for smoking an herb. He was love and forgiveness and compassion, and I was certain He was well pleased with the gentle folk here.

"How are we ever going to find Jean?" I said to Saffron.

We were interrupted by the announcer onstage, reading from some notes in his hand. "Randy White, please go to the medic tent immediately, man. Your old lady's having a baby. Randy White, right away, man, you're about to be a papa." After a spontaneous round of applause and whistles, the announcer carried on. "Sandra, please meet Sam at the left of the stage, he has your medication, and Gerry Kern, call home, your parents are freaking, man."

Saffron pulled her notebook and pen out of her oversized woven bamboo bag. "Here's how we'll find Jean," she said as she began scribbling a note.

"Okay, everybody, hang tough," the announcer said, "we are about to bring on Ritchie Havens. He's just doing his sound checks, but listen up, I'm Wavy Gravy, and me and the members of the Hog Farm and the Phurst Church of Phun are here to be your Please Force.

"There are half a million people here, man, and there's no guns, and no trouble. It's biblical, man, biblical! This generation, man— we all pull together and we're changing the world!" The crowd was on their feet cheering. He shouted over the crowd, "I was rapping with the fuzz, and they say that the New York State Thruway is closed, man. It's closed! Can you dig it?"

He was rewarded with a roar from the crowd.

The announcer grinned from ear to ear, then shouted into his mic, "Ladies and gentlemen, Ritchie Havens!"

A tall, thin man in a flowing light-brown robe began strumming an acoustic guitar with his bandmate playing bongo drums behind. His first words thrilled me to my core. They were all about freedom.

Saffron grabbed my hand, and the four of us started picking our way through the massive crowd, slowly working our way to the stage. No one seemed the slightest bit bothered by us when we occasionally lost our coordination and stumbled onto a blanket or a foot. We apologised, but people just smiled and gave us the peace sign. Feelings of love and acceptance wreathed us like smoke.

At one point Saffron and I accidentally crashed into each other, going down hard, then rolling into someone's big dog who was snoozing in the sun. We lay there stunned for a minute until the dog got up, sauntered over, and began to lick our faces. His thick tongue and velvety jowls tickled. It was hilarious. We couldn't stop laughing.

It took us forever to reach the stage framed by giant scaffolding towers holding speakers amplifying the incredible music, so we danced and grooved to the performance the whole way. Once we were there, we asked around for Wavy Gravy but we needn't have. He was not hard to find. A tall man, he stood out with his big red clown nose and weather-beaten cowboy hat.

Saffron caught his sleeve and handed Wavy her note. Just then, two helicopters came roaring in to land just behind the stage, bringing big-name groups who couldn't drive in. For a few minutes they made so much noise we couldn't hear anything.

Wavy read her note, nodded, and gave her a toothy smile, showing off dentures that were tie-dyed bright red, yellow, and blue. He turned and tacked the note to a large bulletin board behind him. In a minute he was back up onstage, and we waited for Ritchie to finish his set.

"Jean, please meet Saffron and Daisy in the bus parking area. Just look for your van, man." Wavy said it in a loud, clear voice while the stagehands were setting up Joan Baez.

Joan was singing a soulful song about the labour organizer Joe Hill as we worked our way back towards the field where we'd left the van. Eventually we found a spot of unclaimed ground nearby to settle and watch the show.

Some of the biggest acts in rock and roll hit the stage. I knew some of them from my volunteer radio gig, *Daisy's Disks*, which ran every Thursday evening at nine o'clock. It was my favourite time of the week, an hour when I was free to play the music I loved. Woodstock was showing me that there was so much more out there than I knew.

Carlos Santana came onstage to deliver his funky Latin-Cuban rhythms, and Sly and the Family Stone had us all standing and singing "Higher," but for me, Janis Joplin stole the show. She was the young singer I had heard on late-night radio out of Texas when I was a kid. She'd made me realise that girls on the outside could have a career and do something with their life other than being a mother.

Her voice had matured; she was a seasoned performer now. She held the audience spellbound with her throaty, deeply emotional voice. It was as if she could reach down inside me and pull trapped feelings out of the dark recesses of my very being. When she sang "To Love Somebody," she made me want to weep with longing.

I closed my eyes and saw Tobias.

Yes, I still thought about Tobias from time to time, about the kiss we shared, and the future I almost had with him.

But each time I thought of him, it hurt less.

Hours later, we were thinking of packing it in for a while and going back to the van again to cook up a meal and find the long line of porta-potties when a sudden strong wind blew in out of the north. We turned and craned our necks in time to see a monster of a storm cloud swirling down upon us.

"Take cover!" the announcer shouted from the stage. "Gentlemen, please climb down from the towers. Please move away from the towers."

I could hear slight panic in his voice. And supposed that the seventy-foot scaffolding towers were not designed to take big winds or the extra weight of enthusiastic fans.

People dropped down off the towers like rats off a sinking ship when the skies opened up and we were hit with a deluge. Everyone scrambled to try to find some protection. Saffron dug into her giant bag and pulled out a large plastic poncho for the four of us to huddle under.

The free and joyful spirit of the festival was not dampened, though, and the entire crowd began to chant, "No rain, no rain." People emerged from their hiding places to do an anti-rain dance and play their own "instruments" made out of sticks and tin cans. We laughed and clapped along until we finally agreed that we needed a change of clothes and something hot to drink.

Dinner was a pot of my thrown-together chili. Nick and Sam were ravenous and very grateful. After supper, Sam rooted around in his backpack and brought out a Tupperware container filled with brownies. "They're *special* brownies," he said with a wink. I knew what he meant but didn't hesitate. I had two.

Sounds of cheering and laughter brought us out of the van, to a sloped clearing where a group of young men and women had created a mud slide. As with a toboggan run, they made a running start, jumped onto a piece of cardboard at the top of the slope, and then hurtled downhill, slipping and sliding on the thick mud.

Everyone in the vicinity stripped down to their underpants to give it a try. It wasn't long before mud covered us head to toe. Nick and I shared a piece of cardboard on the way down, my arms around his neck and my legs around his torso. At the bottom, we were a tangled, giggling, muddy mess of entwined arms and legs.

I felt so light I thought I must have been flying, and my belly ached from laughing. Nick's warm breath next to my ear brought me back to earth. That and his hard body pressing against mine. His lips nudged mine in a long muddy kiss and I felt my insides melt. I'm not sure how long we stayed there, but people started shouting at us to get out of the way for the others coming down. Smiling shyly, we broke apart, grabbed our cardboard, and made a run for the sidelines.

Saffron was there, her smile glowing brightly from a mud-covered face. "Look who's here," she said.

I wasn't sure at first. It had been three years. He'd cut his hair to the bottom of his ears and shaved off most of his curly beard. He'd clearly been spending lots of time outdoors. His golden hair was streaked with sun-bleached highlights, and his face was deeply tanned, the skin pulled tight across his cheekbones where the last hints of baby fat had once lingered.

I stood before him, semi-naked and covered in mud. He caught my eye and broke into a wide smile, then took a step back to get a good look. "There you are, Little Mushroom." His eyes crinkled and there was just a hint of teasing in his smile. "You've grown up. It looks like I am going to have to stop calling you that."

I think I must have blushed to the roots of my hair. Except he wouldn't be able to see that, I realised, because I was covered in mud. It was even in my ears. I laughed and held out my arms as if to embrace him. "Jean! Welcome to the mudslide."

He dodged me and laughed, and danced Saffron around in a circle. It was great to see him again.

When the rain quit a few hours later, we cleaned up, said good-bye to Nick and Sam, and headed out in search of another spot to settle and watch more of the show. A helicopter hovered briefly overhead, dropping dry clothes and flowers to the grateful people below. Saffron had her pen and notebook out, stopping to ask festivalgoers what they thought of the whole event. She needed personal stories to add to her articles for the *Georgia Straight* to provide a human element.

After watching her interview others, a bearded man stopped her, pointing skyward. "Did you see them, man, just before the storm? The planes? That's what the press should be writing about. I saw those planes circling not long before the rain hit. They were seeding the clouds, man. Those establishment assholes can't stand to see us hippies have a good time."

Saffron took notes, and Jean looked over her shoulder, pretending to read them while winking and twitching his mouth at me.

The bearded man's face darkened with anger, and he stomped off.

We moved on and found a place to sit just as the sun went down and the evening grew velvety and dark. The show was much more dramatic in the night as big stage lights lit up the performers, making them seem larger-than-life. We grooved to Creedence Clearwater Revival and Arlo Guthrie, but when the announcer said, "Ladies and gentlemen, the Who," I felt a shiver go down my spine.

I loved their rock opera *Tommy*, about a boy who becomes the messiah of a religious cult, and when their lead singer, Roger Daltrey, leapt onto the stage, I was transported. He was dressed in a white buckskin leather suit with knee-length white leather fringe that flashed, catching the light, when he danced and grooved. Backlit, and with his thick, curly blond hair, he looked like an angel descended from heaven, like the messiah he was singing about.

It was then that it struck me. Growing up, I had been afraid of the Great Destruction, where all but the righteous would perish

in a horrific burning apocalypse according to the will of a venge-
ful god. But this new generation really did know the truth—that
God is all about peace, love, and freedom, and that doctrines to the
contrary were about control, not salvation. I saw it clearly: God
wanted us all to be happy and to spread love and compassion. The
entire foundation of the Fundamentalist church in Redemption,
that we alone were God's Chosen people and had to embrace
the Principle in order to be fruitful and multiply, was completely
wrong.

Someone needed to tell them.

We drove back to Nkwala the way we came, flushed with the afterglow of the bliss that was Woodstock. Rolling through the vast
plains shadowed by the towering mountain ranges of Montana, I
started giving voice to what I'd been thinking about.

"That was just the most astonishing experience, guys. I mean, I
was really knocked out by it. I felt like we transcended something
back there, don't you? We transcended war and greed and competition and—"

"And our clothes," Saffron said, grinning.

"Those too," I agreed. "I'm just saying that there is huge power
in the hippie movement. We all saw it. Peace and love! I think
that's all I need to help Brighten and my mom and the others in
Redemption find their freedom."

It was Jean's turn to drive, and I saw his eyes shift from the road
as he glanced over at me. "What are we talking about here?"

I told him about growing up in a strict religious community

and escaping a forced marriage. Now that I controlled my own future, I was no longer ashamed of my past. The shame belonged to the Bishop and the priesthood men, not me.

Jean listened, saying little.

"If the people in Redemption could see for themselves that God wants us all to live free lives," I continued, "outside the influence of false prophets who want to control and dominate in His name, I think they would choose the path of peace and love. I think they would turn their backs on the Bishop's teachings. The Bishop determines the course of their lives, like who and when they marry, but most people there crave the freedom of choice. They just need to see the path towards it."

Saffron clasped her hands together and then clapped wildly. "Oh, that's brilliant," she called from the middle seat. "I love it."

I could tell from the look on Jean's face that he was sceptical. "But how would you do that?"

"We organize a love-in at Redemption. Encourage people there to join us, to walk away from their old lives. The Bishop won't be able to stop us, because our message will be undeniable."

Saffron laughed. "This is so brilliant, Daisy! We can spread the word about the love-in through my articles in the *Georgia Straight*. We'll pull together a group of friends who want to help. I can see it now." She held up her hands to span an imaginary headline: "'Flower Power Breaks Up Polygamous Cult.'"

"I don't know," Jean said. "It's just not going to be that easy."

"But maybe it's true," I said, swaying in my seat to imaginary music, "maybe all you need is love."

I read, later, that even before the brilliant Jimi Hendrix had closed Woodstock, concertgoers had departed in droves, leaving mountains of garbage behind. Our generation had achieved a remarkable feat of coming together for one glorious weekend where peace and love ruled, but when the fun was over, we left Max Yasgur's acres of lush countryside a muddy, polluted mess.

Chapter Twenty-Three

The joke around Nkwala was that Mrs. Graham named the Apple Dumpling after herself. Round, soft, and dimpled, she was the personification of the treat and just as sweet. She was almost always dressed in a grey housedress with a white apron. Her stiff, plump legs were encased in thick nylon stockings that were rolled at the top just above her knees, while her swollen feet were laced into sensible brown leather shoes.

She tucked a flyaway wisp of white hair into the neat bun on the top of her head and looked thoughtful at my question. "Myrtle? I think she has gas. How far are you going?"

"Not far, a place near here. It's off the old logging road about ten miles from town."

"Should be fine," she said, "but mind that stick shift, remember."

I heard the tinkle of the shop bell and braced myself for a crowd of demanding kids. They rushed the counter, elbowing one another and yelling.

"I was here first."

"No you weren't. I'll have a double scoop of chocolate."

"I want strawberry."

"What other flavours do you have?"

I groaned inwardly and strapped on my wrist guard that, in theory, prevented wrist strain when I dug out the hard ice cream. I checked the clock. Relief. Only fifteen minutes till closing time.

With the shop locked up and Mrs. Graham safely tucked upstairs with her tea and television favourites, *The Ed Sullivan Show* and *Bonanza*, in the lineup, I fetched the keys and carefully backed the old Volkswagen Wagoneer from the garage out back. I grimaced at the teeth-tingling grind of gears as I depressed the clutch and tried to pop the car out of reverse and into first.

The car was a stubborn old donkey. If you tried to force her, she bucked. I felt my frustration building, but I took a deep breath and stroked the dash. "Come on, baby, you can do it." This time it worked, and we were on our way. Heading out of town, I picked up speed, sliding the gears easily into second, then third.

I'd rarely ventured far from the safety of the village. Though it had been over five years since I'd run away from Redemption, I'd continue to worry until Bishop Thorsen either died or was stripped of his power. Instinct told me that he was never going to let it go. He'd haul me back to Redemption just like he did Brighten if he ever had the chance.

Myrtle protested the steep incline I took her up. Even with my foot pressing the gas pedal to the floor, the car was rapidly losing speed, and I realised she would never make it up the hill in third gear. The car was close to stalling, so I had to come to a complete stop in order to shift back into first gear. I cursed the carmaker who had engineered this weird system. I was a sitting duck in the middle of the road, battling a stick shift that didn't want to find its groove.

A deafening blast from a truck horn made me jump right out of my skin. My eyes flew to the rearview mirror. A fully loaded logging truck had just come around the curve a quarter of a mile back and was trying to brake hard while blasting a warning. My hand shaking, I refocused all my attention on the gear shift.

"Nooo," I shouted, cringing at the sound of grinding metal on metal. There was another ear-splitting blast, closer now, as my damp hand slipped off the gear shift. Looking in the rearview mirror again I could see the panicked driver's face. Despite the blind curve in the road ahead, the heavily laden truck swerved into the oncoming lane and screamed past Myrtle, disappearing into a cloud of wood chips and road dust.

I was left with a pounding heart and shaking hands. I took a long, slow breath and finally got the car in gear. After a few more shaky moments of driving, I found my destination.

A barking German shepherd bounded off the front porch of a small house with faded white paint and weather-bleached window shutters. The porch itself had a distinct slant, and I wondered if it was just the porch or the whole house that was listing. I waited in the car as the dog jumped up to bark at me through the driver's window. Looking around, I hoped its owner would show up soon. I heard a sharp whistle, and the dog finally made itself scarce.

I worked up the nerve to step out of the car just as a tall, deeply suntanned man walked in from the deep-green vineyards that surrounded the house in neat rows.

"If you're selling something, I'm not interested," he called out.

"Jean, it's me, Daisy."

He squinted and came closer in a pair of dirt- and grease-stained overalls. He pulled the ancient straw hat off his head, wiped his brow with the back of his hand, and gave my face a searching look.

"Daisy? Nice surprise. Everything okay?" His eyes scanned the interior of the car, looking for Saffron. "You've never been out here before. Where'd you get the car?"

"It belongs to Mrs. Graham."

He nodded. "Ah."

In all the time that Jean had been away, he'd only been back once. Three years ago, he'd arrived from France with the rootstock he'd convinced his brothers to give him. He'd spent three months planting and setting up his water systems and then was gone again. He left his new vineyard under Hardeep's care while the vines matured and he went to vintner's school.

Ever since Saffron had told me that we'd be picking up Jean at Woodstock, he'd been on my mind. But meeting him there, the way I did, well . . . it left me so confused and uneasy that I could barely look him in the eye. Now, without Saffron flitting around to distract us, I felt the full weight of his stare on me. "I've come to pick your brain. Can we sit for a few minutes?"

Jean shrugged. "Sure. Let's sit in the shade on the porch." He led and I followed.

We sat on old wicker chairs that tilted with the floor.

"I remember your dream of planting a vineyard, of proving good wine can come from here. Looks like it's happening." I gestured towards the rows of healthy-looking vines.

Jean's face cracked into a grin. "Thanks for that, but the jury's still out. The vines are just old enough to start producing. Hardeep brought in a small harvest for me last year, and I've bottled some Cab Franc and Pinot Gris." His eyes twinkled and he looked like a proud papa. "The Cab has to age, but would you like to try the Pinot? Let me know what you think. Be honest."

"Sure. I don't know much about wine, but I'll try some."

Jean disappeared into the house and returned with two large crystal wineglasses, each with a small amount of salmon-coloured liquid inside. "Oh, I wasn't expecting the colour." I held the wine to the sun.

"I leave the skins on and cold soak them for about thirty-six hours in the first crush before I press them off. That's what gives it the slight pink hue, but it's still a white wine, not a rosé. The grapes came in at 24.4 Brix, just about what I was hoping for."

"Brix?"

"Sugar content, basically."

I took a sip and felt the layers of flavour unwrap in my mouth. "Oh, wow. So many different tastes." I thought for a moment. "Makes me think of peach stones, you know, when you suck on them after you've eaten the peach?"

Jean looked pleased. "You get that? You have a good nose."

"Nose?"

"The sense of smell tells the tongue what to taste. Congratulations. Your nose may be small, but it works well." He gave me a mischievous wink and I felt something stir deep inside me.

I took another sip. I liked the feel of the wine rolling across my tongue, but I knew I had to get serious and focus.

"I've been looking into the laws around polygamy—trying to see if we can find a legal way to stop the Bishop and his men. I think it's time I talked to a lawyer, and I remembered you have an uncle who's a lawyer."

He took a sip of wine. "Pierre Dupont—my mom's brother. He's with a big law firm in Vancouver. I lived with him for three years when I was a teenager, when my mom got sick. He's the one who got us the Beatles tickets. Remember?"

It was such a happy memory. I gave Jean a warm smile. "Of course, how could I forget?"

"Some lawyers take on cases for free," Jean said, "pro bono. No charge. I could talk to him."

"That would be so far-out. The thing is, I've looked into it. Polygamy is against the law both in Canada and the U.S. So I can't figure out why the police don't do anything. The women must have rights. Why won't anyone take action?"

"I don't know the answer to that. We can ask my uncle. You know, I hated law school so much that I quit. Sometimes I think maybe you should be the one to go."

"To law school?"

"Yeah, why not?"

I blinked hard, startled by Jean's comment. I shrugged it off and didn't answer him directly.

"Polygamy hurts people in lots of ways." I held up four fingers, counting points off one at a time. "Children don't get a proper education despite what the school inspectors think. The Bishop won't allow medical treatment, not even for difficult births. Some of the brides are just kids themselves, and very few of them are happy. In fact, the Bishop is medicating sister-wives who are low in the pecking order. Something needs to be done." I felt my throat tighten and looked over at the vineyard until I could collect myself.

"In some ways I think Redemption is more of a cult than a religion," Jean said.

I thought about it. Talk of cults was all over the newspapers since a famous movie star and her baby were murdered by a weird group in southern California. According to what I'd read, cult leaders were highly charismatic but warped by excessive self-love. They were champion-level manipulators. They persuaded their followers to put away common sense and prove their devotion by repeatedly performing tasks that were harmful to themselves. These tasks benefited the leader, often sexually and financially.

Bishop Thorsen was a little like that. I mean, people fell all over themselves to please him. He had everyone eating out of his hand; even the chief of police and the mayor of Stewart's Landing thought he was a terrific guy. He preached that having babies was the most important thing that the community could do, and that meant lots of sex, for himself and a few select men chosen by him to spread their superior seed. I didn't know if the Bishop was benefiting financially from his iron grip on Redemption, but it was a good question. He certainly seemed to live better than anyone else there.

"Yes," I said. "In some ways it does sound more like a cult than a real religion."

Jean held his wineglass up to his nose, sniffed, then took a long sip. "I'll talk to my uncle. He mostly does securities law, but he may know someone who could help, or give us a name." He paused, looking up at wispy clouds flushed red by the setting sun. "I'll ask on one condition."

"What's that?"

"Finish your wine and then let me show you my vineyard. The old ranch was called Paradise, so I'm keeping the name. Paradise Wines. Blasphemy?"

I laughed. "Not at all."

"It fits well, if I do say so myself." He held both arms wide, palms up, and laughed. "What can I say, I'm proud of what I've done to the place."

"I'd love to see it," I said, and took another big sip of wine. "Saffron and I are going ahead with my plan to have a love-in near Redemption in the fall, sort of a harvest festival. Music, poetry, storytelling; it's going to be a real trip. Lots to do yet, but we've already picked out some crown land next to Redemption and applied for a permit."

Jean's eyes flickered. "Okay . . ." I could hear the reservation in his voice.

I felt a sudden flash of anger. After all this time, I just needed to find a way forward. I needed support, not doubts. "You don't think it's a good idea, do you?"

Jean held up his hand. "Whoa. It's not that. It's just that—I think it's going to be more complicated than you realise. You want people to come and hear about freedom and then be convinced that leaving Redemption will make them happier, right?"

"Basically, yes."

"How will you get them to come to the love-in?"

"Brighten and my mother will let people know about it and encourage them. A lot of the mothers are unhappy, and they know which ones. And some members of the church have doubts about Bishop Thorsen's leadership."

"Okay, but why would the Bishop let them pack up and leave? You've already told me how he does everything he can to stop women from leaving. Without all the women, he has no power, right?"

"Yes, that's right. The women do everything."

"So he's not going to let them just wander off, then, is he?"

I set my wine down and folded my arms across my chest. I tried to keep the sharp edge out of my voice without success. "I hoped you would support me."

He reached over, gently squeezed my knee, and held my gaze. "Don't get me wrong. I'm a hundred percent behind you and I'll do anything I can to help. I just want to make sure you've thought all this through. With this vineyard, I've learned a lot about careful planning." A shadow crossed Jean's face. "Sometimes I'm all action and no thinking. I've made mistakes. It's one of the things about me that drives my dad crazy."

∽◯

A sage-scented breeze blew in off the surrounding hills as we sauntered in the direction of the lake through the long, neat rows of young vines. He pointed out the drip lines woven among them. "The key is to control the water. I didn't want sprinklers, so I tried these lines instead."

"What's wrong with sprinklers? All the orchards use them."

"So, you think easier and cheaper?"

"Yep."

"Rookie mistake. Once the vines get to a certain point, you have to be careful not to over-water. You want the plant to sense drought, so that it stops putting its energy into new leaf growth and focuses on maturing and sweetening the fruit. Survival of the species."

We arrived at the edge of a cliff that dropped a hundred yards into the inviting deep blue of Okanagan Lake.

I looked up and down the lake at the shadowy cascade of clay banks in the distance and their steep drops plunging into the clear water below. "Wow, this has to be one of the best views anywhere. Stunning. I can see why it's called Paradise."

"And it's perfect for grape growing. Long, hot, sunny summers, the right soil, and irrigation water from the lake. Even these cliffs are a bonus."

"How so?"

"The water table is low here, so the vine roots don't stand in damp soil. They're just like us; they don't like to get their feet wet."

"But what about the winter? Isn't it too cold for the vines?"

"Rarely, but if there is a cold snap, I have a way to manage it. I'm building wind machines, like windmills, that keep the air circulating, bringing warmer air down from above and stopping the cold air from settling close to the ground."

"Sounds like you're proving your father wrong. Have you told him? Can he come and see for himself?"

One glance at Jean's face and I knew I'd said the wrong thing. "My dad and I aren't really talking these days. If Mom was still here, she'd have pushed him to call me, but now? I rarely hear from him."

"I'm sorry." I worried Jean would close in on himself again, but he surprised me by laughing.

"What is it about you that I find myself spilling my guts to you again?"

I smiled. "I learned to be a good listener when I was a kid. The less I talked, the less people noticed me, and that kept me out of trouble."

"Doesn't sound like a very happy childhood."

"Mostly it wasn't."

We stared at the shimmering water for a while. "There's a path to the lake," Jean said. "At this time of day, I usually head down for a swim. It's a hot climb back up, but it's still worth it. You want to come along?"

"Sounds great, but I don't have my bathing suit with me."

Jean shrugged. "So what?"

I felt a hot creeping flush as it made its way from my neck to my cheeks. I knew what he was thinking: It hadn't stopped me at Woodstock, so why now? "I really should be getting Mrs. Graham's car back."

Jean glanced at my reddening face and looked amused. "It's cool," he said. We turned and he walked me back to my car. The German shepherd bounded out to greet us. "This is Bijou. It means 'jewel' in French. He only responds to French commands." He turned to me. "Say 'Bonjour, Bijou,' and he'll let you shake his paw."

"Bonjour, Bijou!" I found myself caressing a soft warm paw.

Jean clicked his tongue. "Ah, bien, you see how easy it is to learn French?"

"Thanks again, Jean. I really appreciate you making the call to your uncle."

"I can't promise anything, but we'll see if he can suggest something or someone to help."

I jumped into the car and put my head out the driver's-side window. "Thanks for showing me Paradise and congrats on your wine. I really think it's good."

Jean leaned on the window ledge. "Thank you, but if I can't find a buyer for the end product, my father will have the last laugh. I didn't do my homework before I chose this place. No one drinks wine here. The restaurants don't offer it. Ladies sip gin-and-tonics at their bridge clubs, and the men drink beer after work or rye and ginger with the evening paper. I have no buyers. I'm not sure my little winery is going to survive." He stepped back from the window before I could make any attempt to console him and waved me away.

I took it slow on the way home. I'd only had a little wine, but I wasn't going to take any chances. And after my near miss with the logging truck, I kept an eye on the rearview mirror.

Switching on the radio for company, I laughed out loud when the familiar sound of Wolfman Jack filled the car. A happy memory, one of the few from Redemption.

"Susie in Pasadena wants 'White Rabbit' by Jefferson Airplane," growled the Wolfman. "Groove on this, sweet little Susie."

I rolled my window all the way down, letting in the hot, dry air, and sang along with Grace Slick. Glancing in the rearview mirror, I noticed a brown Dodge not far behind. I took my foot off the gas and edged to the side of the isolated, narrow road to let it pass. But when I slowed, it slowed, never pulling out and going by.

"Dear Lord," I said out loud. "What now?"

The next time I checked my rearview mirror, the brown Dodge was gone.

Chapter Twenty-Four

"Daisy, I don't have much time and I have to tell you something important. It's about the Utah brides." Brighten's voice carried a note of desperation.

I flicked my microphone switch on. "Did you find something?"

"Yes, I need to talk fast, someone might come looking for me any moment."

This could be it, I thought. The break we'd been waiting for.

The year after I left, Bishop Thorsen began shipping Redemption girls to the Utah chapter. But requests from the Utah church for new brides from Canada had been nonstop, so the Bishop had had a revelation from God that *all* women must have babies as often as possible, including the celestial sisters. It was the only way the Bishop could stabilize the population of Redemption when so many young women were being sent away.

Blossom, like the other celestial sisters, had been married off last year. She was soon pregnant with twins. She couldn't cope with all the demands on her time so, naturally, she stopped caring about her job as a celestial sister. Brighten, who was still childless, had offered to take over many of her financial duties. Blossom had simply handed her the keys to the locked file cabinets and walked out the office door.

Brighten's new role was bittersweet. How long had she coveted the role of celestial sister? Well, now she had it. But this presented me with an opportunity: access to the Bishop's financial affairs. I'd wondered why the Bishop was so anxious to send all the young brides south, so I'd asked Brighten to go through the files and look for answers.

Now, maybe she'd found them.

"I'm listening."

"An invoice came in the other day from Sister Marigold, who handles the books for the Utah church. It was a demand for a refund for undelivered goods." Brighten's voice caught on the last word.

"Okay." I knew that the Bishop shipped forest products to the southern churches. "What sort of undelivered goods? Lumber? Roof shingles?"

"The invoice didn't specify, but I checked it off against the shipping dates of different products in the official books. Nothing was recorded as shipped on that date. I puzzled about it, and after I went home that night it hit me. The date of the shipment was the same day that a large group of brides left here for Utah. Daisy, the 'thing' that was undelivered was one of the new brides from Redemption. She died in transit." Brighten sobbed.

I put my head in my heads and rubbed my forehead. "Oh my Lord. Who?"

"Tulip."

Hot tears stung my eyes. I couldn't believe that Tulip, one of the little girls from my assigned family, was old enough to be married, let alone dead in transit. I remembered a little chubby-cheeked thing, one of my favourites, so fun-loving except for laundry duty, when Mother Rose punished her for wetting the bed.

"What happened?"

"I don't really know. Mother Hyacinth was told just that she died, but I do know she was rebellious and she didn't want to go. She was openly defiant. Maybe she tried to run away."

I slouched forward, cradling my stomach. "This is awful. Do you think she died trying to escape, or do you think they killed her?"

"I don't want to think about it, Daisy. It's too horrible. But do you see what I'm telling you here? Utah is sending money in exchange for the brides. They call it a dowry for the benefit of God's work in Redemption, but I traced the paperwork. The money is going into a holding company that Bishop Thorsen set up. He is the company's sole owner. I tried to put the evidence together, but when I went to make a copy of the original invoice, I couldn't find it anywhere. Obviously, none of this shows up in the books that the Bishop gives the government tax auditors."

I could hardly speak. Was there no end to the evil this man was capable of?

I heard static over the radio, then: "I've got to get out of here, now. Over and out."

"Wait, before you go, I've got something to tell you—I've got a plan to get you and others out of there."

"Tell me quick." I heard a hint of excitement in her voice.

I told her of my plan to hold the love-in near Redemption in the fall, a celebration of peace, love, and freedom. A large crowd of hippies would be there to support and protect the mothers who could gather up their kids and just walk away.

"It sounds beautiful, Daisy, but anything could happen before then." Brighten's voice had flattened again. "I really gotta go. Your mom sends her love. She's going to set up another phone call with you soon."

Brighten's mic went dead.

I slowly turned off my own radio and said a silent prayer.

I brooded all day until Saffron appeared at the end of my shift. She always managed to raise my spirits. The door to the radio room burst open in a flood of light and she twirled into the room.

"Look at these new threads I scored at the thrift shop. Can you believe it?" She did a little pirouette that made the beaded fringes on her leather vest dance and her long, homespun skirt billow over her ankle-high Beatle boots.

"Awesome. How do you find this stuff?"

"You have to be strategic. It's all in the timing. They bring in new stuff from Kelowna the first Monday of the month. As soon as I see it unloaded from the ferry, I head over to the thrift store so I'm the first in line. I get the cream of the crop."

I looked down at my own plain white tee and faded Lee jeans. "Maybe I should go with you next time. I could use a makeover."

"Why are you suddenly so interested in your look? Does this have to do with a certain someone back in town? A very sexy, very moody Frenchman?"

I couldn't resist a smile. Saffron could always see right through me. "I did go out to see Jean, but we're just friends. He likes the Marilyn type, anyhow—you know, the type with curves, not like me."

Saffron stood back and looked me up and down. "Guys were always crazy about Marilyn, but don't be so hard on yourself. You've got a certain something going on, a Twiggy kind of look. It's hot right now. You should wear shorts to show off your great legs."

I looked down at my old, faded jeans with their wide ballroom legs. "I guess."

"Did I tell you that I heard from Marilyn? She's fine, been living on a commune in southern Alberta—has had enough of that, so she's going to San Francisco—was wondering how we're all doing. I filled her in." Saffron looked at me coyly. "How's Jean managing out on his ranch all alone? Is he grumpy, Mr. Sad-Sack, or is he happier?"

"Seems okay, a little lonely maybe. He's worried about his new wine. I tried it and it's good, but he can't find any buyers."

"What's the deal with that?"

I shrugged. "No one drinks wine around here. Not like in France. He didn't get that when he decided to move here. Could be the fatal flaw in his whole plan."

"That doesn't sound good."

"I wish I could think of something to do to help him. I'd hate to see his winery fail. It just seems so crappy, after all his hard work."

"Hmm." Saffron sat down, opened her bag, and took out a pouch and a packet of slim white papers. She carefully pinched a small amount of tobacco from the pouch, stuffed it into one of the papers, licked it, and pinched the ends. "Light?"

I reached over and handed her the ashtray and lighter from the desk. "I know better than to offer you one of these," Saffron said as she took a long, slow drag and let out a sudden sharp cough like a gunshot.

"I don't know why you smoke. All it does is make you cough."

"I smoke because I can. It's a freedom thing. No one call tell me not to. It's why I do a lot of things."

"What about Jean? If his dream fails, he'll have to crawl home with his tail between his legs. His dad will be proven right. We can't let that happen."

"Agreed." Saffron sat and smoked in silence while I got up and kept watch over the harbour. The ferry wasn't due for twenty minutes yet, but it was occasionally early. A small water bomber that had been doing practise runs came in slow, dropped hard on its belly, and taxied to its mooring buoy. Both sailors and houseboats kept a wide berth, as bombers had priority.

I turned just in time to see Saffron drop her head back, curl her tongue, and blow an elaborate smoke ring. "When Lance and I went to California last winter, we got jobs in something called a pizza parlour," she said.

"What's that?"

"Pizza is so far-out. Everyone digs it. It's a kind of pie, but not sweet, made with things like tomato sauce, spicy meat, and cheese—lots of cheese. And they even have one called the Hawaiian, made with ham and pineapple."

"Pineapple in a pie with cheese sounds gross."

"Trust me, it's not. The Italians thought the whole thing up, and they know food."

I shrugged. "I've never been to an Italian restaurant."

"Look, why don't we introduce happy hour at the Apple Dumpling? After all the little tots head home with their mouths and hands happily slimed with ice cream, we make it adults-only from five to seven and serve pizza and Jean's wine? People will find out how good his wine is and start buying it, and we'll have a load of fun."

Mrs. Graham had changed into her frilly white apron and black patent heels. She wore a single string of white pearls around her neck. "Come in, ladies, pick any seat you like," she called to the first arrivals as she hustled over with menu cards, beaming. "Good afternoon, Miss Braid, Miss Getty," she said to the two women as they settled themselves, removing their white gloves and safely stowing them and their handbags on the empty chair beside them.

"This is so exciting," Miss Braid said. "I can't honestly remember the last time we've had occasion to dress up for an event in town." Looking at the menu card, she said, "I'm going to be bold and try the pepperoni pie with a glass of wine, of course."

Miss Getty nodded her head vigorously like a nervous duckling. "Make that two," she giggled, her hand covering her mouth.

A steady stream of customers began arriving. I smiled a greeting as I recognized my first employer, Hardeep Singh, and his wife, Sally. Mrs. Wong from the Canadian Chinese Café down the street waved me over. She squeezed my hand and confided in me that she was so sick of her own cooking that she couldn't wait to try something new.

It wasn't long before the small café filled, and as the evening approached, candles were lit, giving the whole scene the feel of a real Italian café.

Saffron expertly twirled the pizza dough, ladled the tomato sauce and swirled it around, and added the toppings, while I hustled about serving and refilling glasses. Jean arrived looking well-scrubbed in a freshly laundered white shirt and black dress pants. He visited the tables, describing to customers how he had grown the grapes and made the wine.

I could see scepticism on some faces, and I overheard Miss Getty explain to Jean that she too had homemade wine and he should be careful that it didn't turn to wine vinegar as hers had. But it wasn't long before the compliments started flowing along with the wine. People ordered more glasses and even whole bottles to take home for Sunday supper.

As seven rolled around, no one looked ready to leave until Mrs. Graham, her face dewy and flushed, flicked the lights. "Closing time," she called. "Please join us next Thursday for another happy hour."

Jean leaned in close to me and I got a faint whiff of Brut aftershave. His breath held a hint of parsley. "Tonight was a huge success, Daisy. Both the general store and the pub are going to start carrying my wine. Next week I'm going up to Kelowna to see if I can find some buyers. You've inspired me, Daisy." He smiled warmly at me, his eyes glistening in the candlelight.

"Saffron and I were happy to help, and I don't think Mrs. Graham has had so much fun in years."

"Me too. I mean, I want to help you. I talked to my uncle."

Sucking in my breath, I set down the tray of dirty glasses I was holding and waited for Jean's news. "Uncle Pierre said something about it being an important legal question. He can't do it himself, but he'll give you a name to call once he's set things up from his end. Not a junior lawyer, someone senior, with some clout."

The relief I felt was mixed with naked fear. I was terrified to talk to powerful people, but I knew I had to. If they were willing to listen and actually do something, it could be a turning point. Between this and the love-in, the thought of success was almost overwhelming. I reached over and gave Jean a hug, feeling his muscled body momentarily yield to my touch.

He gave me a brotherly pat on the back. "Hold on, let's wait and see what comes of it before we celebrate."

Both Mrs. Graham and Saffron looked beat, so I offered to finish the cleanup while Jean loaded the leftover wine and empties into his truck. Alone in the café, I turned the OPEN sign to CLOSED and blew out the candles. The room took on a satisfied, after-the-party feel.

I stepped outside with the last box of empties and set them on the front porch for Jean. I paused, breathing deeply the clean, fragrant evening air with its heady mix of pine, lavender, and sage. Looking up, I could see the bright North Star off to my left and the Big Dipper almost directly overhead. It reminded me of the evenings five years ago with my new friends, Saffron and Jean, when we sat on lawn chairs at Hardeep's farm, admiring this same brilliant night sky.

Now they were old friends. Sometimes, I felt there had been some unseen hand in my coming here. After all, Saffron had been a guardian angel, saving me twice. If there was, I hoped it was the same benevolent God who was keeping watch over my mom and Brighten. Turning to the North Star, I put my hand over my heart.

"I swear to find a way for Mom and Brighten to have the kind of freedom and happy life that I enjoy here."

And then I went to bed.

Chapter Twenty-Five

Jean phoned the Apple Dumpling and asked me to meet him at his place, so I changed out of my old sundress into a pair of white shorts and a bright yellow sun-top, borrowed Myrtle, and set out for Paradise.

Jean had told me on the phone that he'd had a long talk with his uncle and wanted to fill me in on what he'd had to say. My clammy hands trembled with anticipation as I struggled to get the car into gear and be off.

It was another beautiful, hot, dry, cloudless day in the Okanagan Valley. Perfect for the tourists who arrived in sleek metal Airstream trailers packed full of kids in swimsuits. Perfect for grapes.

"The question is," Jean said when we were seated on his porch sipping his latest, perfectly chilled Pinot Gris, "how far does protecting freedom of religion go? What if I told you that I believed that lovely young virgins should be sacrificed to the great wine god, Pinot, and then I picked you up, carried you to the cliff, and dropped you over? Would I have a reasonable defence if I claimed freedom of religion?"

I swallowed hard and blushed deeply. "I—I'm not sure I'm following."

"Think of all the crazy and awful things that have been done in the name of religion—the Crusades, the Spanish Inquisition, the Holocaust."

There was a time when I would have had no idea what Jean was talking about.

The only history worth learning is the history of the one true church.

I pushed the thought away.

"Yes, I know—terrible." I was proud of my newly acquired knowledge and the hard work it took to get it. It made me feel like I fit in, that I belonged in the outside world.

"The point is, there are limits. I remember that from law school. So, when and how should there be limits on the freedom of religion?"

"I've done some reading too, and I wondered the same thing. Perhaps when it infringes on the rights of others, of women and children."

Jean nodded. "My uncle told me that retired Chief Justice Frank Adams is taking on interesting causes for his retirement project. He especially likes to fight for the underdog. Uncle Pierre thought your case would be right up his alley." Jean paused and smiled at me, his eyes twinkling. "Justice Adams wants to meet you. His retirement home is right across the lake in Peachland."

I hugged myself in glee. "I can't believe this is happening. Wait till I tell Mom and Brighten."

Jean laughed and stood up. "Let's celebrate. How about a swim? I promise to wear swim trunks, and you can wear what you have on. By the time we climb up the cliff afterwards, they'll be dry—trust me."

This time I didn't hesitate. "You're on."

The beach below the cliff was narrow but sandy, the water very enticing. I plunged in, then stood in waist-deep water and yelled, "You could have warned me!"

"Ha ha, not as warm as Willow Beach, but it's fine, you just have to get used to it. It's a big, deep lake. Lots of warm and cold currents. Swim around till you find a warm spot."

I did just that. Having found a warm eddy, I didn't want to budge.

"Ah, Daisy."

"Yeah?"

"If you feel something slimy brush against your legs, don't panic. It's just the Ogopogo."

"What?"

"You know, the Ogopogo. It's like the Loch Ness Monster, only uglier and slimier. Remember how I said this is a really deep lake?"

"You're kidding, right?"

Jean dived under the water. I watched his sleek form as he swam towards me. I shrieked and tried to swim away but got nowhere in the deep water. Jean grabbed my ankle, giving it a tug. I slipped under the water, and we both came up laughing and sputtering. He swam closer, put his arm around my waist, and pulled me to him before gently kissing me. A thrill rippled through my body. The lake suddenly didn't feel so cold.

His kiss tasted like strawberries dipped in chocolate, and I wanted more. I lost myself in the moment, but he pulled away, diving under the water again and slowly swimming towards shore, leaving me confused and insecure.

If I didn't count the Bishop, Jean was only my third kiss. Most twenty-one-year-old girls had a lot more experience than me. Was I doing it all wrong? Maybe he didn't feel anything. Maybe my suspicions had been right in the first place. I wasn't really his type.

The climb up the cliff was long and hot. By the time we neared the top, my clothes were dry as a bone and felt scratchy against my irritated skin. Sand had found its way under my waistband and into my bra. I pulled at my clothing, trying to get rid of it.

Bijou bounded along ahead of us. "Don't let him stick his head in the big pile of rocks up ahead. It's a rattlesnake den," Jean called from behind.

"You got me once. I'm not falling for it this time."

"Seriously. This is the northern part of the desert that comes all the way up from Utah and Nevada. There's lots of weird things around here like cactuses and black widow spiders—and rattlers."

I shivered. "I should get back," I told him. I had felt the sting of rejection and now I just wanted to go home. I started towards the car.

"Wait," Jean said. "Let me give you Justice Adams's phone number." He walked up onto the porch and held the screen door open for me. I stepped across the threshold of the cottage but stayed by the door, in a small dining area off an ancient-looking kitchen.

Jean was leafing through a stack of papers on the dining table. "You know, it could help if you also worked at getting public opinion on your side," he said. "It would put pressure on the government to do something. Why don't you get Saffron to write articles in her paper on the subject? You could give her some examples of what life is really like in Redemption."

"We haven't got much extra time. We're working really hard on the love-in. Between that and the legal angle, something's gotta give."

He handed me a phone number on a scrap of paper. "My uncle says to call the judge when he's at his Peachland beach house in two weeks." Jean looked thoughtful, scrubbing the short whiskers on his chin with one hand. "How *is* the planning for the love-in going?"

I started out the door. "Really well. We've got a couple of bands from Kelowna signed on and the Summerland Poets Society will do a reading, the Peachland Drummers group will do two sets, and we'll have beadwork and macramé workshops. That's just for start-ers." I turned on my heel and headed towards the car, wanting to cut the conversation short and leave.

Jean followed me out. "Saffron is going to Vancouver next weekend to see Jerry Rubin speak at UBC, maybe you should come along. It might do you good to hear his message."

I kept walking. "What do you mean?"

"He says making social change through peace and love—the hippie mantra—doesn't really work in the real world. He calls him-self a yippie and says the only way to get change is to take control and occupy, demand change."

Jean was walking a few paces behind me, and I rounded on him.

"You've never really supported the idea of a love-in, have you, Jean? You think it's all airy-fairy crap, don't you?" I surprised myself at my sudden temper. We stood in the withering, bone-dry heat of the late afternoon, but my face felt several degrees hotter than the air. I rubbed my throbbing temple. My face and my fingertips felt scorched.

Jean held up his hands in surrender. "Whoa, don't shoot the messenger. All I'm trying to say is I think you're a little naïve. You haven't been out in the world like I have. People don't do what's right, they do what's in their own self-interest."

"I'm sorry you're such a cynic, Jean, and that you have so little faith in what I'm trying to achieve. I expected more of you."

I jumped into Myrtle, ground the gears, and slowly puttered down the driveway, leaving Jean in a dusty swirl.

⋟⋟⋎⋏⋎⋏⋎⋏⋏

Chapter Twenty-Six

"And this is Daisy signing off from *Daisy's Disks*. Groove with me next time when I bring you the very latest in rock-and-roll LPs. Peace and love, everyone." I switched the dial and watched it bob and dance. "Hey, Brighten, how's it going? Any better?"

"I've been over the morning sickness for a while, but I'm still not feeling very well. Guess I'm into the second trimester. Could even be in the beginning of my third, I don't know." She paused and cleared her throat.

"To be honest, Daisy, in the early weeks of the pregnancy I was in denial. I'm pretty sure I'm quite a lot further along than I let on. I refused to believe it until the bulge in my belly became obvious. They won't let me have any tests, so I don't know my due date.

"Something seems wrong, but sickness is just a state of mind, they tell me. All I need to do is pray."

"No way you could see a doctor in town?"

"Not a chance. I'm being punished again. My husband tried to have his turn with me even though I'm pregnant. One of the other wives caught him trying to sneak into my room, and she told the Bishop. It's a sin for a member of the priesthood to sleep with his pregnant wife, and somehow it's all my fault. According to the Bishop, I'm a temptress. So now I'm not allowed to visit my mother for two whole months."

"How *is* your mom?"

"Not good. Her moods are worse, and this isn't going to help."

We spoke quickly, as we always did, never knowing how long we had. "I've got news. Things are happening."

"What do you mean?"

I told her about the retired judge who might help, but she seemed unimpressed. "I don't know, Daisy. Don't think I'm not grateful for what you're trying to do, but the legal system can take years. You remember when the Bishop's oldest son got charged in that hit-and-run in town? It took two years to go through all the courts, and in the end, he got off. We have to do something now, before my baby is born. I have a feeling it's not going to go full-term."

"I get it. I've thought it through. First, the love-in will open the doors to people hearing a new message of love and hope for a better life. The Bishop won't be able to stop a mass exodus. It will weaken the Bishop's power, and then the legal fight will shut Redemption down for good."

"That sounds promising. Good luck. I better hang up." Brighten sounded unconvinced and weary. I switched off my mic and dropped my head down onto the desk in the radio room, struggling with fear and creeping doubts of my own.

Chapter Twenty-Seven

"What's got you so down in the mouth, Daisy-flower? You look like a pothead who's lost his weed." Saffron and I were sitting at a table in the Apple Dumpling, pencils in hand, scratching out a list of supplies we needed for the posters we were making for the love-in. I wasn't making much progress, as I'd spent most of my time staring vacantly out the window at the huge cotton-candy clouds that billowed on the horizon.

"Jean and I had a fight. I mean, I had a fight with him because he behaved like a jerk. At least, that's the way I saw it."

Saffron dropped her pencil and leaned away from the table, stretching. "So, like a friends kind of fight or a lovers kind of fight?" She looked at me from under her eyelashes and gave me a coy smile.

I sighed and tossed my pencil on the table. "I think that's part of the problem. I don't know. He kissed me, and then—nothing. He didn't come near me after that—like he hadn't felt anything, like he wasn't interested after all." Jean was the first man I'd had real, grown-up feelings for since Tobias, and I felt rejected.

"I know Jean pretty well and I think he's interested," Saffron said.

"He's not acting like it, and there's more. I was mad that he has doubts about the love-in."

"And you told him that?"

"Sort of. It was more like yelling than talking."

"How did he take it?"

"I didn't wait around to find out."

"Well, I think you're going to find out," Saffron said, looking over my shoulder and out into the parking area in front of the café. "Here he comes now."

I watched Jean struggle with the front door as he juggled a box he was carrying, but I didn't rise to help him. Saffron jumped up, let him in, and called back to me, "Gotta go, see you later." She left.

I pretended to be busy working on the shopping list, my head bent low over paper and pencil, but I was forced to sit up and acknowledge him when a glass bowl filled with delicate flowers was pushed under my nose.

"Nice. What are they?" I said without looking up.

"Wild cactus flowers. I learned an important lesson as I picked these for you. Never wear sandals in a cactus patch." He laughed but I didn't join in. I returned to my work.

"Aren't you going to thank me?" Jean sat down in Saffron's vacated chair and leaned low to make eye contact. "They're a peace offering and an apology. I was an ass the other day and I'm really sorry."

I didn't know if he was talking about the kiss or not but decided not to go there. "You're allowed to have an opinion."

He paused, holding my gaze. "It was spontaneous. I should have checked with you first, that you wanted to, ah, *hear* it, before I blurted it out—the opinion, I mean. Don't be mad at me. Forgive me?"

"I'll think about it."

"How long?"

"A while."

"Okay, I'll wait." Jean sat back and folded his hands on the table.

I ignored him in favour of my shopping list, until I looked up and found him grinning at me.

"You're just going to sit there and wait?"

"Yup."

I sighed. "Listen, Jean. Thank you. I really owe you. The contact with the retired judge that your uncle arranged is terrific. Hopefully something'll come of it. I can't thank you both enough. But we are strictly friends. Nothing more. Okay?"

"Fine, and I promise that the next time I kiss you I will ask your permission first."

"There isn't going to be a next time."

"Oh yes, there is."

A crowd of children burst through the door, their sticky little hands clutching dimes, and they raced to the ice cream counter to jostle for space. I found myself unconsciously rubbing my wrist as I got up to serve them. I was happy to have my conversation with Jean interrupted. He took the hint.

"I'm off, then. Did you tell Saffron that you're coming with us to hear Jerry Rubin?"

"See you," I said, turning my back, pretending to hunt for the scoop. I waited until I heard the screen door slap before I faced the room again. After patiently serving the kids, I wandered out onto the front porch to sit and think.

My thoughts turned to Tobias, my first real crush. I had truly cared for him once, but I was such an innocent, still a kid myself. I was not at all ready for a physical relationship with him. My feelings for Jean were different. I felt a strong desire for him, but at the same time, I didn't want to get hurt.

In the outside world, men and women had relations all the time, and then they moved on. I wasn't sure I could handle that. It was far from everything I'd been taught growing up, like that was a reasonable benchmark. Would I ever truly leave Redemption behind?

I wondered if everything was the same there as it always had been, or if the Bishop had received more messages from God. Maybe if there were changes, I could use them to my advantage. I decided to talk to Brighten again.

⤜⤛

"I've been thinking about Redemption—wondering if Bishop Thorsen has changed much since I left. If he's afraid that people are questioning his leadership, maybe he feels that he has to lighten up a bit or face a rebellion. What do you think?"

Brighten laughed bitterly. "No way. If anything, he's worse. He's like a cornered animal. He's *pretending* to be easygoing, but in many ways he's doubled down."

"How so?"

"Daisy, I never really told you about what happened to me after I was caught trying to run away with you. I knew the truth would upset you, so I buried it—never spoke of it to anyone."

My stomach did a somersault, my voice dropped to barely a whisper. "Did he beat you?"

"Worse. At least a beating would have been over quickly. My punishment wasn't physical at all. He had my husband's family lock me in a room with just a bed, no window. They brought me meals but cut my food rations in half. No one but the Bishop spoke to me for weeks. I thought I would go mad."

Isolation and re-education—so cruel. My mom had been

shunned, but this was different, worse in a way. I felt my temples begin to throb and leaned forward to massage them.

"He told me that I needed re-education. The only thing in the room was a book of his sermons. Other than reading the book, there was absolutely nothing to do all day. I got so sad and lonely. I could tell I was losing weight. My hair even began to fall out in spots. After a while I just lay in bed all day and slept."

I felt the urge to cry and took a moment to try to pull myself together. My voice was hoarse. "Oh, Brighten, I am so, so sorry." This was all my fault.

"Don't be sorry. I knew what I was doing. I just didn't understand how horrible the Bishop could be. Every Sunday evening, he came to my room and asked me if I was ready to repent and be rebaptised." Brighten's voice fell. "I just couldn't take it anymore. I thought I would die alone in that room if I didn't get out of it soon. I told him I was ready."

"What else could you do? You had to say it. There was no real harm. The Bishop can't know what's truly in your heart."

"It's not that, Daisy." Brighten's voice dropped to a whisper. "The Bishop told me that the only way to truly repent was to become a mother of Zion. I had to sleep with Brother Earl until I became pregnant. Only then would he let me out of the room."

I didn't speak for several seconds. Of course, I knew that Brighten had had to sleep with Brother Earl. How else could she have gotten pregnant three times? But we'd never talked about it. Only the pregnancies and miscarriages. I looked out at the view from the radio room just as the fiery ball of sun came out from behind a cloud, hanging low in the west. My dry eyes burnt.

"That's so terrible, Brighten," I whispered. "I can't imagine what you went through."

I heard a sob. "My body was too weak. The midwife explained that I was malnourished, and that's why I didn't hold that little life inside me for long."

I burst into tears, and soon we were both crying. I told myself to be strong for Brighten and willed myself to stop, but before I could console her, she said she had to go. I shut down the radio and headed back to the Apple Dumpling. I did all my best thinking on the front porch there.

The late-afternoon heat had just about reached its peak, and it was too hot to leave the shade of the porch. Too hot for anything much, except sleep. I pushed my dreary thoughts away and briefly closed my eyes.

When I awoke, the sun's final rays winked at me from behind spun-cotton clouds that had taken on an impressive array of shapes as they loomed higher and higher overhead.

As the glowing orb of sun completely disappeared behind the distant hills, the heat of the day eased. Twilight came quickly. The high-level winds picked up and teased wisps from the loftiest clouds, creating pale witches with wild hair flying. The breeze stirred the large, dry tumbleweeds, sending them careening recklessly down the main street, crashing into cars and bouncing off fence posts.

Clouds exchanged moody mumbles followed by scattered pulses of sound and light, like popcorn before the main event. The white flash came several seconds later. I felt a vibration, a low rumble in the ground, followed by a cracking clap of thunder.

The late-summer storms were always the most dramatic—

something about the jet stream in the upper atmosphere, I had heard on the radio.

More dry lightning and thunder followed, the gap between the two shortening. A brilliant flash of light left me with spots in front of my eyes, while the frightening crack directly overhead lifted me from my chair.

I sat still, waiting and worrying while my vision cleared. Everyone dreaded the storms that produced lightning but no rain. Usually, summer thunderstorms came in from the west, across the lake between Summerland and Peachland, but not this one. It was coming in from the east, directly over the provincial park with its giant old pine trees.

Shielding my eyes, I got up and walked to the edge of the porch and turned, straining to see the low mountain ridge behind me. In the distance, another lightning strike produced a shower of bright yellow sparks that shot skywards before raining back down. Then the lights went out.

At first, I couldn't see a thing—the contrast of the darkness to the flash of lightning was too great—but slowly my eyes adjusted. Thankfully, there was a three-quarter moon visible between the thunderheads. It, and the headlights from the few cars driving down Main Street, cast enough light for me to make my way back inside the restaurant and light candles.

I checked the stove and grill to make sure everything was off. I grabbed a flashlight for backup and blew out the candles, standing in darkness as I double-locked the café front door.

Looking through the door window, my attention was caught by a slow-moving car. It was a solid vehicle, fancy-looking, I thought, sleek and black, not the sort of thing people around

Nkwala drove. The car pulled into the parking area in front of the café, shining its lights directly into the building through the front windows.

Something about it didn't feel right. I shrank back, hiding behind the door, occasionally peeking to see if anyone got out of the car. The car cut its lights, but no one got out. After a bit, it silently backed away, turned its lights on, and rolled on down Main Street. I let out a breath.

I headed upstairs to bed and much-needed sleep, but worries kept bugging me and I lay awake long into the night. Who was in that car? Was it Tobias again? The Bishop himself? Would Redemption ever stop coming for me? Or was it someone else?

I gave up trying to sleep at about two in the morning and wandered over to my little attic window. Opening the shade, I pushed my window wide and looking up, gave a start. The night sky pulsed with an ominous orange glow.

⟶ↂↂↂↂↂ⟵

Chapter Twenty-Eight

By six I got up, dressed, and headed downstairs to the café. The power was back on, so I started cleaning and setting up for the day. At seven I flipped the CLOSED sign to OPEN and almost immediately the door swung back on its hinges. A lone figure emerged from the smoky haze and stepped inside.

"Grab a seat anywhere," I called over my shoulder as I went to fetch the coffee urn. "Coffee?"

"No, thank you. I don't drink coffee."

I knew the voice. Frozen in disbelief, I managed to turn on my heel to stare at the man.

Tobias leaned backwards and snapped the front door lock into place. "It would be best if we weren't disturbed."

I struggled to recover from the shock, then found my voice. "Tobias. It's been years. Why now? What do you want?"

He glanced around the room, making sure we were alone. "Daisy, this thing between us—it's never been settled."

"There's no 'thing' between us. That was over a long time ago."

He looked at me hard, his smile carrying a hint of condescension. "You're lying. We both feel it, we always will. You are denying it because Satan has his hooks into you." He paused, gesturing towards the little bar where Jean's wines were on display. "You serve alcohol here? You're wearing shorts and a low-cut top? How could you sink so low?"

Despite my outward calm, I felt fear and I struggled to breathe. It was as though I'd forgotten how. I stared at Tobias, fighting the shock of seeing him again after five years. The last time I saw him, I was fighting him for my freedom.

For my dignity as a woman.

He was no longer the sweet-faced, dimpled boy of my childish dreams. His whiskers had grown in, giving his face a dark shadow, but he was still handsome, and he still gave off a sense of confidence and entitlement. He was the son of church royalty. People didn't say no to him.

"How did you find me?"

"Your new driver's licence, of course."

I clutched the dishcloth I was holding and twisted it into a knot. "You're wasting your time and energy coming here. I'm unworthy. Remember? Like I told Rainbow, I'm not going back. I'm staying right here. Tell the Bishop."

"But it won't be like it was before," Tobias said. "The Bishop has changed. Some say he's not the same since his *accident*. For whatever reason, he's much more easygoing. He's forgiven you."

"Really? I find that hard to believe."

Tobias took a step towards me and put his hand out, seeking mine. An image flashed through my mind of the day when we had boldly held hands and talked of marriage. I pushed it away and moved back, creating distance between us.

He persisted. "I'm here to tell you some wonderful news. The Bishop has agreed to reassign you to me. I have permission to marry you. You'll be my third wife, my celestial wife. When we die, you'll be able to join me in the highest kingdom of heaven, the Celestial Kingdom, for time and all eternity." Tobias clasped his hands as if praying and rolled his eyes skyward. "Don't you see, Daisy? I'm going to save you after all."

I knew Mrs. Graham was just upstairs in her room. If I called her, would she hear?

"I'm not the same person I was five years ago," I said. "Back then, I had a schoolgirl crush on you. But I've been over you for a long time and I don't want to marry you."

He stepped closer, his hot breath against my cheek, his large body dwarfing mine. "It wasn't a crush. We were meant to be together, promised as partners in the pre-life. I still love you and I know you love me."

"No, I . . ." I heard a persistent rattle from the front door. Someone was trying to get in, no doubt wondering why the door was locked when the sign said OPEN.

I had an urge to call out, but Tobias gripped my arm hard and leaned in very close, his prickly chin scratching my ear. "Just let whoever it is go. We're not done here."

I heard the echo of retreating steps on the old wooden porch floor. Tobias squeezed my arm painfully.

The whites of his eyes were glistening with fervor. "Don't you get it, Daisy? The Bishop is losing his grip. There's talk of the need for a new, devoted, younger leader, someone like me. If I'm able to stake my claim as the new Bishop of Redemption, you would have all the power and prestige of a favourite wife."

"Those things don't matter to me anymore. They never did. What should matter to you are Rainbow's feelings."

"The only option you have is to come with me now. 'Sinners shall be destroyed in the flesh and shall be delivered unto the buffetings of Satan unto the day of redemption, saith the Lord God.'" He pulled me hard against him, pressing his body into mine, trying to kiss me. I struggled to turn my head away. I tried to push him back, but he wouldn't budge.

A wailing siren startled both of us. He dropped my arm and stepped back in surprise. I knew the sound. It came from the radio room, a hand-cranked siren alerting the village to an emergency. Drowning, heart attack, boat accident, or fire; the call to the volunteer firefighters was the same.

Chapter Twenty-Nine

I took advantage of the surprise and pushed past Tobias, unlocking the door to the café and stepping outside. I smelled thick, prickly wood smoke just as my lungs erupted in a coughing fit. Blinking the burn from my eyes, I saw that the orange glow in the dawn sky was now filtered through a thick, hazy layer of smoke.

Holding the door wide behind me, I turned back to Tobias. "Just leave," I said. "I'm not going back and never will. You don't need another wife to get into heaven, you just need to be good to the ones you have."

The wailing alarm sounded again, and I turned and ran in the direction it came from.

Out into the street I rushed along with the others who had emerged from their homes. They were all headed to the fire hall across from the general store. A group of young men were already there, in various states of readiness, as they pulled on heavy padded pants and jackets and slapped bright yellow helmets on their heads. Several large trucks and two fire engines blocked the main drag as men threw shovels, picks axes, and large bags of sand into the backs of their vehicles.

I saw Jean, his face flushed, jaw tight, an angry pulse throbbing in his neck. He was shouting into the two-way radio in the fire truck. "No, you listen to *me*—we need the Martin Mars, *now*, while the lake's calm. We can't wait and see. Get it airborne before it's too late—before we lose properties." I felt the baking sun on the back of my neck. The morning was already hot and sticky because of the smoke. Jean was sweating, cursing with frustration under his breath.

"What's happening?" I asked him as he slammed the radio mic back in its cradle.

"Forest fire. Out of control and building fast. It'll be crowning in no time, and I had to convince Forestry to send in the big boy. They were just going to use choppers. Can you believe it?"

His eyes bulged with disbelief as he glanced about at the frantic preparations going on around him.

"Hold on, back up," I said. "Big boy? Crowning?"

Jean sighed and wiped his dripping forehead with the back of his hand. "The Martin Mars is the biggest water bomber in the fleet. It's expensive to run, so they only bring it in when trees are crowning, when the fire is so hot that is skips along the treetops, and the trunks below just explode."

"Yikes. Where's the fire?"

He took a deep breath, trying to control his emotions. "In the dry sage brush and pine forest about five miles back of my place. If it jumps Dead Horse Canyon, I've had it." Jean pressed the corners of his eyes with his forefingers, blinking and swallowing hard. His voice tightened. "Everything I've built, everything I've worked for—my vineyard, the winery—my mother's legacy, could all be gone in a day. My father—he'd never speak to me again."

I instantly forgot my anger at Jean. I only wanted to comfort him. "It'll be okay, don't worry." I reached up and rubbed his shoulder. "Everyone is pitching in to help. We'll get this done. What can I do to help?"

Jean nodded. "Saffron's going to need you as backup. She'll coordinate the bomber's water pickup—you call in the-all clear when she's sure there's no ferry or any other boat in the way. It'll be tense and hectic."

"Okay, I'm on it." I turned to go but stopped. Reaching up, I gave Jean a hug. "Everything'll be all right, it really will."

Jean wrapped his arms around me, squeezing hard. "Thanks. I've left Bijou at Saffron's place. Check on him later, okay? I won't be back till late. He'll need a walk, fresh water."

"For sure. Good luck."

Saffron was seated at the radio, her pink slipper-clad feet up on the desk. She wore a Japanese silk kimono, with her thick, curly hair piled on top of her head, held in place with two chopsticks. "Your idea of sleepwear?" I asked.

"Of course. Did you honestly expect a flannelette nightie?"

"Not from you. So, I guess you've been up for a while?"

Saffron stretched. "Got a call from Forestry at first light to come in and start making calls to the fire captains. Now they want me to stay and help with the water bomber. I'm pooped already."

"I'm here to help. You go get a shower and something to eat. I'll keep an eye on things for a while. Oh, and could you stop in at the Apple Dumpling and tell Mrs. Graham what's going on?"

"No prob. I'll bring you back a doughnut. I don't expect much'll happen for a while yet but keep an eye out for the big water bomber, just in case. Jean told me it can pick up thirty tons of water in twenty-two seconds. When it comes in to scoop water from the lake, we don't want it to suck up some poor kayaker or Miss Braid when she's out for her early swim."

I shuddered.

Saffron giggled. "I'm kidding, Dais."

"I knew that."

"No, you didn't."

Saffron left and I scanned the horizon just to be sure it was all clear. The first ferry wouldn't be in for a couple of hours yet, and there was no sign of early-morning boaters or swimmers. My lack of sleep was already weighing heavily on me. *I'm lucky if I got two hours*, I thought, as my body folded forward, and I let my head drop slowly down onto the table. "I'll just rest my eyes for a minute or two."

A sudden cacophony jolted me wide awake. Looking up through the large window, I saw a great metal albatross coming in dead-on for the bay, seconds from laying its blood-orange belly down on the smooth surface of the lake. It reminded me of a dancing elephant, massive, lumbering, yet somehow graceful.

It cut its engines and dropped from the air. Without the lift from the propellers, the plane sank low in the water, its two massive wings supported by pontoons. I watched it taxi to a mooring buoy. A small window in the nose of the plane popped open and a head and arm emerged from the hatch, clipping a line to the buoy.

I grabbed binoculars and trained them on the pilot. He sat with a clipboard, checking dials on the dashboard and scribbling notes. I scanned the dock and surrounding beaches. All clear.

The radio crackled to life. "Martin bomber to Nkwala base. Come in, Nkwala base."

"Nkwala base here. Come in, Martin bomber."

"I'm just finishing my flight check and then I'll start a series of pickups and drops. I'll have my mic open at all times. If you see something I should look out for, just give me a shout."

"Ten-four." I felt a small thrill of self-importance. I had a major role. Back in Redemption, the women were always told to make sandwiches when there was any kind of emergency or crisis.

Feed the men, and above all, keep sweet.

Not anymore. An out-of-control forest fire threatened Nkwala, demanding that everyone do everything they could to fight it.

Chapter Thirty

I watched in awe as the great beast lumbered into a takeoff, then circled back around. Coming in low, it skimmed its belly along the surface of the water, sucking up gallons and leaving a dragon's tail of mist. I wished I could see the drop, but my view was obscured by a low range of mountains.

Saffron came back a while later, dressed in a miniskirt and Indian peasant blouse. She tossed me a doughnut and took over the radio. I wandered outside to sit on my favourite bench under the weeping willow and eat my breakfast.

There were several large boats at the government dock, not unusual for this time of year. I guessed they had chosen to tie up to keep out of the way of the water bomber and helicopters.

Houseboats were common, but my attention was drawn to an unusually large craft, at least twice the size of the others. I squinted to read the name stencilled on the bow but couldn't quite make it out. As I watched, a man dressed in a grey suit stepped off the houseboat and walked directly towards me. I stiffened and looked around. There was no one nearby.

I tried to make myself small, ducking behind the elegant sweeping tendrils of the massive willow tree, but the man walked deliberately towards me, removing his sunglasses before squinting through the branches.

"Daisy? Daisy Shoemaker?" He was fiftyish, bushy eyebrows and greying hair. My skin pricked. I'd seen him before, but where?

"Sorry. Wrong Daisy," I said. "I'm Daisy Ford. You've made a mistake."

"I know who you are. There's someone here who wants to see you."

I could only sit and stare, frozen in place.

"I'm Bill." The man inclined his head towards the large house-boat. "And my boss is waiting for you on board. Come with me."

My first instinct was to run, but Bill reached in and placed a vise grip on my upper arm. "This way," he said, pulling me to my feet. He was twice my size and easily propelled me towards the boat, just as the massive water bomber came in for another pickup. If I tried to shout, not a soul would hear me. All eyes and ears were drawn to the aerial ballet taking place in the bay.

Suddenly I remembered where I'd seen Bill before. He was the man who'd come looking for me years ago, the day of the pickers barbeque on the beach, when he'd offered money to the others for information about my whereabouts. My blood ran cold.

The Bishop had found me.

Bill guided me down the stairs from the dock to the boat, through an open door and down a narrow, low-ceilinged hallway. Bill knocked softly on a cabin door. It was opened by a nurse in the traditional white uniform and thick-soled shoes. She reached for me, pulling me into the room and shutting the door on Bill.

She spoke softly. "Your father is very frail. Don't say or do anything to upset him. There's not much time. His heart is failing. I've just given him an injection. He'll rally for a while, but not for long."

My jaw dropped. "My father? Dan Shoemaker? Not Bishop Thorsen?"

The nurse nodded, her mouth grim.

The room was dim, with the shades drawn and the lights very

low. It smelled of strong disinfectant and eucalyptus. A large hospital bed dominated the room, and I could just make out a shadowy, white-haired figure lying inert in the bed. The only sound was the hypnotic sighs of an oxygen-condenser pump set on a low table by the bed.

A flash of light filled the room, and I turned just in time to see the nurse disappear into the hallway before darkness descended once more. I forced myself forward.

He moved. "Daisy? Is that you?"

My heart skipped a beat. I slowly approached the bed. He was partially sitting up, supported by a mound of pillows. His gaunt face had puffy, doughy bags under the eyes, and his skin was mottled with dark patches that looked like bruising. Thinning white hair was plastered to his head. Despite the oxygen tubes in each nostril, his breathing was laboured.

Images of a younger version of my father flashed through my mind. Dad, with a large, warm smile, gently tossing a ball to me, cuddling me as he read me bedtime stories, lifting me up to peer inside a bird's nest, presenting me with a large stuffed teddy bear for my birthday. The memories brought a flood of warm feelings.

"It's me, Daddy. I tried to find you after I escaped from Redemption—"

He lifted a shaky hand and tried to touch my arm. I took his hand and gave it a gentle squeeze before carefully placing it back on the bed.

His voice was a hoarse whisper. "I wanted so much to see you, to talk to you while I still can. I hope Bill didn't scare you. He tried to drop by the café last night to tell you I was here, but it was closed. He's an old army buddy of mine—a private detective. He offered to help me try to find you. It's been years, and he didn't have much luck. Until you got a driver's licence, then it was easy."

First Tobias, now my father. I'd had no idea I'd be traceable so quickly.

The colour seemed to return to his face and his milky eyes brightened as the injected drug did its thing. "Come closer, let me see you. Turn up the light a little." His voice had some strength now. I raised a dimmer switch on the wall and soft, golden light replaced the gloom. I leaned forward over the bed as my father studied me. "You look more like your mother than me. Lucky you."

A million questions ran through my mind. Why did he leave Mom and me? What happened between him and the Bishop? But I knew I had to put my questions away for now. How long would his strength last?

"Daddy, I'm sorry we didn't get a chance to meet before this. I didn't know how to reach you. I even asked Miss Braid, but it's really hard to find a houseboat."

He was suddenly agitated, and I winced, remembering the nurse's warning. "That's the Bishop's doing. I had no choice. It matters so much to me that you understand—that you don't blame me."

"I don't blame you, Dad. I'm proud of you. You're a war hero. I read an article about you. You helped free your fellow prisoners and led them to safety. Tell me what happened to you."

"Help me sit up a bit better." I pushed another pillow behind him for support. He coughed and cleared his throat. "I was hurt in the war, beaten and starved for organizing the escape. When I finally got back home after, I was lost, and I struggled. I was look-ing for a better way of life, a simpler way of life, guided by spirit. I thought I'd found it in Redemption. When I married your mom and we had you, I was the happiest man alive."

He took a moment to rest, his eyes searching my face, as if he were looking for confirmation that I was really listening and accepting what he had to say.

I nodded, urging him on. "What changed?"

"Everything and nothing. Bishop Thorsen took over the leadership from his father. The son had a massive ego. He was greedy and power hungry. Seemed to have a lot of new revelations from God, or so he claimed.

"He proclaimed that everyone had to hand over their assets to support the community. People gave him everything or risked being excommunicated. Houses, cottages, farms, boats, vehicles, and businesses, they were all signed over to him."

"What happened to it all?"

"The Bishop sold some of it for cash, which he pocketed. He reassigned homes and vehicles to the more worthy priesthood men who blindly followed his every word." He said "worthy" like it left a bad taste in his mouth.

I leaned in closer. "Did he do that to you too?"

Dad paused, catching his breath one more time.

"I had poured everything into building up Shoemaker Forest Products. I worked hard, and it was a success. I think I knew deep down that I wouldn't have a long life. My health was poor. I wanted to leave something for you, Daisy. Something to help you through life when I wasn't there any longer."

I had to suck back tears and force myself not to cry. He let out another long, ragged cough. A trembling hand brought a tissue to his mouth.

"Take your time, Daddy. Don't tire yourself."

"Bishop Thorsen wanted my business, but I refused to sign the transfer-of-ownership papers, so he and his thugs forced me out. Even though they didn't own it, they took it anyway."

"Did you go to the police?"

"I couldn't. He threatened you and Ruth if I tried to do anything. He told everyone that I'd sold the company to him for a fair price, and I didn't contradict him. I was forced to go along with the lie. He quietly cut all my employees' wages, but he kept two sets of books, so no one knew.

"Once I left Redemption and became a nonbeliever, an apostate, Ruth's father threatened her with a blood atonement if she ran away with me. My beautiful little family was torn apart."

I reached across the bed and did my best to hug him despite the many lines and tubes running in and out of him. "I understand, Daddy. I really do. Mom explained it to me the best she could. She didn't tell me what Bishop Thorsen did to you, but I know she loves you. She used to sneak off to see you in town, right?"

"She did, but one time we were almost caught. That was the last time we tried it." Large tears began to roll down my father's cheeks, but he made no move to rub them away. They left a spidery pattern across his powder-white skin.

I moved closer to the bed, ready to give him another gentle hug, but a slight shake of his head stopped me. His eyes gleamed bright with a sudden urgency.

"Daisy, I haven't got long in this world." He pointed to the table beside the bed and a blue velvet box. "Take that. It's the deed to my sawmill and lumber business. When I'm gone, get back what's rightfully yours. Don't try to do it yourself, hire a lawyer. There's no telling what Thorsen might do. The business is a moneymaker. He won't give it up without a real fight—and he fights dirty."

"Dad, I don't care about deeds and money. I just want to be with you." I held his hand as tears poured down my cheeks. "I just want to be a family again."

Chapter Thirty-One

The high-pitched shriek of aircraft engines hit me like a blow to the head as I stepped onto the blistering-hot deck of the houseboat. Directly above me, the massive Martin Mars rolled over and banked sharply as it fought for lift. I wiped my tears, and the headache threatening my brain exploded.

The sunlight, even muted as it was by the smoke, made me squint and shield my eyes after the gloomy, oppressive stateroom. With the blue velvet box tucked tight under my arm, I groped my way across the deck and down the steps to the dock.

When my eyes adjusted to the light, I was startled by what appeared to be snow falling in the middle of summer. I stared uncomprehendingly at the large white feathery flakes until I breathed in a small piece and choked. It was ash.

The flakes stuck to my hair and clothes as I walked with my head down over to Saffron's tiny, one-room cottage on Third Street. The door was never locked, so I let myself in after shaking off the soot.

Bijou barked until he saw who it was and then came bounding out to greet me. I gave him fresh water, then let him out in the backyard for a quick pee.

While he was touring the garden, I took a few moments to try and process what had just happened. I had been overjoyed to see my dad again after all these years, but at the same time I was heartbroken that his health was failing and I wouldn't have much more time with him. At least I got to hear his story, from his own lips.

In our short time together, I'd felt something special—a deeper connection that reached back to my early childhood. We were alike, my father and I. Neither of us was afraid to take a chance in life, and we were leaders, not followers.

Bijou scratched at the door, and I let him in, then hunted through Saffron's cupboards for an aspirin. I didn't find one, but I did discover something else, the perfect hiding spot. It was a long, narrow cupboard close to the ceiling. I pulled an old wooden kitchen chair over and stood on it, balancing with the blue velvet box in one hand. Opening the cupboard, I found an odd assortment of things, a teapot with a broken spout, a fondue pot, and a macramé plant holder. I placed the velvet box behind them before rearranging them like they were, then I hurried back to work.

It was an exhausting day and when the fiery red ball of sun finally sank behind the mountains, we were relieved that the blistering heat was gone as well. The water bomber's pilot wiggled the wings in salute as he headed back to his base for the night, and Saffron and I packed up and headed to the Apple Dumpling.

Four soot-blackened Forestry trucks were parked outside the café, and a group of thirty or so exhausted men sprawled on the small lawn beside the café's front door. No one was talking. They slurped steaming cups of coffee and took great bites of sandwiches and hot dogs, chewing voraciously and swallowing hard.

Saffron walked over to a man in a fire captain's uniform and asked for the latest news. He slowly pulled himself upright and helped himself to another sandwich from the tray perched on a low stool. When he looked down at Saffron, he reminded me of an old horse being pushed to plow one more field long after its strength had gone. He spoke slowly and quietly, as if parcelling out his last morsel of energy.

"Don't know the latest. When we were pulled off the fire, it was sixty percent contained—still on the far side of Dead Horse Canyon, but who knows? Ugly out there. Depends on the winds. The crews'll be here soon. Ask them."

Saffron and I nodded our thanks, and the firefighter sank back down to his spot on the lawn.

The dusk was deepening, and it was getting hard to see. Saffron and I lit some candles, then grabbed a couple of cold root beers. I drank mine in one long pull just as two trucks drove up, cutting their lights, and parking on the street. Several men got out. I knew instantly that one of them was Jean. It was his walk. I'd know it anywhere.

"You guys look like you could use a cold drink," I called out to them and pointed to the cooler heaping with ice, pop, and beer.

I wanted news. As they got closer, I scanned the men's faces, my eyebrows raised, questioning. No one spoke. Jean walked over to the sprinkler on the edge of the lawn, uncoupled the hose, and turned on the tap. Bending from the waist, he scrubbed his face and hands before collapsing onto the far corner of the lawn.

I heard him let out a loud groan as I hunted in the cooler for a beer for each of us. Returning with two tall brown bottles, I dropped down beside him. I felt the heat of his body through his jeans. He turned, his weary smile inches from my face.

"I'm guessing from your smile that the news isn't bad?"

"We're not out of the woods yet, but we held the line for most of the day and then made some real headway. If the winds are in the right direction tomorrow, I think we can completely beat the fire. The Martin Mars made all the difference."

I used an opener to flip off the beer caps and gave Jean one. I tapped his bottle with the neck of mine. "To saving your vineyard."

"To my vineyard," he said before tipping his head back and swallowing two-thirds of the cold drink in one long gulp.

"So, tell me about the fire. What happened?"

Jean slowly exhaled and leaned back on his elbows. "Oh man, it was intense. When we got there, the fire was right up against the far side of the canyon and the wind was tossing embers. I stayed on the edge of my property and put out spot fires while everyone else cleared the brush in the canyon. Then the water bomber came. It was so, so cool, like a great guardian angel dropping out of the sky. It spread load after load and then the helicopters came in with retardant. We managed to keep the fire from jumping onto my land."

"The crew that came off the fire first told me that the fire was partly contained."

"Yeah, another group of firefighters came at it from behind and built a firebreak, but they were pulled out when the wind changed—which turned out to be the best thing."

"How so?"

"The wind blew the fire back on itself, and since it had already burnt all the fuel there, it snuffed itself out—or mostly out. There'll be hot spots that could flare up at any time. We'll have to go after them tomorrow."

I looked over at him. He reminded me of a warrior back from a big battle, relieved, but still wary, exhausted and emotionally fragile. I reached up, took his head in my hands, and gave him a long, slow kiss.

When I broke away, I said, "I figured you weren't going to get around to it."

He laughed. "I was going slow," he said. "I didn't want to scare you away."

I smiled. "You didn't." I paused. "I saw my dad today. For the first time in eighteen years. He's dying." The tears started. I couldn't stop them. "He's loved me this whole time, and he really didn't want to leave my mom and me. The Bishop made him do it."

Without a word, Jean wrapped his arms around me and drew me to him. I cried harder, but it felt so good. "How about I come back to your place tonight? You can sleep and I'll stay up—take a shift of fire spotting."

Jean kissed me on the forehead. He didn't need convincing. When we got to his place, he hit the shower then walked like a zombie straight to his bed. He threw back the bedcovers and dropped the towel from around his waist before crash-landing into bed; he held open his arms for me, and I lay down at his side. He was fast asleep in seconds. It wasn't what I'd had in mind when I'd offered to stay over, but it was lovely.

I got up and moved out onto his side deck with binoculars glued to my eyes, scanning the horizon looking for flare-ups. I spotted several but they always snuffed themselves out. By four in the morning, all was quiet.

I headed back to bed. Dropping my clothes in a heap on the floor, I crawled into bed beside Jean, who was lying on his side. Running the palm of my hand slowly down the smooth skin of his back, I traced the curve of his spine, then rested my hand on his hip, waiting for a response. He stirred, mumbled something, then was lost to sleep again.

This time I propped myself up on one elbow, reached over him, and ran my hand across the wide expanse of his chest. It had grown hard and flat from all his work in the vineyard, the skin tight. I heard him groan.

I slid my hand past his navel. "Daisy?" He rolled over to face me. "Nice wakeup call."

I laughed. He reached over and stroked my hair. "Are you sure about this?"

"Very sure."

He smiled in the soft half-light of early dawn. "You're wonderful, Daisy," he whispered softly in my ear. "There's no one quite like you. I'm so happy to have you in my life." Pulling me to him, he kissed me deeply, then his mouth travelled slowly down my neck and beyond.

∽◦

On my slow drive home, the beautiful soul ballad "I've Been Loving You Too Long" by Otis Redding came on the radio. I turned it up and sang along as I thought about my lovemaking with Jean.

I smiled when I thought about my girlish fears about sex. Short and brutish was how I saw it. According to the farmyard animals I'd seen and the game of "*Father and the Mothers*," the males chose the females, and the act was simply a release for male urges.

Jean knew it was my first experience and he made sure to be kind and gentle and patient. It was pure joy, like the secret novel I had read in my mother's basement. If I hadn't left Redemption, I'd never have known what it was to have my desires satisfied, or to have a deep connection with a man.

But more than that, being with Jean felt like my final break from Redemption. I chose the man I wanted, not the other way around. It was not Tobias, and it certainly wasn't the Bishop. I had chosen Jean of my free will and it left me feeling strong and empowered.

Chapter Thirty-Two

When I got home, I decided to try to catch Brighten on the shortwave. I wanted to tell her about meeting my dad, and Jean and me, how our relationship was getting more serious. With all that had been going on I hadn't talked to her in a while. That made me nervous. Nothing good seemed to happen in Redemption these days.

A little while ago, Mom had managed to call me collect from the public library in Stewart's Landing. She told me that the Bishop and others were taking on younger and younger wives. Among women of childbearing age, the birth rate was astonishing, and mothers had less and less time to give their kids the love and attention they needed.

I set my coffee cup down on the desk in the radio room and brought the shortwave to life. Brighten was at work and easy to find. We switched to a more private channel.

"Daisy, I'm so glad you called. We have to talk." A new desperation had crept into Brighten's voice.

"What happened?"

I heard a long, slow exhale. "I was feeling lousy again, not like morning sickness—different. I snuck over to your mom's and talked to her."

"What'd she think?"

"She figured that I might have a UTI, and said I needed to see a real doctor in town, not the one who gives the Bishop the sedatives for all the mothers.

"I told her that there was no way. That I was watched way too closely. So we came up with an idea. I gave her a sample of my urine and she took it to the doctor, saying it was hers. She got a prescription and passed it to me."

"Great idea. I hope you're okay?"

"I am now, thanks to the pills. The problem is, I got caught. I threw away the prescription bottle, but I didn't know that they search my garbage."

"Oh no!"

"I've been assigned a punishment."

"I'm scared to ask."

"My faith is not pure, according to the Bishop. After the baby is born, the other sister-wives will take care of it for four months, and I will be sent away for a period of reflection and spiritual growth at one of the isolation trailers in the woods. I won't get to see my baby till I get out, and by then it won't even know me." Brighten began to cry softly.

"I can't believe the Bishop could be so cruel. That's not good for the baby. He's sick," I said.

Brighten spoke in a thick, husky voice. "It's not just me. Others are feeling it too. He's got scapegoats. He kicked two families out of their homes because they refused the special levy for the new school. They'd given so much already they couldn't put food on the table, and now they have no place to live."

"Brighten, I—"

She interrupted me with a fierce whisper. "Gotta go, Daisy."

The radio channel went silent. I dropped my head down onto the desk and closed my eyes. My poor father. Those poor families. Poor Brighten. After all this time, the Bishop was still destroying lives and livelihoods to enrich himself and no one was doing a thing about it. I had to do something to get Brighten out and soon. The legal route was taking too long, and she might have the baby before the fall love-in. There had to be something else I could do to stop her suffering.

Chapter Thirty-Three

It only took twenty minutes to cross the lake on the ferry. When it let me off at Peachland's main dock, I compulsively smoothed the skirt of my paisley-print A-line dress and adjusted my sunglasses with their round granny frames. Scanning the parking lot, I looked for the older model black Volvo that the judge's wife, Mrs. Florence Adams, said she'd be driving.

She had been warm and easygoing when I called for the appointment with her husband, generously offering to pick me up at the ferry. "Just look for an old Volvo and the even older grey-haired battle-axe driving it," she'd joked.

A tall woman in a large sun hat waved to me as she stood by the open door of her car. I made a beeline for her. She gripped my hand warmly and we were off. It was no more than a ten-minute drive through the small village to the beach on the far side of town.

I had expected that a retired judge would live in style in some ultra-cool beach house, but as we pulled up beside a small, weathered cottage, Mrs. Adams explained, "This is where I grew up. My father built it himself after he came back from the first war. We love it and we haven't changed a thing—other than taking out the outhouse and installing an indoor bathroom, that is," she said, laughing.

Once inside, I could see why they loved it, with its large front windows that looked directly out over the lake. The living room was cool and inviting in summer, but I guessed it would be a sanctuary on a cold winter's day with its huge river-rock fireplace and wooden walls and ceilings that reflected a warm, cozy light. Seated in a well-padded leather recliner, beside a large coffee table covered in family photos, retired Chief Justice Adams waited for me.

I guessed him to be in his early eighties, a big man with a pale round face, puffy cheeks, and a large prominent nose. I doubted he had ever been handsome, even in his youth, but there was something about his bright, intense eyes. I saw energy and intelligence and maybe just a little mischief in them.

"Please excuse me if I don't get up," he said in a deep, throaty voice. "I'm afraid these old pins of mine have never worked quite right since my childhood bout with polio." I noticed the crutches beside his chair and urged him to stay seated. I perched on a small wooden chair with rose-coloured embroidered pillows, next to him.

"I'll make tea," Mrs. Adams said, and disappeared behind a swinging door.

I had expected to be tied up in knots meeting the judge; after all, he was legal royalty and an outsider of the worst kind, according to Bishop Thorsen. But as he sat surrounded by pictures of his loved ones, his smiling face had a kind and thoughtful expression and I relaxed. I glanced at the photographs with envy. It struck me that he was the sort of grandfather I wished I could claim.

He made me think about my father and my eyes threatened to fill with tears.

"Let me start by saying how sorry I am that you've had to endure so many awful things in your young life, Daisy. Florence has taken a great interest in your case ever since I first heard about it from Pierre Dupont, and she has found some articles and a few books written on the subject for me to read. I agree with you that some of the practises of polygamous communities are truly horrendous. Now we just need to convince the attorney general of that."

I hadn't prepared myself for kindness and compassion from someone like him. I thought he'd see me as a curiosity, a strange bird who brought an interesting legal question along with her weird religious background. It made me feel bold. I felt I would be heard.

"Judge Adams, I can't thank you enough for agreeing to give me some legal advice. I've tried to figure it out myself by reading articles and things, but I just don't know enough about law."

He held up a hand and I stopped speaking. "Just to clarify, once I became a judge, I ceased to be a lawyer. I can't give legal advice. But never fear, I've set you up with a young woman lawyer I know who'll help you pro bono—no charge. You'll like her. She's smart and she'll be sensitive to the difficult issues you'll discuss with her."

I didn't like the idea of telling strangers about Redemption, but I swallowed my discomfort. I'd do anything for my mom and Brighten. "Thank you so much."

"Happy to help. This is going to be a very interesting case for me. Let's start with your questions. You must have some?"

"Yes, thank you. For a long time, I've been trying to understand why both Canada and the U.S. outlawed polygamy in 1890, then didn't do much to stop it."

"Good point. I can't speak to the U.S. government's lack of action, but the situation became more complex in Canada when Parliament approved the Canadian Bill of Rights in 1960," the judge said.

"Yes, I read a bit about that."

"The Bill of Rights ensures that all people, no matter who, have the right to freedom of religion. It's a cornerstone of our democracy."

"But how can the government make a law forbidding polygamy on one hand and on the other, guarantee freedom of religion? Don't they contradict each other when polygamy is part of a religion?"

"Excellent question and it gets even more complicated. The Bill of Rights also guarantees the right of the individual to life, liberty, security of person, and enjoyment of property. Which right has the greater need of protection, the right to freedom of religion or the rights of the individual? How can the government guarantee both rights when they can conflict?"

"You've got me there."

"That's the really intriguing legal question before us. I called John McPhee, the AG, and had a chat with him about it."

I sat up straight in my chair. "You talked to the attorney general about this?"

He laughed. "I've known John since he was in diapers. His father and I were in the same class at law school, and we've been friends ever since. I pushed John to lay charges against Bishop Thorsen but he's hesitant. He'd considered it before and decided against it. I told him that I think the path forward is to establish harm."

Mrs. Adams came in with a tea tray and I jumped up to help her. We set it on the corner of the large coffee table, and she poured a cup for each of us and pushed the cream and sugar in my direction. "Has Frank got to the part about establishing harm yet?" She looked eager, excited about the discussion.

"Hold your horses, Florence dear," the judge said, "just getting to that."

She winked at me. "This is the good part."

Judge Adams slurped his tea and carried on. "I'm convinced that the way to establish that the right of the individual outranks the right to freedom of religion, in this case, is to consider harms. From what I understand there are many harms that the women and children in these communities can and do suffer."

I felt my pulse pick up, my optimism building. I nodded vigorously. "The child brides have no choice whom they marry, the children are neglected, there's no proper schooling, or access to medical care. The list goes on and on. I can write it all up for you if you like."

Mrs. Adams exhaled with a sigh as she set her teacup down heavily. She looked at me with sympathy. "There's a catch, dear. John tells me that you can't just write out a list. You must swear an affidavit in front of the lawyer. And you can only swear to things that you have personally experienced, otherwise it's hearsay and it doesn't count, right, Frank?"

"Florence is correct. For us to get the AG to take all this seriously, we need to clearly establish harm without hearsay."

"I can swear a statement. Before I escaped, I was married at fifteen to a man forty years my senior, and my education was a complete sham. You can ask Miss Braid at the Nkwala library. Would that be enough?"

"That would be good, but, we'll need others as well. Can you convince some of the other women in Redemption to give statements about their lives? It's the key to moving this forward."

My optimism vanished. Why did I have to hit roadblocks at every turn? How could I possibly convince the women to testify and sign an affidavit before the lawyer? Even if I could somehow convince them, the logistics of collecting their testimonies blew my mind.

Justice and Mrs. Adams looked at me expectantly. "I can set up a phone call with my mother. It's not easy but we've done it before. I could see if she'd talk to some of the women, try to convince them."

"I would love to get involved and help any way I can," said Mrs. Adams. "I'm a big advocate for the rights of women."

I told her about the love-in, and she immediately offered to be an organizer.

I accepted gratefully. "The love-in will give the people of Redemption an opportunity to see for themselves that not all outsiders are godless devil worshipers, and that life here can be full of love and peace."

But even as I described my plan, I realised that the love-in would be a one-time event, with limited effect. Some of the disaffected might take advantage of the opportunity and leave Redemption, but others would be too afraid. Then things would return to the status quo, with Bishop Thorsen making all the decisions. I needed the government to step up and enforce the law. To do that I needed public opinion on my side, and that required testimonials about the harms that girls and women suffered that would stand up in court.

The Adamses nodded their heads encouragingly, but I worried the chance of success was dismal. My mom was formidable, but she was also an outcast, a nonperson. She was the one that the other women told their troubles to, but she was not a leader. She had no power, and they wouldn't follow her. The whole idea was doomed from the start.

I put on my Daisy-face: fake, plastered smile; my eyes wide and unblinking. It was the face I'd used for years to cover my feelings, my hurts. As we said goodbye, the Adamses couldn't have known how I felt inside; that my hope was crumbling, that I felt the creeping sense of the futility in it all. Despite my best efforts, I was looking failure right in the eye.

Chapter Thirty-Four

After my shift the next day, I had a quick chat with Brighten and finally told her about my dad. She was astonished to hear what the Bishop had done to him and cried with me. I locked up the radio room, had a short visit with Dad, and then went to find Saffron and hand over the keys. I found her sprawled on the grass by the giant willow. She flipped up the brim of the oversized sun hat so she could see.

"There you are, looking sad like you always do after you talk to your friend. Come on. It's a phantasmagoric day and you should be groovin' on a sunny afternoon, like the song says. Turn that frown upside down, Daisy my friend. I have some fun in store for us."

I couldn't help but smile. Saffron always managed to make me feel better. "What kind of trouble are you going to get us into now?"

"Not trouble exactly. We're going to a sit-in."

"What's a sit-in?"

"I keep forgetting you grew up in a cave. A sit-in is a happening." Saffron was chewing a large wad of bubble gum and paused to blow a perfect pink bubble.

"Okay, what do we do at a happening?"

Saffron let out an exasperated sigh. "Come with me and learn at the feet of the master. Jean has lent me his van and we are driving to Vancouver to hear the leader of the yippie movement, Jerry Rubin, speak at the Faculty Club at UBC. I'm going to write it up for my newspaper and you are coming along as my photographer. It'll be a blast."

"Jean's not coming?" I tried not to sound too disappointed.

"He's worried that the forest fire might not be completely snuffed, so it's a girls' weekend."

◌

As we walked through a dense grove of mammoth evergreen trees, we heard music before we even saw the Faculty Club. It was a throbbing, pounding bass beat that we felt in our teeth and bones. The Beatles' "Revolution" screamed at us from outdoor hi-fi speakers.

The building was spectacular, an elegant modern structure of glass and wood. The nearby parking lot was jammed with vehicles. We found a path through, inching past several vans, old beat-up cars, and a Silver Shadow Rolls-Royce painted bright yellow.

A long-haired man dressed in crushed-velvet bell-bottom pants and an unbuttoned, flowing white shirt sashayed by. "Cigars, cigarettes, weed, hash, LSD?" He stopped in front of us and held up two fingers in the sign of a V. "Peace, love, dope," he said.

Saffron and I shook our heads, and I looked around for cops and security guards. I didn't see any, none that were obvious, anyway. We followed the music and came to a clearing where hundreds of students were gathered, most sitting cross-legged on the ground or on concrete ledges. A few were wearing rubber Richard Nixon masks, while one shirtless guy had *Fuck the Man* painted across his bare back. The mood was an odd mix of defiance and humour.

A young woman stood in the centre of the circle. In one hand she held a mic, in the other she clutched a little girl on her hip who looked just like her. People near her held up signs saying ZARA FOR MAYOR.

"And if I'm elected, I promise to repeal the law of gravity. That way, everyone can get high."

The crowd cheered and roared with laughter. I guessed that half the audience was already stoned. I closely followed Saffron as she worked her way to the front, just as Jerry Rubin was introduced.

He took the mic from Zara, pumped his fist in the air, and shouted, "Liberate! Liberate now!" Curly dark hair covered his head and most of his face, and it was held in place by a tie-dyed bandanna looped around his forehead. He wore a patterned shirt with flowing sleeves and a cape was tied around his shoulders. When I looked closer, I could see a white *X* painted on one cheek and a lightning bolt on the other.

"My father worked all year at a job he hated, just for his two weeks of vacation every summer. Fuck that, man, fuck that." The crowd cheered. "This is a revolution, man, and TV is the link. Get yourselves on the nightly news, man, and that will spread the word. Don't ask me what to do, you know what to do. We are all leaders."

People began to stand, clapping and cheering. I took Saffron's 35-millimetre camera from around my neck, focused it, and heard the sharp click as I snapped some shots.

More fist-pumping. "Don't trust anyone over thirty," Jerry said. "Take the power. Take control. Liberate something!"

He was a showman, charismatic and somehow very cool. I knew from experience that these kinds of people could be forces of good as well as evil. I wasn't sure which he was.

The door to the Faculty Club was suddenly flung open and the crowd surged forward, taking Saffron and me with it. I entered through large double wood-and-glass doors, and strolled into a sitting room. People flopped onto couches and chairs while someone found the liquor cabinet and began liberating its contents.

Someone else set up a stack of records for automatic play on the hi-fi, and the first one dropped onto the turntable. It was a Buffalo Springfield song: "For What It's Worth." I had heard it on rotation on all the rock stations. I found its dark, brooding lyrics oppressive.

The room was getting uncomfortably crowded and I began to feel claustrophobic, a rising panic taking hold. Fighting a human tide, I squeezed out the door of the sitting room and into the hall. I spotted a quiet library next door, and I pushed my way through the throng towards it.

A group of young people was gathered around a TV, watching a horrific scene play out on the news. Protesters were being beaten on the head by police with billy clubs, and then dragged to waiting police vans by their blood-soaked hair.

"What's happening?"

The man standing next to me turned his head and looked at me with a cold, dark stare.

"You don't know? Wake up and smell the coffee, little girl. You need to tune in and be part of the solution, or you're part of the problem."

A large woman looked down on me with kinder eyes. "It's an antiwar demonstration. The pigs are everywhere, beating up the yippies. It's like Jerry said, you have to fight for what you want. It's the only way to change the system."

I wanted to leave, but I was rooted to the spot, watching the gruesome violence.

When had the hippies become angry and turned into yippies? How had it all become so grim? The news coverage flipped to scenes of the Vietnam War, and I realised that I was staring at the answer.

The government wasn't listening to the cries of injustice and demands for change from their own people. Their answer was to beat back the protestors and keep everything the way it was— just like in Redemption. Maybe peace and love weren't enough to bring the change I wanted. Maybe change required something a whole lot darker.

On the drive home, it finally became clear to me what I had to do.

I was afraid and didn't want to do it—it was the *last* thing I wanted to do—but I had no choice. It wasn't about me anymore. It was about Brighten, and my mom and dad. I told Saffron my intention, and she was furious at first, but the more I explained, the more she listened. After an hour of argument, we started making plans.

Chapter Thirty-Five

I lay awake all night, tossing and turning, thinking and worrying about what I was about to do. I had to tell Jean, of course—not that anything he could say would change my mind—but out of respect for him and our relationship.

I was up at the crack of dawn, knowing that I had to catch him before he went off into the vineyard to work for the day. I found a wicker picnic basket on an upper shelf in the kitchen of the café, lined it with a cloth napkin, and filled it with fresh-baked cinnamon buns. Next, I brewed coffee and filled an old thermos, then I loaded up Myrtle and set off.

Out on the narrow logging road, I drove fast but paid extra attention, watching for crews that were still coming and going to the fire site for mop-up.

Bijou streaked off the porch to see who had invaded his territory. When he caught a whiff of my scent through the open window, he began to bark ecstatically. I put the parking brake on and jumped out of the car. "Hello, boy, good to see you too. If your master was trying to sleep late, he's going to be up now, that's for sure."

Bijou danced circles beside me as I made my way up onto the porch. I was about to try the door when Jean came flying out of the cottage and we almost collided.

"Good morning. Fancy some breakfast?" I held up the picnic basket.

I'd clearly woken him. He was unshaven, his sun-bleached hair tousled. It looked like he'd just pulled on an old T-shirt and rumpled shorts. "Guess I should have called first. I figured you farmer types were usually up early to catch the coolest part of the day."

"No problem. What's up?" He crossed his arms over his chest and stood there, looking expectant, not offering me a seat on the porch.

"We need to talk." I held up the basket again and pulled back the cover cloth. The caramelized sugar aroma of warm cinnamon buns and fresh coffee wafted up. I didn't tell him that I hoped the food would help to lessen the blow of what I had to say. I knew he wasn't going to take it well.

Jean seemed confused, scratched his head thoughtfully for a moment, but said nothing.

"How about we sit on the porch and have breakfast while we talk?" I suggested.

"Yes, bien sûr, sit." Jean made an expansive wave towards the outdoor table and chairs. I laid out the buns on the small plates I had brought and poured the coffee into mugs.

"Black, right?"

"*Oui*, thank you." Jean seemed to wake up and focus with his first few sips of coffee. We sat silently for a while, savouring our brew.

"Jean," I began, "I've made an important decision. I need to do something bold, drastic even, if I'm ever going to get Brighten out of Redemption."

His eyes narrowed, a slight frown tugging at the corners of his mouth. He seemed edgy, nervous, shifting in his chair uncomfortably.

I startled at the sound of a kitchen cupboard door slamming

shut. My eyes darted in the direction of the house and back to Jean. His faced darkened, his eyes not meeting mine.

"Someone's here?"

"An old friend dropped by for a visit yesterday."

"Do I know him?" We both looked at the front door as it swung open. A woman emerged, wrapped in nothing but a short terry robe. I knew the jet-black hair and unusual green eyes immediately. Marilyn.

"I thought I asked you to wait inside," Jean said through gritted teeth.

"I know," she said, "but when I realised it was our old friend Daisy, I just had to come and say hello." Marilyn wore no makeup, and her hair was dishevelled, but she still managed to look gorgeous. She turned to me, smiling. "You've grown up. Not the little string bean anymore."

"I—I thought you were going to San Francisco," I stammered.

She sighed heavily. "So did I, but those pigs at the border wouldn't let me in. Some crap about a previous drug charge—so then Saffron told me how well Jean was doing with his vineyard, and I decided to see for myself. And the wine's great, don't you think? I may have had a bit too much of it last night, though." She laughed and massaged her forehead.

"Yeah, it's great." I got to my feet. "I should definitely have called first. Didn't mean to barge in. I'd better get back anyway. My radio shift starts soon." With a trembling hand, I tossed my half-drunk coffee onto the ground near the deck and began to pack up the picnic.

"Oh, yum, cinnamon buns," Marilyn said. "Let me grab one before you go." She dug into the basket and pulled out a sticky bun.

"You make these? I remember you were a good cook." She licked her fingers.

I turned to Jean. "You done with your coffee?"

"I'll finish it while I walk you to your car."

I repacked the basket quickly, dumping the plates and my mug on top of the buns. "I don't need an escort. Just drop your mug off at the Apple Dumpling next time you're in town."

"I *want* to walk you to the car," Jean said firmly and stood up, taking the basket and carrying it for me. Once we were out of earshot, Jean said, "This isn't what you think. I didn't invite her, she just showed up."

I stopped walking and pulled the basket out of Jean's hand. "And you didn't send her away, did you? Look, Jean, you don't owe me any explanation. You're free to do whatever you want with your life. And so am I."

"What's that supposed to mean?"

I rounded on him and looked him hard in the eye. "I'm leaving, Jean. I'm going to put on an ankle-length dress, pin my hair back into the old style, and go back to Redemption."

He looked as if he'd been slapped. "What? Wait!"

I didn't stop to hear what he had to say. I just got in the car and drove off without another word.

PART FOUR

Redemption

October 1969

Chapter Thirty-Six

Ihad a moment of disconnection, as if I had somehow skipped back in time. I stood at the side of the road and watched Saffron and Myrtle disappear into the distance. A wooden sign—PRIVATE PROPERTY, KEEP OUT—was stuck lopsided into the dirt beside me.

Jean had offered to drive me, but I'd said no. I'd gotten over the whole Marilyn melodrama when he explained how she had arrived late at night after paying someone to drop her at his place. She was tired, hungry, and broke. She stayed the night, but he'd slept on the couch. He drove her to the ferry after she finished my cinnamon bun.

The new source of friction between us was my plan to return to Redemption. Jean was even angrier than Saffron had been when he heard the details. Now we were barely speaking, which added to my general feeling of doom and gloom, and I hadn't bargained for the intense emotion I would feel as I set foot here—a sense that I would never escape, and the outside world would forget about me.

In the last week, the summer in Nkwala had settled into a dreary inertia. Everything seemed old and faded, the grasses scorched brown, the drooping trees weary of their burden.

Here in Redemption, it was the same.

But I saw it now through mature eyes. Some of the larger houses looked like they were in the middle of renovations to expand. None of the modest homes were putting on additions. The disparity between the wealth of the priesthood and the rest of the men was conspicuous. Those closest to the Bishop—those who pledged unquestioning obedience and loyalty, the deserving—were rewarded with huge houses and many young wives to fill them.

Identically dressed boys in long-sleeved shirts and black pants with suspenders drifted out from houses and playgrounds, watching me. They circled menacingly, like watchdogs nipping at my heels.

"Hey, lady, get out of here," one of the bolder ones yelled. "Can't you read?" A pebble hit me in the knee, and I turned in time to see a small boy hide his giggle in cupped hands and run away.

Dressed as I was in a jacket and jeans, no one recognized me. I did my best to ignore the boys and made a beeline for the Hall of Worship and its adjoining offices. As I approached the scene of my disastrous Placement five years earlier, a flood of unhappy memories threatened to overwhelm me.

Oh, how I longed to see my mother's face.

I forced myself forward.

A sign on the side of the building read, RAY THORSEN AND SONS, LOGGING, MILLING & CONSTRUCTION. I'd seen that sign a million times, but now that I knew the history, I imagined the original name—Shoemaker Forest Products. My heart lodged in my throat as I lifted my shaking hand and knocked softly.

I tried to talk myself down. I wouldn't be here long, I reminded myself. By January, I would be back at the community college in Peachland, taking the introduction to law classes I was looking forward to. And I had a general plan with plenty of strategies and ideas on how to achieve it. I just had to implement it. For instance, I knew that several women and some men were disillusioned and unhappy with the Bishop's leadership. That was my starting-off place. I had to till their seeds of doubt.

My goals were clear. I pulled a piece of paper from my pocket and reread it for the hundredth time. It helped me to focus, but at the same time, I felt a little daunted by all I had to achieve. *Get in and get out quickly,* I reminded myself.

Get Brighten out of Redemption before the baby is born.
Convince my mother to leave with me.
Hold a fall festival love-in. Find a way to prevent the Bishop from banning it.
Talk to the women, face-to-face, and encourage them to tell their stories of harm.

I knocked with more confidence.

The door flew open. Brighten stood before me. Her face shifted as waves of surprise, joy, and concern washed over her. She stepped outside and closed the door firmly behind her. We held each other in a tight, teary hug.

"Daisy! The Bishop told me to expect you, but I couldn't believe it. I thought it was just one of his lies to keep me in line. What's going on? I can't believe it was your idea to come back!"

Brighten had aged ten years in five. Despite her obvious pregnancy, her face was thin and her eyes hooded. Her hair was limp, lackluster. Her skinny arms dropped protectively to her belly, but her shoulders slumped as if she carried a burden.

I spoke in a low voice. "I'll tell you everything when we can talk. I have a plan to help you, and this is part of it."

She gestured to the jam-packed parking lot next to the building.

The sight of all the black pickup trucks made me instantly uneasy. "We can't be seen talking," she said as she reopened the door and pulled me inside the large office.

Her eyes floated to the office across the room. A sign on the closed door was a warning. BISHOP THORSEN.

"Welcome back, Daisy," Brighten said in a loud stiff voice. She gestured towards the washroom door on the opposite side of the room. "Bishop Thorsen has received word from God that you must not mingle with His Chosen people until you have been purified through rebaptism. Everyone has been summoned to witness your rebirth, and all is ready. I will help you dress."

In the washroom, Brighten's eyes grew moist and very round, holding my gaze. She leaned close, her breath hot. "I hope you know what you are doing. This is very dangerous. You're playing with fire."

I took her clammy hands in mine. "You have to trust me that I know what I am doing. The Bishop thinks he's infallible, but he's not. He's made lots of mistakes—and committed outright crimes. That makes him vulnerable, and I'm going to expose him. Death by a thousand cuts."

Brighten gave me a sad, bewildered look. "I'm terrified for you, Daisy. Bishop Thorsen was bad before, but he's much worse now. He pretends to be a kind, thoughtful, fatherly figure, but he's not. He's driven by greed and lust. I can see it. He'll do anything to keep his power and control over us. It was a mistake coming back here, Daisy. If you make the tiniest slipup, you'll be in serious danger."

"I'll be very careful. I promise."

Without another word, Brighten began to help me out of my clothes and into the rebaptism gown. With a shudder, I realised it was my old wedding gown. It was way too tight and too short. I looked ridiculous, but I was to wear it all the same. The Bishop was going to make a spectacle of me.

And I had agreed to all of it.

***

Chapter Thirty-Seven

I caught sight of myself in a large dressing room mirror backstage. I looked like Mini Pearl, a comedienne I'd seen on TV in her down-home country dresses. But I was an adult dressed like a child, squeezed into a dress that was bursting at the seams. I looked silly with my long, thick leggings sticking out from under the calf-length skirt. Years ago, it was ankle-length and, I thought, elegant. I clomped onstage with heavy, thick-soled sandals.

The crowd of several hundred roared with laughter.

The Bishop at centre stage was bathed in soft overhead light as if a star shone down on him from heaven. He had been preaching about the coming apocalypse when the Chosen would be called home by God. I recognized the seven-foot-deep "rebaptism bath-tub" at his side, and grimaced at what I knew was coming, a brief but complete dunking under water during the redemption ceremony.

"We have a stray who has wondered home—a sinner who has lived the worst kind of life. I am sorry to have to tell you this, and I know it will be shocking to our sweet young brides-to-be, but this sinner—Daisy—chose to live on the outside, where she behaved like a harlot. I understand that she had a boyfriend and is no longer a virgin."

The women gasped. The men murmured among themselves in low, disapproving tones.

"She thinks that all she has to do to get into the kingdom of heaven is to say she's sorry. Is that true?" he asked his congregation and cupped a hand behind his ear.

"No!" the congregation thundered.

"Do we want hippies in our midst?" he shouted.

I felt the hairs prickle on the back of my neck.

"No," the crowd roared.

"If we relent and show mercy, should she atone for her sins before she can achieve redemption?"

"Yes," the crowd cheered.

The Bishop raised his hands skyward. I noticed his left hand trembled. "And I say unto you, God has spoken to me and He hath condemned the ways of the outsiders. The so-called hippie generation is an abomination in His eyes. And drugs, free sex, and the devil music rock and roll are but instruments with which they destroy themselves. The world will be purged. There will be a great ascension into heaven. A Rapture. And we will be saved, oh people of Redemption, while all the outsiders will be destroyed."

"Amen," the crowd prayed.

Rapturous faces looked up at the Bishop. Scrubbed, attentive, weary faces, all white. It struck me that this was a religion that excluded others—and made a virtue of it.

Ray Thorsen lowered his hands to calm the crowd. "Many of you men will be called to the highest level of heaven, the Celestial Kingdom, where you will live like gods for all eternity. It is reserved for those of you who have lived the Principle, a plural life with at least three wives. And you ladies out there who have prayed the

hardest and been the most obedient, those of you who are loving sister-wives, you will be pulled into heaven by your spiritual
adviser, your husband. You will sit beside him on a celestial throne,
and together you will be gods and goddesses for all eternity."

Several women stood and clapped, while the Bishop smiled and
gestured to them. "You young girls take note. If you do as you are
told and work hard, you will receive a blessing and marry one of
the priests, just like these saintly mothers here.

"This brings me to the important item of business." The Bishop
paused for effect, taking a drink of water and clearing his throat. The
women took their seats and the Bishop pointed dramatically to me.

"We are here to witness the rebaptism of Daisy Shoemaker and
her reintroduction to our community. Many are surprised to see
her back. I was surprised too, when she called me a few days ago.
And *begged* me to let her come back to Redemption, to the loving
bosom of her family, because she is *terrified* for her immortal soul."
The Bishop was really playing it up now.

"Let that be a lesson to you all. Life on the outside brings only
ruin and regret. And let me tell you, the holy water in the baptism
tub will wash away her sins, but it cannot make her whole again. I
cannot make her whole again. I am your Bishop, at one with God.
I am set apart from all mortals. Only the purest of women can be
my wives. I *recant* the marriage vows I made to her years ago. After
a period of re-education, I will assign Daisy to another worthy
member of the priesthood."

A wave of murmurs swept through the room. Men sat tall, cran-
ing their necks, trying to get a good look at me. Perversely, my too-
short bridal dress that hugged my breasts and stretched across my
hips made me look like some sort of strangely dressed sex worker.

Suddenly I understood the real reason the Bishop had agreed to the terms of my return. He was no longer sexually interested in me. I was not what he preferred, an innocent, timid, fifteen-year-old (or even better, a twelve-year-old). I felt a wave of relief that he was sticking to our agreement, but I shuddered at the thought of the poor girls who would come after me. *Get in and get out quickly,* I reminded myself. I would have to be gone from here before I was "married." I felt emboldened. Things were falling into place.

The Bishop grasped my hand and led me to the tub, the size of a small aboveground pool. He motioned for me to climb a small set of steps with him and then kneel down on a wooden platform.

He said a prayer begging the Lord for a sign that I was redeemed, then told me to slide off the platform into the tub. The water was at room temperature, but I began to shiver uncontrollably. I gripped the plastic edge of the tub to keep from sinking over my head, my dress billowing around me.

"Do you, Daisy, repent your sins and beg for redemption?"

I looked out at the audience. "Y-yes, I do," I stammered softly.

The Bishop rolled up his shirtsleeves and turned to the crowd. "Count with me, people." Kneeling on the platform, he grasped a knot of my hair with his right hand and thrust me under the water. I could hear their chanting even as bubbles raced past my ears.

"One, two, three . . ."

At the count of ten I tried to surface, but the Bishop was powerful. With his one-handed grip, he held me down while I struggled and panicked.

"Eleven, twelve, thirteen . . ."

At the count of fifteen, he released me. I burst from the water, gasping for breath. Gripping the edge of the tub on one hand, I yanked my hair out of my eyes with the other.

"Do you think you have achieved redemption, woman?" the Bishop bellowed in my face.

"Yes," I coughed.

The Bishop turned to the crowd again. "What say you? Remember, suffering is an important prelude to redemption."

"No," came shouts from every corner of the room.

Once again, the Bishop gripped the knot of my hair—I took a big breath—and pushed me hard under the water. I opened my eyes wide as bubbles rose and popped all around me. The muffled, slow counting started again.

"One, two, three . . ."

After ten seconds, I struggled to hold my breath. My puffed cheeks began to ache. The count of fifteen came and went. I fought panic. My mind flashed to a memory of reading an article on the microfiche in the library in Nkwala. Was this how Lavender drowned?

I tried to break free of the water by kicking my feet, but the Bishop pushed me down even harder, using the weight of his entire body.

At the count of eighteen, I was finally freed. Gasping and sputtering, I broke through the surface and tried to tread water, but my foot struck the wall of the fibreglass tub, sending pain shooting up my leg. I threw an arm over the edge of the tub and hung on, panting for air.

My wet garments clung to me obscenely, and my hair was plastered to my face so I could barely see.

"Can you imagine the evil that this woman entertained on the outside? Brother Tobias found her working in a café that serves alcohol. And she was wearing the devil's clothes, tight garments that flaunted her body to tempt innocent men."

The Bishop called to the crowd one more time. "Has she achieved redemption?"

"No!" the crowd roared.

The Bishop turned to me. "And what do you have to say?"

"Y-yes. I—for sure I feel redeemed."

The Bishop held his right arm over his head and looked skyward, beseeching the Lord for direction. After a moment he said, "God has spoken to me. One more time."

The men applauded and hollered.

But the women had grown quiet.

This time, the Bishop dug his hands painfully into my shoulders to thrust me under. It happened so fast I didn't have time to take a big gulp of air first. My lungs screamed and panic gripped me. I struggled, but the pressure on me was too great. Instinct took over.

I dove down, deep into the tub where the Bishop couldn't reach me, swimming sideways to escape his hold entirely. When I surfaced, I was across the width of the tub from him, staring into his red, angry face. If I had been within reach, he would have struck me.

"We are not done," he roared. He stood and turned to the crowd. "In order to be truly redeemed, Daisy must pray nonstop while she undergoes a period of re-education. She will repent from afar in a seclusion trailer set out in the woods for two weeks. She must pray for the Lord to make her worthy—only then will she be welcomed back into our community."

The crowd cheered as the Bishop walked away, leaving me to drag my sodden, exhausted self from the tub.

Chapter Thirty-Eight

I sat sandwiched between Mother Rose and Mother Hyacinth in my wet, itchy clothes as they drove me along the dusty old track that led to one of the isolation trailers. I remembered them both.

When I was young, Mother Rose was mean and never missed an opportunity to remind me that I was the spawn of an apostate. Mother Hyacinth, on the other hand, was always kind. One of Mom's regulars, she secretly visited my mother despite the rules against it.

In the back seat of the car were all the supplies I would need for my two-week period of re-education—two small boxes of food, a change of clothes, and a can of gas for the generator.

My heart had sunk when Bishop Thorsen had pronounced my fate. This was not part of our agreement. How would I be able to work towards my goals if I was locked away in the wilderness by myself for two whole weeks?

Isolation was what Brighten had had to endure too, but hers had lasted for weeks on end and it was followed by forced sex with Brother Earl until she conceived. At least I knew there was an end to mine. Two weeks—I could do it. I would just have to put my head down and get through it.

I tried to look on the bright side. Out here in the country, I could look out the trailer windows and watch birds and wild-life, even enjoy the unseasonably warm autumn weather. It was so much better than what Brighten had suffered, locked in a window-less room with absolutely nothing to do.

I had to squint at first when I caught sight of the small, silver trailer as it glistened in the hot afternoon sun. Set just off the dirt road, in the middle of a grassy field, it looked small and shabby. It rested on deflated tires.

With just a couple of narrow, cracked windows and no shade trees nearby, I guessed it would be hot, so I was relieved to see that there was a screen door. If I left the main door open, I would be able to get some breeze through in the heat of the day. I could have done worse, much worse, knowing Bishop's Thorsen's cruel streak.

We parked and got out. I stretched my neck and shoulders, still sore from the Bishop pressing down hard on me in the tub. Mother Rose handed me the two boxes of supplies from the back seat, while Mother Hyacinth grabbed the gas can and topped up the generator.

I was concerned that two weeks' worth of food weighed so little. The two cartons felt like about twenty pounds. I had a quick look inside the top box: canned beans and peas, and bags of rice, oatmeal, and pasta. Pretty crappy meals. I would be lonely and bored, but at least I wouldn't starve.

Mother Rose interrupted my thoughts. "The generator is on a timer. Six o'clock in the evening—you'll get one hour. That's when you can cook, shower, and flush the toilet, so don't dillydally like you used to. Remember to fill your water jugs then, also. The tap is on an electric pump."

She gave me a queer, smug look, but I saw something else as well. She had a nervous tick in one eye. Odd, I thought. Mother Rose had always been so confident.

Mother Hyacinth came back from filling the generator and stowed the empty gas can in the car. I tried to catch her eye and give her a quick smile, but she kept her head down, refusing to look at me.

"We'll leave you now," Mother Rose said. "We'll be back in two weeks, and in the meantime, we'll pray for you every day." She stepped forward and opened the screen door for me. I struggled, trying to balance the food boxes while opening the heavy metal main door to the trailer. It eventually swung wide, and I stepped into the moldy, airless space. Dropping the boxes on a small plastic table, I turned around just in time to see Mother Rose close the door behind me. Then I heard a dead bolt slide into place.

I did all right for the first two days, but on the third evening, the generator sputtered, then quit.

Chapter Thirty-Nine

I read somewhere that people die of thirst before they die of hunger. I wondered how long that would take. The evening the generator died I had to fight blind panic. I had already learned that the windows were rusted shut and the one window big enough to break and crawl through had a metal grill nailed over it. Catching rainwater was impossible.

Being in the small metal trailer was like being locked in a hot car in the sun with the windows closed. All I could do in the heat of the day was to lie on the bed with my clothes stripped off, sweating.

At night, after the hot autumn sun dropped below the hills in the west, the temperature plummeted, and I was so cold I couldn't sleep. There were no blankets, but I found a tablecloth stashed in one cupboard that I managed to cover myself with. It helped me get some sleep.

I had searched the trailer from top to bottom, looking for anything that I could use to pry the door open and force the lock, but the only "tools" I could find were a plastic fork, knife, and spoon. On the fifth day I managed to use the handle of the single cooking pot to break a piece of glass out of a window. It helped with the heat, but it made the cold nights worse.

To help with my anxiety, I tried to do some gentle, calming exercises that Saffron had taught me. She called them yoga, and had learned them on a trip to Los Angeles a few years ago. The fluid stretches and poses helped me feel less panicked, but they built my thirst.

I rationed what little water I had managed to save before the generator failed. Added to this was the fluid in the cans of beans and peas but, by day six, my thirst was an all-consuming agony. My throat was so dry that swallowing had become slow and painful. My pee had turned to a dark orange, a sure sign of dehydration.

Not wanting to lose any precious fluid from my body, I tried not to cry as I battled despair. One evening I thought I saw a moving light on the dirt road, and I tried to call out despite my hoarse and aching throat, but if anyone was there, they were too far away to hear me.

Once I had eaten all the tinned food, there was nothing left but the rice, pasta, and oatmeal. I had no way of cooking them and trying to chew on them when I had no saliva was impossible. The first time I tried, I ended up tossing the hard, dry spaghetti onto the floor in angry exasperation. I stared off into the setting sun as twilight descended. Dark thoughts crowded my brain.

I was going to die.

God was punishing me.

For lusting after Tobias, for lusting after Jean.

For being disobedient.

On the seventh night my thirst felt like a raging fire inside me, one that I couldn't extinguish. All I could think about was having a long drink of something, anything that was wet and cool.

After several hours of fitful thrashing about in my bed, I dropped into a strange dream-filled sleep, one that I had trouble rousing myself from when I heard a noise followed by the gentle swaying of the trailer on its deflated rubber tires. Either I was hallucinating, or someone or something was moving beside me. I struggled to pull my eyelids open, but the effort seemed too great.

I heard the strike of a match, and the sudden light felt like it was burning my eyeballs as I managed to drag myself from a semiconscious state. Someone was speaking to me; I struggled through my deep fog, trying to hear.

"Daisy, it's me. Try to have a little sip of water. I'm holding up a cup to your lips, take it slow and steady, just a little bit to start or you'll be sick."

Mom?

"Mom? How?" My voice sounded like it belonged to someone else. Someone old and feeble. Mom's face was illuminated from behind in a halo of white light. Was she real or was I hallucinating?

Please, God, make this real.

"Shush. I'll tell you everything in a minute. Just take some small sips for now."

I felt the soothing touch of her hand on my forehead, a gesture I'd known from my earliest days. It was as if an angel were reaching down from heaven, caressing my very soul. In that moment we were so deeply joined I didn't know where she ended and I began.

The warmth of her touch was replaced by a cool, wet cloth on my head. I was floating through water as if I had been gently dropped into an arctic sea filled with ice crystals and magical creatures that swam alongside me, drawing me into the shimmering light that beckoned from above.

God was in the soothing hand of a woman on the brow of a child.

I pursed my lips and sipped. My parched throat reacted with repulsion at first, the liquid causing painful spasms as I swallowed, but soon it felt as though I was drinking the nectar of the gods. It was all I could do to stop myself from wrenching the cup from Mom's hand and drinking great gulps.

Blinking with newfound consciousness, my vison cleared, and I looked at Mom. "How did you know?"

"Mother Hyacinth. She was very worried about you. She often sets up these trailers for seclusion re-education. She said there wasn't the usual amount of gas in the can—not enough for two weeks, anyway. She could tell as soon as she picked it up. When she spoke to the Bishop about it, he told her that it was none of her business and to just do as she was told."

"But how did you find me?"

"She drew me a map and gave me her key to the padlock on the door. You weren't hard to find, once I knew the route—only an hour's hike from my place, but still, I got lost the first time I tried. Maybe you saw my flashlight in the dark? I talked to Hyacinth again, and that's how I found you."

We cried and hugged each other as my strength began to return.

She filled my saucepan with water and left fruit and bologna sand-wiches. Promising to come back every night until I was released, she set off well before dawn so she would be home before anyone was up and around.

The days and nights passed much more easily after that. During Mom's visits I told her about seeing Dad again, about my life in Nkwala, about my struggles to get an education, about Saffron and Jean, but mostly we talked about how the Bishop's corruption was ruining people's lives and it had to stop.

I consoled myself that my seclusion was coming to an end. Who would come to fetch me? The Bishop? Would he come alone, expect-ing me to be dead, having died of thirst? What would he do to me when he found me healthy and well? Revived by a mother's love?

I tried not to dwell on my scary thoughts. Instead, I thought about what I would do to bring down the Bishop and help the people to reject him and leave Redemption. I remembered my one meeting with my dad and what he'd told me about Bishop Thor-sen's takeover of Shoemaker Forest Products. Dad had said that the Bishop had "quietly cut all my employees' wages, but he kept two sets of books, so no one knew."

∞◯

On my last night in the trailer, Mom and I had a heart-to-heart. Sit-ting on my little bed, wrapped in the blankets that Mom had brought from home, we held cups of steaming tea and I told her all my plans.

"A love-in? I'm not sure what you mean by that," she said.

"It's like a festival of peace and love. I want the people of Redemp-tion to see the outside for all the good it has to offer. I want them to choose to leave for the chance of a better life, and I want to sow seeds of distrust about the Bishop so they feel compelled to leave."

Mom got up, opened the door to the trailer, and checked outside for a minute. Convinced that no one was lurking out there, she sat back down, wrapping the blanket around her one more time. "How are you going to manage that?"

"Brighten is my spy on the inside. She's looking for evidence of financial wrongdoing, and I want you to help me organize some of the women to tell their stories. The world needs to know what goes on in here."

Mom took a sip of her tea and was silent for a minute. "Whatever I can do to help, just tell me."

"I need you to do two things for me. Saffron's written an article about the abuse that goes on here. It's in the *Georgia Straight*. It's going to make the whole world sit up and take notice. I need to see it. You could get a copy from the library in Stewart's Landing, and while you're there, use the public pay phone to make a special call for me. You'll have to be careful. No one can know what you're doing. It's the key to everything."

"No problem. Give me all the details and I'll do it tomorrow."

⊱✦✧✦✧✦⊰

Chapter Forty

I was roused by the sound of a pickup truck skidding on gravel and stopping just outside the trailer. I heard the sharp metallic sound of the dead bolt snapping back. The trailer door slowly opened. The silhouette of a tall man standing in the doorway was backlit by the bright sunshine.

"Daisy?"

"Tobias?" Thank God it wasn't the Bishop. I could handle Tobias.

"The Bishop sent me to get you. Are you okay?"

My heart skipped a beat. I was floored by the depths of the Bishop's depravity. He'd told Tobias to come and get me, thinking that Tobias would find me dead. He knew full well that Tobias claimed to love me and that finding me dead would be a terrible blow. Had he planned to inflict pain on Tobias, or was he setting up Tobias to take the blame for my death?

"I'm all right. We can go now." All I wanted to do was to get out of the trailer that had been my prison for two weeks, and stretch and move, but Tobias's large body filled the doorway. He wore an intense look. Like he had something to say.

"Daisy, I'm taking you to Utah with me."

I felt my throat constrict. "What are you talking about?"

"My father's given me permission to bring you south—to meet you."

"Why me?"

"Because I'm going to make you my third wife, my celestial wife. The Bishop has assigned you to me. You are under my priestly direction and care from now on."

Five and a half years ago, nothing on earth would have made me happier. My ambition had been to marry Tobias and give him many children. Now, the idea of consulting a schedule for my slot with my husband made me shudder. I refused to be placed in a position like that, where I was resentful of my sister-wives and consumed with petty jealousies that eroded our sisterhood.

I tried to smile and look pleased. I had to play along. "That's wonderful, Tobias. After all this time we can finally be together, and Rainbow and I will be so happy being sister-wives."

It struck me that the Bishop had agreed to give Tobias everything he'd asked for, thinking his promises didn't matter. I was supposed to be dead. I shuddered at Tobias's words, but I told myself that none of this mattered; I would be leaving Redemption soon. I would never go to Utah or become Tobias's wife.

I tried to push past him, to get out of the trailer, but he took my hand. "I can't wait for you to meet my mother. She's going to love you as much as I do."

I felt my stomach tighten painfully. "You've never mentioned your mother before."

"She's my father's favourite—petite and pretty like you. I owe her so much. Even though she was his twentieth wife, she's had more influence than his first one. She's doing everything she can to promote me over the other sons of the Council of Seven fathers."

"Promote you how?"

"She talks about me all the time—tells everyone that God has spoken to her in a dream. He told her that I was the new Nephi, the next prophet."

For a moment, Tobias looked like the dimpled heartthrob of my girlhood dreams, with his rosy face and eyes wide with excitement—before my dreams turned into nightmares. "I've got big things in my future, Daisy. You'll be the favourite wife of the newest member of the Council of Seven. People will treat you like you're somebody. It's all set. Nothing can stop me now."

Chapter Forty-One

I was surprised to see cars parked along the road to Redemption. There was even a large van with a cone-shaped superstructure on the roof, *Canadian Broadcasting Corporation* blazoned on the side. Beside the sign that told the world to keep out, a crowd of people had gathered. They were packing up gear and heading for the Hall of Worship. I kept myself partly hidden as I quietly followed them.

I was on my way to meet Tobias and bring him his lunch while he was organizing the construction of an addition to the Hall of Worship. We were to have a platonic relationship until our wedding in Utah, so I was happy to live in the relative safety of Tobias's house for now. I had good reason to be very afraid of the Bishop, and living with Tobias offered me protection.

The shocked look on Bishop Thorsen's face when he saw me alive and well after my re-education and seclusion had been priceless. Tobias and I were taking his little toddler, Luke (Rainbow's child), to play on the swings when we saw the Bishop walking across the playground on his way to his office. Tobias had waved a friendly greeting and the Bishop had stopped short, not even trying to cover his astonishment. He had stared at us until he recovered himself, rubbing his head with his hand before turning and walking slowly away.

Inside the huge community hall, I saw the Bishop in the middle of a crowd. I ducked into the cloakroom where I could hear what

LESLIE HOWARD

was said but couldn't be seen. I peeked through the open door and saw microphones and cameras. I felt a shiver of excitement. Reporters! Someone had exposed him!

But to my surprise, the Bishop was laughing. "It's hard work keeping all my ladies happy. It takes me a month to recover from Mother's Day." Some of the reporters repressed smiles, covering their mouths or turning away.

"I don't know where that newspaper woman, what's her name? Saffron something? What kind of name is that? I don't know where she got her story. Didn't call me or any of my ladies for our take on things. Not very professional, if you ask me. So I brought out two of our mothers to talk to you and answer any of your questions. We've got nothing to hide."

I looked around at the small group that the Bishop was putting on display for the benefit of the cameras. Adorable little girls, scrubbed and in their Sunday best, were making colourful crepe-paper flowers on a long art table while the boys were laughing and tussling in a game of Red Rover.

Mother Rose and Mother Rainbow stepped forward. Both were clearly pregnant, and Rainbow had Luke perched on one hip. Looking slightly aloof, they introduced themselves.

"How old were you when you got married?" a reporter with a pad and pencil called out. "And what's it like being a plural wife?"

"I was eighteen," Rose said, "and I love having sister-wives. We have lots of children, so there's plenty to do—cooking, cleaning, and tending kids. Who wouldn't want sister-wives to help with all the work—and to have fun and share things with?"

I watched with disbelief as one of the female reporters nodded her head encouragingly.

284

Rainbow spoke up. "I was young when I married—sixteen—but I was hopelessly in love with my husband, Tobias." At the mention of his father's name, the child on Rainbow's hip turned and looked shyly at the cameras before burying his face in his mother's bosom.

"I look back now and realise I must have hounded our poor Bishop half to death," Rainbow said. "I was so determined to get married that I begged and begged him to let me."

"All lies," I murmured under my breath. "You were fifteen and had no say in your Placement."

Bishop Thorsen chuckled. "She was persistent, that's for sure. I finally had to give in. I figured she wasn't going to take no for an answer. Most of the girls are older when they marry, but I made an exception, and it's worked out pretty well." He tousled the child's hair. "This little fellow already has three brothers." A photographer with a camera stepped forward and took a picture of the toddler hugging his mother. I was close enough to hear the flashbulb's hot sizzle and pop and smell the acrid smoke.

Rainbow patted her belly. "And another on the way. Thankfully I already have one sister-wife, and there'll be another one soon."

Several of the reporters turned to one another, grinning.

What was I seeing? Was this little show all it took for people to forget about Saffron's story? The reporters seemed to think it was all a big joke and that nothing bad was going on. It was like they *wanted* to believe the Bishop, because the truth—that child marriage was child sexual abuse—was too uncomfortable to consider. Did they think that the welfare of these particular women and children wasn't important? Or not of their concern?

"Rainbow's wonderful, don't you think?"

I turned to see Tobias standing beside me.

"She's a good person," I said.

We both gazed at Rainbow as more reporters snapped pictures. "I know I've made her happy, and she's everything a man could want in a wife—loyal, hardworking, obedient," Tobias said. "There's just one thing she's not."

"What's that?"

"You." Tobias turned and looked deep into my eyes.

The reporters began packing up their equipment and the press conference appeared to be winding down. Tobias took his lunch and headed back to work.

Relieved to be free of him, I took a shortcut on a leaf-strewn path across the old playground with its rusty swings and warped aluminum slide. My earlier, catastrophic fear—that no one would come for me, that I would be trapped in my old life forever— haunted me. Collapsing on a swing, I welcomed the silence of the empty playground and a chance to think.

Lost in thought, I startled when someone climbed onto the swing beside me. A freckle-faced girl, perhaps eleven or twelve, hung listlessly from her seat, looking shyly at me. "I've been look- ing for you," she said. "I need to talk to you. I'm Holly, by the way."

"Hi, Holly." I wasn't much in the mood for a chat but said, "What's up?"

"My cousin Hank. He's older than me, twenty. I hate him. He bullies me."

"Yeah—well, there's lots of those types around here. The boys are all taught that girls are snakes, so it's not too surprising. What did he do to you?"

"Used to just call me names like *stupid* and *dumbass*, then he started pushing me around. Last week he punched me in the back. Hurt like heck."

"He sounds like a big jerk. Maybe you just need to avoid him."

"I can't avoid him. The Bishop assigned me to marry Hank next month. He says the apocalypse is coming soon. Righteous men need wives to get into heaven."

I turned and looked at her square on. "How old are you?"

"I'm thirteen, but I'll be fourteen when I marry Hank. I don't want to get married yet." We were silent for a moment while I tried to get my head around what I'd just heard. Holly kicked listlessly at the dirt under the swing.

"You're way too young for marriage."

"I think so too. I know this sounds crazy, but my mom gave me an old violin for my tenth birthday. It was my grandpa's. I was just so in love with it, right from the first. Mother Orchid gave me lessons, and I used to sneak into the woods and practise all the time instead of doing my chores." She looked sideways at me.

"Good for you," I said, giving her an encouraging smile.

"The violin, it's special—worth lots. Hank told me that he's going to make me sell it as soon as we're married, and he'll keep the money."

My face felt hot. "I'm so sorry, Holly. I wish there were something I could do."

"My mom, Mother Hyacinth, told me that you and your mom are going to try to help some of the other ladies with their problems. You have to help me. I'm scared of Hank." Holly began to cry softly. I reached over and put an arm around her. "He told me how babies are made, and he says he can't wait to make me pregnant. I don't want to do what it takes to make a baby, and I don't want a kid yet. I'm too young. I want to work on my music."

I thought for a few minutes. "Would you be willing to tell your story?"

She nodded, wide-eyed.

"Go to the radio hut tomorrow morning, really early, before anyone's up, and Brighten'll help you tell your story over the radio to my friend Saffron. She'll record what you say and then type it up for her newspaper. She won't use your real name. Just our lawyer will know that. No one will know it's you. Does that sound okay?"

"I'd be willing to do anything if it meant I didn't have to marry Hank."

"You can't breathe a word of this to anyone. I'm going to get others to testify as well, but I'm going to carefully choose them. Promise you won't tell?"

She made a cross on her heart with her finger and a zipping motion across her lips.

I smiled. "I'm going to try to help you, Holly. Don't worry." I hurried off to the radio hut with the idea of leaving a note for Brighten, telling her that we needed to talk, but when I opened the door to the hut, Brighten's head popped up from where it had been resting on the desk.

We hugged, my arms reaching around her distended belly, and I then told her everything. She happily agreed to help Holly and any other women who wanted to testify.

"There's one more thing," I said.

She stretched her back, then settled heavily on the backrest of her chair. "Anything, if it gets me one step closer to getting out of here before my baby is born. I'm worried that I've guessed the wrong due date. I just have this feeling that something's changing, that my body is getting ready."

"Okay, hold on. If I can get what I came for, we'll leave with my friends right after the love-in. It's all organized. Just a little bit longer. But first, I need to know about the work you do for the Bishop—how you help Blossom with the bookkeeping."

"It's pretty straightforward. I keep the ledger of accounts payable and accounts receivable. I've been doing it for over two years now. The Bishop is a fanatic about records, he records everything."

"While I was in seclusion, I didn't have much to do but think. I remembered a comment my father made to me, that the Bishop keeps two sets of books, one that shows all his real transactions and one that he shows the government tax auditors."

"I'm not surprised. He thinks that cheating the government is a point of pride. 'Bleeding the beast,' as he calls it."

"Right, and I expect there's a third set of books, one where he keeps the records of his income from *dowries*, or whatever he calls it, for the child brides sent to the Utah church."

Brighten sighed heavily. We both paused for a moment, thinking of the death of my little sister, Tulip, and her mother's heartbreak.

"The point is," I said, breaking the silence, "I have been trying to find a way to go after the Bishop and have him charged with polygamy. It's a really hard thing to do. The government is not taking the situation seriously. And the press, except for Saffron, aren't helping to raise awareness. But charges for tax evasion are always taken seriously. People get prosecuted for that all the time. I've been making things hard when they could be easy. I just need to prove that the Bishop keeps two sets of books."

Chapter Forty-Two

Rainbow woke me a few days later with the "cheery" news that Brighten was in labour. It was all I could do to not shout *No!* at the top of my lungs. The escape was all set, but the love-in wasn't until this weekend, and my plan didn't include a newborn.

Tobias had believed me when I'd told him that I couldn't wait to get married to him, so he wasn't watching my everyday movements closely. The plan was that Brighten and I would sneak off on Sunday and get lost in the festival crowd, then make a run for it with Jean and Saffron's help.

"Can you make do without my help this morning?" I asked Rainbow as she sat bottle-feeding her youngest. "I want to see how Brighten is and find out if I can do anything to help with the birth. I'm worried that the baby might be premature. There could be complications."

"Of course, and don't worry, I've been praying for a special blessing for Brighten. I know that the Lord has heard me. All will be well."

"Thank you, I'll tell her that," I said as I grabbed a piece of toast and hurried to the door.

"Wait—Daisy! The Bishop's away, so Tobias is in charge. He wants you to drop by the office and let Blossom know that Brighten won't be in today. Blossom will just have to muddle through the best she can until Brighten's back."

When I stuck my head in the office, I found Blossom bent over the ledgers with papers scattered all over the desk while simultaneously rocking a cradle with her foot. Two identical crying babies crowded the extra-wide hand-made wooden cot.

"Keep sweet, Sister Blossom," I said.

She looked up at me with tired eyes. All her fire was gone. In its place, exhaustion and overwhelm. Blossom was alone in the office, trying to juggle the phones, the paperwork, and her twins. I told her the news about Brighten. She looked like she might start crying along with her babies, but I couldn't stop and help her. I had to find out how Brighten was. I reached out and touched her hands, promised I'd be back, then turned, picked up my skirts, and ran in the direction of Brother Earl's massive house.

The "deserving" Brother Earl had clearly done well over the years. The freshly painted house was even bigger than I remembered, with a large addition on the north side that featured three gables and picture windows overlooking the Hall of Worship. A truck and two cars were parked in the front beside a rider-mower and several children's bikes.

I entered through the kitchen, a madhouse of heat, noise, and activity as Brother Earl's fifty-six children and eighteen wives finished a breakfast of bacon, eggs, and toast. One of the toddlers began to cry loudly when an older boy stole her toast. I had to sidestep when a furious mother jumped up and slapped the boy hard across the face, sending him howling from the room.

No one noticed me, and I quietly exited the kitchen and rushed upstairs to Brighten's room. Fourth door on the right, she'd told me. I knocked gently and went in.

"Thank the Lord, it's you." Brighten was sitting up in bed, with Robin, the midwife, massaging her back.

A heavyset woman of about fifty, Robin was dressed in a long pastel-pink dress and thick white sandals. She had the outward calm of a woman who had seen many things and helped guide a lot of babies into the world.

"I just heard." I turned to Robin. "Thank you for being here, Mother. How's she doing?"

Robin spoke in the manner of many of the older generation of women in Redemption, a slow, soft, halting voice, with eyes lowered. "Everything seems to be pretty ordinary, which is what you want at a time like this. It's early, though, and it might be a false alarm. Nothing's going to happen for quite a while yet."

I pulled a chair up to the edge of the bed and sat down.

"I have to get a few things that I'll need for the birth. Are you okay to stay with Brighten for a bit?" Robin asked in her quiet way.

"For sure."

Brighten watched Robin leave before she spoke. "I've waited so long for this moment. I can't wait to see my baby, but at the same time, I don't want it to happen yet. I don't want to have complications from an early birth, and I can't bear the thought of being sent away."

I leaned forward and grasped both of Brighten's hands in mine. "We'll make it work. The thing is to act quickly, soon after the baby's born," I said. "Just follow my lead."

We went quiet as Robin returned carrying a basket of clean linen and began folding.

"How long have you been a midwife, Mother Robin?" I had to get Robin talking while I had the opportunity—and steer the conversation in the direction I wanted it to go.

Robin was guarded, slow to answer. "Thirty years."

"That's a long time. You must have seen a lot of births. How many would you guess?"

She seemed reluctant to be drawn into a conversation. "Too many to count."

"There must have been all kinds—of births, I mean. Some easy, some hard?"

"Yup, all kinds."

"I was wondering about the hard ones—some of the new mothers are pretty young, I mean, maybe a bit too young?"

Robin looked up and held my gaze. I thought I saw distrust, but in the next moment the midwife's attitude softened.

She spoke so quietly that I had to strain to hear her. "Yes, that's true. Their bodies aren't mature. There can be complications. Some're really too young to give birth."

"How do you feel about . . . ?" We were interrupted by Brighten, who groaned softly and rubbed her belly.

"You'll be holding your new baby in your arms before you know it," Robin said. She looked taken aback when Brighten began to cry.

I saw my chance. "Do you know what's going to happen after Brighten's baby is born?"

Robin looked away. "There's gossip."

"And what do you think about it?"

"I feel bad for Brighten, but it's not up to me. We do what we're told, as you well know." Robin began to refold the linen she had already folded.

I put my hand on Robin's arm, stopping her. "How can it be right to separate a mother and baby?"

Robin dropped the cloth and sighed heavily. "It isn't. It's the worst thing—bonding, nursing—lots of reasons."

"And babies can have other complications as well, right?"

"They can."

"Like jaundice?"

"Sure—if it gets bad, they have to go into the hospital for a week or so. They put the babies under special lights. We can't do that here. Don't have the facilities." We stopped talking again as we helped Brighten shift her position and recline more comfortably.

Once Brighten was more relaxed, I said, "I think this baby is going to have jaundice and need those special lights."

Robin snorted. "You can't know that before the baby is born."

I looked at her intently, willing her to understand me. "I get that. What I'm saying is, if you tell Brother Earl that the baby has to go to the hospital for life-saving treatment, he'll agree. The babies can go even if mothers can't, right?"

Robin set the linen down and looked directly at me. "I know what you're doing. The mothers are talking. You're trying to stir up trouble for the Bishop, aren't you? Get some of the women to break the covenant—to be disobedient."

I reached out and gently touched Robin's shoulder. "No—please don't misunderstand. I just want to do what's best for Brighten and for her baby. I desperately need your help. It's harmful to separate them, you said so yourself, but Brother Earl won't listen to me if I tell him so."

Robin looked at me with wide eyes, then blinked and looked away. "Over the years, I've tried to take courses to improve my skills, but still, I've lost some mothers. They could have been saved if I'd been allowed to take them to the hospital." Robin paused and rubbed her eyes, wiping away a tear. "I've tried so many times to talk to the Bishop, but he won't hear it—tells me to mind my own business."

"But this is very much your business."

"Yes, it is."

"When babies and mothers need help, maybe it's time we stopped being unquestioningly obedient," I said.

"Maybe it is," Robin said.

Chapter Forty-Three

The midwife assured me that she would send someone to fetch me when Brighten was getting ready to deliver, so I headed back to the office to let Blossom know.

I was about to enter the office building when I was brought up short. A small white car parked just outside the door seemed familiar. I stepped around it to get a better look and I knew at once who was inside the office. I whispered a little prayer of thanks to Mom for making the phone call I'd asked her to. The stars had aligned, and I now had a huge opportunity.

Blossom gave me a weary wave. "How's Brighten?"

"She's making some progress, but it's slow." I looked over at the two men sitting at a table just outside the Bishop's office. Blossom followed my gaze, rolling her eyes.

"Just what I need right now, a surprise audit. Apparently, they received some sort of anonymous complaint from a disgruntled employee at the mill."

I sat down in the chair next to her desk and said quietly, "Blossom, you're looking beat, and your babies need attention. Why don't I watch the phones and you find a place to nurse them in private and change their diapers."

Blossom looked relieved and immediately packed up her twins. "Just tell everyone who calls for the Bishop that he's gone to Cardston and will be back tomorrow." She was out the door in minutes. Neither of the two men working at the nearby table looked up or even seemed to notice the personnel change.

I got up, took a deep breath, and confidently strode across the room. Entering the Bishop's private sanctuary, I closed the door firmly behind me. Brighten had told me which filing cabinet I needed and where the keys were hidden. I had it open in minutes. I went back to the office door and opened it wide.

I knew him immediately by the balding head, baby-blue polyester suit, and wide white leather belt with matching loafers. The other man wore the obligatory grey flannel suit, his dark hair trimmed very short and carefully parted on one side.

"Hello, Matt," I said. "Remember me?"

The two heads shot up in unison and turned to look at me. Matt looked flustered, confused. The other man looked wary.

"I'm sorry?" Matt said. "I'm afraid I'm at a loss."

I gave him my sweetest smile. "I'm Daisy. You gave me a ride when I was a teenage runaway, near here, five years ago, remember?"

Matt's face positively pulsed with red heat. He glanced at his colleague and gave a nervous giggle. The other man's eyebrows shot up, his eyes wide.

"Always ready to help out a stranded young woman."

Matt was sweating now. He pulled a crumpled linen handkerchief from his wide pocket and swiped at his mouth.

I stepped just outside the office door. "Great to see you again. I wonder if you could do me another favour. I need some advice on the tax papers I've been collecting for your audit. Could you step into the Bishop's office with me and take a look at something?"

Both men shifted uneasily, but I hadn't really given Matt an option. In my next breath I could expose him as the opportunistic creep that he was—a man trying to pick up young, lost girls in hopes of sexual favours, while he was supposed to be on the job in a government-issued vehicle. Matt's career was on the line, and he knew it.

"This is a little irregular," Matt said. "Tax auditors aren't really supposed to speak to staff while they're doing an official audit." He glanced at his partner and gave him a reassuring smile. "But depending on what you need, I might be able to help you without breaking any rules."

In the time it took to cross the room and retreat into the Bishop's office, the door firmly shut behind him, Matt gained confidence. "What's your game, little lady? What are you trying to pull?" He was full of righteous indignation.

I was taller than Matt and I stepped closer, looking down on him. "If I remember correctly, your pickup line was something like, 'When I'm home I'm the perfect husband and father, but when I'm away I'm a bad boy.' I was fifteen, Matt, a child in the eyes of the law."

The haughty look slid from Matt's face.

I put one finger to the side of my cheek, pretending to think. "You asked me if I was a bra burner, remember? And, ah, you suggested I should wear a miniskirt to show off my legs."

Matt had the good grace to hang his head and look ashamed. "I really don't want my family or my boss to hear about any of this." His voice was a whisper.

"And they don't need to. It's up to you. I just need you to look at a second set of books and tell me if they are the same as the ones that you are auditing."

Matt blinked in surprise.

⁕⁕⁕⁕⁕⁕

Chapter Forty-Four

I knocked on the door to Brother Earl's private den. Women were seldom admitted, but this was a special occasion.

"Come," said a curt voice. I pushed the door open but hesitated on the threshold.

"What is it?"

"I have happy news, Brother Earl."

He looked up from his desk and squinted at me. "Daisy, is that you? Come in. What's happening?"

"Congratulations, you have a daughter."

"Another girl! Wonderful. A future mother of Zion." He pushed back in his chair and looked thoughtful. "Who's the mother?"

"Brighten."

"Ah, Brighten." He sighed. "She's done well by me. I'll be sorry to see her sent away. It was the other wives; they get so jealous. The favourites get targeted. You'll soon learn about that." He leaned forward and peered at me. "Come on in, let me see you."

I would have been happier to stay by the door, but I obeyed and stepped into the room.

"Over here, let me get a good look at you."

The room was heavily draped and had little natural light. An old oak desk and large brown leather couch dominated. I moved closer to the desk and stood with my eyes cast down demurely as women were taught.

Women must lower their eyes when speaking with a man.

"Don't stare at the floor. Look up."

I forced a shy smile and did as instructed. Brother Earl was like many priesthood men. His salt-and-pepper hair, thinning on top, was parted and brushed back, held in place with a thick gob of Brylcreem. His eyes, chin, and belly all protruded. The cheap suit he wore didn't do his greying complexion any favours. There was nothing that marked him as special, even though he was said to be a future god of the Celestial Kingdom.

He looked me up and down, then his face cut in a Cheshire-cat smile. "You're cute. I like that. Tobias is a fortunate man. I tried to convince the Bishop to assign you to me, but Tobias beat me to it."

I changed the subject. "Your daughter—I need to talk to you about her. It's important."

"Sure, let's give the little one a name. I'm giving all my kids names that start with the same letter of the alphabet. I change the letter every year. It helps me keep track of who's who and how old they are. Let's see, last year was *R*, so this year must be *S*. I don't think we have a Sunny, so I'll name her that."

"Don't you want to ask Brighten what she thinks first?"

"Why would I do that? Mothers don't have a say."

I took a deep breath. "Okay, then, we need to talk about Sunny. She's quite jaundiced."

"That's happened before with some of the others. It clears up. Nothing to worry about. You know, Daisy, if you think you'd like to be one of Brighten's sister-wives, I could still talk to the Bishop. Tobias thinks he's got it all locked up, but the Bishop owes me.

I just bought him a brand-new truck a few months back." Earl's teeth were the colour of weak tea.

I forced myself to be flirty. "I'm so flattered, Brother Earl, but we need to talk about Sunny."

"Humph." Earl puffed out his cheeks in a pout. He looked up sharply. "You on about her again?"

"The jaundice, it's really bad. Robin, the midwife, says she should go to the hospital. They'll have to put her under special lights for a few days. You can check with Robin if you like. I need your permission to take Sunny for the treatment."

"Fine," Earl said as he waved dismissively. "Go deal with it."

I had to work to hide my smile. "Thank you, Brother Earl."

"Keep sweet, Daisy."

I backed out of the room, but just before I closed the door behind me, Brother Earl called me back. "The nurses—they'll expect Sunny's mother and father to bring her in. If you show up, they'll start asking questions about who and where her parents are. We don't want them poking into our business. Brighten and I'll take her in together."

I couldn't think of anything to say to make him see it differently. The success of my plan hinged on Brighten and me taking Sunny to the hospital. "Y-yes, Brother Earl."

Chapter Forty-Five

"What's the suitcase for?" Brother Earl asked as I stowed the bulging, heavy bag in the trunk of the car.

"Diapers mainly, and a few clothes. Mother Robin said

Sunny will probably have to stay in the hospital for a few days."

Earl frowned and shrugged. He climbed into the driver's seat beside Brighten, who was holding Sunny on her lap. I slid quickly into the back seat of the car. Earl turned around and looked at me, his face flushed with irritation. "Where do you think you're going?"

"I thought I'd come along to help Brighten. She can't carry both the baby and the suitcase."

He turned his head and started the car. "You thought that, did you? Well, forget it. Stay behind and do your chores. I'll carry the suitcase." Brighten turned in her seat to look at me, her eyes imploring.

If Earl picked up the bag, he'd know that there was something more than baby clothes and diapers in it.

I made no move to leave the car. "It's just that, you know, the Bishop is trying to avoid attention, criticism of the way we live the Principle, after those stories in the newspaper—and it's just that you'll attract attention if you go in with Brighten."

"What do you mean?"

I squirmed in my seat. "Most married couples are about the same age and you're, ah, thirty years older than Brighten. The hospital staff will wonder. They'll gossip."

"I suppose." He banged the flat of his hand on the steering wheel. "Let's just get going. I've got more important things to do today."

Brighten closed her eyes and mouthed a short prayer before turning in her seat and cuddling her baby.

The drive into town that had seemed so short before was interminable today. We got stuck behind a farm vehicle, an old DDT sprayer, as it lumbered along from one farm to the next. Brother Earl honked impatiently, but the driver, wearing noise-reduction earmuffs, heard nothing.

There was little we could do on the narrow, winding road other than wait it out. Earl leaned forward and switched on the radio. Hank Snow was singing his country heart out and Earl turned up the volume, singing along, mimicking the country twang. I had to fight the urge to roll my eyes.

The song ended and the news came on. I lost interest as the newsreader, a man with clipped nasal tones, droned on about some problem in the Suez Canal. As I watched the endless parade of pine trees pass my window, I felt a shot of adrenaline ripple through me. *My plan is too simple*, I thought. *Someone in the hospital will stop us.*

Brighten turned in her seat and stole a look at me, her face betraying the same worries. I nodded and tried to smile, but my lower lip trembled.

At the edge of town, the farm vehicle finally turned off the road, and Earl rolled to a stop at the first set of traffic lights by the Crazy 8 motel. He reached up to turn off the radio but stopped, his hand frozen in midair. The radio announcer's voice filled the car.

"Long-time Stewart's Landing resident and war hero, Dan Shoemaker, died today on his houseboat, the *Ruthie*. Dan was a well-known and beloved member of the community, but was most remembered for his bravery in the Second World War, when he heroically led a group of fellow prisoners to safety. He is survived by his wife, Ruth, and daughter, Daisy, of Redemption. The Stewart's Landing chapter of the Royal Canadian Legion will be hosting a memorial next Saturday afternoon in the Legion Hall on Front Street, two p.m. All are welcome."

I was stunned. I struggled to keep my composure. I'd known my dad didn't have much time, but I'd hoped to have more visits with him. It was so ironic that my need to return to Redemption had robbed me of my final chance to be with my father. The Bishop had torn my loving family apart right to the bitter end.

Earl looked in the rearview mirror and caught my eye. "I heard about him, your father."

Brighten turned and gave me a warning look.

"The Bishop's big forest products company—it used to belong to your father. Good thing the Bishop got control of it before your dad left. It's what keeps Redemption rolling in the dough—a real moneymaker."

For some reason, this struck Brother Earl as very funny. He guffawed out loud and slapped his knee. I felt a burn at the back of my neck.

We finally pulled up in front of the hospital at a spot marked FOR DROPOFF AND PICKUP ONLY, FIFTEEN MINUTES MAXIMUM. "Don't make me get a parking ticket. Be back here in no later than fifteen minutes," Brother Earl told us.

"Yes, husband," Brighten said as she gathered Sunny up in her arms and struggled with the car door. Brighten's hands were trembling, so I jumped out and held the door open for her. She was perspiring heavily; her face was damp and flushed as she emerged from the car.

"I'll get the suitcase," I called out quickly, working to keep my voice even. I heaved the heavy bag from the trunk, then took Brighten's free arm, guiding her to the main door of the hospital. We walked haltingly up the steps.

Earl leaned out the driver's-side window. "Fifteen minutes. Got that?"

I turned and waved pleasantly at him, then I practically dragged Brighten through the double glass doors of the large white stucco building. Halls went off in three directions from the circular lobby. I frantically searched for the hallway I wanted, until I saw bright light shining from the back of the farthest hall on the right-hand side.

"This must be it," I whispered to Brighten. "Don't stop. Act like you know where you're going." We walked confidently down the corridor, but when we got to the end, the rear exit door I'd been expecting wasn't there. I stopped, confused, looking for a map or directional sign on any of the walls.

"Can I help you?"

I turned and came face-to-face with a white-haired man in a black security guard's uniform.

Chapter Forty-Six

"Yes, thank you. We're going to the back parking lot. I thought it was this way."

The security guard didn't respond. Instead, he bent over and examined Sunny. "Cute little duffer. How old?"

Brighten cleared her throat. "Four days."

The guard straightened up and studied her. "Being sent home already? Seems too soon. They kept my wife in for two whole weeks after she gave birth."

"Really? I guess things have changed since then," I said.

"Follow me," the guard said, and turned abruptly on his heel. Brighten and I exchanged wide-eyed looks as we stumbled after the man, retracing our steps back to the lobby and the main reception desk. I felt my stomach flip as we approached the official-looking woman sitting at the circular desk, but we bypassed her with a sharp right turn and came to a bank of elevators.

The guard pushed the button, and we stood in silence, waiting. He glanced at our clothes. "Looks like you girls are from Redemption. We don't get a lot of you here. I hear the Bishop thinks good old-fashioned home births are best."

Sunny started to fret, and Brighten busied herself with her while I was saved from answering by the arrival of the elevator. Once inside, the guard picked up where he left off. "That Bishop Thorsen, he's a good man—I played golf with him at a charity fundraiser for the hospital last month—a real family-values kind of guy. I like that."

I nodded and smiled.

The guard reached into his back pocket and pulled out his wallet. Opening it he took out a business card and showed it to us. *Ray Thorsen and Sons, Ray Thorsen, President and CEO.* The guard beamed. "Gave me his card, said to call if the hospital had another charity event. Even offered me a job if I wanted to make a move. A real nice guy."

"Where are we going?" I asked when the elevator doors opened, but the guard either didn't hear or ignored the question. We made a left turn, walked down another long hallway, and found ourselves standing next to the rear door of the hospital. I was elated. "Perfect. Thanks a lot. Not sure we would have found it on our own."

The guard chuckled. "Everyone says that. I keep telling the hospital they need more signs." He opened the door for us and looked around the parking lot. "Don't see anyone waiting for you. I'm almost off shift. I'd be happy to drop you at Redemption. I go right by."

"Someone should be here any minute, but thanks."

The guard's walkie-talkie squawked, and he put it to his ear. "Got to go check on something at the ER. After that I'll come right back and make sure you girls have been picked up. I'll call Bishop Thorsen first to let him know. Can't just leave you standing here with a brand-new baby and all."

"Oh, that won't be necessary. Please don't trouble him, he's a busy man. But thanks again for all your help." I smiled at him again and hurried after Brighten. Once outside, I was momentarily blinded by the bright sun and had to squint as I checked the parking lot for Saffron and Myrtle's bright-green paint job. I saw no sign of either of them. I put my hand over my fluttering heart and waited, scanning the parking lot.

And then I saw it. A van I knew well, the one with the psychedelic paint job. It suddenly sprang into life with an engine roar. It took a sharp turn and came to a shuddering stop in front of the hospital's back steps.

Saffron was out of the passenger seat in an instant, running up the steps and drowning me in a bear hug. "Oh my God, Dais, I'm so glad to see you. This whole thing's been like a bad trip. Time to get you home." She let me go and focused on Brighten. "You're Brighten! Daisy's told me so much about you. Come on, hurry. Let's get you and your little bambino into the van. It's time to blow this joint."

Jean jumped down from the driver's seat and grabbed the suitcase I was holding. "I'll take that." I felt a huge relief to see it set safely inside the van. Jean slid the side panel back to let me into the vehicle.

I made no move to get in. "Jean, what are you doing here?"

"Just what it looks like, helping Saffron." He nuzzled my neck. "I've missed you so much. Nothing could keep me away."

I hung back. "I'm not coming with you."

"Mon Dieu! Why not?"

"I have to go back to Redemption to get my mom. It's a long story. It's about my dad. I'll fill you in later. Trust me."

"No! It's way too dangerous for you now that we've grabbed Brighten and her baby. They'll know you set it up!"

"They won't know for a few days, not until it's time for Brighten and Sunny to be discharged from the hospital. Look for my mom and me at the love-in on Sunday. We'll leave for Nkwala with you then."

"I'll be back for sure on Sunday. But I still don't like it." Jean's big arms enveloped me in an embrace. His smell was a comforting mixture of soap and wine yeast. I breathed deeply. I felt the prick of his whiskers as his lips brushed my cheek.

When he pulled back to look at me, Jean's wide blue eyes were full of concern. "Stay safe. I don't know what I'd do if anything happened to you."

I kissed him. "Tell the others what's going on." Before anyone else could protest, I turned and ran back into the hospital.

∽

Brother Earl, his mouth drooping open and his head back, let out a sharp snore and startled awake as I slid into the passenger seat beside him. "Where in God's green earth is Brighten?"

"She has to stay with the baby. Doctor's orders. The nurses don't want to introduce bottle feeding, so Brighten has to nurse her. Just a few days. They'll call you when Sunny and Brighten are ready to go home."

Earl slapped the steering wheel with the flat of his hand. "For crying out loud. None of my other kids ever caused this much trouble." He turned the key, stepped on the clutch, and shifted the car into gear. "We've wasted half the blasted day. It's getting dark already, almost suppertime."

"I'm sorry, Brother Earl."

He flushed. "Fudge. What a day this's turned out to be!"

We drove on in silence until we reached the turnoff into Redemption. I pointed to the path. "Would you mind pulling over and letting me out here?" Brother Earl stopped the car, and I jumped out. "Thank you, Brother Earl," I said as sweetly as I could manage under the circumstances.

Dusk was settling in as I left the path and hurried into Mom's yard. I approached the house and saw the yellow porch light on. *Mom must know about Dad*, I thought. And the Bishop will hear the news soon. What will he do? I wondered. And when will he do it?

※

Chapter Forty-Seven

I threw myself into Mom's outstretched arms, and we hugged and cried together for a long time. When we finally broke apart and sat on the sofa calming ourselves, she said, "I loved your dad and was very happily married to him. I thought I had grieved his loss years ago, but today it feels as fresh as the day we agreed we had to stop seeing each other. I'm so sorry he didn't get to live a good long life." She sighed and shook her head. "He never seemed to get much of a break. I hope he has peace now."

She made tea and we moved to her kitchen table. She reached across the table and squeezed my hand. "While I'm sad for your father, I'm feeling hopeful for us."

I wrapped my hands around my cup of tea, feeling its warm hug. "How so?"

"The blood atonement my father swore on me if I ever left Redemption to live with your dad is over. I'm free now, free to leave with you. My father is old and feeble. I'm not afraid of him anymore, or the Bishop. They have no control over us anymore."

"Brighten and her baby are on their way to Nkwala with Jean," I said. "We don't have to worry that the Bishop might do something to *her* anymore, either. On top of that, I've done something to ensure that the Bishop leaves us alone once and for all."

"What've you done?"

"Wait until it's all in place, then I'll tell you the whole story. I just have one more little detail to iron out."

Mom smiled wearily and dabbed her eyes with a Kleenex. "For the first time in years I feel real hope—hope for the future, hope for both of us. I've started to fantasize about doing things I've always wanted to do. I could have a real job; one I enjoy and that pays me a proper wage. I could travel, go to concerts and theatres. I could practically live at the library."

We both laughed at the image. "I'd love it if you came and lived with me in Nkwala. You could start over and build your own life as you want it. And we've got a fantastic library there. You'll love Miss

Braid." I got up and wrapped my arms around her. "Pack up your things and we'll leave tomorrow with Jean and Saffron."

"I don't have much I want to take from here. I'll be so happy to leave it all behind."

She took a long, slow breath. "Daisy, after you were born, it took me a while before the reality of being a mother really sank in. I clearly remember the day I realised that for the rest of my life, I would be responsible for you, that I'd need to protect you, no matter what. I've had to make some very hard choices, like losing your father. I feel like today is my vindication for all the tough choices I've made."

I kissed her cheek tenderly. "I know that, Mom, and I love you. We'll be out of this awful place soon. I just have one last thing to do, and then we'll be free to go. Lock your door while I'm gone and don't let anyone in. I'll be back before you know it."

❧❧❧❧❧❧

Chapter Forty-Eight

I left Mom and went straight to the Hall of Worship. I figured that the best place to confront the Bishop would be at the rehearsal for next week's communal wedding for the new brides from Cardston. I wanted to avoid a private meeting in his office because I was afraid of him.

He had tried to kill me twice, I was certain. First by baptism, then by re-education in seclusion. He would dismiss the incidents as accidents, but he would never convince me of that. I was about to make him very, very angry and I wanted the protection of others nearby in case he became violent.

When I stepped into the Hall it was a scene right out of my past. The young brides were sitting in a tight circle, talking and giggling while one of them stepped from behind a screen, wearing her wedding dress.

The girl on display was blushing, her damp face growing darker and darker as the others voiced opinions about her chosen colour and style modifications. I felt weary at the sight of it. Nothing had changed in over five years, and nothing ever would unless something drastic was done.

The Bishop was onstage with a group of mothers who were in the process of setting up the bridal arch. He stood in the middle of them, waving one arm and giving directions.

I slowly climbed the steps to the stage, feeling heavy with the knowledge of what I was about to do. I startled him by coming up on him from behind. He turned sharply, looking at me fiercely. The pure hatred on his face stopped me cold.

I lost my nerve. I'd practised my speech many times, but now the words were frozen in my head, and I couldn't seem to unstick them. The setting had unnerved me, thrown me back into my former self. I was little Daisy once again, the runt, everyone's scapegoat.

The Bishop snapped, "What do *you* want?"

I took a deep breath, thought of my mom, and pressed on. "Brighten is gone. She and her baby left hours ago. She's safe where you'll never find her—and there's more. In Brighten's suitcase is a copy of the accounting books you keep on Ray Thorsen and Sons, or should I say, Shoemaker Forest Products, the company you stole from my father. There were two sets of books, right? The ones you showed the government auditors, and the real set."

The skin around the Bishop's eyes grew tight, his jaw hard. "Of course there are two sets. One is a backup for the other in case the original is lost or damaged. You've got nothing on me, Daisy."

I stepped forward. We were toe to toe. "But the two sets of books aren't the same, are they? One set for the auditors shows meagre profits to keep your taxes low. The other shows the real profit figures. After you pay all your workers starvation wages, the company makes huge profits year after year, doesn't it? I've seen both sets of books. The auditor showed me his copy. Tax evasion is a crime. You could go to jail."

The Bishop raised his right hand sharply as if to strike me, but I didn't back away. I gestured to the mothers and brides nearby. "Is the loving and kindly Bishop going to strike a woman in front of all these witnesses?" His hand hovered for a moment, then dropped to his side.

His voice seethed. "All I've ever done is look after you and your mother. I've fed and clothed you for free after your deadbeat dad took off. I even offered to give your children the privilege of my name, and this is how you repay me? What do you want from me?"

"Sunday, at morning church services, I want you to announce to the whole congregation that everyone is free to attend a love-in that afternoon. In fact, I want you to encourage it. You will say that it is a celebration of the kind of love and family harmony that Redemption is well known for."

The Bishop laughed. "That's it? That's all you want? Fine. My flock will attend your little love-in, but they're not going to be swayed by a bunch of hippie crap. You think they'll hear your message of promiscuity and drug use and decide to leave Redemption in droves?" He laughed again. "They're afraid for their souls, Daisy.

They're afraid of eternal damnation. They aren't going to leave here, ever."

He paused for a moment, pretending to think. "You know, you look like your mother, but you're more like your father. You're stupid. I grabbed his forest products company right out from under him, and he was too dumb to do anything about it. He deserved to lose it."

Something inside me snapped. I could barely control my temper, and when I spoke my voice was flat and low. "My father was a hero and a loving husband and father. Despite your many wives and children, that's something you have never been. The only reason he didn't fight you was because he was protecting Mom and me—but I'm going to fight you now. Dad left me the deed to the company and I'm going to get it back from you—and if you ever bother Mom or me again, I'll go to the police and give them my copy of the company books."

I turned on my heel and marched off the stage with a heady feeling of triumph. I'd stood up to the Bishop, and my plan had worked. The people of Redemption were going to be free to hear the words that I wanted them to hear. If they chose to leave this place, they could find a community on the outside that spoke to their values.

I'd done what I came here to do, but my feeling of elation slowly waned as I began to worry that I'd said too much. My father's words echoed in my brain.

"Let the lawyers go after the Bishop to get the company back. Stay out of it. There's no telling what the Bishop might do. He's dangerous."

Chapter Forty-Nine

Sunday was perfect. It dawned warm and sunny, with golden-leafed poplar trees shimmering against a pale blue sky in the gentle fall breezes. As Mom and I crested the hill that separated Redemption from the Human Be-in (as Saffron had named it), I was thrilled at the sight before me.

The first sounds that stood out in the murmuring crowd were of laughter, not something I often heard in Redemption. I guessed there were at least a thousand people hanging out, their faces stretched to the welcome sun as they lay on blankets on the low grass. Settled in small groups, most of the crowd were grooving to the acoustic folk trio on the small stage that was set against a back-drop of trembling aspens.

Others were taking in the cool vibe of love, peace, and harmony by dancing or swaying to the gentle rhythms. A group of children had formed a line that snaked through the crowd, laughing and dancing as they went. I held my breath in wonder as several mothers from Redemption let their giggling children catch up and join in.

In tents all along the perimeter were arts-and-crafts booths where artisans had set up small workshops and anyone was free to try their hand at things like face painting, pottery-making, and macramé.

Hippies dressed in brightly coloured kaftans, their cheeks coloured with flower petals and with small mirrors pasted to their foreheads, meandered through the crowd. They sought out those from Redemption and handed them long-stemmed carnations.

"It's incredible, don't you think, Mom?"

Mom was wide-eyed and flushed with excitement. "Fabulous. I've never seen anything like it, and it seems like the people from Redemption are blending in. It's just what you wanted, isn't it, dear?"

"Absolutely!" I put my hand over my eyes like a visor and searched the crowd. "Come on, I want to introduce you to my friends. Let's find Saffron and Jean. We can ditch our backpacks in one of their cars." I spotted Saffron talking to a group of the mothers and pulled Mom towards her.

A tight group of women was hanging on Saffron's every word. "Lots of people on the outside have an alternative lifestyle," she was saying. "The point is, you're free to choose how you want to live. Maybe that means one husband. Or no husband at all."

I recognized Blossom among them, listening closely, her face tight and serious. "But how do single mothers get by?" she said.

"It can be tough at first," Saffron answered honestly, "but there're charities that can help until you get a foothold. In Nkwala, where I live, it's pretty easy to get a job, and neighbours help each other with childcare and stuff."

Blossom relaxed a little, nodding her head slowly.

Saffron caught sight of me, and her face opened in joy. She immediately enveloped me in a great bear hug. "Sweet Daisy-flower! You're safe and sound."

She looked over my shoulder and saw my mom standing uncertainly behind me. Spreading her arms wider, she scooped up my mom. "And Daisy-flower's mom! I'm so excited to finally meet you."

The three of us squeezed one another hard, until I broke away, catching my breath. "How are Brighten and Sunny? Are they settled in with Mrs. Graham okay?"

Saffron held up her hands in a calming gesture. "All good. Brighten said she didn't want to do anything but rest and feed her little bambino for a while, and Mrs. Graham's thrilled to have a baby in the house."

I felt the air release from my lungs in one long, slow exhale. Finally, after all this time and all my planning, Brighten and her baby were safe from the Bishop's endless punishments and Brother Earl's demands for sex. I'd never really let go of the idea that what happened to Brighten was my fault, at least partly. Now I could finally put the guilt to rest.

"We need to stash our backpacks in Myrtle," I told her. Saffron I scanned the crowd, looking for a curly blond head tall enough to be above most others. "Have you seen Jean? I want him to meet my mom."

"He was looking for you earlier, now he's helping to set up the pancake griddle. He should be back any minute. I'll tell him where to find you." She handed me the key to Myrtle, and we set off for the makeshift parking lot.

Myrtle was easy to locate, and I was just relocking the trunk after we'd tossed in our stuff when I sensed someone standing close behind me. There was a shadow, large and cool, blocking the sun. I shivered.

"Were you just going to leave me without so much as a word of goodbye?"

I turned to calmly confront him. "Hello, Tobias."

I couldn't quite read the expression on his flushed face. I could see anger and disappointment there, even some hurt, but there was something else that left me uneasy.

Tobias looked me in the eye. "Rainbow and I have welcomed you into our house, treated you like a loved member of our family. She spent hours making a beautiful quilt for your bed, and matching curtains. We were both so excited for you to become my new wife, my celestial wife." He paused for effect.

He was trying to shame me. I knew the tactic.

"My parents had planned a big family dinner to welcome you when we drove to Utah next week." His voice rose with anger. "But now you've made them look like fools for trusting the daughter of an apostate. You know, Daisy—you've got a cruel streak."

I was about to defend myself and launch a counterattack, but there was a kernel of truth to what he had to say. I had taken advantage of him, and I'd lied.

Before I could acknowledge my sins, Mom appeared, coming around from the far side of the car. "Leave her alone, Tobias."

He looked startled. "This doesn't concern you, Mother Ruth. Go back and join the crowd. Daisy will be along soon enough."

Mom stepped around the back of the car to join us, planting her feet wide and placing her fists on her hips. "The days of you, or any man in Redemption, telling me what to do are over, Tobias—and my name is just plain Ruth now. The only person who can call me 'Mother' is Daisy."

Tobias pursed his lips and stroked his chin. He seemed to be thinking, then shrugged his shoulders. "I'll pray for your soul, Mother Ruth."

He turned and spoke directly to me, acting as though my mother was suddenly invisible. "The Bishop sent me to find you. He wants the deed to the sawmill and lumber business."

"I'll bet. I hope he's miserable."

Tobias flushed and cleared his tight throat. "The Bishop isn't worried about himself; he's worried about the jobs of two hundred employees. And it's not just them. All the other businesses that the Bishop owns depend on the wood products that the mill produces, the two-by-fours for construction, roofing shingles, kitchen cabinets, hardwood flooring. If the mill stops, it all stops."

"Well, I guess that's tough news for the Bishop. Why should I care?"

Tobias shook his head. Anger was replaced by pity. "Because all the workers depend on those jobs. You know that the devoted give healthy tithes to the church. People in Redemption don't have savings. If they lose their employment, they usually turn to their community for help. But when the whole community goes down, children go hungry. Is that what you want?"

His comments brought me up short. "I hadn't really thought of that."

"It seems like you haven't thought any of this through very well, Daisy. That's what husbands are for. Look, the Bishop is meeting with his lawyers right now. They're at the sawmill, trying to come up with an interim plan so they can keep things running for now. We need some sort of agreement where the Bishop hands control over to you, if you can produce the deed, without hardship for the workers. Can you at least drive over and hear what he's offering you?"

All I wanted to do was to find Jean and get the hell out of there. I hated Redemption and just wanted to be gone—away from all the awful memories, away from the Bishop's power and control. The thought of delay killed me, but what could I do? I couldn't let the children of Redemption go hungry.

∽◦

I drove with Tobias beside me and Mom in the back. We sat in silence until I glanced sideways at him and spoke up. "Have you never questioned? Never doubted?"

Tobias looked at me. "What do you mean?"

"The blind obedience. Does it sit well with you? The ban on music, art, books. There's no joy in Redemption. The outside isn't perfect, but you can think for yourself, make your own choices. There's joy in everyday life. Don't you ever question if your life in Redemption is a meaningful one?"

"We must be patient and wait for our reward in heaven."

I tried again. "You've had good friends who've been pushed out of the community, boys that have no hope. The outsiders call them 'lost boys.' The Bishop said that they were undeserving. Don't you think that's cruel?"

"It just shows that God saw their undeserving nature and directed the Bishop to force them out—for the good of everyone."

"What about the mothers? Most of them are unhappy. Lots take drugs just to get through their days. The Bishop gets prescriptions for them."

"I don't believe that. Why would they be unhappy? They're achieving the highest calling; they're becoming mothers of Zion. Remember Rainbow talking to the press? She's happy. She told everyone."

"Rainbow's hopelessly in love with you. She may be happy

319

now, but how do you suppose she's going to feel when you bring new and younger wives into the family—women whose beds you choose over hers?"

Tobias's face flushed and he looked up sharply. "What do you know about it? You've never been a sister-wife."

"While I was away, I read a lot—about the Mormon religion and about laws. Polygamy was outlawed in both Canada and the U.S. in 1890. You're breaking the law by having more than one wife. You could be arrested and charged."

Tobias scoffed. "You're letting the government tell you what to do now? You've swapped one master for another. And the new one doesn't care about your eternal soul. You call the police. I'm not holding my breath. If polygamy was outlawed in 1890, it looks like nobody really cares in 1969." He spoke calmly but forcefully. "Polygamy is not against *our* law, Daisy. Ours is the highest law. We answer directly to God."

His last comment left me troubled. I scanned the horizon and was relieved to see the odd-shaped sawmill with its tall, smoldering, cone-shaped chimney not far ahead. I just wanted to get this done and get out of here.

I put my indicator on and turned left into the parking lot. It was empty, except for the Bishop's big black Dodge.

"I thought the mill would be full of people working. Where are the lawyers' cars?"

Tobias looked long and hard at me. I saw a heavy sadness creep into the corners of his eyes. He blinked several times. He spoke quietly. "It's all arranged."

I felt a terrible prickle of fear creep up my insides. I caught my mom's wide, frightened eyes in the rearview mirror.

Putting the car in park, I turned to Tobias. "I'm not comfortable with this, so I'm dropping you off here. Mom and I are going back. If the Bishop has a deal he wants to discuss, his lawyers can call mine."

Tobias made no move to exit the car. He seemed to be in a trance, his voice taking on a faraway tone. "Do you remember the story of Nephi, from the Book of Mormon?"

"What are you talking about? No."

Tobias put his right hand over his heart as he spoke. "God commanded Nephi to kill, but Nephi said, 'In my heart, never at any time have I shed the blood of man, and I would that I might not slay him.' But God said, 'It is better that one man should perish, than a nation should dwindle and perish in unbelief.'"

I swallowed nervously. "What's that got to do with this?"

"Nephi followed God's direction and slayed the nonbeliever, proving he was worthy to be a prophet."

"So?"

Tobias turned and held my gaze. "I've been chosen to be the next prophet, Daisy. I'll replace Bishop Thorsen when he dies and is lifted up to the Celestial Kingdom for all eternity. I am the new Nephi."

Tobias reached into his jacket pocket and pulled out a gun.

Chapter Fifty

Mom and I stumbled into the huge barnlike structure that was the sawmill. The hot air inside was smothering, with sawdust so thick it was hard to breathe. It felt as though someone was holding a cloth tightly over my nose and mouth.

The whole place had an earthy, primeval smell to it. Stacks of fresh-cut two-by-fours were piled everywhere, and huge, harvested trees lay ready for cutting by a series of massive circular saws with ragged teeth that reminded me of dinosaur jaws.

Tobias waved his gun at us and pointed at a low stack of two-by-fours. "Sit over there and wait for the Bishop."

Mom and I did as we were told. "I don't know what you want, but you don't need both of us," I said. "At least let my mother go. Just take one of us."

"No!" Mom shouted. "It should be me. Let Daisy go. This is all just talk, right, Tobias? You can't—"

A door banged open and closed and the hollow echo of the Bishop's cowboy boots filled the vast space. Seconds later, the Bishop walked in.

He clutched papers, waving them at me. Sweeping sawdust off a drafting table, he slapped them down on the rough plywood surface and pulled a pen from his pocket. "Daisy, over here. Sign these papers."

I took a tentative step forward. "What am I signing?"

"You're selling me what used to be known as Shoemaker Forest Products for the grand sum of one dollar. Effective today."

"If I sign, will you let Mom and me go?"

"Of course. What else?"

I wanted to believe him. But I didn't. Not for a second. I pushed myself to walk the few feet to the table. I stood next to the Bishop, and he pointed to where I should sign. I noticed his left hand had a slight palsy and I wondered if it was from the fractured skull I'd given him. He must have hated me for it.

I bent over the table and scribbled my signature beside a large

X. I set the pen down. There was a heavy stillness. Nobody moved for a heartbeat.

Tobias turned to me with unseeing eyes, raising his gaze to a heavenly vision that only he could visualize. "The Lord has called for a blood atonement. It is the way for us to love you, to cleanse you of your sins, to give you a chance for eternal life. The spilled blood on the ground is an offering, the smoking incense of your atonement."

Tobias lowered his gun on me, and I froze, a scream caught in my throat.

I struggled with a surreal feeling that this was not really happening, and that if I were to respond in any way, it would be an overreaction. It was a dream, a very bad one, but one that I would wake from soon. I pinched myself, but the dreadful scene continued to play out.

"This is all your fault, Daisy." Tobias's eyes were full of tears, and he shook his head as if trying to ignore a voice only he could hear. "I thought you loved me, but you were just using me the whole time. I would have married you and I could have protected you from all this."

I loved him once, or thought I did, and I had sought his protection, but then, on the bridge that night of the Placement, I saw what a stifling thing that protection really was.

And it finally registered that Mom and I were in mortal danger.

"It was all just a game to you—pretending you cared for me, saying you wanted to be my celestial wife—but all the while you were planning to go back to your old life and your boyfriend. How could you betray me like that? Humiliate me in front my congregation?"

"Hold on there, sonny," the Bishop interjected.

I hadn't guessed at the depth of Tobias's emotions after all this time. In my mind, after that conversation on the bridge, he had become like all the other priesthood men. Reviled. But to him, upon my return to Redemption, I had become a possibility. A celestial wife who would guarantee his place in the Celestial Kingdom. "Listen, Tobias, I—"

"All I ever wanted," Tobias interrupted me, "was for us to live for time and all eternity, a loving god and goddess, together forever in the highest Celestial Kingdom." Large tears began to slide down Tobias's cheeks.

I felt suspended in time and space. Floating. Closing my eyes, I then slowly reopened then.

"You don't have to do this, Tobias."

"Tobias!" Bishop Thorsen shouted. "Get it done. You've been chomping at the bit to replace me. You claim to be the new Nephi. Prove it!"

Tobias stepped forward and put the gun to my head, holding my gaze. "I loved you from the first time I saw you and I've never stopped. My heart was pure. There has only ever been you."

Seconds seemed like hours. I waited for the crack of the gunshot, the last sound I would ever hear.

Tobias lifted the gun from my temple and raised it high in the air, firing one—two—three. He let his hand fall limply at his side, dropped the gun, then crumpled to the floor, weeping but unhurt.

"Tobias!" I felt like a statue; my feet were bricks, cemented to the spot. In my peripheral vision I caught a movement. The Bishop stepped forward and picked up the gun. With his back to Mom and Tobias, he pointed it directly at me.

"Never send a boy to do a man's job," he said with a cold focus. He glanced back at Tobias and shouted at him, "The only thing you've done today is prove that you aren't the new Nephi. I'll make sure everyone hears about this. You'll never replace me, you idiot."

"Wait," I said. "My friends, they have the real books. If something happens to me, they'll go to the police."

The Bishop shook his head. "Problem with you, girl, is that you think you're smarter than everyone else. The police will be paying your friends a visit very soon. I'm going to show them the paper trail I've set up. It seems that my trusted bookkeeper, Brighten, has been embezzling from me for years. I had no way of knowing it because the official audit didn't uncover it. She recently ran off with the evidence to try to cover her tracks. Brighten will be the one to go to prison, not me."

"Oh, Lord," I whispered. "Not Brighten . . ."

Somewhere nearby a heavy door banged shut, followed by the sound of running steps in the hallway. "Daisy? Daisy? Are you here? Are you okay?"

It was Jean's voice. We all turned our heads to the inside door, expecting Jean to burst in any moment, and that's when it happened. In a flash, Mom hoisted up a two-foot length of two-by-four and hit the Bishop in the back of the head with all her might.

The same spot I had cracked years ago.

His knees buckled and he wavered like a drunk. The hand that held the gun began to shake uncontrollably. The rest happened in a blur. Tobias leapt forward and wrestled the gun from the Bishop. A gunshot ricocheted, echoing in the vast building.

Jean burst in. Together we watched the Bishop collapse to his knees, then fall flat on his face. The back of his head was gone.

Mom looked up at me, her face contorted in rage. She still held the blood-spattered two-by-four. "I damn well swore to protect you when you were a baby, Daisy, and I did just that. I always will."

Tobias dropped the hot, smoking gun. No one moved. "Go," he finally said. "Get out of here and never come back. Nobody will find out. I'll take care of it."

Jean reached for my hand and then my mother's, and slowly guided us to the door. Just before exiting, I dropped Jean's hand and ran back to grab the documents that had signed away my father's business. On the way to the car, I clutched them to my chest.

PART FIVE

Nkwala

September 1971

Chapter Fifty-One

"New Beginnings," I said into the phone. "How can we help?" I nodded as I listened. "That's right. The Cherry Tree Motel, near the ferry dock. There are two rooms booked for you and your children. The manager is expecting you—oh, and you'll find groceries, new clothes, and some toys for the kids in the rooms."

It was a conversation I'd had many times before. "No, it's all free. The society covers everything. Nothing to worry about." I paused. "You're very welcome. Get settled in and I'll be over to check on you later." I listened again. "We're very happy to help. That's what we're here for. Please don't cry."

New Beginnings was the charity I'd set up with the profits from Shoemaker Forest Products. My father's legacy had become mine, my source of funds to support those who chose to leave their past and start over as I had. This was the last and crucial part of my plan, the final piece of the puzzle that would allow the women and children of Redemption to live their lives in peace, love, and freedom.

After all the legal work was done and I was the new owner, I hired my old friend Donald to run the place. He'd worked in the forest industry ever since he ran away from Redemption years ago. After I paid all the workers a living wage, there was still plenty left over for my nonprofit work.

I'd bought a slightly run-down bungalow on the edge of town and converted it to office space. It was just big enough to hold all the volunteers. We took out as many walls as we could to create one big working space. We also had a fully loaded kitchen and two bathrooms.

Florence Adams sat across the large room from me pecking away at her typewriter. It was her job to lobby the authorities to act, to enforce existing laws, and ultimately to end the practise of polygamy in the province. In reality, it was child sexual abuse. We'd made some headway, but it was a constant fight. Governments and police found it easier to take the path of least resistance, to follow rather than to lead.

I watched the office door open and Carol Braid, the librarian, walk in. I motioned for her to sit at Mom's empty desk. I made more reassuring noises into the phone and then gently hung up.

"Another new guest?" she asked, her eyes beaming behind her cat's-eyes glasses. "How many is that now?"

"Orchid makes it fifteen so far and fifty-six children. Not bad for the first year. And it's not just mothers fleeing Redemption; lost boys have contacted us as well, from all over Canada and the U.S. We even had a call from Mexico the other day."

Carol set two coffees and a basket of cinnamon buns from the Apple Dumpling on my desk. "That's wonderful. Everyone's so proud of you, but you work too hard. Let's take a break."

"Talked me into it," I said. I pushed the chair back from my desk and reached for the steaming hot brew.

"When I think about the first day we met, when you came into the library, a scared little waif, I can hardly believe the changes in you," Carol said. "And here you are, the executive director of a nonprofit society, helping people to start their lives over."

"I wouldn't be here without your help. You gave me a chance at a real education and walked me through all the hurdles. I'll never forget that."

The door swung open again and Brighten popped her head in.

"I just wanted to check and see if you need any help today. Oh, cinnamon buns, perfect." She stepped inside, pushing a stroller. I was struck by how much Brighten had become her old self since coming to Nkwala.

Her aura of quiet self-confidence had returned. I hadn't seen her this happy in years, not since our childhood. Little Samantha (Brighten hated the name Sunny and changed it) struggled to be set free from the stroller as she reached for a bun.

"She's always hungry," Brighten said with a laugh, and settled Samantha on her lap in the office visitor's chair to feed her.

"Oh, I almost forgot." Miss Braid leaned across the table and handed me an envelope. "I've been watching the newspapers and magazines that come across my desk for articles that pertain to your former area of study. I found a newspaper clipping that I think you'll be interested in."

I pulled the clipping free, held it up to the light and scanned the headline. It was from the *Vancouver Sun*. "New Prophet Chosen by Polygamous Sect."

We sat in silence as I read and digested the news. Flashbacks of that terrible day in the sawmill still haunted me, but they had grown less frequent. The news in the article helped to bring some closure.

"Tobias has been selected as the new Bishop of Redemption," I said. "Apparently, he's the youngest-ever leader of the church in North America. It says he is to replace Bishop Thorsen, who died of a stroke last year."

The others quietly nodded as they absorbed the information.

I examined the article more closely. "He has five wives now and vows to continue to live the Principle, even though Brother Earl was arrested on polygamy charges. The girls' testimonials of harm were read out in court, and Earl was convicted. He's serving one year of house arrest."

The others groaned and shook their heads.

Brighten cooed at little Samantha. "How long until he's back at it?"

"Don't be discouraged," Florence said. "It's actually a big win for us. It provides a precedent. People can and will be charged and convicted of polygamy."

Murmurs of approval passed through the group.

"Maybe Tobias'll bring some humanity to the role," Brighten said. "He's not like Bishop Thorsen."

I sighed and pushed back in my chair. "Tobias isn't a bad man deep down," I said, "but he is a product of his upbringing. He has no understanding of the outside world—no way of thinking or behaving differently—because living the Principle is all he knows. He has no frame of reference other than what has been drilled into him since the day he was born."

Florence spoke up again. "Yeah, and if everyone told you that you were a saint with a direct line to God, and that you would live forever as a god in the celestial kingdom, you're not going to fight it, right?"

We all had a good laugh.

The day was blustery, and it seemed that everyone was looking for something to do indoors. The little office was already crowded when Mom arrived. She was the society's bookkeeper, a job that she loved. Then Saffron dropped by at lunch with a pizza.

"Daisy-Flower Flower-Power!"

I enjoyed the companionship, but I relished the end of the day when everyone left me alone to finish up my work in peace and quiet. Just as I was closing my files and getting ready to leave, the office door swung open. I squinted, peering into the grey shadows.

I hadn't been expecting anyone. Shifting uneasily in my chair, I saw a lone figure slowly emerge from behind the door.

"Holly!" I exclaimed.

"Hi, Daisy. I hope I didn't startle you. My mom and I are settled into the new house now and I just wanted to come by and thank you for everything."

"Come in," I beckoned. Holly stepped forward. She was dressed in red pedal pushers with a matching sweater draped over her shoulders and held in place with a sweater pin. She clutched a violin case in one hand.

"What's this?" I pointed to the case.

Holly put the case on the floor and opened it, pulling out the instrument. "This was my grandfather's, the one I told you about when I asked you to help me—to save me from having to marry my cousin Hank? Because of you, I still have it."

"I'm so glad, Holly. It's gorgeous."

"I applied to the music school in Kelowna. I got in. I start next month."

"Wonderful!"

Holly looked up at me, her freckled face unfolding into a shy smile. "For my audition, I did a classical arrangement of 'I Want to Hold Your Hand.' Brighten told me it's one of your favourites."

At the mention of the song, I was transported back in time to my fifteen-year-old self, when worries and troubles were unrecognizable shadows in the distance and I struggled to accept the future that others had chosen for me.

"How are you making out? I'm sure it's not easy for you. It's hard to see the way forward at your age," I said.

"I'm okay. Sometimes fitting in is hard, but I'm pretty sure it'll get easier."

"It will. Trust me."

"I do trust you, Daisy," Holly said softly. She gave me an awkward hug, squeezing hard, before returning her violin to its case and then bolting for the door. "Mom's waiting. See you soon," she shouted over her shoulder, and was gone.

I closed the door but didn't latch it. My old fear—that somehow I would be pulled back into my old life, that someone from Redemption would come and drag me back—was gone for good.

Epilogue

"It's not like I'm dreading Jean's big celebration, Mom. It's just that Jean's dad is coming all the way from France. At least he says he's coming. The only thing worse than him coming is him *not* coming. Jean is tied up in knots over it. They haven't seen each other since their big fight years ago, just after his mom died. I don't want a blowup to ruin his big day."

We were taking it easy in Mom's garden after a long day. "He sounds like a bit of a jerk, if you ask me," she said as she swirled her glass of iced tea, listening to the summery sound of ice cubes colliding. "He should be proud of Jean. How can he be so hard on him?"

"Jean thinks he's never gotten over losing his wife. It's complicated—Jean is a lot like his mom. It's misplaced grief, or something."

"Maybe he's met someone new, gotten over it by now."

"No such luck. He's coming solo—that's why I want you to sit next to him at the dinner and talk to him—just for a while. You don't have to stay with him all evening. We want him to try to relax, have a little fun even—otherwise, I'll worry."

"Don't fuss. Leave the miserable old fart to me. I'll keep him in line."

I laughed and gave Mom a hug. "Thanks, I owe you."

"No—no, you don't, dear. Believe me, it's the other way around."

A few days before the big event, Mom had announced that she was going to Kelowna to shop and see a hairdresser. She hadn't cut her waist-length hair in years. "It's time," she'd said.

She had arrived home laden with packages, transformed. Her hair was trimmed into a short, stylish pixie cut, and the new clothes were London mod. Today, for the party, she wore a chartreuse pant-suit with wide bell-bottom pants and a long purple chiffon scarf draped around her neck. She reminded me of Petula Clark.

That evening, I noticed a middle-aged man drive up Jean's driveway and park a rental car. Could this be Jean's father? I wondered. He bore little resemblance to Jean. Dark-haired with a high forehead, receding hairline, and long, aquiline nose, he couldn't be Jean's dad, I thought, until the man looked up and caught my eye. His face split into a wide grin and I knew at once that it was. Their smiles were identical. I smiled shyly as I felt a quiver of anxiety. I knew how much Jean craved his father's approval. Would he be disappointed yet again?

Jean looped his arm through mine and led me over to meet his father.

"*Enchanté*," Philippe said. He startled me by kissing me on both cheeks. "I am so happy to see my son settled down with a nice girl. I wasn't sure it would ever happen. He's been a bit of a rebel."

"I wouldn't say that, Papa," Jean said, flushing. "I just chose a different path, that's all."

Philippe shrugged and gestured expansively with his hands. "Growing grapes and trying to make wine in Canada. I'm not sure what you'd call that, but—"

I interrupted. "You'll try some of Jean's new Merlot at dinner. Jean says he found a way to manipulate the fermentation so the smoke from the big fire didn't taint it. I'm no expert but I love it, and everyone around here thinks it's great too."

"A ringing endorsement," Philippe said dryly. Jean swallowed hard and looked away. Mom was passing by, and I grabbed her, pulling her into the group. "Mom, come meet Jean's father. Philippe, this is my mother, Ruth."

Mom offered her hand. "You've come all the way from France. Imagine that. I hear it's a beautiful place," she said. "I hope to see it myself someday."

Instead of shaking Mom's hand, Philippe raised it to his mouth and brushed her fingers with his lips.

"Oh!" Mom said, flushing and smiling up at Philippe. She leaned close to me and whispered, "He's not what I was expecting."

Philippe's eyes were bright. "Our family's land is in Provence; it's lovely there." Then he paused and looked about. "And this place is beautiful too. Surprisingly, there are similarities—the landscape, the dry heat, even some of the trees and flowers—the arborvitae, for instance. They're everywhere back home."

"Exactly," Jean said. "Similar soil and climate. That's why I can grow grapes here—and make good wine."

Philippe's smile tightened. "We shall see."

At dinner, I felt a mixture of dread and fascination as Philippe finally brought the glass of wine to his lips and took a sip. He rolled the liquid around his tongue and mouth for several seconds before finally swallowing. My stomach tightened. I searched his expression, but he gave nothing away. Instead, he turned and spoke to Mom beside him.

I tried to focus on my meal but kept stealing nervous glances at Philippe. Mom was doing a good job, I decided, a *really* good job. I watched with growing surprise as our parents clinked glasses and laughed loudly at shared jokes. Jean put his arm around my waist and leaned in close. "What's up with my dad and your mom?"

"Nice, isn't it?" I smiled innocently, but worried that Mom needed a break from "babysitting" Jean's father. I headed to the bathroom, but paused as I passed Mom. "Don't think that you're stuck here, Mom. Feel free to mingle," I whispered.

"I'm not going anywhere. Philippe is charming—and so funny, not to mention he's so good-looking for a man his age."

My eyes widened as I patted her arm. "Oh-kay."

As I dropped back into my chair beside Jean, I squeezed his thigh and said, "I checked in on my mom. She says they're getting along like a house on fire."

Jean looked amused, but in the next moment I felt him tense as

Philippe reached over to the wine carafe and poured himself and Mom another glass.

Mom giggled, then picked up a spoon and tapped it on the side of her wineglass.

Philippe rose. "Ladies and gentlemen, I would like to say a few words." It took a moment or two for the laughter and chatter to quiet. "Most of you will not know this, but Jean and I have been at loggerheads over his choice to come here and become a winemaker. It struck me as a harebrained idea, one likely to put him in the poorhouse, as the English say."

There were a few nervous laughs until the silence became deafening. The story of the tension between Jean and his father was well known. All eyes were on them.

Philippe took a white cotton handkerchief from his breast pocket and wiped his eyes. "I would like to say that I was dead wrong about Jean and about this place. Jean has worked diligently and produced a wine that I expect his older brothers would be proud to have grown and produced in France. More than that, his Merlot was good enough to beat out many others and win a silver medal in the New World Wines annual competition."

He raised his glass. "To Jean and to Paradise Wines."

Everyone cheered their agreement, got to their feet, and raised their glasses in a toast.

Saffron set up her portable record player and placed a large box of forty-fives and LPs beside it. She set the volume on maximum as everyone left the table and headed out onto the lawn to dance. Philippe offered me his hand and led me out onto the dance floor. We danced a slow waltz, ignoring others around us who were doing the twist.

"You and Jean must come and spend Christmas with me in France this year. You should meet the family. My treat," he said.

"We would love that; so kind and generous of you," I said, smiling.

"Be sure to bring your mother."

As the evening wore on, I told Jean I would be back for a midnight swim and snuck off, driving the van into town. I parked it in front of the church and climbed the long flights of steps up to the radio room, one last time.

I kept the room dark, turning on just one low-watt desk lamp and opened the window wide to let in the warm, fragrant, late-summer evening air. The moon had left a long shimmering silver reflection on the glossy lake below.

Switching on the radio, I felt the familiar thrill as I watched the dials bob and dance. The frequency strength had been increased recently, and now my show, *Daisy's Disks*, could be heard all over western Canada and the western United States.

I reached into my purse and pulled out the letter, spread it out on the desk, and read the opening paragraph for the hundredth time.

We are very pleased to inform you that we have accepted your application to law school starting September 1972.

I smoothed the letter flat and kept it in front of me the whole time I did my show.

Listeners regularly sent me their song requests by postcard; Jenn and Dan in Spokane, Andy in Medicine Hat, and Annabel in Laguna Beach wrote and told me a little about their lives and their love of music.

Often, when I was on air, I imagined that I was physically travelling the airwaves along with my voice, and that I could reach out and touch my listeners. We were all connecting through the sheer joy of listening to rock-and-roll music.

The hour flew by. "Here's an oldie but a goodie," I said as the clock counted down. "Groove on this, everyone, from way back in 1964. This is for you, Sal in Portland. The Beatles and 'I Want to Hold Your Hand.'" I closed my eyes, not moving. The music swept me away, as if I had stepped through a portal into another dimension.

As the song faded, I clicked on my mic. "This is Daisy from *Daisy's Disks* signing off one last time.

"Peace and love, everyone. Peace and love."

Acknowledgments

The Celestial Wife, my second novel, was my Covid project, written in the isolation of that time without the usual opportunities to gather feedback from friends and writing colleagues, and so I was immensely grateful to Simon & Schuster for agreeing to take it on. In particular, I would like to thank Sarah St. Pierre for having faith in the story and facilitating the acceptance process.

My editor, Adrienne Kerr, was indispensable with her astute editorial suggestions that made the novel a much better read than it would have been. I would like to thank her for her support, dedication, and hard work. I would also like to thank Brittany Lavery for her editorial input.

Thank you to my agent, Andrew Lownie of the Andrew Lownie Literary Agency in London, England.

Several people lent support with the information-gathering and research I did for the novel. I would like to thank the following:

Angela Harrop gave me a firsthand account of weather information and emergency radio operators in remote areas of the country in the 1960s and '70s.

Maureen Devine provided background on the workings of a library in the 1960s, the use of microfilm for research, and the Canadian Library Association's Microfilm Project in 1960–61.

Bob and Colleen Ferguson of Kettle Valley Winery answered my questions on the wine-making industry in the Okanagan Valley and the effect of wildfire smoke on a grape harvest.

My sister, Allison Howard, and her friend Heather Johns offered a firsthand account of the Beatles concert in Vancouver in 1964. (I'm still mad that I didn't get to go.) Their memories of that iconic night allowed me to add the kind of small details that can mean so much.

My son, Tom, told me of his summer picking fruit in the Okanagan, of the hard work and the fun and games.

Please note that all factual errors in the novel are mine and mine alone.

Thank you to my fellow author Roberta Rich for generously passing along a trove of articles regarding the FLDS in North America.

The members of my writing group have provided suggestions and recommended edits over the course of many months, and I would like to thank them for their ongoing support and generosity. They are Felicity Schweitzer, Petra Mach, Francis Fee, and Jessica Chan.

I'd like to thank my family: my husband, Austin; my daughter, Katherine, and son-in-law, Colin; my son, Tom, and daughter-in-law, Kat; and most importantly, the little ones, Ellie, Arthur, and Lily.

And finally, thank you to my chocolate lab, August, who is getting a little long in the tooth but who still lies curled at my feet while I write, keeping me focused and my toes warm.

Author's Note

One of the books that inspired me to become a writer of fiction was Daphne Bramham's *The Secret Lives of Saints: Child Brides and Lost Boys in Canada's Polygamous Mormon Sect*. Daphne is a journalist who wrote a remarkably detailed account of the history and beliefs of the Mormon sect of Bountiful, British Columbia. This sect (the Fundamentalist Church of Jesus Christ of Latter-Day Saints, FLDS) is closely aligned with sister sects in Hildale, Utah; Colorado City, Arizona; and other sects in Texas and Mexico—including those who embraced the notorious leader and self-proclaimed prophet Warren Jeffs (now serving life plus twenty years in prison for the sexual assault of two of his seventy-eight wives—who were twelve and fifteen at the time).

It troubled me that the shocking abuse that these sects perpetrate on women and children in the name of religious freedom could be tolerated in our modern societies. I wondered why there wasn't more hue and cry. Researching the subject, I discovered that much of the material written about the FLDS and similar cults is nonfiction; there were precious few historical fictions.

Human beings are hardwired to remember and connect with stories more than facts. Stories help us to relate to others and develop empathy, so I decided to bring the tales of these victims to life in a novel. After two early drafts that eventually found permanent homes in my desk drawer, I found *Daisy* and my story took flight. To help me bring Daisy to life, I turned to Rachel Jeffs's memoir, *Breaking Free*.

Rachel is the daughter of Warren Jeffs. In her memoir, she tells of suffering sexual abuse by her father at a young age. Her life story helped me to understand the everyday trauma that women suffer in polygamist cults as they struggle for an emotional connection with the husband they share with other women, and the jealousy, infighting, and cruelty that naturally flows from that.

In spite of everything, leaving the sect was horrible for Rachel to contemplate. She knew that her children would never see their father again and that she would be forced to permanently cut ties with a large network of loving relatives and friends only to face the terrifying unknown.

In some ways, *Keep Sweet: Children of Polygamy*, a memoir of the life of Debbie Palmer, had the deepest emotional impact on me. Debbie was raised by sister-wives after her mother died. The story unfolds as a stark demonstration of the depths of emotional abuse that some children suffer in polygamous communities when raised by unhappy and overworked sister-wives who don't love them and are forced to care for them.

Redemption is a fictional place, but it is fashioned from a mix of the real towns of Bountiful, British Columbia; Hildale, Utah; and Colorado City, Arizona. Most of the events that I portray in Redemption are based on real life. The strife between the bishops of the Canadian FLDS and the American branches has happened, as has the illegal cross-border transportation of young brides between communities.

Different FLDS communities structure their beliefs and lives according to their bishop's (or prophet's) self-proclaimed revelations received directly from God. Unlike formal religions, the beliefs and lifestyles are not harmonious but vary from place to place. To the best of my knowledge, there are no celestial sisters in these communities. There are a few relatively powerful women who take leadership positions in running the financial and business affairs for their locations, but they do not have a formal title.

I chose to set my novel in the 1960s as I felt that the contrast between Daisy's life in Redemption and her life on the outside during the cultural revolution of the 1960s would be extreme, creating tension in the story. The hedonistic youth of the day, with their focus on "drugs, sex, and rock and roll" made Daisy's decision to flee her deeply religious upbringing all the more daunting.

Music was a hallmark of the time and I enjoyed choosing some of my favourites for inclusion in the novel. I also drew on my fond memories of driving on backcountry roads near my Okanagan home with my friends and picking up *the* Wolfman from some exotic-seeming radio station south of the border.

The village of Nkwala is fictional but some may argue (correctly) that my model for it is the village of Naramata on the east side of Okanagan Lake, British Columbia, with ferry-only access a thing of the distant past. I named my town for the mountain that I look out at each day from my writing desk. The original Nkwala (1785–1859, Hwistesmetxē'qen, also called Shiwelean or N'Kuala) was head chief of the Okanagans.

Kelowna, Peachland, Rattlesnake Island, Paradise Ranch, and Commando Bay (where Nkwala is situated) are all real places. Paradise Ranch continues to live up to its name but is no longer a ranch as it is entirely planted with grapes. In the 1960s it was owned by family friends, the Wilson family, and I visited it as a child. Sandy Wilson is a well-known Canadian film director (*My American Cousin*). Today, Paradise is owned by Anthony von Mandl, who founded one of the earliest Okanagan wineries in 1966: Mission Hill near Kelowna. Commando Bay earned its name during World War II. It was a secret location where a group of Chinese Canadian solders were trained in guerrilla warfare before being dropped behind Japanese lines in Operation Oblivion.

I have taken liberties with my depiction of the fledgling wine industry in BC in the 1960s. From the 1930s to the 1970s, most BC wines were fruit wines. The Pinot Gris that Jean planted in the novel was not introduced in Canada until 1976. Today, the Okanagan is the second-largest wine producer in Canada with over three hundred licensed grape wineries. While some winters have been cold enough to cause damage to grape vines, the northern latitude offers an advantage over California in that the area receives up to fourteen hours of direct sun in the summer with temperatures surpassing 40°C (104°F).

Finally, a note on the legal argument Daisy sets forth in the novel. The Canadian Parliament enacted the Bill of Rights in 1960 and the Charter of Rights and Freedoms took effect in 1982. The legal challenges to the defense of polygamy as a right of religious freedom have been made in recent years under the Charter. Because I set the novel in the 1960s, I have used the Bill of Rights as the legal backbone of Daisy's argument against the legality of the practise of polygamy.

In spite of the fact that Warren Jeffs was convicted of sexual assault of a child in the US in 2011 and Winston Blackmore was convicted in Canada of polygamy in 2017, both men continue as their community's spiritual leaders and condone polygamy. While the legal route has not served to halt the practise, the support and education that nonprofit organizations provide to those who are considering leaving and those who have left the sects is growing and proving to be highly effective.

Dear reader, thank you for joining Daisy on her quest for freedom and self-discovery. I hope you found it both entertaining and enlightening. Peace and love, everyone, peace and love.

Leslie Howard

Sources

The following publications provided factual information about the story's time and place and allowed me a glimpse into the everyday lives of the women and children of the FLDS and religious cults in general.

BOOKS

Blackmore, Mary Jayne. *Balancing Bountiful: What I Learned about Feminism from My Polygamist Grandmothers*: Caitlin Press Inc., 2020.

Bramham, Daphne. *The Secret Lives of Saints: Child Brides and Lost Boys in Canada's Polygamous Mormon Sect*: Vintage Canada, 2009.

Cutler, Max with Conley, Kevin. *Cults: Inside the World's Most Notorious Groups and Understanding the People Who Joined Them*: Gallery Books, 2022.

Jeffs, Rachel. *Breaking Free: How I Escaped Polygamy, the FLDS Cult, and My Father, Warren Jeffs*: Harper, 2017.

Krakauer, Jon. *Under the Banner of Heaven: A Story of Violent Faith*: Anchor Books, 2004.

Mackert, Mary. *The Sixth of Seven Wives: Escape from Modern Day Polygamy*: xpolygamist.com, 2000.

Palmer, Debbie with Perrin, Dave. *Keep Sweet: Children of Polygamy*: Dave's Press Inc., 2004.

Toews, Miriam. *Women Talking*: Vintage Canada, 2019.

Westover, Tara. *Educated*: HarperCollins Publishers Ltd., 2018.

LEGAL

Bauman, R.J. C.J.S.C., reference re: Criminal Code of Canada (B.C.) [2011], B.C.J. No. 2211. British Columbia Judgments, British Columbia Supreme Court. Docket S097767.

ARTICLES

Adams, Brooke. "Kingston Inc.: Polygamy's Entrepreneurial Empire: A Company, a Clan, a Corp. with a plan." *Salt Lake City Observer*, August 14–17, 1998.

Bramham, Daphne. "Bountiful schools need a closer look." *Vancouver Sun*, September 20, 2004.

Bramham, Daphne. "What's down the road for Bountiful: A Special Report." *Vancouver Sun*, August 7, 2004.

Gregory, David. "Summerland's Battle of AQSKEPKINA SECWÉPEMC versus SYILX." *Archivos*, no. 4 (Spring 2018).

The Committee on Polygamous Issues. "Life in Bountiful: A Report on the Lifestyle in a Polygamous Community." April 1993.

Walker, Linda. "The Genetic Gene Pool May Be Weak and Flawed Due to Polygamous Practices: Fatal Inheritance: Mormon Eugenics." Child Protection Project, 1991.

Wright, Lawrence. "Lives of the Saints: At a Time When Mormonism Is Booming, the Church Is Struggling with a Troubled Legacy." *The New Yorker*, January 21, 2002.

MEDIA

CKNW radio. The Beatles live recording of the Vancouver concert, August 22, 1964.

Wadleigh, Michael, director. *Woodstock: 3 Days of Peace & Music*.

Netflix. *Keep Sweet: Pray and Obey* docuseries.

CBC. *As It Happens*. Polygamy Decision, interview with Jane Blackmore. March 9, 2018.

The
Celestial
Wife

LESLIE HOWARD

A Reading Group Guide

Questions for Book Clubs

1. The novel follows Daisy Shoemaker, a young Mormon girl born into a fundamentalist polygamist community. Did you know about the history of polygamy in North America before reading this book?

2. Daisy lives in a closed society where interaction with outsiders is severely limited, so she has few opportunities to see how other people live. But she has access to library books through her mother, who lives apart from the polygamist households of Redemption, and she has access to popular music through her shortwave radio job relaying morning road reports. Books and music expand Daisy's ideas of what's possible. Have books and music had the same influence on you?

3. As the novel opens, Daisy awaits the Placement, the ceremony where the Bishop chooses her husband from among the men of the priesthood. She wants to marry Tobias, the handsome young newcomer from Arizona, but she's also thinking about life outside of Redemption if she's not matched with him. What does this say about the options available to women in this community?

4. Daisy's mother is unique among the women of Redemption; she lives alone and leads an independent life. Though Daisy is told to avoid her, she visits her often and she learns that other

mothers do too. What does Daisy's mother offer these women? Why do they seek her out?

5. Daisy and Brighten live in polygamist households marred by jealousy, competition, and bullying between sister-wives, and neither wants to be forced to compete for affection. Who benefits from these tensions? Who is hurt by them?

6. Brighten hopes to be made a celestial sister at the Placement and play a managerial role in the community before being married to a priesthood man. What do you make of her preference?

7. Daisy is caught between the need to be accepted by the members of her community and her need to think for herself and reject the dogma of the Bishop. Are these needs incompatible? How does she resolve the tension of these needs?

8. Daisy and Tobias have different ideas of what marriage should be. How is Daisy a product of her environment and upbringing? How is Tobias a product of his?

9. Even when Daisy escapes Redemption and the Bishop's influence, she can't escape his teachings. How does she start to unlearn the damaging lessons of her religious education?

10. Daisy's first experience with an outsider after her escape from Redemption confirms the Bishop's teachings that all people outside are evil, but her next meeting changes everything. How does Saffron win over Daisy?

11. When Daisy first meets Jean, she is intimidated by him and embarrassed by her narrow upbringing. When and why do her feelings for him start to change?

12. Miss Braid, the librarian in Nkwala, has a tremendous influence on Daisy, helping her attain her high school equivalency

and start pre-law classes at a local community college. What else does Miss Braid offer her?

13. Jean is the black sheep of his family and suffers under his father's disapproval, while Saffron is the black sheep of hers and manages to thrive. How do Daisy's friends' situations help her figure out her own?

14. When Daisy hears Brighten's voice over the shortwave radio, her memories of the Placement come roaring back, and she resolves to do something to help her best friend. For a while, she gets caught up in the ideals of the 1960s protest movements to create lasting change in Redemption, but then explores a legal remedy. Where does each avenue take her?

15. Daisy is disappointed to learn that the right of religious freedom seems to be held in higher esteem than the practice of polygamy is condemned, leaving women and girls vulnerable to sexual abuse and trafficking. Do you think that the right of the individual outranks the right to freedom of religion? Why or why not?

16. Judge Adams thinks the way to establish that the right of the individual trumps the right to freedom of religion, in this case, is to consider harms. What harms do the women and children of Redemption suffer under polygamy?

17. How does Daisy's idea of God change from the beginning of the novel to the end?

18. Discuss the significance of the title *The Celestial Wife*.

Enhance Your Book Club

1. Want to learn more about the legality of polygamy in Canada? Read the CBC's interview with Jane Blackmore, ex-wife of Winston Blackmore, on *As It Happens*: https://www.cbc.ca /radio/asithappens/as-it-happens-friday-edition-1.4569603 /it-needs-to-be-stopped-bountiful-b-c-leader-s-ex-wife -welcomes-polygamy-ruling-1.4569606.

2. To pull back the curtain on polygamy in the United States, watch this docuseries on Netflix: *Keep Sweet: Pray and Obey*.

3. If the scene of the Beatles' first Canadian concert at the Empire Stadium in Vancouver whet your appetite for more, check out highlights from *The Beatles Bible*: https:// www.beatlesbible.com/1964/08/22/live-empire-stadium -vancouver-canada/.

About the Author

Leslie Howard is the bestselling author of *The Brideship Wife*. She grew up in British Columbia and developed a passion for the province's history. A graduate of Ottawa's Carleton University with a degree in economics and political science, she divides her time between Vancouver and Penticton, where she and her husband grow cider apples. Connect with her on Twitter @AuthorLeslieH or on her website at LeslieHoward.ca.